Praise For Jim Nesbitt's Latest Work, The Dead Certain Doubt: An Ed Earl Burch Novel

"Jim Nesbitt delivers his best West Texas hard-boiled crime novel yet with the fourth installment in his Ed Earl Burch series, *The Dead Certain Doubt*. Nesbitt has a way with titles, as he has a way with crackling language that carries you into the darkest places populated by unforgettable characters. Ed Earl is a private eye of a certain vintage, though not the kind you find in the best wine cellars. Feeling his age and his sins, he seeks redemption by helping a dying woman he should have aided years earlier. He heads into the West Texas badlands looking for the woman's granddaughter. This stark yet beautiful world is populated by gun runners, cartel killers, rustlers, thieves and crooked lawmen. Problem is, the granddaughter looks to have hooked up with even worse: white supremacists. Ed Earl is in for a fight. He's always in for a fight. That's what makes him such a compelling character, battling time, tides and too many bad guys. *The Dead Certain Doubt* is a thrilling, lightning-paced, ferocious crime novel. Highly recommended!"

> — Rich Zahradnik, author of *The Bone Records* and *Lights Out Summer*, winner of the 2018 Shamus Award for Best Paperback Private Eye Novel

"If you hear fans of author Jim Nesbitt's hardboiled novels tell you that he pulls no punches, believe them. Series protagonist, Ed Earl Burch, occupies terrain staked out by genre legends like James Crumley and Jim Thompson, but with a distinct Texas accent and tooled leather boots crusted with blood and caliche dust. The prose is powerful and beautifully gritty, the dialogue authentic and raw. I won't sugarcoat it; I am not impartial–I am a fan. *The Dead Certain*

Doubt is authentic contemporary cowboy noir, where the language is rough, the characters are rougher, and the dividing line between the heroes and the villains is often in the eye of the beholder. Ed Earl Burch is one tough SOB, and author Jim Nesbitt knows how to write him. If this book was a movie, you'd be deep in Sam Peckinpah territory, and you'd want to watch it again and again. This book is a hardboiled winner."
> — Baron R. Birtcher, *Los Angeles Times* best selling author of literary thrillers *Fistful of Rain* and *South California Purples*

"You're searching for redemption in a sunbaked West Texas hellscape - without mercy. You're Ed Earl Burch, canned Dallas homicide cop, on a quest to right what might not even have been wrong. Burch is pure joint-damaged cholla cactus, surrounded by water-sucking cartel murderers, cash dazzled border grifters and sun-bent, double-crossing law dogs. Taking a mission from a dying old woman to rescue from this burnt world a granddaughter fallen among Kluxers and neo-Nazi gunrunners, he's all gears on go. Behind every reflective Ray-Ban, sporting stolen automatics and the occasional Zapata moustache, you'll find shooters, wire pullers and human scorpions. Ed Earl and his ghostly conscience buddy Wynn Moore, will guide you through the last arroyo with wit, truly memorable dialogue and locations you'd like to visit… with a gun."
> — John William Davis, author of *Rainy Street Stories* and *Around the Corner*

"This is hard Texas stuff, savage at times in its realism, perceptive in its recognition of the things that can drive men to violence when they feel their way of life disappearing. Or, perhaps, if they fall prey to sugary recollections of a past time. Dallas ex-cop Ed Earl Burch is still alive, but the list of people who want to change that is depressingly long. Burch decides to save a young woman who's gone over to the dark side… drugs, gun-running, sex and revenge. And the list of people who want her dead is even longer. Burch will soon find himself surrounded by bullets and the smell of death. Just the sort of odds the old Texan needs.

Out the door. Into the cool, night air of The D, a mirthless and merciless city that ate the weak and only smiled at money.

Tough, bold and relentless, Burch always answers the bell. And yes, Ed Earl Burch is pure entertainment.

Maybe tell a war story or two. It's the way old soldiers and ex-cops remind themselves of who they once were before time and lousy choices took it all away."

— Michael Ludden, author of *Alfredo's Luck* and *Tate Drawdy*

"Great title, great read! Ed Earl Burch is back, and the ex-homicide cop takes us on a no-holds barred mission of revenge, redemption and righting wrongs from the past through a hellish West Texas world he knows only too well. This is classic hard-boiled fiction, and no one does it better than award-winning author Jim Nesbitt. Get ready for another wild ride with Ed Earl!"

— R.G. Belsky, author of the Clare Carlson mysteries

"*The Dead Certain Doubt* is a noir gem, peppered with American muscle cars, Kentucky bourbon and universal life lessons. Written in author Jim Nesbitt's powerfully lyrical and staccato prose, the hunt for a troubled young woman who is marked for death by gunrunners and a Mexican drug cartel puts Dallas private detective Ed Earl Burch – and the reader – through the wringer. The pace is swift, the action is raw and the characters are intense and visual. The compelling power of remorse drives the page-turning pace even as the glorious phrasing makes you want to stop and savor the work of a master wordsmith. Nesbitt's prose, characters and gritty authenticity make him one of today's most talented and stylish noir writers."

— Carmen Amato, author of the Emilia Cruz and Galliano Club mystery series

"Lawman turned PI Ed Earl Burch is like a pair of old boots. Worn around the edges, scuffed a bit, but more than serviceable. If you like your mysteries hard boiled – and who doesn't? – they don't come any harder than Ed Earl Burch. Gritty and tough with enough despicable West Texas hombres to fill a tour bus, Jim Nesbitt's *The Dead Certain Doubt* is impossible to put down. A must read!"
> — Bruce Robert Coffin, award-winning author of the Detective Byron mysteries

"Dallas has plenty of bottomless pits, and Ed Earl Burch, the washed-up detective in Jim Nesbitt's Texas crime thriller series, has managed to fall into most of them. Usually trying to do the right thing, as if that exists in Nesbitt's extra-hard-boiled tales. And when the attempted good deeds run bad, as always, they quickly move to West Texas, where Burch's rough days and harsh nights seem like paradise before it's all over."
> — Rod Davis, author of the Southern noir novels, *South, America* and *East of Texas, West of Hell*

What Fellow Authors Say About Jim Nesbitt's The Last Second Chance, The Right Wrong Number *and* The Best Lousy Choice

"If you're looking for gritty, *The Right Wrong Number* is as gritty as Number 36 sandpaper."
> — Bill Crider, author of the Sheriff Dan Rhodes mysteries

"If Chandler's noir was a neon sign in the LA sunset, Nesbitt's noir is the Shiner Bock sign buzzing outside the last honky-tonk you'll hit before the long drive to the next one. On the way you'll pass towns with names like Crumley and Portis. Roll down the window; it's a hot night. It's a fast ride."
> — James Lileks, author of *The Casablanca Tango*, columnist for the *National Review* and *Star Tribune* of Minneapolis, creator of LILEKS.com

"In *The Right Wrong Number*, Jim Nesbitt writes like an angel about devilish deals, bloody murder and nasty sex. His beat is Dallas – not the glitzy spires of J.R. Ewing, but the back alley bars and brothels of Jack Ruby and Candy Barr. His PI, Ed Earl Burch, is steeped in Coke-chased bourbon; cured in the smoke of Zippo-lit Luckies; and longing for hard-bitten girls who got away. Nesbitt channels the lyricism of James Crumley, the twisted kick of Jim Thompson and the cold, dark heart of Mickey Spillane."
> — Jayne Loader, author of *Between Pictures* and *Wild America*, director of *The Atomic Café*

"In *The Last Second Chance*, Jim Nesbitt gives readers a splendid first opportunity to meet Ed Earl Burch, as flawed a Luckies-smoking, whiskey-drinking, serial-married hero as ever walked the scarred earth of Dirty Texas... In Burch, Nesbitt has created a more angst-ridden and bad-ass version of Michael Connelly's Harry Bosch and a Tex-Mex landscape much meaner than the streets of L.A. Add hate-worthy lowlifes and a diminutive dame, Carla Sue Cantrell, who cracks wiser than the guys, and you've got a book with gumption."

— Bob Morris, Edgar finalist, author of *Baja Florida* and *A Deadly Silver Sea*

"If you like to read, if you appreciate words and the people who run them brilliantly through their paces, give Jim Nesbitt's *The Last Second Chance* a read. And his next one, and the one after that. You'll be enthralled, like I was."

— Cheryl Pellerin, author of *Trips: How Hallucinogens Work in Your Brain* and *Healing With Cannabis*

"Jim Nesbitt's latest hard-boiled Texas thriller is another masterpiece. *The Right Wrong Number* has everything to keep the reader turning the page – vivid characters, stark Texas landscape, non-stop action and a classic American anti-hero in Ed Earl Burch, Nesbitt's battered but dogged Dallas PI. Buckle up and brace yourself for another wild ride."

— Paul Finebaum, ESPN college football analyst, author, host of *The Paul Finebaum Show*

"Cowboy noir for the cartel era... *The Last Second Chance* is a gripping read with a cathartic ending, and it takes you places you've likely never been."

— Jeannette Cooperman, author of *A Circumstance of Blood*

THE DEAD CERTAIN DOUBT

AN ED EARL BURCH NOVEL

JIM NESBITT

THE DEAD CERTAIN DOUBT
An Ed Earl Burch Novel

Copyright © 2023 By Jim Nesbitt
Published by SPOTTED MULE PRESS

Paperback
ISBN 13: 978-0-9983294-5-1
E-Book
ISBN 13: 978-0-9983294-6-8

Cover photograph by Joel Ruiz Salcido
Used with exclusive permission.
Author photograph by Pam Nesbitt
Used with exclusive permission.
Cover design by SelfPubBookCovers.com/Island
Interior formatting and proofreading by Pen2publishing

Jim Nesbitt Web site: https://jimnesbittbooks.com

Author's Note

If you've read any of my earlier Ed Earl Burch novels, you know I have an abiding love for the harsh, stark beauty of the border country of West Texas and northern Mexico where the mountains rise from the sun-scorched desert like the bones of the earth ripped open for all to see. The primordial power of that land first hooked me in the late 1980s and early 1990s when I was out there chasing stories as a roving correspondent for various news outfits. What I heard, saw, smelled and felt forms the backbone of all four of my Ed Earl Burch novels – partly because I'm a firm believer in creating a keen sense of place, but mostly because the land is so evocative that it becomes a character unto itself. And while there is no Faver, Texas and Cuervo County is also a figment of my imagination, my descriptions of those fictitious places are rooted in what I saw in real towns like Sanderson, Marathon, Marfa, Alpine, Valentine and Fort Davis.

Writing a novel is both a lonely road and a collaborative effort and I'd like to thank the people who helped keep me on track, gave wise counsel, kicked me in the butt when needed and helped shape and polish the finished product. Special thanks to my editor, Cheryl Pellerin, a damn good writer in her own right who kept dogging me to publish my first two novels, and my old border running buddy, photographer Joel Ruiz Salcido, whose marvelous photo graces the cover of this book and the previous Ed Earl saga, *The Best Lousy Choice*.

Thanks and a tip o' the Resistol to my semi-irregular cadre of reviewers, fellow writers, beta readers and smart-ass buddies who didn't sugarcoat their opinions. The crew includes writers Dick Belsky, Baron R. Birtcher, Rich Zahradnik, John Davis, Carmen Amato, Michael Ludden, Mike Seely; and my nephew, Patrick Lee. Thanks also to Texas ace reviewer Kevin Tipple; my old friend, Richard Beene, the Czar of Bakersfield, who hosts a great podcast; North Carolina political operative Ray Martin, who is a graphics, marketing and social media wizard; and fellow whisky-slinger and history buff Stanley Hitchens, who ceaselessly touts my work to our Delco high school pals.

Most of all, many thanks and much love to my wife, Pam, who believes in me even when I don't.

For Pam and The Panther

One

The screams stopped them in their tracks, frozen in mid stride by the cresting, falling wails of a terrified creature in deep pain, carried on the harsh night wind as it slid up and down the scale of torment, rage and fear.

They listened, adrenalin surging, hearts slamming a staccato, senses filtering out the rushing current of cold and the answering cries of coyotes, pinpointing the location of agony's call.

A death song in the dark. It didn't sound human but they knew it was. And they knew where it came from – the darkened ranch house below. Without a glance or a word, they stepped out of the moonlit middle of the steep dirt track they were descending and into the shadows of the rocky wall that loomed above them.

They even knew who it was. Not a guess. A certainty. They listened. Seconds seemed like hours. The screams stopped. Sticking to the shadows, they edged down the shoulder of the track, feet slipping in the loose rock and gravel, each cursing silently as they stopped to listen again.

Nerves taut, they reached a spot that overlooked the house then crossed the track to a boulder that gave them cover. Close enough to see the flicker of flashlights and hear laughter and low voices. And the bang of metal on metal.

A whisper in her ear. A rank puff of stale cigarette smoke and sour coffee in her nostrils.

"We close enough to hear 'em, they close enough to hear us."

She nodded, then tightened the scratchy wool scarf that covered her nose and mouth and pulled the black felt Resistol a little lower over her bottled blonde hair. They watched and listened.

They heard the chop of metal on meat. The sound of the butcher shop, not the woodpile. Then the low, guttural laughter of men sharing a task they couldn't see.

Engines cranking then catching. Rumbles, deep and uneven, smoothing out as drivers rapped the pipes then let the revs die down. Running lights popping on, outlining the dark forms of three backcountry rigs, jacked up and sporting spotlights and chrome roll bars that reflected the amber beams.

Then the deeper roar of a larger rig. A humpbacked beast waddling out of the deep darkness behind the house, back where the barn stood that served as storage for lethal product headed south. A six-by-six, mil surplus or stolen from the Mexican army – maybe a loaner from a corrupt colonel or general. There go the guns and ammo, she thought. Our guns and ammo. Kiss our money-maker bye-bye.

Panic shattered the farewell. Fatal if these machos headed this way. But they didn't. In trail, the three rigs and the bigger beast rolled toward the far end of the mesa and the gravel switchback that led miles of rough ranch road and the highway beyond. They watched and listened until the beast slipped over the distant edge and the sound of engines faded away.

Rhonda Mae heard him let out a long breath and mutter to himself in Spanish. Armando reached into his coat and pulled out a pack of *Delicados*. He shook out two unfiltered nails, lit them both with a Bic knockoff and handed one to her.

She nodded a thanks and took a deep drag of strong, honest smoke. Delicate, this ain't, usually amused by the machos who puffed a tough-guy brand with such a feminine name.

Not tonight, though. Her lover was dead. His screams still echoed in her head. No time for tears. Save those for later.

Time to get gone. Over the uncharted route a dead man taught her, always warning her to stop just before the last turn and down-hill grade to the house to scope things out on foot. After a rocky, three-hour grind bouncing through axle-busting arroyos and up steep gravel traces that provided narrow grace between a cliff face and the black nothing below. A ride better made on a mule than in a rusty CJ5.

"You still want to go down there?"

"Oh, hell no – the guns are gone and those bastards might come back. And we don't want to leave sign for no law to find. I don't need to see the body to know he's dead."

"Okay, then. We go back to the Jeep."

"*Si*, we go back to the Jeep."

"They will come for you."

"I know, but they'll have to find me first."

"It was crazy what he did. Rat out rivals then go back into business with their customers."

"Worked for a while."

"*Si*, with you out front and him in the shadows. Until somebody figured it out."

"That's why I left. I knew it was only a matter of time."

"Then why come back? You know they'll do to you what they did to him."

Rhonda Mae stopped walking and stared at Armando until he also came to a halt. She thought but didn't say: *I loved him. I missed his craziness. I missed how he made me laugh. I missed the danger, the action, the juice. I missed the way his cock made me cum like a runaway rollercoaster rocketing off the rails.*

"You can stop talking now."

"*Si.*"

3

Two

It was well past the frozen hour of midnight when Sudden Doggett turned off U.S. Highway 90, braking to a slow stop on the gravel side road, jumping out into lung-searing night air to lock the front hubs, then sliding back behind the wheel and shifting the Bronco into four-wheel drive.

He banged the dashboard with the heel of his gloved right hand, cussing softly at a heater with a wheezy fan but little warmth. The cold caused his left leg to throb right where surgical pins held together the femur he shattered at a rodeo in Pocatello. Only high heat would help. The Bronco didn't have it. And he didn't have any coffee.

Hell, it's a wonder the wheels on this rig still spin. County bought the damn thing in '83. Used.

Duct tape on the dash and front seat cushion. Yellow foam pads playing peek-a-boo through a split. Transfer case that needed an overhaul a year ago.

Ain't nothin' wrong with the engine, thank Christ. Sumbitch is still strong enough to power the rig over rough ground. Guess that'll have to do.

He knew where he was going – down miles of gravel and potholes that would rattle his teeth, then up a rutted switchback carved into the western face of a nameless mesa to a long, low adobe house on the topside with a tin shed roof.

Hadn't been there in years, but it once belonged to a distant cousin, Carlos Lucas, a horseman just like most of the Doggett clan, killed in the pre-dawn darkness when a semi blew through the stop sign of a four-way outside Van Horn.

Turned the cousin and three of the four horses he was hauling into so much strawberry jam and butchered bits of meat. Bad way to die, but quick. The fourth horse survived, a claybank gelding. Got named Lucky by his new owner.

Closed casket funeral for a man most people called Charley. Doggett attended in Class A Army green and a piss-cutter garrison cap. That made it fifteen years ago. Try twenty. Back when he was an MP. Before he did a tour as an Army C.I.D. special agent.

When Doggett got to the house, he'd be ten miles over the Cuervo County line. Hardly worth a mention for most Texans. Like cruising down to the corner Gas N' Go for a six-pack of Pearl.

Didn't matter. He'd still be outside his jurisdiction. In Jeff Davis County. Sheriff Lamar Blondell's turf.

Blondell called him two hours ago, jangling him out of deep sleep, yanking him out of an iron-framed bed with a warm woman snoring lightly beside him, extending a terse invitation that meant the Cuervo County badge he wore wouldn't be totally useless.

"Got a killin' I want you to eyeball. Pretty grisly. Might be someone you know."

Gave Doggett the location, then hung up. Blondell hated talking on the phone. Didn't say much face to face, either. Laconic. A lawman of few words. A pure-dee Gary Cooper pose that played well with the good people of Jeff Davis County. For four terms.

Also, a damn wise practice for a sheriff rumored to have his fingers in more than a few semi-illicit pies. Not an out-and-out crook. Not a killer. Not a shill for the *narcos* across the river. To Doggett's knowledge.

Mostly kickbacks on county road projects and inmates loaned out as work crews. A rambling stone house built for Blondell by a big backer. A mortgage to make it look legit, paid by another campaign contributor. A friendly DA kept sweet by skim from the same money streams.

That was the talk. Almost quaint by the scumbag standards of today's bent border sheriffs, more than a few of them wholly owned and operated by the cartels.

He fishtailed through the last switchback and gunned the Bronco through the ruts of the final rise. A hammering gust rocked the rig, shooting icy nails through dry-rotted window seals, causing his bum leg to kick back with a sharp pain he could feel in his teeth.

When he reached the top and turned toward the house, his high beams swept across that lawdog circus he knew so well. County four-bys with light bars strobing red and blue against cracked adobe walls. Portable lamps countering with harsh white beams that didn't blink.

Lawmen milling around, striking tough guy poses, watching the crime scene crew do their work and keeping their distance. Cigarette smoke and breath vapor billowing above their heads. Stretched yellow crime scene tape snapping in the wind, guarding against any marauding coyotes or javelinas that might breeze by and drop some scat that might confuse investigators.

Those boys'll be talking low about me soon as I step out of this rig.

Damn half-breed – half nigger, half pepperbelly.

Been hearin' that horseshit all my life. At a rodeo, waitin' to rope a calf. In the latrine of an Army barracks. Walking up the courthouse steps past a group of solid citizens. Never to my damn face. Fist sandwich to those who did back in the day.

Flip that half-breed coin and call it semi-true. Granddaddy was an ex-slave who made a name for himself charming, coaxing and capturing wild mustangs for ranchers all over West Texas.

Wrapped himself in a horsehair blanket and eased his way into a herd. Became part of the family. Gained their trust then led them right into captivity. He married a Mexican woman. So did my daddy.

More horseshit: Goddam joke him wearin' a sheriff's badge. He ain't no Blue Willingham, that's for damn sure.

That's right, I ain't Blue Willingham. I ain't an ex-Ranger who talks tough about waging a one-man war on drugs while raking in cartel money. I ain't a traitor to the badge. That would be your boy Blue, honest as a carny barker, true as Judas, living the loud lie everybody believed. Even Larry King.

Until Blue ate his gun. Used the thumb-buster his granddaddy carried as a Texas Ranger just before their descendants closed in. Kept his Big Adios in the family.

Now I'm wearin' his badge. Tough titty if you assholes don't like that. Voters in Cuervo County like me just fine. Almost sixty percent of them last election. Not bad for a pepperbelly nigger.

He pointed the Bronco toward a rectangle of ground on the southern flank of the house, lit brighter than high noon by the portable lamps posted at each corner. Looked like a half-ass patio with iron chairs and two picnic tables scattered around a mammoth black smoker hulking in the center.

Also looked like Ground Zero of the killing, judging by the number of evidence techs buzzing around the grill, wearing masks and Latex gloves.

A lawman broke away from the pack as Doggett nosed the Bronco next to a bigger, shinier Jeff Davis County rig.

Blondell.

Tall, lanky and long-faced. Squinting into the high beams as he walked up. A stag-gripped thumb buster riding low on his left hip. His badge danced and glittered in the glare, marking the time of his slow stroll. So did the satin finish of his insulated, olive-green jacket.

"Sheriff, thanks for comin'. Sorry to jerk you out of bed on a night like this."

"You sure can pick 'em. Night like this would freeze the balls off a billy goat. Hope you boys brought some coffee."

Blondell chuckled as Doggett stamped his feet, trying to jar the stiffness out of his legs. The bum one fired back. Doggett winced, pulled straight the stiff, unruly canvas of his Filson barn coat and pushed his hat down tighter, slipping the braided horsehair stampede strap under his chin.

"Come ahead on. The boys will fix you up. Might even have some ninety-proof sweet'ner, if you're so inclined."

"Straight black coffee will do, Sheriff."

"How long you had that hat?"

"Since my rodeo days. Just gettin' it good and broke in."

"'Bout time to trade it in for a new lid, ain't it? Now that you're the sheriff."

"No need to toss something that works on the scrap heap just because it shows a little wear and tear. Folks in my county might think I was puttin' on airs. They like me to at least appear to be poor, humble and honest."

"Everything your predecessor wasn't."

"You bet. So, what we got up here? You said 'grisly.'"

The wind shifted, carrying a stench that caught Doggett full in the throat and made him gag, a familiar smell known and dreaded by any lawman or firefighter. Sickly sweet and musky, coppery and metallic, bolstered by the meaty scent of spoiled steak sizzling in a frying pan with rancid fatback thrown in.

Thick enough to chew on then puke.

That was the good part. Mix in a choking backbeat of burnt liver peppered with sulfur and the marinade of a backed-up sewage line. Then top it with a sharp, acrid foulness that grabbed the nose hairs by the roots, rattled the palate and ripped the throat before rocketing into the smallest pockets of both lungs.

Burnt hair. Nothing quite like it. Nothing Doggett hated more. A smell and taste that cigarettes couldn't mask; mouthwash couldn't kill and the memory could never forget. He knew it would ruin any meal he choked down for the next two or three days.

He coughed twice and tried to clear his throat, then spat in the dirt. That made it worse. He fished a pouch of Red Man out of his coat pocket and forked two full fingers of chaw into his cheek, working up a thick dollop of tobacco juice that soon joined the phlegm.

"That help any?"

"Not hardly, but a man can hope. May take you up on that coffee sweet'ner after we take a closer look at what you got."

"Doesn't look any prettier than it smells."

The two sheriffs walked toward the harsh light and the hulking black steel showcased in the square – Doggett, short and barrel chested, a Mutt to Blondell's Jeff. He pocketed his leather gloves and shook out a Latex pair, pulling them over his hands and giving the bottom opening a snap that stung each wrist.

The stench got worse as they got closer to what looked like a tribute to the Texas obsession with oversized overkill and barbecue. A massive smoker with a firebox and grill, one on each side, and a width Doggett guessed broke twenty feet and a height that topped half that, maybe a little more.

A capped, sheet metal chimney poked skyward from the top of the rig, looking like a dark plea for mercy in the glare.

"Anybody but the vic livin' up here?"

"Nobody recent. Found some girlie stuff in the bathroom. Box of tampons. Some bras and panties. Hairbrush and hand mirror. Some Clairol, which makes whoever she is a blonde from a bottle. Hairs in the brush the same color."

"That it?"

"For the house, yes. Just some odds and ends left behind. Cleared out otherwise. We'll bag that stuff just in case another body shows up, but it looks like she lit out for the territories before this little hoe-down."

"Lucky girl. She best stay long gone. Find anything else?"

"Barn out back. No livestock. Looks like it was used for storage. Found tire tracks for a big rig out back and signs of some heavy loads dragged through the dirt."

"Horse or coke?"

"C'ain't really tell, but I doubt either. Looks like crates or cargo boxes."

"That ain't good."

"Nope. Bang sticks that play bush time rock n' roll, I'd wager."

"Who called this in?"

"Anonymous tip."

"Phoned in by the killers, more'n likely."

"Agree with you on that, Sheriff. Wanted us to see this sooner rather than later."

"Bodies stackin' up like cord wood over the river. Believe it's a fracas between those Monterrey boys what blew Malo Garza out of his socks a few years back and another outfit. Now we're gettin' the spillover."

Blondell grunted.

"Ain't that always the way? Open the sumbitch up and let Sheriff Doggett take a peek."

Two techs slipped work gloves over their Latex. One looked back at Blondell.

"He ain't gonna like what he sees, Sheriff."

"No, don't imagine he will. I sure as hell didn't so what's your damn point, Blackie? Just open that damn smoker for the man."

Blackie hung his head, then stepped up and lifted the left-side lid and locked it in place while a grinning tech buddy muscled and locked the right. Smoke and a stronger wave of stench rolled out.

"Not a goddam thing to smile about, is there, Jack? Give the man some light and stay out of his way."

Doggett held up a six-cell Kel-Lite.

"Got my own, boys. Make a hole."

Three heavy-gauge racks stretched the length of the smoker interior, stacked vertical with about two feet of space in between. Enough room to smoke a whole butchered cow. But smoked beef wasn't on tonight's menu. Mesquite-cured manflesh was.

Doggett leaned close and fanned the beam along the bottom rack, flashing across the blackened torso of a slim man with stumps just below the shoulders and hips where the arms and legs were severed. Beneath the charring was smoked flesh with a reddish brown cast. The light caught the ivory gleam of the severed neck bone.

There was a darker blotch on the left side of the chest. Tattoo, maybe. Lucky if it was. Made the ID easier. The abdomen was split down the middle with well-muscled flesh peeled to both sides. Lean and tough to chew, if that was your craving.

The guts were gone. So were the cock and balls. Doggett knew where he'd find those. He hacked up another wad of phlegm and tobacco juice and turned his head to spit.

"Hey, you're fuckin' up my crime scene, Sheriff."

Blackie's bleat. Doggett turned his head, looked the tech up and down, then snorted. He spoke low, slow and soft, like he would to an unruly gelding.

"Shit, son, did the Good Lord make you this dumb or did you have to work at it? Forensics will help us ID the guest of honor here, but it won't find the fuckheads who did this. They're back in Mexico by now. They set up this little freak show to leave a callin' card and got gone. So, me spittin' in the dirt at your crime scene is a no-nevermind, *sabe?*"

Nobody answered.

Doggett turned back to the smoker and passed the beam across the second rack. Charred legs and arms, ropy with the russet-colored muscles of a man who had known hard work. Another dark blotch on the right biceps. Maybe another tattoo. Feet and hands attached but missing a few toes and fingers. The fuckheads took their time and had their fun, snipping digits and snapping questions.

11

Doggett saved the worst for last.

At the center of the top rack was the victim's severed head, the hair burned off, leaving a smoke-cured scalp and the gagging sulfur scent now lodged in Doggett's lungs. The mouth had been pried open to stuff the dead man's pride and twin joys inside.

Nearly every *narco* question-and-answer session he'd ever sifted featured this final touch. Almost a cliché, but he still felt his own balls try to crawl deeper inside his body than the cold had already driven them.

The eyelids were razored away.

The better to see us clip your toes and fingers, manflora, then cut off your pene y los huevos. Manflora, maricon, mayate, joto – yup, they always question your manhood just before they slice it away.

Like the faint touch of a feather, Doggett felt a vague sense of recognition creep into the back of his brainpan. Very slight and ready to bolt if he studied on it too hard to force it to the surface. He relaxed and ignored the thought, treating it like a colt reluctant to enter the corral.

It'll walk on in when it's ready and give me a nudge.

He looked at Blackie, who tried to avoid his eyes.

"You got forceps and an evidence baggie handy?"

"What you want with those?"

"To gently remove the man's cock and balls to preserve for posterity, then look inside his mouth."

"Best wait on Doc Green before we do something like that."

"Doc Green your coroner?"

"Yup."

"Did you boys photo the body? Get all the angles you need to document the crime scene?"

"Yup."

"Then I doubt Doc Green will give much of a shit about me doin' what I want to do."

Blondell's voice, with a razor-wire riding the words.

"Quit fuckin' with the man, Blackie. Get him the forceps and baggie. Then thank him for doin' some of your dirty work."

Blackie did as he was told. He even held the evidence baggie open as Doggett used the forceps to fish out the victim's shriveled family jewels and drop them inside.

"Take my flashlight and shine it so I can see inside his mouth."

No backtalk this time. Blackie centered the beam. Doggett used the forceps to lift the lips and study the man's top row of teeth. Gold flashed where two central incisors used to live. That vague sense of recognition took another step into the corral.

"Got anything else for me to look at?"

Blondell answered.

"Sumbitches took his wallet, so no ID. Piled his clothes over there. Used that plastic barrel as a gut bucket."

Doggett looked at the barrel. It was baby blue with the top quarter sawed off. Dark blood stained the sides, quick frozen into place after a short vertical run. Broad black stain in the dirt where the body was butchered. He spotted the pile of clothes and walked that way. He could see the outline of a harder lump of something buried underneath.

He pulled at the pile. Dark blue boxers. White undershirt. Faded Wranglers. A dark green rancher shirt with faux pearl speed snaps. An insulated vest, tan with grease stains. And a denim jacket with a quilt lining. No hat or cap.

Boots buried at the bottom. He picked one up. The feather became a finger poking his brain. Or a colt nudging his back. Snakeskin with garish purple inlays cut into the tall yellow calfskin top. Black piping down the sides. Needle-nose toe perfect for killing cornered scorpions. Two-inch underslung horseman heel with a spur shelf.

Seen these before. Where? Who was wearing them? Gold teeth and snakeskin boots.

He dropped the boot and picked up the faded jeans, weighted by a belt buckle big enough to be a hood ornament on a Cowboy

Cadillac. He flipped the buckle so he could eyeball the raised script on the front. Two words, stacked: Texas Secede.

Bang. The colt was in the corral and the gate slammed shut. He turned and walked back to Blondell.

"Tommy Juan Jaeckel."

"How can you tell?"

"He was wearin' those boots and the same belt buckle when I busted him two years ago for runnin' stolen guns. And those two gold teeth in his head? One of my deputies knocked out the originals when he cold-cocked Tommy Juan for comin' up behind me with a pig sticker. He had a Texas flag tattoo on his chest with some kinda Latin underneath and some other ink on his biceps. His file will have what they say if we can raise them up on the body."

Blondell grinned.

"Good job, Sheriff."

"Sumbitch. You knew, didn't you?"

"I suspected but didn't know for sure. That's why I called you. Wanted to see if you confirmed my suspicion but wanted you to come up with it natural."

"You're a sly bastard, Sheriff."

"Ain't we all?"

"I'll take that coffee now."

"Sweet'ner?"

"You bet. A double shot."

Sumbitch. Tommy Juan Jaeckel. What the hell are you doing here? Thought I sent you to the stony lonesome for a long stretch. Ten years. Which meant six with good time tallied up.

What did you have to trade to get your ass out of the joint? Must've been gold. Or fool's gold. Whatever it was, it got you dead and smoked like the main course of a long pig feast.

Three

When the walls close in and the mind plays an endless loop of past sins, losses, monumental fuckups, frozen moments of terror and faces of the dead and long gone, a man of a certain vintage has two options.

Stare at the furniture what talks, hoping an old movie or the yakheads of CNN override the bad memories. Sleep won't be dropping by this night and only a deeper, wide-awake darkness beckons.

Or, get your ass out of that ratty recliner with the sprung springs and split seat cushion. Slip on your boots, your shoulder rig and scuffed leather blazer. Grab your keys, your Luckies and a battered Zippo.

Get gone.

Get out into the night, looking for strong drink, noise, neon and a fellow insomniac or three to chat up about sports, ex-wives, absent friends and good times that curdled way too soon.

Maybe tell a war story or two. It's the way old soldiers and ex-cops remind themselves of who they once were before time and lousy choices took it all away.

Ed Earl Burch used to have two other options. Pop a Percodan and wash it down with four fingers of Maker's Mark. Or dial up a woman who believed in the healing grace of carnal salvation as much as he did.

Both choices were off the table these days. He weaned himself from the mother's little helpers six years ago and white-knuckled the night terrors until they became old friends. Still had the

Maker's – peerless Kentucky bourbon, whisky without the 'e.' But the women who used to be willing to share his lonely bed were either married or looked right through him when they walked on by. One or two still dropped in, but their visits were few and infrequent.

No pharmaceuticals and a dearth of carnal distractions made Burch feel like he had been kidnapped by redneck monks. His life in The D – his nickname for Dallas – was once gaudy, guilt-tinged and lit by saloon neon. Now it was dull, shopworn and stale. Which made the remorse of past sins harder to ignore.

He was making more money than ever before, chasing down fugitive partners of real estate deals gone sour, digging up hidden assets and dropping paper on deadbeat developers. It was a specialty born out of the savings-and-loan bust of the previous decade and Burch was good at it, able to finally pay back the large debt he owed his shyster lawyer, Fat Willie Nofzinger.

Put a little coin in the bank, open an IRA, play the market a little. Be a citizen. A civilian. Just like all those John and Jane Does he was once sworn to serve and protect.

Bored the shit out of Burch. Had him thinking about the stark, harsh badlands of West Texas, where the high desert mountains collided and crashed, looking like the bones of the earth revealed for all to see.

Every time he went out there, people tried to kill him. And he never felt more alive, thrilled to be a manhunter again. Cuff 'em or smoke 'em, kill or be killed. Just like the days when he carried a gold detective's shield, hooked on the juice of the chase and the live-wire jolt of a showdown.

Cuffs were useless accessories in that frozen moment when the bad guy twitched the wrong way, the play got dealt and the brain recorded each split second of muzzle flash, burnt powder stench and the slap of a slug striking flesh.

Another scumbag smoked. Burch still standing.

Never felt more alive.

Burch shook himself from this fantasy and fished his car keys from the bowl centered on a tall and narrow oak table by the front door of his crib. A tap to the left pocket of his blazer confirmed the Zippo and pack of Luckies were inside.

A touch under his right armpit told him his Colt 1911 was secure. One round in the pipe. Eight in the mag, a mix of hardball and 200-grain, wide-mouthed hollow-points – Corbon Flying Ashtrays. Extra mag in the blazer pocket that didn't hold the Zippo. No rattling telltale for an ex-street cop.

A glance in the hallway mirror – granddaddy white shot through the coal black of his beard like unchecked mold on a stale loaf of pumpernickel. Same for the fringe of hair that bordered his bald pate. The white was winning on both fronts but hadn't invaded his eyebrows. Yet.

Burch could count a solitary win in this ceaseless war on creeping decrepitude – cataract surgery that gave him near 20/20 vision for the first time since the third grade. Offset the cigarette-smoke whisp of blindness in his right eye that lingered after the surgeon's fix of a detached retina.

Semi-sharp vision meant he could ditch the thick-lensed glasses he had worn since he was a kid, even on the gridiron – ugly, shatter-proof lenses protected by the bars of a full facemask cage. Also meant he was free to buy cheap sunglasses like every other American. And lose them with cavalier impunity.

But he had worn Ray-Bans with prescription lenses so long he was as snobbish as a Navy Tomcat pilot. Burch was flat-out disgusted by the notion of buying the same convenience store shades as the great unwashed.

Still had to have his Ray-Bans. Still felt naked without eyewear. He slipped on a pair of special-order Aviators with the pale yellow Kalichrome lenses made for driving and shooting. Wore these at night and indoors – a second pair with dark, smoke-green lenses tucked inside his jacket for the blinding Texas sun.

Out the door. Into the cool, night air of The D, a mirthless and merciless city that ate the weak and only smiled at money.

Same key to trip twin dead bolts. Short stroll to the four-car garage behind his Marquita Street digs – one for every tenant of the tan-bricked, two-story walkup with the blood red tile roof. Muscle up the door. And slip the cover off the shiny beast that was an aging Boomer's wet dream.

A '68 Olds 442 in deep nocturne blue. Four coats of color covered by twelve coats of clear. A 455 Rocket under the hood. Biggest block alive. So says the Gillian Welch and David Rawlings song.

With a four-barrel Quadrajet, oversized pistons and a performance crank. Muncie four-speed gearbox and dual exhaust with Flowmasters. Gave a throaty rumble at idle and a tiger's scream any time he dropped the hammer.

Burch called her Betty Lou because that wasn't the first name of any of his ex-wives, girlfriends or once semi-steady bedmates. And it wasn't the handle of the long-gone woman of short, bittersweet memories who still walked his dreams.

The car used to be hers, fitting for a petite blonde with a roving eye for other people's cash. She was an up-holler Tennessee hellcat with a little North Dallas gloss. Loved muscle cars, crystal meth and running the high-wire double-cross on nasty *narcos*, bikers and stone-cold killers. Saved his life in Mexico when a voodoo-crazed drug lord tried to carve out his heart – parked a .45 slug in the man's right eye.

She came as close to owning him as any woman could.

Tagging the Olds with a two-first-name moniker was a nod to her. Brushing as close as he could stand without turning into a maudlin basket case with a bad case of terminal longing that would have him grabbing for the whiskey fire hose.

Burch smiled when he fired up Betty Lou and rapped her twin pipes. A twinge of sadness undercut the smile, bringing up the memory of the knock on his door two years ago and the instant spikes of lost love and regret that stabbed his heart when he saw the big Olds gleaming in the harsh Texas sun, parked curbside in front of his building.

A lanky guy with limp, greasy hair was at his door. His arms were covered in jailhouse tatts. An ink spider web snaked around his neck. He handed Burch two sets of keys and a thick manila envelope with a Tennessee title signed over to him, an owner's manual and a doctored bill of sale with his name as the buyer.

The letterhead on the bill of sale said Smoky Mountain Classics. Probably a chop shop owned by family.

The guy cleared his voice and spoke. He had her mountain twang.

"I was tole' to deliver this sweet ride to you and hand over the keys and such, up close and personal like. Why I didn't just keep going straight to Mexico and keep this jewel for myse'f I'll never know."

"Because you know someone would track you down and kill your sorry ass if you did – probably me. Or one of her cousins."

"Shit, mister, didn't mean to piss you off. I'm one of her cousins, but that wouldn't keep her from sending someone to blow me down. Or pullin' the trigger herse'f. She can be hard on kin."

"Yup. I know the story of what she did to that cousin who killed her Uncle Harlan."

"That cousin was my older brother. Mister Harlan was my uncle, too."

"Then you know talk of takin' this car down to Mexico was either a bad joke or the confession of a guilty conscience."

Burch looked up from the documents and pinned the cousin with the dead-eyed stare of a cop. The cousin stood there with his mouth open, then shook himself and handed Burch a folded piece of paper.

"I'm also 'sposed to give you this note and watch you burn it after you read it."

The note said: "Take good care of this ride and it'll take good care of you, Big 'Un. Can't think of anybody else I'd rather have the keys. Think of me when you crank her up."

"Where'd you get this note?"

"Lawyer down in Knoxville. He got it from a lawyer in Atlanta with instructions about giving it to you with the title and the dummy bill of sale."

"Means she's either dead or still runnin' from folks who want her that way."

The cousin didn't hazard a guess. He asked for a ride to the airport. Burch fired up his Zippo to burn the note, then cranked the Olds and barreled up the North Central Expressway and across the LBJ to DFW.

Faded memory. Burch headed the Olds toward Louie's with one name on his mind – Carla Sue Cantrell.

A wall cloud of tobacco smoke and noise met Burch as he walked into the front door of Louie's and ducked around the sharp corner that led to the bar. He glanced at his charcoal portrait hanging at the bottom left corner of a rogue's gallery of regulars.

He paused to look over the Friday night crowd packing the tables and running three-deep at the rails, then lit a Lucky to jet his contribution to the second-hand smoke that dimmed the soft glow of the ceiling lights. He let the loud talk and laughter wash over him like a revival blessing.

Whitey was behind the stick. Burch caught his eye and raised his right hand, flashing four fingers on the horizontal like a cockscomb then two on the vertical like Churchill's V-for-Victory signal.

Semaphore for four fingers of Maker's Mark, neat. Same pour in two glasses.

A nod from Whitey, who didn't have to be told to bring two ice-water chasers. Burch ducked into the back room, which was darker, somewhat less smoky and didn't force a man to shout at his friends.

Friends. Maybe yes, maybe no for the four men he joined at a back corner table. Comrades-in-arms was the better phrase, old warhorses who once wore the badge of a cop or deputy.

All of them knew the grueling hazards of the street – the stark terror and adrenalin rush of a gunfight; the constant demand to be quick of eye, fists and wits; the painful rage when one of their own was killed; the temptation of a hooker's freebie or a fat envelope of cash from a drug dealer, a bent pol or a mobster's mouthpiece.

That was the common bond. Friendship was optional. They shared one other experience – each had been bounced, forced to turn in badge and gun, cashiered and ex-communicated from the job that gave them a higher sense of duty and purpose. A calling rather than a career.

Fallen angels. That fit.

Burch grabbed a chair, spun it backwards and straddled it, resting his forearms on the top rung. Right on cue, Whitey walked in, balancing a tray, and placed two tall ice waters and two rocks glasses three-quarters full of Maker's on the table. Burch slipped a twenty and a ten on the tray.

"Many thanks, Whitey. Keep 'em comin'. Got a powerful thirst tonight."

"How's that different from any other night?"

"Let's put it this way – you might give serious thought to running up the gale warning flag. Keep the change and lemme know when you need another twenty."

"Hell, Double E, we got a goddam tab open."

A voice from the table. Burch answered.

"Don't doubt it for a second, but you never can tell when it might be better for a man to sit alone in a corner and do some deep whiskey meditation. Good to see you boys, though, and I aim to stay as sociable as I can."

"Anybody got a stopwatch? The boy ain't long on table manners."

That drew snorts and guffaws. Burch took a long pull of Maker's and looked at the speaker.

John "Cactus Jack" McKinney, ex-Dallas County sheriff's investigator and rumored bagman and occasional muscle for the Campisi outfit. Mostly, Jack used to spread the gelt to keep brethren lawmen off the backs of Campisi bookies and high-stakes poker games. He also beat hell out of welchers and threatened long-term parking under the sod if they didn't pay up.

Jack was crooked on crimes like gambling, prostitution and bootlegging. Considered them harmful by-products of the Bible thumper's eternal quest to deny a good time to a working man. But he was straight as a Baptist deacon's backbone on murder and became one of Dallas County DA Henry Wade's favorite investigators. He was one of the lead lawdogs who tracked down the two men wanted for the execution-style slaying of three plainclothes deputies in what became known as The Trinity River Massacre.

That wasn't enough to save him from the blowback on a hard interrogation gone bad and bloody. Jack was roughing up the running buddy of a nasty piece of work named Lucius Simpson, wanted for gunning down a Harry Hines Boulevard liquor store owner and a cashier during a holdup.

Jack was getting nowhere fast with fists and a telephone book, so upped the ante by jamming the barrel of his Smith & Wesson Model 24 into the man's mouth and cocking the hammer. The man jerked his head back, Jack's finger slipped and a .44 Special slug blew brains, blood and skull fragments across the interrogation room, splattering Jack's partner.

The dead man was named Jimmy Carlton. Nobody's angel. Had a lengthy yellow sheet for car theft, break-ins, strong-arm robberies and stick-ups. He was also the wayward but beloved nephew of a prominent South Dallas Baptist preacher who had backed the campaign of the new sheriff, Carl Thomas, the first Republican elected since Reconstruction.

Jack was part of the old Democrat crowd, hired by Bill Decker and promoted by Clarence Jones. He was indicted for manslaughter and got the chop after being acquitted. Lost his badge but landed on his feet with a sweetheart gig as security chief at Texas Instruments. Still had enough extra time to moonlight for the Campisis and do a little investigative work for anybody else with enough long green.

Burch liked Jack, a rawboned, florid-faced man with a pug nose, an easy smile offset by icy blue eyes and a thick, swoopy pompadour that was once reddish blond, but now had the yellowed tint of old ivory.

Back before he lost his own gold shield, Burch and his partner, Wynn Moore, had teamed up with Jack on a couple of homicides, including the slasher slaying of one of Abe Weinstein's favorite strippers, a Colony Club headliner-turned-hooker with the stage name of Peppermint Pop. Agnes Crowley was the name on her driver's license.

They nailed her pimp, George "Be-Bop" Gibson, who confessed he cut her up because she stole his money and hooked up with another pimp. No remorse. No leniency. A date with the Big Spike deferred until the Supremes in DeeCee started letting states legally kill a man again.

After Burch finally got kicked off the force for beating the shit out of a pimp in front of his lawyer, Jack helped him get his PI license and spoon fed him jobs that helped him crank up the business. He became Burch's 'rabbi', a mentor who helped him navigate the treacherous ground of life without a badge.

"Evenin', Jack. You the vicar for this little prayer meeting?"

"That's the Reverend Jack to a heathen and sinner like you, Double E. Are you ready to repent and join the fellowship this very night as we drink deep, tell each other lies and penetrate the mysteries of life?"

"Is there a membership fee?"

"Yes, you pick up next week's tab."

"Sounds expensive, but I do believe I have the credentials to qualify."

"Believe me, son, when I tell you that's a true fact."

Everyone at the table qualified. Looming on Jack's left, at the shadowed corner of the table, sat Wilbert "Big Cat" Thompson, the first black cop to win a gold detective's shield. The Cat also had the dubious distinction of being the first black detective bounced from the force for breaking the fingers, wrists and kneecaps of a kidnapping suspect to get him to spill the location of nine-year-old Carlotta Sanchez.

Saved the girl. Lost the shield.

On the Cat's left sprawled a bald, big-bellied ex-deputy named Bobby Carl Schmid, great-nephew of Sheriff Smoot Schmid, whose deputies helped ex-Rangers Frank Hamer and Manny Gault track down and kill Bonnie Parker and Clyde Barrow.

Burch couldn't quite recall how Bobby Carl lost his badge, but it had something to do with a dead hooker, a gambler, a cock-fight and a state senator. He didn't much like Schmid. The feeling was mutual but simmered on a back burner as long as Jack was around.

Burch and Schmid made it a point not to look at each other.

Burch did look at the man to his right and smile. Johnny Del Rio, thin as a rake handle, still sporting an extravagant Zapata moustache, still flashing the gold jewelry and pimp swagger that made him so convincing an undercover cop when he and Burch were on the vice squad.

They partnered up and worked an inside-outside game, with Johnny playing the Mex mack daddy to get next to pimps, mad-ams and *coyotes* bringing teenage girls to *El Norte* to be turned out as whores. Burch would run the paper trail, grab the warrants and watch Johnny's back until it was takedown time.

They were a good team and put solid cases together that helped ease Burch's pain from being exiled from homicide after his partner, Wynn Moore, got killed. The brass blamed him for Moore's death, but not as much as Burch blamed himself.

When murders started spiking in The D, Burch was called back to homicide because they needed experienced manhunters.

Back to The Show. But never forgiven.

He danced on the trap door for a few more years and solved a string of murders that pissed off the suits even more. They were waiting with double-bit axes when he bounced Ronnie Bedoin, a skinny-ass Cajun pimp, off the cinderblock wall of a downtown dive and punched out most of his teeth for dismissing the death of one of his hookers as the unavoidable cost of doing business.

Burch liked her, a gal from Nacogdoches named Ruby Sweat who worked the streets as Candy Slice. She once gave him a freebie mercy fuck after finding him seriously behind the whiskey curve in a hotel bar shortly after his third and final divorce. The only time he took a freebie from a working girl while wearing a badge.

An act of sentimental violence wasn't much excuse for a terminal fuckup, so Burch turned in his shield. Johnny didn't last much longer. He got framed for a hooker's murder by the friends of the same assholes he and Burch put away for shanghaiing Mexican girls for Dallas hot-pillow joints.

The frame was iron-clad and detailed – Johnny's fingerprints in the vic's apartment; wire transfers from Mexico to a Fort Worth account in Johnny's name; Johnny's scrawl forged on the signature cards; witnesses who said he and the vic, Traci Fuentes, were a hot item who had screaming matches that quickly turned violent.

And the clincher – a scarf found in Johnny's apartment that matched fibers found in the abrasions on the strangled woman's neck.

A dirty cop with a violent temper. Didn't look good. But Johnny had a rich uncle in Albuquerque who hired one of Racehorse

Haynes' proteges, a smart, charismatic lawyer named Randall Sharp, who had learned many of the master's moves and was out to make a name for himself in The D.

Sharp hired Jack and Burch. They knocked holes in the prosecution's case, unearthing the fingerprints of a Tex-Mex hitter at the vic's apartment. Crime scene boys found them but they weren't in the murder book. Friend of Jack's slipped the prints from the deep freeze of the frame.

They also lined up the branch manager at that Fort Worth bank who testified Johnny wasn't the man who opened the account that bore his name. Got the victim's sister, who put on a tearful show at trial, insisting Johnny was a kind and gentle lover who was going to rescue Traci from a life of perdition.

With a catch in her voice, the sister even used the Spanish phrase *la perdición*. Which was a nice touch the jurors loved.

Good enough for two mistrials and an acquittal, but Johnny was done as a lawman. He went to work for Sharp and enjoyed wrecking flimsy case work by cops and prosecutors intent on railroading the semi-innocent. Which won him no friends in the DA's office or the Dallas Police Department and the Dallas County Sheriff's Office.

Johnny didn't give a shit. He stood up, arms open wide. Burch did the same, stepping into a manly *abrazo*. Johnny stepped back and gave Burch the full up-and-down assessment.

"*Te ves próspero, mi hermano.*"

"*Esa es solo otra manera de decirme que estoy gordo, cabron.*

Johnny laughed, feigned a pained and surprised look, then pointed at Jack.

"*Estoy herido, mi hermano. En verdad, te ves casi tan distinguido como nuestro Líder sin Miedo.*"

"*En inglés, pendejos,*" Jack growled. "*Por favor, en inglés.*"

"I was just telling our old friend Ed Earl how prosperous and distinguished he looks with all that white hair in his beard. Almost as distinguished as you."

"He was trying to tell me how fat and old I looked without pissing you off. Now, he's let the cat out of the bag."

Jack grunted.

"Enough of this happy horseshit. Let's get serious about telling each other tall tales and true lies. You know, there's a helluva lot of facts floating around out there, but very little truth. Let's see if we can find some at this very table."

The stories started to flow, each one reminding somebody else of another. Burch listened, laughed and chipped in a few of his own legends and one or two about Wynn Moore. Carla Sue's memory faded away and his other demons stayed curled up in their holes. He relaxed and his bloodlust for strong whiskey throttled down.

The tales bouncing around the table were tinged with gunsmoke and gallows humor, off-hand admissions of stark terror followed by the electric jolt of life unexpectedly reborn, bawdy moments with cop groupies in the back of a squad car. And the absolute worst – the deep cut of the one case that was never solved or brought to trial and gnawed at the soul like a rat chewing through the insulation of a 220-volt power cable.

The Cat growled out the story of one that still haunted him, his voice rumbling like chunks of coal tumbling down a sheet metal chute, sharpened by the pain of memory.

"You know how we do what we do," he said, pausing to drain a tall glass of vodka on the rocks. "We like a guy for a kill but it might be somebody else. We work the leads. Things start pointing his way. Then we sit across the table with that guy, look him in the eye and just know. Know it down deep in that lizard brain we got that this motherfucker iced the vic. We motherfuckin' KNOW."

He lit a Newport with a gold Ronson Varaflame, sucking down the smoke and picking up the story in a softer voice.

"Vic was named Loretta Smalls. Pretty little thing. Blonde, petite, everybody's little sister. Studying to be a nurse at Texas

27

Women's. Found her raped and strangled in her apartment. Eyes gouged out of her skull with a linoleum knife. Post-mortem."

The Cat grimaced and stubbed out his smoke.

"Scumbag we liked for it looked like a Joe Straight Arrow, an accountant who worked financial services at the school, Christopher Norris. Lived alone not far from the vic. Loner type. Glasses and bow tie. Hung around the coffee shop and tried to chat up the gals. Geeky but harmless, the gals said. Until he zeroed in on Loretta and started pestering her. Wouldn't stop. Dude got dark and a little scary."

Flame to another Newport and a deep drag.

"She filed a complaint. They gave him a warning but he kept at it. They let him go. That night, he shows up at her apartment, banging on the door, raging mad, seriously unhinged. Calls her a bitch and a whore. Says she ruined his life. Neighbors hear all of this and call the cops. Gave them his punchline – 'You're a pretty little prick-teaser but I'm gonna fix you so you ain't pretty no more.' That earned him some time in county and a psych eval. Three weeks after he gets out, Loretta gets dead."

The Cat leaned forward, out of the shadows and into the dim light, resting his elbows on the table. His head lowered, his eyes seeing nothing but the flickering images of his memory, a movie they all knew but only he could see because nobody owned it but him.

"You know, fellas – when I looked that motherfucker in the eye, it was like plugging into the main line. Brain gets lit up, spine starts tingling, synapses start firing. And you can see right inside the man's head, see what he done to that girl. You know and you know that motherfucker KNOWS you seen what he done."

The Cat sighed and paused, like he was weighing whether to keep telling his story or shut the hell up. He spotted Whitey and whipped an index finger in an air circle to signal another lap around the hard liquor track.

"Never could nail that pencil-necked motherfucker. Evidence went sideways. Witnesses crawdaddied. Couldn't even get his ass indicted. Drove my partner and me crazy. So I started staking out his house off McKinney. From dark thirty till the wee hours. Two, three nights one week. Then disappear the next. Back two weeks later."

Whitey placed another vodka highball in front of The Cat. A long sip drained half the glass.

"Wasn't subtle about it. Let him know I was there. Tail him to the Tom Thumb. Grab a cart and do my own shoppin', let him see me at the cashier's. He's gettin' brisket at Sonny Bryan's, there I am in line gettin' a sausage plate. Worked other cases, but always found time for my man. After two years, it finally paid off. Man hung himself in his closet."

Burch understood the Cat's obsession. Knew it all too well. Driven by bone-deep certainty about a killer's guilt and boiling impotence over the failure to find enough evidence to fill a prosecutor's checklist, a cop became trapped in a vicious and corrosive dynamic – certainty ramped up the rage while the rage gave the certainty deeper roots.

Deep enough to cause some cops to take the ultimate step with a throw-down piece that couldn't be traced.

The Cat got lucky – the object of his fierce compulsion took his own life before the cop did it for him. But Burch knew that with the end of the furious obsession, the certainty withered and the doubt came roaring back. He knew the Cat would never know whether the hangman's knot was a confession of guilt or mad terror about a true-to-life Grim Reaper who haunted his every step.

Burch kept his own counsel about this, sipping Maker's and lighting another Lucky. He should have known his dead partner would weigh in with a ghostly whisper.

"We know a thing or two about believing a man's guilt beyond a mortal certainty, but not being able to prove it, don't we, Sport Model?"

"*You bet, partner. We know it's a trap, danglin' a tempting short cut that keeps you from doin' what you need to keep doin' – dig deeper.*"

"*Easy to be self-righteous about that, Sport Model.*"

"*I'm not gettin' on no high horse to throw down on another man's choice. I understand why my man here did what he did. But I was never so certain about a man's guilt that doubt was totally snuffed out. Doubt kept me up at night. Doubt kept me diggin'. Did the same for you, too.*"

"*Didn't know you were taught by the Jesuits.*"

"*Never had that privilege, partner. But I do know the Brothers say doubt is not the denial of faith, but the struggle to believe. They say it's an ongoing tussle and the older I get, the more I believe that faith never wins and doubt never dies.*"

"*Lemme tell you one or two things about doubt, Sport Model. Doubt is your friend. It's second cousin to the hairs standing up on the back of your neck that make you duck that bullet headed for your brainpan. Long as it don't freeze you up, doubt keeps you alive and doubt makes you a good cop.*"

"*Hell, tell me somethin' I don't know, partner. Doubt is the only thing I'm dead certain of.*"

Four

Back at his own crib. In the hushed and lonely hours closer to dawn than midnight. With almost enough whiskey under his belt for a snooze.

Betty Lou safely tucked away with The Club ratcheted through the steering wheel, the hidden ignition kill switch flipped to OFF and the alarm armed. Dust cover tucked in place. Leather blazer and shoulder rig shrugged off and hung on hallway pegs.

He toted the Colt, the Zippo and the Luckies to the spindle-legged cedar side table by his recliner. He shucked his snakeskin Justins while standing, then padded into the galley kitchen to crack open a fresh fifth of Maker's and pour a three-fingered nightcap.

Settled in with his feet up and jetting smoke toward the ceiling light, Burch replayed the evening's banter, war stories, lies and tall tales. He sipped his drink, hugged the soothing familiarity of all that talk and spiked the knowledge that memories wouldn't bring back the badge he lost.

He even found comfort in the imagined words of a dead man and his own response.

"Doubt is your friend...doubt keeps you alive and makes you a good cop."

"Doubt is the only thing I'm dead certain of."

A snort, a shake of the head and another sip. Burch let his mind drift, once an open invitation for those demons to come calling. The winged serpent. The knife pointed at his heart. The terror that

31

once stalked his days and nights, driving him to self-medicate with Percodan and e-less whisky.

No longer.

A memory he didn't share at Louie's rose to the surface.

Night stakeout in East Dallas. Late-70s, maybe. Year or two before Wynn Moore's death. Cold, winter rain coming down hard enough to slap down frogs and ducks. Then strangle them.

Watching the clapboard bungalow of a skell named Butch McKelvey. Red-headed dealer and KA of Scooter Short, a guy they liked for popping a jewelry store owner during a heist gone bad.

Short had a taste for Mexican brown. Specialty on the bill of fare at Chez McKelvey. Burch and Moore hoped he'd show up hungry.

Camped out in Moore's '69 Merc Marauder X-100. Black two-door with a 429 engine that never met a gas station it didn't like. Blackwall tires. Bucket seats. Console shift for the automatic tranny. Fastback hardtop.

Beast of a car. Moore called her Black Maria. She wasn't that pretty but the color was right.

Parked on a side street with a view of McKelvey's front porch and yard. Lights were on. Anybody home? Anybody's guess.

Burger wrappers on the dashboard. Cold coffee in the cupholders that rode the transmission hump. Body heat and breath fogging up the windows. Bitching back and forth.

"Can't see a fuckin' thing. Can we crank up the car and fire up the defroster?"

"Shit no. What's the matter with you, Sport Model?"

Crack the windows to let some exhaled air escape. Gut out the cold and keep the front glass clear with a bandana.

"Keep the Luckies in your pocket, Sport Model. Break out the Red Man to chew instead of smoke."

"Yeah, yeah – no smoke signals that scare the settlers. Colder'n shit tonight and we're outta coffee."

"Suck it up, Sport Model."

Chew chaw. Shoot the breeze.

Bitch about that new lieutenant with a broomstick up his ass and a hard-on for them both. Bitch about the Rangers – ol' Fergie Jenkins and pray for rain, a hurricane and the healing power of DMSO on a Canadian warhorse.

Bitch about the Cowboys missing the playoffs. Bitch about alimony and ex-wives – Burch's second, Moore's third. Bitch about the cold and rain and no damn coffee.

McKelvey's front door bangs open. He stumbles out, buck naked. Fish-belly white skin and spiky red hair. Staggers and falls off the front porch. Pops upright, mud covering his face and torso. Tries to run, dragging his left leg.

Moore fires up the Black Maria and swings a hard left onto McKelvey's street. Flips on the peekaboo headlamps. High beam. White glare on McKelvey as the front door to the house bangs open again.

Harsh white lights up a tall, big-chested woman, just as naked, storming off the porch, screaming "Motherfucker!" at the top of her lungs. Rays catch the wet and shiny black of a big revolver in her right hand.

Large breasts swinging as her long strides close the distance.

McKelvey slips in the mud. Rights himself in a crouch. Turns toward her, hands splayed out in a silent plea. She raises the revolver. A .357 Colt Trooper, they find out later.

"Last time you ever knock me around, you cockbite motherfucker."

She fires four rounds. Burch can see each one strike home as he and Wynn pull their pieces and step out of the Marquis.

Burch keeps himself behind the car door, .45 in his left hand. Wynn leans across the left fender, braces his .44 Special across the top of the hood. They both yell: "Police! Freeze!"

The woman looks their way, her black hair a drenched tangle plastered to her face and neck, her amber, wolfish eyes flashing in the headlight glare.

Burch feels a shock of recognition. He knows her from his days in vice. Theda Bayer, part-time hooker, receptionist, cocktail waitress, poker and blackjack dealer.

"Oh, fuck no – you're not gonna bring me in for killin' this piece of shit."

She jams the barrel under her chin and fires a round that blows off the top of her skull.

Body stands for a two-count before collapsing like a ruined skyscraper.

Helluva nightcap memory.

He could still see Theda's corpse. Up close in the mud. Rain-soaked raven hair against what was left of an acne-scarred face. Almond-shaped, eight-ball eyes blackened by a lover's fists. A broken nose sharply slanting left of center. Picasso paints the death mask of a raccoon woman.

Might as well kiss the ass end of sleep goodbye. Won't come now.

Guilt knocked on his brainpan, though. Serving up a reminder of a promise ignored and unfulfilled. To an old woman who might be dead by now.

Burch hoped not. He liked her. Salt of Texas type. Believer in the sweet grace of Jesus, but still liked a snort or two at sundown. Cattle and a few pumpjacks scattered around the back forty. Not filthy rich, but comfortable.

Juanita Mutscher, Theda Bayer's ex-mother-in-law, grand-mother to Theda's only child, Rhonda Mae Bayer. Burch was the one who tracked her down after Theda's last bloody testament to the power of truly rancid love.

Burch put Juanita in touch with the county child welfare folks who had Rhonda Mae, maybe all of six or seven at the time. Checked in a few times to make sure the county didn't fuck up such an easy handoff to a grandmother's loving arms. Called in a few markers when it looked like they would, including an

I.O.U. from the county judge for keeping his son out of jail after a brothel raid.

Got invited out to the Mutscher home for a face-to-face thanks. Telling Juanita 'no' was not in the cards. Nice, breezy afternoon cruise in Ol' Blue, his faded red '73 F-100 with the big six banger and the granny creeper first gear. Out U.S. 67 to Ellis County and a place in the country between Midlothian and Venus.

Wood-framed farmhouse with a tin roof, painted dove gray with navy trim on the false shutters and the frames for the doors and windows. Shook paws with Juanita's husband, J.D., a burly but quiet man with a waxed handlebar moustache who slipped away to work on a balky tractor.

Settled in with iced sweet tea on the wide front porch because sundown was still a few hours away. Burch and Juanita in matching metal patio chairs, white metal tubes with the seats and clam shell seatbacks painted the same navy as the trim.

"Miz Mutscher…"

"Call me Juanita. I'm older than you, but not THAT much older."

Said it with a smile. She was a handsome woman in her late 50s, with thick black hair shot through with white, a strong jawline and big hazel eyes that stayed dead level and didn't miss a thing.

"Detective Burch…"

"If I got to call you Juanita, you got to call me Ed Earl."

She tilted her head back and laughed, slapping her knee.

"Done deal."

Then she locked him down with those dead level eyes.

"We sure do appreciate what you did to smooth out the rough spots and get the county to do the right thing and give Rhonda Mae to us."

"Just made a few calls."

"Don't kid a kidder, Ed Earl. My husband's kin still have some fingers in the political pie up in Dallas County. We know you pulled a string or two with the right people. We're grateful. And we're not ones to forget a kindness like this. You're welcome here any time."

For five or six years, Burch took them up on their offer. Sunday chicken dinners, mostly. Invites to local shindigs. Barbecues. True Texas style. No burgers. Just smoked beef brisket, ribs and sausage. White bread, white onion slices and bread-and-butter pickles. Bottles of Lone Star, Pearl and Cokes iced down in washtubs.

The Mutschers might be Baptist, but they were also Texas German. Beer was in the blood.

It was damn near idyllic, a refuge from the murders, the mayhem and the bourbon-soaked neon. Watched Rhonda Mae grow up. Tall like her mother. Long, coltish legs. Heartbreaker smile. Smart and funny. Black hair and amber, wolfish eyes, like Juanita. Eyes you remembered. Eyes that never blinked.

Met his second ex, Faye Bonner, at one of the shindigs, a wild-game supper at the end of deer season. The marriage barely survived her move to The D. His visits to Ellis County tapered off after splitting the blanket with Faye. He still checked in with Juanita by phone, promising to visit soon. But he rarely did, shading the failure as giving Faye elbow room in her old hometown. The lies you tell yourself.

Idyllic turned to shit shortly after Danny Ray Mutscher moved back to The D from Vegas, towing a big bankroll of dubious provenance. Got a good lawyer. Crooked but sharp. Asserted Danny Ray's parental rights. Took his own mother to court.

And won.

The fix was in. The right people got greased. Not a damn thing anybody could do, including Burch, who was rarely sober by then and barely holding onto his gold shield.

Rhonda Mae moved in with her father. Juanita called and made Burch promise he'd keep an eye on granddaughter. It was a promise he kept as the girl hit her teens and took the first baby steps toward the wild side of life.

Burch got her off the hook for underage drinking, getting caught with a baggie of weed and getting swept up in a raid on a party known for maximum decibel music and a smorgasbord of pharmaceutical delights.

She wasn't holding that time. Next time she was – baggies of Black Beauties and Quaaludes. At an after-hours joint in the West End, in a back room pulling a train with some bikers. He had a word with the vice honcho on that one, his old partner, Johnny Del Rio, who had a word with the narcotics honcho, who ditched the baggies and helped Burch get her into court-ordered rehab.

Burch was out of markers. By this time, he was off the force, too, his PI shingle hung above the door of a ratty office just off Mockingbird with a view of the Dr. Pepper clock. He called Juanita and said he could do no more for Rhonda Mae. He promised to visit, but never did. He turned his back on them both. Rhonda Mae turned 17 and skipped town.

There was one last bitter memory that bit him right in his guilt-riddled heart, an earwig of Juanita's voice on his office answering machine, pleading with him, cursing his name and, finally, breaking down and sobbing out one more S.O.S. for Rhonda Mae.

Instead of adding a few more bricks of whiskey and pain pills to the wall of self-medication like he used to, he listened to his memory playback and let the shame claw his heart, twist his guts and sear his brain.

It was the howl of a wild animal in pain, a she-wolf with her paw crushed in the iron jaws of a trap. It ended with a cold curse on his already bleak future.

"Goddam your soul to hell and back, Ed Earl Burch. I wish you had never darkened my door."

He never returned that call. She never called again.

Burch poured himself a second nightcap and lit one of the last Luckies in the pack. He hadn't thought of Juanita Mutscher and

Rhonda Mae Bayer in a long time. Nearly fifteen years. Hadn't listened to that shameful playback of an old woman's anger and fear.

Hadn't called up the images of Theda Bayer's suicide after murdering her drug-dealing boyfriend, either. Tack another five years to that memory going AWOL.

Guilt told him he needed to remedy that. Guilt told him to call Juanita Mutscher, if she was still alive. He snorted again and nodded.

"Can't call her now. Tomorrow will have to do."

"It's already tomorrow, Sport Model."

"Today, then. But not now. If she's still alive, she's asleep."

"You'll forget."

"I doubt that. Between you and a guilty conscience, I'll manage to be reminded."

"Doubt's the only thing you're dead certain of, right Sport Model?"

Burch shook his head. Nothing like a ghost using your own words against you.

Five

Time had not been a friend to Juanita Mutscher.

Her thick hair was yellowed like curdled cream, peppered with a few strands of the black of youth. A gauzy patch covered her right eye and the right side of her face and mouth were frozen in place.

She leaned heavily on a silvery metal cane with a four-footed tip when she met Burch at her screen door. She dragged her right leg while slowly moving back to an overstuffed easy chair that gave her a long view through the door's wire mesh and the pasture and gravel driveway that led up from the road.

A stroke for sure. A strong, handsome woman now ruined. She batted away his hand when he tried to help her into the chair.

"Pshaw! I ain't dead. Yet. Grab yourself that chair over there and keep an old woman company."

Burch did as he was told, spinning a hoop-backed chair with a cane bottom into place so he could sit close under the gaze of her good eye. Still hazel. Still able to pin him with a dead level stare. He slid the Ray-Bans off his face and slipped them into his pocket.

"That's some kind of car you're drivin'. Last time I saw you, it was an old Ford pickup. Now this shiny thing. How'd you come by it."

"Long story, Juanita. Lot of water under that bridge."

"Bet there was a woman under there, too."

Burch smiled: "You'd win that bet."

"Go ahead and light up. I like the smell and enjoy watching a man taking his ease with a good smoke. Haven't had much of that since J.D. passed."

"I'm sorry for your loss. I didn't know. I liked J.D. Liked tinkering on the tractors with him. How long has he been gone?"

"Be ten year come January. Not exactly like you've been darkening our door to know such things, though."

Burch blushed. Her good eye didn't blink and didn't let him off the hook. Her words did that.

"I hated you for a good long while. Damned your soul and wished you an early grave and a fast trip to hell."

"You had every right. I turned my back on you, J.D. and Rhonda Mae."

"Seeing you here and now, I can't stay mad at you, Ed Earl. Not too much. You did everything you could for Rhonda Mae and then some. And I know you had your own life to live after you and Faye broke up. But we considered you a friend and it hurt when you didn't call or visit."

"I'd like to think I'm still a friend. A sorry one, maybe, but still a friend."

She stayed quiet, holding him in place with focused hazel, forcing him to raise his eyes to meet her stare. She broke first, tears filling that single eye.

"Dammit to hell, I missed you. What made you come back now?"

He fished a dark blue bandana out of the back pocket of his Wranglers. A clean one. She took it with her left hand, wiped away the tears and honked her nose once before handing it back.

"Why now? It was easy for me to pretend you were just another loved one who had passed on."

Burch blushed again but smiled.

"Simple. I owe you for being that sorry friend."

"You don't owe me a thing."

"You're wrong about that."

"Don't argue with an old woman. I'll hit you in the head with this cane."

They both laughed and both enjoyed him smoking a Lucky in the twilight quiet that followed.

"The doc don't give me long. Says the next one will do me in. Could happen any day now. Or tomorrow or next week or next month. Like a piano wire stretched to breakin'. Least little thing might set it off. And that'll be the end of me."

"They can't do anything?"

"Oh, they could saw open my skull and root around in my brain some and patch some blood vessels. Might buy me a little time. Or it might turn me into a pot of overcooked string beans. Said no thank you to that mess."

"You would."

"So would you."

"That's a true fact. Don't we make a pair?"

"Couple of stubborn ol' mules. Too old to pull a plow. Might as well shoot the both of us."

She laughed again and slapped her knee. That drew a chuckle from Burch that turned into a smoker's hack and a ball of phlegm. He pulled out the bandana and spat.

"Not very sanitary after I blew my nose in there."

"What are friends for? Let me ask this – got anybody lookin' after you?"

"Don't need no damn body lookin' after me. I can still get around. Slow as hell, but still able. I can even cook and take a shower bath. I still got Carlos comin' round to tend to the place and his wife Luz to come in and clean."

"Anybody else?"

"Got a girl named Lucy who comes from town to do my hair because I still have my vanity. She likes to sit with me on the porch, have a beer or two and listen to me talk about the old days. Sometimes she sleeps on the couch if it gets too late and I fix her breakfast. Girl's family is pure-dee white trash, but she seems set on makin' somethin' of herself. Works in a beauty parlor in the daylight. Takes accounting courses at night."

"I'm sure they're all fine people, but they ain't kin."

"No, they're a damn sight better than my blood kin. All but one."

Her lone eye swept his face, searching. Burch met her stare but needed to do something with his hands. He lit another Lucky, snapping the Zippo shut with a flick of his wrist.

"You came here to make amends for being such a sorry friend, right? Let me tell you straight out that I don't want your charity, Ed Earl Burch. Or your pity. But I do believe in the power of redemption and a man trying to right something he thinks he done wrong. Doesn't matter if I think he done wrong. He does. And wants to do something about it."

"That about says it. Don't know if it would have made a damn bit of difference if I'da been around, but I wasn't. I wasn't a friend when you could have used one. I know that now and I'd like to make it up to you."

"Shut up before you get me to cryin' again. Since you've got your cap set on makin' things right between us, let an old woman tell you what you can do. No, I ain't about to tell you to go to hell. Just West Texas, which some folks think is the same thing."

Burch grunted. She saw a darkness flicker across his face.

"Did I say somethin' wrong?"

"No, ma'am. You're fine."

"I saw that look. Don't try to spare an old woman's feelin's."

"You said West Texas is all. Brings up some memories. Not all of 'em good ones."

"You been out there?"

"A time or two. A case or two. Every time I've been there, some folks have tried to punch my ticket. Some of them wore a badge."

He didn't tell the old woman about the broken jaw that still crackled and popped where it had been wired together or the white scar that ran just above his forehead where his hairline used to be.

Lovely parting gifts from a *narco* named Teddy Roy Bonafacio, who saw winged serpents and Aztec leopard knights in his nightmares and was raising a knife to cut out Burch's heart when he got blown down by hollow-points from the .45 of the woman who gave him that dark blue Cutlass.

He didn't tell her how T-Roy's nightmares became his own or how those midnight terrors stalked him during the day, giving him vertigo and a howling lust for Percodan and bourbon to hose down those demons and slam them back into their holes.

Took him a long time to lose that pharmaceutical and corn distillate crutch and face those fiends cold sober. A long time. And he still kept the bourbon handy.

"If what I want you to do involves West Texas, the deal is off?"

"I didn't say that. Truth is, I've been thinking about that place a lot lately. Somethin' about it speaks to me in spite of almost gettin' killed out there. I'm just surprised that whatever it is you want me to do means headin' back there again. I don't think that's coincidence."

"Sounds more like fate."

"Yes'm, it does. Mind tellin' me what it is you want me to do?"

"Find Rhonda Mae. Haven't heard from her in more than a year. Not a card or a phone call. Used to hear from her right regular. Now, nothing. That's how I know she's in trouble."

Trouble and West Texas. To Burch, they were one and the same.

Burch burned a third Lucky while Juanita told him what she could about Rhonda Mae.

It wasn't much. The granddaughter was mixed up with one of those Texas secession groups that hated the federal government and wanted to revive an independent republic. Bring back the Lone Star as a national flag.

"Bunch of damn foolishness. Next thing you know, they'll want to dig up the bones of Sam Houston and turn the Alamo into the state capitol," she said. "Tried to tell her that but you know it don't do no good talkin' sense to a true believer."

Burch knew the type and their line of talk. Brushed up against them as a cop and a shamus. They wanted to save Texas from those godless sodomites in Washington, D.C. Put Texas back on track to fulfill a manifest destiny that would be smiled upon by a righteous and almighty God.

They rarely said it plain in public, but they meant a God for whites only. Blacks and Mexicans need not apply. And no damn Jews.

Peddling a bunch of addled-brained bullshit, by Burch's lights, with their crazy-quilt interpretations of the Constitution, the Treaty of Guadalupe Hidalgo and the questionable legality of the joint House-Senate resolution used to sidestep the need for a Senate-ratified treaty to annex Texas in 1845.

The Texas Secede bunch papered state and federal courthouses with lawsuits claiming the Republic of Texas was never legally dissolved and filed warrants and subpoenas against judges and elected officials in the name of a sovereign Texian republic that existed in their minds only.

With their tortured legalisms, they appeared little different from the other anti-government groups that fired up across the Midwest, the Great Plains and the Mountain West, fueled by outrage over the 1992 killing of Randy Weaver's wife and son by federal agents besieging the white supremacist's hilltop home on Ruby Ridge, near Naples, Idaho.

Never mind that a U.S. marshal, Bill Degan, was also killed. The siege was portrayed as an act of paramilitary murder by a malevolent federal government. Randy Weaver became a hero, Vicky and

Sam Weaver martyred saints and Ruby Ridge a battle cry and a bloody shirt for recruiting.

With the fiery end of the Branch Davidian siege near Waco, Texas the following year, anti-government hatred shifted into overdrive, swelling the ranks of self-declared militias, Christian Patriot and Posse Comitatus groups, tax protestors and secessionists – of both the Texas kind and those neo-Nazis calling for a whites-only homeland in the Pacific Northwest.

Burch had a second cousin, Jerry Pace, a McLennan County sheriff's investigator who knew David Koresh, pegged him as a bat-shit crazy cockhound with a messiah complex and bitterly resented the brutal federal shit show that turned the man into a patron saint and Exhibit A that the federal government was at war with its own people.

"Right or wrong, these crazies got all the evidence they need to sell their happy horseshit. Goddam trigger-happy feds served it up on a bloody platter with all their military hardware and dynamic entry SWAT bullshit. It's like these assholes have let loose a plague on the land that us locals will have to clean up. And if you're wearin' a badge, you best get into their crazy shit and learn the lingo so you'll know what you're up against."

His cousin was right. These rag-tag bands found ready converts among the disaffected and down-and-out, mainly but not exclusively white, willing to buy their bent interpretation of the Constitution and their babbling about One-World Government, black U.N. helicopters and sovereign citizens who didn't need to pay taxes and didn't need to have a driver's license or auto tag. Their top draw was a shared zeal for unfettered gun rights, calling on citizens to arm themselves so they wouldn't be the victims of the next Waco or Ruby Ridge.

Others took a darker turn, finding a home with white supremacist outfits like Aryan Nations and their Christian Identity dogma that preached hatred of Jews, blacks, Mexicans, Asians – anybody who wasn't white and didn't share their lust for a race war to cleanse America. To these crazies, the feds were the main enemy – the Zionist Occupation Government, or Z.O.G., the hated protector of the Mud People.

While some just played at the anti-government game, a splinter group of Aryan Nations known as The Order, or Brüder Schweigen – The Silent Brotherhood – took action. They pulled off a string of armored car heists in the early 1980s to raise funds to turn their call for a race war into reality.

One of their members was convicted of the 1984 murder of Denver radio talk show host Alan Berg, an outspoken Jewish lawyer who regularly ridiculed their anti-Semitic beliefs. Their leader, Robert Jay Matthews, was killed in a shootout with FBI agents on Whidbey Island, Washington that same year.

That bit of bloody history reminded Burch of two things. *Just because you think they're crazy doesn't mean they won't kill you. And this: Never, ever underestimate the lethal potential of dogma no matter how loony it sounds.*

A corollary also crossed his mind: *Don't laugh in their face – that'll get you dead.* After all, this was Texas and everybody had the gun even if they didn't have the dogma. And few Texans expressed any love for the federal government, no matter how much green milk they sucked from the taxpayer's tit.

Burch didn't need a roadmap to see it wasn't that long a drive from the benign sounding anti-government rhetoric of Ronald Reagan to the more militant talk of gun-toting yahoos running around the woods in surplus fatigues getting ready to fend off black helicopters carrying jackbooted federal thugs. Strip away the Constitutional and sovereign citizen gibberish and you could clearly see they were at different exit ramps on the same highway.

It was even a shorter trip between the closeted Klansman with the Rebel flag sticker on the bumper of his pickup and the Christian Identity adherent. They both hated Jews, blacks, Mexicans and the federal government; one was just more willing to take direct and deadly action.

And it didn't surprise Burch one bit when mainstream politicians, almost all of them Republican, began catering to the less onerous beliefs these groups held with sharper, more overt rhetoric damning the feds, embracing God and guns and giving a knowing wink to some of the loonier beliefs.

Tim McVeigh slammed the door shut on all that shameless suck-up when he blew up the Alfred P. Murrah Federal Building in Oklahoma City on April 19, 1995, a date with heavy meaning for the Z.O.G. zealots, the second anniversary of the bloody end to the Waco siege.

When McVeigh set off a rented truck packed with ammonium nitrate and diesel fuel, he killed 168 people in the worst act of domestic terrorism in U.S. history. An Army veteran of the Gulf War and a militia believer, he also made it far less fashionable for politicians to kiss the ass of militia types and go too far in their own anti-government rhetoric.

Still had to sift through the stubborn losers with nowhere to go, filtering out the loudmouths and yard bitches to find the dead-eyed *seriosos* who would gun down a mixed-race couple or an abortion doc. Or drive a truck bomb into a courthouse or synagogue. Might only be two or three in any group, but Burch knew they were there.

Also had to be mindful of this dangerous border truth: in the desolate West Texas outback, any gaggle of outcasts might be using the aggressive insistence on sovereign citizenship and high-decibel anti-government preaching to keep solid citizens at bay. In a place where folks naturally tended to mind their own business and hate *federales* of any stripe, this was damned good cover for gun-running and drug smuggling, particularly if the gaggle was gathered at a remote ranch miles from the nearest crossroads community and close to the Rio Grande.

And that looped back to spotting the hard cases. From his days as a cop, Burch knew it was rarely the loudmouth or barnyard strutter. Whether he was dealing with a street gang, a car theft ring or a bunch of drug smugglers, Burch always eyed the quiet ones who stuck to the shadows, the ones unwilling to let a cop see their lethal innards or the cold look that marked a killer.

Lawmen who dealt with these anti-government groups said the same dynamic was in play. The motor mouth was usually the front guy, chattering the Christian Patriot or Texas Secede dogma like a chipmunk with Dixie Crystal roaring through a peanut-sized brain. You kept an eye on that one just in case you were wrong, but you were cutting sign to find the muscle and brains of an outfit that might have a far more lucrative and criminal calling.

You kept looking for telltales, some that tickled the subconscious, others subtle as a Louisville Slugger to the snout. Like spotting somebody in a gaggle of Kluxers sporting an Alice Baker tattoo – maybe a green shamrock with the letters A and B in the middle.

Cute little tatt like that would cause your pucker meter to max out. You knew you weren't dealing with your basic, homegrown scooter scum or trailer park meth cooker.

Not hardly. Alice Baker ink meant you were going up against the worst of the worst, the Aryan Brotherhood, the powerful prison gang that preached white supremacy and the Aryan Nation's Christian Identity beliefs and had a long reach that stretched beyond the walls of the stony lonesome.

Anybody sporting an AB tatt rode for The Brand and was using dogma as cover. What The Brand really stood for was money, greed and a violent means to grab and maintain their power over any outfit they infiltrated. Gun-running, prostitution, drug smuggling, murder-for-hire – you name it, they did it, ditching the dogma in a heartbeat to align with anybody who helped them get what they wanted. Didn't matter if they were black, red, yellow or brown.

"You're awful damn quiet."

"Just thinking. Did Rhonda Mae tell you much about the folks she was with?"

"Not a lot beyond that restore-the-Texas-Republic bushwa. In one letter, she mentioned there being a squabble. Sounded like Baptists arguing over doctrine just before splitting the church in two. Said it had her thinking about moving on. Next note I got from her, she said it was all sweetness and light again and she decided to stay."

"Still got those notes, Juanita?"

"Middle drawer of J.D.'s rolltop. Tied up with a black ribbon. Go fetch them and bring them here."

Burch did as he was told. His knees popped as he walked across the hardwood floor to find the bundle of letters and hand them to the old woman. She untied the ribbon then, one-by-one, pulled out the envelopes and held them close to her good eye to read the post-mark date. She handed Burch five envelopes.

Three had a Faver postmark, the other two were sent from Van Horn. Inside each was a sheet or two of ruled white paper like you'd find in a school kid's notebook. Burch scanned each one, wincing at the passages that tied the false promises of Texas secession to fiery riffs about Waco and Ruby Ridge and the urgency of creating a bastion of well-armed sovereign citizens.

"My eyes are open now for the first time in my life, grandmother....I truly believe it's time for the people of this country to take a stand against a Federal Government that has betrayed them, leading us down a godless road of One-World Government, Homosexuality and Race-Mixing...The cure for this is building another Texas Republic based on the Bible and the gun, a separate place where Sovereign Citizens can live free..."

Hard to believe the smart, rebellious girl he remembered would buy this bullshit. Harder still to see how she expected to win over Juanita Mutscher. People change, but only the desperate and deeply alienated fed their souls and brainpans with rank hokum and hatred.

Unless.

Unless you were slinging this shit like a snake-oil salesman barking his pitch to the yokels of East Bumfuck. Unless you were filling the yokels with fantasies, scapegoats and false promises to make it easier to pick their pockets. Unless you wanted to make folks believe you were one thing – a half-crazed huckster, best avoided, hustling half-dangerous true believers – while you were really something far different.

"...there are True Believers living here, folks who want to save Texas and keep her separate from a Federal Government that wants to put us under the boot of the U.N. Then there are folks who want to make a quick buck. Lots of quick bucks. I've got a foot in both camps but the tension is thick and I got to make a choice or leave because the middle is no place to be...Everybody has a gun...."

Burch could buy Rhonda Mae as a sovereign citizen grifter who didn't believe a word of what she preached. That matched what he remembered. Then again, he was deeply cynical and quit believing in anything when he lost his gold shield and was always looking for the con behind any preachy rhetoric.

No reason she couldn't be both – a True Believer willing to sell out her own. Judas did it for thirty pieces of silver. He looked again at one of her lines. *...the middle is no place to be...*

Never was in the West Texas border country. Nasty players lurked at either end of that middle – *narcos*, gunrunners, smugglers, rustlers, thieves and greedheads who never, ever had their fill. Had enough money to farm out their wet work and keep their fingernails clean and well-manicured. Soul-less creatures who would bash a baby's skull on a rock before killing the screaming mother then count the greenbacks while fresh-spilled blood gleamed like splattered paint.

Had to be just as nasty as them to survive. Or get yourself long gone. Rhonda Mae made it sound like she chose what was behind Door Number Two.

Be a ghost.

But you never knew what somebody would do when the wolves were at the door, snarling and baring their fangs. Might make you take a different turn on the trail. Might flash your own fangs and find out they were just as sharp and deadly as the other guy's.

Might like the power of your new, lethal self. Might turn you from a charming grifter into something with more murderous intent. Travel down that trail far enough and you became just as cold and dead-eyed as them. And just as beyond grace and redemption.

Burch hoped that wasn't true of Rhonda Mae but knew he could wind up dead if he dismissed the possibility. Be a damn steep price to pay for fulfilling the last wish of a dying old woman.

Another passage brought him up short for its arresting honesty, fired by words that struck a true chord utterly devoid of dogma or hustle, matching what Burch felt about that atavistic country.

"...There is something wonderfully raw and beautiful about the land we live on...At night, you can lose yourself in stars that glitter like diamonds and cover all the sky you can see...It's harsh, arid country with its own stark magic. The mountains rise up rocky and sharp, looking like the bones of an ancient and terrible beast ready to tell you the earth's deepest and darkest secrets....I love it and want to stay out here forever...."

In her final letter, she said she found true love.

"T.J. is a good man who sees the world as I do...we both believe in creating a new Republic of Texas and living our lives out here in freedom and God's grace. We're both ready to sacrifice whatever necessary to build that better place..."

Burch eyed the old woman.

"She ever say more about this T.J. fella?"

"No. Just more of the same of what you've already read. Don't even know his name. Just that they found each other and believe the same thing."

"She ever tell you where she was livin'?"

"Not really. Said it was on an old ranch that had been abandoned. Livin' there with a bunch of other true believers. Runnin' a few head of cattle. Dividin' the chores. Made it sound like a hippie commune. With guns."

"Never said where, though? There's a bunch of places like that out there."

"No, sir. But quite a few of them letters had that Faver postmark. Know the place?"

"I do. Know it well. Even know the sheriff."

"He one of the ones who tried to kill you?"

"No, that would be his predecessor. He tried to set me up for a dirt nap. But he's dead and I'm still standin'."

"You kill him?"

"Didn't get the pleasure. He blew his own brains out when the Rangers started closing in on his crooked ass."

"What's the new one like?"

"Straight-shooter and fairly honest when I knew him, but it's been a few years. Guess I'll find out if he's changed any – for good or bad."

"That your starting point?"

"Only one I've got, so far. You mind me keepin' these and the others? Never know what I might find by givin' each one a careful read."

With a grunt, she handed over the rest of the ribboned stack. She then lifted a Bible with a cracked, brown leather cover from the table at her side and plunked it on her lap. She looked down, moving her head to get focus with her good eye, then pulled out a thick business envelope.

"Leviticus. That's about right," she said before looking up at him. "This here will get you started."

"I don't need your money, Juanita."

"And I won't accept your charity, Ed Earl. You know better than to piss me off. You'll take this envelope and use the money to find

Rhonda Mae. There's four thousand dollars inside. When you need more, you call. There's also a note I wrote to her. Says I want to see her one last time."

He leaned forward in his chair and took the envelope from her shaking, outstretched hand. She flopped back in her chair and took a rattling breath.

"You're a good man to do this, Ed Earl, but I want it to be a square deal between us."

He nodded, tapped the envelope on his left thigh, then stood up to leave. There were tears in Juanita Mutscher's good, left eye.

Six

Wiley Bohannon slammed shut the steel-tubed gate on 200 acres of sorry, rocky and scrub-choked pasture split by a creek bed that stayed dry. Unless a rare storm parked overhead and pissed enough rain to create a sudden raging runoff that just as quickly turned back into a trickle, a mud track then dust.

He rattled the gate chain around an upright metal fence post, pulling the slack through a half-assed half hitch, noting the metallic echo from the rocks of a rise at the far end of the pasture. Shucking greasy cowhide work gloves and slapping them on top of the post, he turned his back to the sharp wind knifing down from the Davis Mountains to roll a homemade of Bugler. Fired it up with a kitchen match raked across a calloused thumb.

With arms draped over the gate's primer red top tube and its speckles of surface rust, Bohannon smoked and watched about fifty head of cattle chow down on hay he had forked out of the bed of a clapped-out '64 International Harvester pickup. The truck coughed and rumbled behind him, a rust bucket no longer licensed for the road.

Cattle looked damn happy to have this feed because the winter had been cold and dry, so far, with little of the rain that called up the bright green of fresh forage. They were mostly Corriente, a breed descended from the herds brought to the New World by the Spaniards, and Corriente-Hereford crosses. With a few Brangus sprinkled in for show.

Snooty ranchers slurred the small-framed Corriente as 'trash cattle,' suitable only as targets for rodeo ropers and bulldoggers, damning their lean meat as too tough and stringy to cut and chew.

Man might dull three knives and chip a tooth for his trouble, so the snoots said. Might be better off staying long hungry. Or sticking to frijoles and tortillas. Less of a hazard to cutlery, crowns and bridgework.

But they were perfect for this harsh country, thriving on less feed and water than larger, beefier breeds and armed with curving horns to fend off wolves and coyotes. They were also wily escape artists that could jump a low fence and stay hidden in thick brush like Comanche raiders.

Other than that, they were easy keepers. Just throw them out on the land and let them be. Which is pretty much all Bohannon and three other hands did for the 300 head scattered across this remote northern corner of Cuervo County.

Perfect for another reason on this place, once a real deal cattle outfit known as the Bar L R, last-name initials for the two men who founded it in the 1870s, Josephus Linton and Titus Raulerson. Perfect window dressing for a ranch in name and brand but not true purpose. No fuss, no muss and cheap to replace for the few sold for slaughter or rodeo stock to maintain a West Texas fiction.

When he kept his mind empty and his eyes on the cattle and the jagged peaks jutting along the long horizon of clear winter air, he could fool himself for a half hour or so and forget the fiction.

He could almost believe he was a sho'nuff cowhand riding for the brand like he did in his younger days. In those stolen moments, he could pretend the Bar L R might be a raggedy-ass outfit but was just as righteous in the beef and blood as the o6 or the Gage Holland.

A short, barrel-chested man with blue eyes, close-cropped gray hair and a luxurious Fu Manchu the color of iron filings, Bohannon was pushing sixty and could still rope and ride like a man twenty years younger.

But back in his hard-drinking days, he fell in with a crowd that rustled cattle and stole tractors, balers, stock trailers and any other kind of ag equipment that wasn't locked down tight. Did a five-spot in Huntsville, keeping his skills sharp with prison rodeo and weaning himself from whiskey.

The mark of an ex-con killed his chances of ever again working for a top cattle outfit. Only the smaller spreads would take him on. And never for very long. More often than not, he hired himself out for day work during busy spells like roundups, when ranchers weren't too choosy about the past of a man with roping skills and cow sense.

When ranch jobs were scarce, he'd sign on with a well-digging or road-building crew – outdoor work to keep some cash in his pocket.

He refused to take an indoor job in town. Refused to drink, too, or look up his old running buddies he had never ratted out.

An old waddie he knew from the Gage Holland, Tom Sartelle, told him about this place. In his younger days, Sartelle had been a top hand. But he wasn't above taking a buck or three to look the other way when Bohannon and his crew cut fence to rustle some cattle or steal a top-end loader.

Sartelle worked the Bar L R for a couple of years until his arthritis left him too stoved up to ride or rope. Quit to run the cash register at a feed store in Faver, entertaining the locals with tall tales when Bohannon chanced upon him a few years back. Sartelle was still wearing a sweat-stained Resistol, a canvas vest and tall boots that day, but his scrawny butt was planted in the bucket seat of a swivel stool instead of a slick-fork saddle.

Bohannon kept his eyes on the cattle as they munched hay and let his mind drift back and run a replay of his chat with a man now resting below the sod of a pauper's grave at the edge of town.

"You'll get three squares, a bunk, a horse or three and a decent wage, but it's ain't what you'd call a real workin' ranch."

"What is it, then?"

"A place where a man what knows how to keep his mouth shut can rope, ride, chase Mex cattle and fix fence for fair pay. They won't ask too many questions about you if you don't ask ANY damn questions about them."

"Shit, Tom – I sure as hell don't want to get in no jackpot. One jolt in the stony lonesome was enough for me."

"And you been scramblin' for piss poor pay ever since, am I right?"

"You know you are, Tom."

A customer, one of those not-from-here dudes chasing his True West dream, stepped up to the counter, his boots a little too shiny, his hat way too clean and his jeans faded by chemicals instead of hard work and a hundred Maytag spin cycles.

"Lemme ring this man up and we'll talk more. Park yourself on a feed bag back there."

Bohannon's eyes followed Sartelle's pointing finger until he spotted bags stacked at the back of the store. He ambled back, parked it where told and pulled out the fixings for another homemade. After the time it took to tell the customer a tall tale ticked by, Sartelle limped down the aisle and joined him.

"Lend me some of that golden leaf."

Bohannon handed over his leather tobacco pouch and watched Sartelle sit on a feed bag opposite his, roll his own then fire it up with a match swiped across the sole of a tall boot.

"That's a damn good smoke."

"I oughta know – it's my 'backy. What else do I need to know about this place?"

"Don't get your panties in a bunch, Wiley. Let me enjoy another drag or two and I'll tell you."

Bohannon smoked his own and tried not to get angry with the old coot. *He'll tell me in his own sweet time and it'll be more than I want to know. Which is bullshit because a man like me, so desperate for money that he'll step into something crooked of his own free will, needs to know as much as he can.*

Sartelle finally wet a thumb and forefinger to snuff out his smoke.

"Here's the deal. You and them cows are all show and no go. So are the hands you ride with. You move just enough stock to make it look like a working outfit. And if you make a little money for them, great, but they really don't give two shits."

"Don't give a shit about making money – what are they, a bunch of Commies?"

"Not Commies, but some of them are True Believers."

"In what?"

"Take your pick. In Texas becoming a freestanding republic again. In splitting the blanket with the rest of America. In setting up a homeland for white folks based on the Bible and bullets. In shipping the niggers and wetbacks back to Africa and Mexico and killin' the ones who won't leave. In driving a car without a license and not payin' taxes. They got it all out there."

"Sounds like a man's gotta believe what they believe to work out there."

"That's the beauty of it – you don't. You might have to learn just enough of their lingo to understand what the hell they're talkin' about, but you don't have to swear a blood oath. Just tend to them cows, smile and nod a lot at those crazy bastards, mind your own business and take their money."

"And I don't have to do anything illegal?"

"Nope. And no side hustles that'll get you in trouble. They get wind of one and you're out. Permanently and forever."

Sartelle paused and stared at him to underline the point.

"That was a warning you needed to hear, Wiley. But I've known you a long time, before and after prison. You've kept your nose clean since getting out and you know how to keep your mouth shut. It pains me the way a top hand like you has to scrape by. Let me call the foreman out there and give him your name. I know they're lookin'."

"Who's the foreman?"

"Fella named Talbot Jackson – Tal for short. He's tight with the owner, but he knows how to run cows. You answer to him and nobody else."

"Not even the owner?"

"No sir, just Tal. That's how the owner wants it. A wall between the cattle business and the rest of what goes on out there. You'll meet the owner once. Thomas "T For Texas" Bondurant. A right innerestin' hombre. Oil money. Former state senator. Can fire up a crowd with this Texas Secede stuff."

"But not a True Believer."

"Not in what he's selling to the suckers. Oh, his group raises hell at rallies up in Austin and files lawsuits against the federal government. And they hold seminars at the ranch to indoctrinate the faithful – 40 or 50 of them at $200 a head. You'll truck in some fat cattle with real beef on 'em for that."

"Because city folk might choke to death on steak from Mex cattle."

"You bet. Sure as hell don't want that. What they also don't want is to rile up the locals. You won't see these folks locking horns with the sheriff or the county judge, which makes them different from these other outfits you read about that seem to always be fuckin' with the local honchos."

"Thought that was the stock in trade for these Texas Secede and militia types."

"Not these folks. Oh, they might show up at a county commission meeting to spout off about godless feds, black helicopters and Ruby Ridge and such. Stuff most folks 'round here already believe. But mostly, they're content to walk the courthouse square and hand out leaflets or buy a booth at the county fair. Hell, Bondurant even makes campaign donations to the county judge and sheriff, which is right peculiar since most of his followers believe this should still be a white man's world and the sheriff's half Mex, half coon."

"So, they keep it on the low burner here and don't shit where they live. That's pretty smart."

The Dead Certain Doubt

"*True, but hustling the suckers is small change for a guy like Bondurant. He only worships one thing – the dinero. And lots of it. You know as well as I do, there's only two or three ways to make a lot of money in this rough-ass country and they're all illegal.*"

"*That's Bondurant's true calling.*"

"*Right as rain. He's in bed with some real bad folk. And you can guess who that might be and what they might be doin' but never get curious. That'll get you dead. Call 'em silent partners. Some of them are out there all the time, watching, but you'll rarely see 'em. They're kind of like them Corrientes you'll be chasin', good at stayin' scarce and hidin' in the brush.*"

"*Something to really worry about instead of these other knotheads.*"

"*I wouldn't say you worry so much as know they're out there and steer clear of 'em. Kinda like a nest of rattlesnakes. You hear 'em or see 'em, you go the other way. But keep a hogleg handy. Just in case.*"

Bohannon stared down at the floor between his boots and thought of his vow to stay out of prison and how hard he worked to stay on the straight and narrow. Then he thought of his empty wallet, the rumble in his belly and the chance to chase cows for a steady wage.

All he had to do was keep his mouth shut.

He looked Sartelle in the eye.

"*Make the call.*"

Bohannon's mind drifted back to the present. He finished his smoke, stubbed out the butt on his boot heel then field stripped the remains, letting the wind catch the loose tobacco and pocketing the scrap of charred rolling paper.

A heart attack took Sartelle down six months ago in the middle of the feed store while telling another one of his tall tales about riding the range. Lucky hombre. Shed of all the worries and cares of this sorry old world. Ghost riding the Devil's herd in the sky now. Cue up the Johnny Cash hit.

The old man was right about this outfit, though. Phony as a three-dollar bill. Right about it paying fair wages and Tal Jackson

60

being a damn good cow boss. Tal let a man stay on the outside of a good horse, babysit cattle nobody cared about but him and his sidekicks and feel better about himself as long as he stayed in the saddle and didn't think too much.

Sartelle was also right about the True Believers drawn to this place. Like it was a Mecca for the angry, the alienated, the dispossessed and the down-and-out, people who were losing their jobs, their way of life and their grip on a country hell-bent on leaving them in the dust.

The men ran from big-bellied and moon-faced to rail-thin and sharp-featured dead ringers for Confederate soldiers yipping the Rebel yell. They were country boys and ranch hands – or one generation removed from rural life. Some were vets – Vietnam or Desert Storm.

They knew how to shoot, show up every Sunday at the Church of Christ, drink beer, skin a buck and punch the clock for factory, oil field and feed mill jobs that were circling the drain or already long gone. Their fathers were Kluxers or Birchers, so they were already hard-wired to hate niggers, greasers, kikes and slanty-eyed Japs, chinks and zip refugees from Southeast Asia.

One or two had the dead-eyed look of someone familiar with taking a man's life. Up close, not by remote. But only one or two.

Their wives were shrill and pinched, with an anger and hatred that often outstripped their men. They were worn down from working two or more minimum-wage jobs in town as waitresses, house cleaners, store clerks, janitors or bookkeepers to keep the family's double-wide or pre-fab home from foreclosure.

Bloated or weathered before their time by too many kids too fast, they were country gals who could once ride and shoot as good as their men – or better. Some still could. More than a few were fierce and scary. They might not have killed yet. But you could bet they damn sure might. And getting yourself dead has always been a gender-neutral fuckup.

They were pissed off, scared, desperate and looking for somebody to blame and something to believe in. Chickens ripe for the plucking. Willing to fork over $200 they had to go to the pawn shop to get for a five-day seminar that showed them tax dodges sure to land them in foreclosure, bankruptcy and prison.

Fueled their fears and hatred with lectures about the evils of the Federal Reserve, One World Government and open borders. Fed them sugar pills about secession and a reborn Republic of Texas that would be a Promised Land for God-fearing, gun-toting white folks just like them.

Center stage was Bondurant, their Messiah, preaching a powerful message of scapegoats and false hope, pumping them up with a delivery that smoothly meshed the familiar cadences of the pulpit and the stump speech, shifting from folksy and friendly to earthy and angry before rocketing into pure brimstone and damnation. And then downshifting into the images of glory, redemption and a Lone Star flag snapping in the breeze.

Bohannon figured it was smart to get to know a little bit about the Devil signing his paychecks, so he'd slip into an empty chair or stand in the back and listen to Bondurant crank up the faithful. The True Believers. The sheep already shorn.

It was like listening to the bastard child of Jim Jones and Aimee Semple McPherson, their union blessed by Nathan Bedford Forrest and George Lincoln Rockwell and their spawn baptized by Charlie Manson.

"You've watched helplessly while the Jew, the nigger and the wetback have taken over this country, claimed the jobs that are rightfully yours or refused to work to suck up the slop of the government welfare trough. Slop that your hard work pays for...

"You've watched as the government of this great land has become a slave of the Anti-Christ and his bloody horns and all-seeing eyes, sending out its jack-booted thugs in black helicopters to crush your freedoms and take away your guns. You've watched as the politicians

you elect turn their backs on you and swear fealty to The Beast and the iron-fisted rule of the U.N. and One-World Government...

Then he fed them steaks as a Last Supper. Prime cuts from cattle bought from other ranches. Not the stringy Corrientes found on this ranch. Butchered at the Bar L R, but not raised here.

There were two disciples Bondurant invited to stay at the ranch and help him run the dog-and-pony hustle, joining a dozen other men and women who cooked, cleaned, ran the membership and fund-raising lists and kept the buildings from falling apart.

Both were Believers. Or talked like they were. Like bright pennies found on a rain-slicked street at midnight, both stood out because they ran against type of the hate-filled lambs Bondurant was fleecing.

One was a long-legged blonde, younger than the rest by a decade or more. She did the paperwork for both the ranch and the hustle and stayed in a double-wide parked on the south side of the big house, screened by mesquite, hackberry and shin oaks.

Her haven was a safe distance from the bunkhouse north of where Bondurant slept. Not that Bohannon and his *compadres* were much of a threat to make any randy advances. Old saddle tramps still had their carnal dreams, but not enough sap to make them real. Unless a wayward wife of a sucker snuck into the bunkhouse, on fire from Bondurant's preaching, leaving her with an itch her sad sack husband was no longer inclined to scratch.

Bohannon liked the girl, who called herself Rita. No last name given. Or asked for. He could tell her blonde hair came from a bottle so the name she used might be just as artificial.

Her business. Not his.

About once a week she would stop by the corrals and ask to borrow a horse. Usually, she rode alone. But sometimes, she asked whether she could tag along if he was loading up a trailer for a horseback loop to check cattle.

She rode well in the backcountry and was good company. Not a motor mouth. Knew when to keep quiet. And asked intelligent questions about the land, the cattle and the horse she was riding.

The other disciple was a little older than the girl, a handsome man named Tommy Juan with coal black hair combed straight back from his forehead and the dark eyes and olive skin of Mexican blood. Which would seem to be a handicap in this crowd but wasn't.

Tommy Juan was a smooth talker with an easy smile and manner. Also, a bit of a peacock, favoring tall boots with stacked heels and loud, unnatural colors. Paisley shirts with faux pearl speed snaps and a belt buckle as big as a pie pan that made his beliefs plain as a sun-scorched day on the hot sands – Texas Secede! embossed on a bas relief outline of the Lone Star flag.

He talked the talk and walked the walk, going out with the flock to hand out pamphlets and driving them up to protests in Austin or Lubbock to raise hell with the like-minded. He was hard not to like and the flock took him in as one of their own, skin-color be damned.

Tommy Juan and Rita were an item, no doubt. Claimed to be engaged. Their business. Not his.

When Tommy Juan was at the ranch, he stayed with Rita. But he came and went and seemed to be a man with a lot of irons in the fire. Some of those irons were on the dark side of Bondurant's interests, helping the shadow partners with their after-midnight runs.

One day Tommy Juan went but didn't come back. Word was he got busted for gun-running.

Shadow partners. When Bohannon first got to the ranch more than two years ago, they were Kluxers and no-necked muscle bossed by a trio of tough, savvy West Texas hombres Bohannon once rubbed elbows with during his outlaw days. They knew the smuggling game and how to cultivate customers across the river.

Those boys were suddenly long gone. Didn't take much imagination to figure out their final destination. Deep desert holes with rocks piled on top to keep the coyotes out. Tommy Juan getting busted probably saved his ass. Not sure about Rita, who disappeared a few weeks before. He hoped she was still alive but knew wishful thinking couldn't stop a bullet.

The new shadows running Bondurant's dark business were several cuts of lethal above the old crew. Hard and much more terminally inclined. You could feel it. Even if you couldn't see them. It was in the wind and the dust. They were out there. And it caused the hairs on the back of your neck to tingle.

Shadows. New or old. Didn't matter. Just keep your mouth shut and give them a wide berth.

He eyed the cattle. A few lingered over a last clump or two of hay. But most were done and trailing back toward the line of thick brush that rimmed the rise a few hundred yards away. They shied away from a clump of creosote and ocotillo dense enough to hide a tank.

Or a man with eyes on him. Meaner and more lethal than a rattlesnake. Always around. Always watching.

Made his scalp itch. He had a Ruger thumb-buster in .45 Long Colt tucked behind the small of his back. He resisted the urge to reach for it. His .30-30 Winchester rested in the gun rack of the idling pickup, the long gun he always kept in a saddle scabbard when mounted.

He remembered Sartelle's advice. *Know they're out there and steer clear of 'em...But keep a hogleg handy. Just in case.* Time to get close to that rifle and get gone the other way.

Cleve Chizik watched the cowboy smoke his cigarette while leaning on the fence gate, sitting cross-legged on sandy soil behind a cover of creosote and ocotillo as cows and steers ambled his way.

His eyes were glued to binoculars he held with his hands cupped above the lenses to prevent any reflection giving him away. A scoped Ruger Mini-14 rested in his lap. He saw the cowboy look once toward his hidey hole, saw the man's jaw set then relax before again sweeping his eyes over the cattle.

Chizik slowly lowered the binoculars and eyed the cattle. They were splitting left and right, avoiding the dense brush where he hid. Cover blown. But fuck it, it's just one of the show cowboys already bought and paid for to keep their mouths shut and their minds on the sorry-ass herd of this sham ranch.

Besides, he knew all about this particular cowboy. Bohannon. An ex-con who knew how to keep that yap zippered when the heat was on. He was a stand-up guy who did his time and didn't rat out the others in his rustling ring.

Chizik knew because he did his homework. Knew cons who did time with the man. Ran down the man's particulars. Knew he never wanted to do anything to wind up in prison again but wasn't above taking dirty money as long as the dirt didn't get on him.

Not a thing to worry about with a guy like that. Keep his belly and bank account full and let him live his cowboy dream.

Don't get cocky. A worm can always turn. So can a solid con.

That was his old Pelican Bay cellmate whispering in his ear. Don Kavanagh. His mentor. A lifer, a Diamond Tooth OG. It was Kavanagh who brought Chizik into the Alice Baker.

Set up the hit that won Chizik his bona fides. Damn near botched it with a shiv that was too dull. Had to strangle the man with his bare hands, eyeball to bulging eyeball, breathing in the man's rank breath even as he shut it the fuck down. Almost puked from the stench of the man shitting and pissing his drawers as he checked out.

Kavanagh laughed and ragged him unmercifully about that. Chizik didn't mind – the rough razzing told him he was in. Made the grade. Got The Brand carved into his chest. A shamrock with A B in the middle.

And the hit told him something about himself he had always suspected – he liked to kill. The closer the better. With shivs, straight razors, sharpened screwdrivers, ice picks and a Gerber lock blade. No stilettos – those were for greasers and pimps.

Kavanagh knew how deep his blood lust ran before he knew it himself. Started calling his number on kills meant to send a special message. Drew him close and started teaching him the ways of Alice Baker.

Righteous Don. Shanked to death in the showers.

Blood in, blood out. No fear of death.

Payback for Don's death was swift and brutal.

Chizik coldcocked the nigger who killed Don with an iron pipe. Fished out his cock and sliced it off with a straight razor smuggled in by a screw on the pad. Stuffed it in the man's mouth before slitting his throat to let him choke on his pride and joy and his own blood. Went nose to nose with the man as he gurgled and gasped, watching the light go out of his eyes, making sure his face was the last one the man would ever see.

Same bill of fare for the boss nigger who ordered the hit. With one twist – gouging the eyeballs out with a sharpened screwdriver before slitting the man's throat. Chizik savored the memory and felt his molars grind – a pleasure reflex that traveled straight to his crotch and gave him a chubby.

Blood in, blood out. The AB avenging their own.

Righteous kills with a grisly signature that made Chizik a Big Stripe nobody fucked with. On the yard or on the block. Not even the niggers and greasers still fighting The Brand's graybar dominance.

Also gave him his pick of the punks who would rather suck and get fucked by a Big Stripe than get gang raped in the shower.

Sure, I fucked punks. Beat fuckin' my fist. A man's got needs and ain't no pussy on the block. Besides, a mouth is a mouth and a hole is a hole. Went right back to pussy when I got out. But every now and then, I get the urge and find me a smooth young boy.

He watched the cowboy climb into the cab of the rust-bucket pickup, bounce through a U-turn and rumble away. His thoughts turned to Bondurant, the greedy gasbag who owned this spread and thought he was top dog.

That made the man a dead wrong dumbass. But as long as Chizik and his crew could keep doing business uninterrupted, he was content to let Bondurant strut around and bark like an alpha never needed to. Guns south, drugs north. Long as the pipeline flowed. Long as Bondurant didn't get too greedy and this Texas secede bullshit kept providing cover.

There was another reason Chizik left the leash loose. They were still rebuilding their network of customers and suppliers, still recovering from a disastrous raid two years ago that took down more than half his crew and shuttered a sweet operation they were running from a *rancho* thirty miles southwest of here, closer to the river but still in Cuervo County.

Ratted out by one of their own – not an AB brother, but a man valued for his contacts across the river and his knowledge of every arroyo, cattle trail and river crossing within a hundred miles. And every bent sheriff, ranch foreman, banker, truck driver and gun dealer along the way.

Chizik was lucky. He was shacked up in El Paso with a whore named Juanita Ruiz when the raid went down. Nasty bitch with cantaloupe tits, a big ass and a pussy that squeezed a man's cock like a velvet vise.

Two other members of the crew were also away from the ranch on a horizontal refreshment run. Feds still had warrants out on all three of them. Forced them to lay low, buy some new names and change their look.

Chizik now called himself Del McCoy. Delbert Lucius McCoy – a name from an infant's grave. A Lubbock boy, so his forged papers said. Texas driver's license photo showed a man with shaggy brown hair, hazel eyes and a close-cropped beard. Covered the shaved head and face he preferred. Also hid the nasty scar along his left jawline, souvenir of a knife fight, and the dent in his skull from a screw's baton.

Took more than a year of staying off the radar and rebuilding the scratch and muscle to get back in business. Guy he only knew as Danny Ray bankrolled him. Took more time and a couple of false starts before they found this place and convinced Bondurant they would be better partners offering a more lucrative payout than the Kluxers he was working with.

Three of those peckerwoods had to get dead first before the deal got done. Two more stupid enough to squawk afterward got a lead Third Eye for their trouble. Bondurant didn't care – he stayed zeroed in on the prize. More greenbacks in his offshore account.

Chizik's new crew all wore The Brand. There were nine of them, including himself and the two veterans of the old crew who weren't netted in that raid. Officially, they were the in-house construction crew of the Bar L R, erecting outbuildings and moving earth with an ancient Cat D4. They rarely went into town and one or two were always near the Big House, working while keeping an eye on the suckers. And Bondurant.

At night, they made their runs to and from the border. They knew the ropes, knew the backtrails and bent lawdogs on both sides of the river. Knew enough border Spanish to get by and get it done.

No need for a local outsider – Chizik wouldn't make that mistake again. They built a bunkhouse shadowed by the rocks of a canyon on the north side of the ranch and a trail to the nearby gate wide enough for a semi. One of the crew was a punk who liked to suck and take it up the dirt trail. At a moment's notice. They called him Eveready. Kept the sap from rising to lethal levels between runs across the river for cheap Mexican pussy.

That northside gate made a nice little escape hatch out there where only the crows, rattlers and jackrabbits kept watch. Made sure Bohannon and his buddies loaded up cattle for market from there on a semi-regular basis to cover the tracks of their border runs.

Once they were open for business. Chizik wasn't surprised to find their old customers hooked up with other suppliers. Nature abhors a vacuum. So do gun runners and drug dealers. And with a war between rival drug factions heating up across the river, there was a rising demand for a steady supply of weapons, which created an opening for his new crew they widened with a killing or three.

But he was none too pleased to find out a half dozen of his best buyers were doing business with the same supplier, an outfit fronted by a tall, blonde Anglo, a woman known as *La Güera*. Took him some time to grease the right palms and break the right arms to figure out who she was and who she was fronting for – Tommy Juan Jaeckel, the asshole who snitched out his old crew.

Had to give the man credit. Jaeckel put on a good show when the raid went down. Went after the Mexi-coon sheriff of this shithole county with a blade. Got clocked by a deputy and wound up spitting teeth. That was the word from one of Chizik's old crew, now stacking a ten-spot in Huntsville, where Tommy Juan wound up for a short cup of coffee.

Way too short. The first clue Tommy Juan had ratted them out. Okay – let the feds build you a new, anonymous life. Stick you out in East Bumfuck. Pray you never cross paths with any swinging dick riding for The Brand. Pray Cleve Chizik never darkens your door.

Life as a scared rabbit. Never relaxed. Always nervous. Always checking the rearview mirror. Always sleeping with a gun under the pillow. Knowing this: That Day would finally arrive. But never knowing when. Hardly a life worth living.

That wasn't the choice Tommy Juan made. Had to give him credit again. Took balls to rat out his old compadres then dial up a string of their best customers and become their new supplier. Balls or a death wish.

Trouble was, Tommy Juan also ratted out the rivals of those best customers. That gave him enemies on both sides of the river. Chizik and his crew. And *sicarios* for one or two of the warring *narco* factions vying for control of the river between Ojinaga and Ciudad Acuña.

Hard to pick the winning side in the middle of a war among five or six factions. And Tommy Juan picked wrong. The side he ratted out was starting to win. Funny thing about that – they were headed by the descendants of the old *narco* king who once ruled this stretch of river, Malo Garza.

Blown to bits by a car bomb courtesy of some boys from Monterrey, young turks tired of the old ways of doing business. Now, the young turks were under the gun, losing to the Garzas and their allies, said to be led by old man Malo's eldest daughter.

The Garzas were the first customers he signed up when he got things rolling at the Bar L R. Tommy Juan's rat work had landed three of their lieutenants in the graybar hotel. Either they would track down Tommy Juan or he would.

Payback lust strengthened the ties between the Garzas and his crew. They double-teamed the search, hunting for months before tracking Tommy Juan down to a stone house atop a frozen mesa in Jeff Davis County.

You always kill a rat slow, first chopping off fingers and toes. Then razoring the eyelids. Tommy Juan's screams: Dee-licious. Pure agony bouncing off the rocks above. Up and down the octaves of pain.

Chizik closed his eyes and felt the chubby grow into a full hard-on, tempting him to rub one out right here in the brush.

Why the hell not? Nobody could see him. He unbuckled his belt and unzipped his jeans. He spit in his palm and pulled out his cock, mind locked on the images of Tommy Juan's death as he stroked himself.

Tommy Juan tied to a metal folding chair as the Garza sicarios kept his pain level high by chopping off toes and skinning strips from his body. Hard questions about the girl, where she was, who she was working with.

Tommy Juan wouldn't say. Too busy screaming. They didn't give much of a shit because maximum pain was their object, not information.

Slice the rope that binds him and pull Tommy Juan from the chair. Carry him to the wooden picnic table and stretch him spread-eagle across the rough planks. One of the sicarios turns to Chizik and offers a straight-edge razor that gleams in the moonlight.

"Señor, we hear you like to sign your kills with the same gesture we like to make."

"Wasn't aware you had the exclusive franchise. I've always thought feeding a man his own cock and balls first was the perfect way to kill a traitor. Or hated enemy."

"Si, it's a just way to kill men without honor. Are you sure you're not part Mexican, señor?"

"I'm sure. But I am happy to be your brother in business. And the way of the razor. Honor's all mine."

Lying out his eye teeth to the man about honor and brotherhood. Mexicans were just another breed of mud people. Sub-human. But sometimes useful to The Brand's business deals. Never let ideology get in the way of the gelt. Kavanagh taught me that.

Razor in his palm. Admire the balance and bone handle. Test the blade with a calloused thumb, drawing a thin line of blood. Sharp as a surgeon's scalpel. Step to Tommy Juan's side, nodding at the sicarios holding down his arms and legs.

Gun hand aims a flashlight at Tommy Juan's naked crotch. Beam lights up his cock and shriveled scrotum. Balls tucked up for warmth. No matter. Stretch Tommy Juan's cock with his left hand. Sever it at the base with one swipe of the razor. Smooth.

Blood spurts from the stump as Tommy Juan's screams bust through a higher octave. Grab and twist the scrotum. Slice away sac and balls with four swipes. Lick the blade clean. Gun hands nod and grunt their approval.

Stuff the bloody mess into Tommy Juan's mouth, muffling the screams. Razor back in his hand. Lean in, nose-to-nose with Tommy Juan as the man gags and gasps. Savor it. Burn the image on the brainpan. Stroke that cock faster.

"This is what we do to a fuckin' rat, Tommy Juan."

Slice Tommy Juan's throat deep, from ear to motherfuckin' ear. The blood pumps and gurgles. The pain and horror flash freeze in Tommy Juan's lidless eyes.

Chizik rewound to the image of himself licking the blood off the blade, pumping his cock hard and fast. He came two seconds later, spurting into the sand.

The enemy of my enemy...

Chizik smiled and finished the phrase out loud – "...is my friend." The smile disappeared as he stood, tucked his cock away and zipped up his jeans. He left his brushy hideout and headed for an ATV parked a half mile north.

We found that bastard and I sent him straight to hell. Scooped up his guns and drugs for a bonus chunk of change. Split the take then turned around in that very instant and gave his share to the Garzas.

Pro move. Playing the long game. Making the grand gesture. The Garza crew ate it up. Their jefe, short and big-bellied, with arms swollen by forced-reps muscle, stepped up, staring into my eyes.

Don't blink, motherfucker. You blink, you die. Lock down that stare. Turn your face to stone.

A slap on the back and a full-throated laugh as the jefe turned to his crew.

"¡Qué jodido hombre tenemos aquí! Un hombre que sabe lidiar con un traidor y tiene el cerebro de un Einstein."

73

An abrazo, *full-bodied and macho. Squeeze tight, motherfucker. Force the air out of his lungs. Pound his back harder than he's pounding yours. Smile like you just found your long-lost brother.*

The jefe *breaks the embrace.*

"Señor, *you may not be a Mexican but you think like one."*

"*I'm honored you think so,* mi carnal. *Consider this a gift to honor our brotherhood and a partnership that will be mutually profitable for years to come. Tell the Garzas of my gift and my hope."*

"*They will be very pleased with the gift and the prospect of doing more business together."*

Right on both counts. Next up – the blonde bitch.

More at stake than straight revenge. And it wasn't a hunch, but a certainty. Tommy Juan buried another cache of weapons and drugs before we caught him. Because that's what the man did when he worked for him. Before he became a rat. Had loads buried out there where only the coyotes roamed.

He could feel it. He could smell it. He knew it. And the bitch knows where it is.

Get her, get the cache and sell it to the Garzas. Make her talk. Cut it out of her. Finger by finger. Toe by toe. Burn it out of her. With a branding iron.

Smell that seared flesh. Make her scream. See the fear in her eyes. Make her give it up.

Then kill her. Slow. With a blade. With his bare hands. I want it to be me. I want to look into her eyes as I snatch her life away. I want my face to be the last thing she sees.

Up close. Know your killer, sweetheart. Know it's me.

Seven

*W*atch your six, Sport Model.

A dead partner's whispered warning. A triggered twitch of muscle memory and street cop reflexes. The split-second dive to the right. The graceless tuck and shoulder roll that slams and skids your ass across the greasy linoleum floor of a roadside tienda.

Left hand full of a Colt's cold comfort. Hammer back. Eight Fat Boys in the mag. One in the pipe. Hardball .45 ACP and Flying Ashtrays. Find the source of that buckshot blast meant to blow your head into red mist, skull fragments, hair and brain matter.

Ignore the screams, shouts, clumping footfalls and Dios Mios of customers and clerks exiting rapido to safety. Smell the cordite but pay it no mind.

Ignore all that shattered bottle glass and the ketchup, mustard, mayo, salsa picante and salsa verde splattered across the floor, your jeans, your belt buckle and your best Nocona boots. A swirling mess of red, green, white and yellow that just doesn't matter.

Find that shooter. Listen for the telltale shing-shing pumping more buckshot into the chamber. Pray he's old school. Pray the shotgun isn't a semi-automatic with the next round already in the pipe.

Shing-shing.

Answered prayer. The sound rises from the next aisle to his front left. The Colt tracks the echo, sights panning across the shelves facing him. Jarritos, Jumex, Sidral Mundet, Big Red, 7 Up. Spam, Underwood Deviled Ham, Starkist. Valvoline, Havoline, Pennzoil.

A boot sole scrapes the linoleum. Front corner of the next aisle. Right behind the 10W30. Colt centers on the sound. Front blade splits a quart of Havoline. Blast five shots. A grunt, a groan and the clatter of dropped gun metal. Ears ring.

Quick crab crawl to the opposite corner.

Sneak a peek. Shooter on his knees. One hand covers his bloody gut. The other reaches for his pump shotgun.

Fuck you, old school. Three more blasts from the Colt. Squeeze the trigger like a lover until the slide locks back and smoke curls from the breech. One round cores a Third Eye in the shooter's forehead.

Quema tu culo en el infierno, pendejo. *No last rites. No absolution. Straight to the flames. Spit a sour green ball of phlegm on the floor.*

Shuck the empty mag. Slap home a fresh one. Trip the slide. Shake out a Lucky and stick it on a dry lip.

Light the nail with a Zippo and a shaky hand. Drag the smoke down deep to smother the stench of gunsmoke and blood. Dial 911 on the black rotary phone next to the cash register and wait for the gaudy post-mortem show to start. No popcorn.

Give thanks to the whiskey gods you survived another gunfight. Thank those old reflexes, too. They're the second cousins of doubt – the only thing you're dead certain of.

Dealer's choice. Jacks or better to open. Check, raise, bluff or call in a round of liar's poker with a lawdog Burch knew but hadn't seen in almost a decade. Didn't know if he could trust the man who held all the high cards. And the badge. Best to play it close to the vest.

"I see you still worship at the Church of John Browning. Bet you still follow the lessons they taught you at the Hollow-Point Charm School."

Raise with a bluff and smartass bluster.

"Dance with who brung ya, Sheriff. And not much charm to this deal. Just a shitload of lead. *Muchacho* there tried to make me a headless horseman with some double-ought. I begged to differ and let Brother John's best do my talking for me."

"Old gun." Call.

"Old man shootin' it. Only gun I can hit anything with." Re-raise.

"And you had to come all the way out to my county to prove you still could. Why the hell is that?"

Burch smiled but didn't answer. A quiet fold. The sheriff was deeply annoyed but wasn't ready to throw him in a jail cell. Yet.

Burch stood about five feet away from the shooter's corpse, dripping ketchup, mustard and salsa on the *tienda* linoleum. Half-assed trying not to fuck up the sheriff's crime scene while smoking another Lucky pacifier.

His eyes scanned the body, sprawled face first in a dark, spreading pool, left arm flexed out like it was plowing a path for a body that would never follow.

His brain automatically picked out and filed the details. Once a murder cop, always a murder cop. Gold badge or not.

Detail: The last hollow-point he fired blew out the back of the man's skull. Filed.

Detail: A scorpion tattoo on the left forearm. Black ink only. Lines still sharp. Filed.

Detail: Shooter's gun a Remington 870 pump. Twelve gauge with a sawed-off barrel. Common as rocks and sand in West Texas. Filed.

He studied the left side of the man's face, the side that wasn't marinating in blood and brain pulp.

Detail: Smooth bronze skin, left eye showing the eight-ball bulge. Detail: Lips locked back over a pearly white grimace. Silver cuff on the left earlobe. *Maricón?* Maybe.

Details and question filed. Nothing rose from his memory banks. Noted and filed.

His eyes returned to the gaping hole in the back of the man's skull.

Gotta love them Flying Ashtrays. Did damage to a man. Hardball knocked him down and hollow-point chewed up his innards and cored out his skull. The Big Adios. One-way ticket. Paid in full.

The sheriff squatted on his boot heels near the dead man's right hip, using the eraser end of a pencil to lift the bloody tail of a denim shirt to study an exit wound. A muttered oath. English or Spanish. Burch couldn't tell.

More muttering. A wallet fished out of a back pocket with a hand gloved in latex. A glance at the driver's license. A quick riffle through a thick sheaf of greenbacks.

Detail: Helluva lot of lettuce in that wallet. More than your average greaseball carries. Noted and filed.

Sheriff Sudden Doggett gave one shake of the head then pinned Burch with dark, angry eyes framed by the underside of a faded, stained and dented Resistol that might have been dark gray in its younger days.

"Why the fuck is it every time you cross the Cuervo County line you have to announce your presence by painting the walls red?"

"Only the second time I've visited your fair jurisdiction, Sheriff. And the first time was a few years back. Seven or was it eight?"

"Not long enough if you ask me. Why can't you be like every other tourist passing through and keep trucking over the river for some bad tequila and cheap pussy?"

"Because I'm on a job. Was on my way to see you when this happened."

"Well, fuck me runnin'. Worst news I've had all day. Fuckin' angel of death is what you are. And my morgue's already full. Last thing I need is another gun hand racking up body count."

"Startin' to sound like your old boss."

"You can just take that talk and jam it straight up your ass, *pendejo*. Go clean yourself up some. You look like Ronald McDonald with that shit smeared all over you."

"Good to see you again, too, Sheriff."

"Bite my ass, Burch."

Risky to poke a stick at Doggett with the thin hand he held. Might wind up in a jail cell for his trouble. But the reaction he got was worth it – genuine pissoff with no hesitation or trace of guilt. Told him he just might be dealing with a straight shooter. *Hope so. We'll see.*

The lawman kept his eyes locked on Burch as he barked an order.

"Get this fuckhead out of my face before I run him in lookin' just like the clown he is. Take him out back. Ruby's got a garden hose out there. Let him use it and get cleaned up while I check out this mess. Leave his Colt on the counter."

A blade-faced deputy with acne scars and the flattened nose of a bad boxer stepped up and grabbed him by the elbow. Burch shook his arm free, gave him a glare and walked toward the back door of the store.

Anger flushed out the shakes. He felt better, but not great. As good as it gets after killing a man.

"Know who the shooter was?"

"Never saw him before I had to kill him."

"You sure you didn't know him?"

"How the fuck am I supposed to know one of your locals, Sheriff? Been some years since the last time I darkened your jail-house door and didn't think I'd made any new enemies."

"As I recollect, that usually don't take you very long. You walkin' into a room of folks is enough to get half of them wishin' you was dead. You openin' that yap of yours seals the deal for the other half."

"Part of my irresistible charm. Now can we stop fiddle fartin' around so you can tell me who my new enemy was so we can start piecin' together the why's of him tryin' to blow my head off?"

Sudden Doggett smiled his sad-eyed smile. Burch noticed some wiry white hairs springing from the brushy Zapata moustache he remembered being ink black.

The sheriff's dark brown face was still smooth, but ditch-deep grooves creased the side of each eye. Hard to tell if those were just from more years of squinting in the desert sun or carved by the stress of dodging *narco* gunsels, backstabbing pols and random troublemakers blowing in from the big city and spilling blood in his county.

Probably an unhealthy dollop of all of the above. And a helluva lot more.

They were seated in the sheriff's office; Doggett slouching in an old wooden swivel chair, tooled black boots with tall riding heels propped on the desk; Burch facing him in fresh, dry clothes, leaning to his left in an armchair with oxblood leather cushions, legs stretched out to quiet his barking knees, boots crossed.

Burch had been here before, back when Doggett was the chief deputy for his predecessor, Blue Willingham, a Texas law-man straight out of central casting. Tall, broad-shouldered and blue-eyed with the fleshy physique of a third-team All-American defensive end gone to seed. Thick, swept-back hair the color of coal and lead with a jaw that could punch through the armor plate of a dreadnaught.

He was also an ex-Texas Ranger with an eye on the governor's mansion and a hand in a *narco's* pocket. Talked Texas tough on law-and-order and the War on Drugs but was crooked as a sidewinder.

Sucker punched Burch while he was chained to a D-ring in an interview room. Wanted Burch to get dead quick but didn't want to get blood on his own hands.

Bad for the public image.

Fobbed the job off to a bent deputy, a skin-popping hophead and ex-Marine sniper named Needle Burnet, the sheriff's enforcer. Burch beat Burnet to the punch in the hallway of Mexican hideaway by emptying a full magazine of fat, slow-moving slugs that hit like runaway dump trucks.

Nothing more terminally certain than hardball and Flying Ashtrays. Saved Doggett's ass from a Burnet killshot. Blood-red icing on a cow shit cake that left the son of one of Doggett's Mexican cousins dead.

Burch took inventory of the office, matching it against what he remembered. Something was missing. Willingham had kept a framed black-and-white print the size of a movie poster hanging on the wall behind his desk.

It was a blow up of the photo that made him famous. A money shot of the big sheriff in his Ranger days, standing on the concrete block steps of a double-wide, blood staining the legs of his whipcord pants, carrying nine-year-old Carmen Gonzalez with his left arm while his right hand gripped the Winchester pump he used to blow down two meth heads who killed her parents in a botched kidnapping attempt.

Willingham's partner, Charley Bowness, got killed in the Carrizo Springs shootout, but Carmen got saved. Meant Blue Willingham was a Lone Star hero who didn't have to share the stage.

Good for the ego and the ambition.

Willingham also kept the break-top Smith & Wesson .44 his grandfather, Albert "One-Eye" Willingham, carried as a Ranger in a glass display case on a side table. When the Rangers tumbled to Willingham's corruption, they closed in quick.

Hell hath no fury like a lawdog tracking down a brother who has betrayed the badge. Before they could cuff him up and drag him through a perp walk with the camera strobes flashing, Willingham loaded up his grandfather's pistol, jammed the barrel into his mouth and blew off the top of his skull.

Burch had a hand in this. A weak one. But like the loose strand of yarn that can unravel a sweater, it was enough for the Rangers to pull on and take down Willingham. Not as satisfying as pumping his sorry ass full of Flying Ashtrays, but it would have to do.

Burch was still standing. Willingham wasn't.

The glass display case was still on the side table. It still held the break-top pistol Willingham's grandfather carried. Burch saw this as a good sign, a deadly reminder of the line a righteous law-dog doesn't cross and the terminal consequences for those who do. More confirmation that Doggett might be the same straight shooter he knew from a long time gone.

Maybe not, though.

In place of the giant Willingham money shot hung an American flag flanked by a couple of framed color glossies from Doggett's rodeo days as a champion calf roper so quick the scribes and fans started calling him Sudden. The nickname stuck even after a badly broken leg ended the man's pursuit of faster runs and belt-buckle glory in Vegas, home of the National Finals Rodeo.

Gone, too, was the raging hostility and undercurrent of lethal menace Willingham served up. Instead, there was the semi-tense air of two savvy alpha dogs who knew each other for a brief spell but needed to circle, sniff and figure out whether to snarl, bite or wag their tails.

Doggett broke the silence.

"I wouldn't call the shooter a new enemy. More like blood kin of an old one. And you know how prickly blood kin can get and how long they can hold a grudge."

"How 'bout a name, Sheriff?"

"You remember Chuy Reynaldo, doncha? Hitter for old man Garza? The late, lamented and blown all to smithereens Malo Garza? Shooter was Chuy's younger brother, Luis."

Sweet Jesus. Chuy Reynaldo.

Moon-faced, puzzle-gutted shambler with stringy hair, a scraggly beard and the clueless look of a terminal dumbass. Kind of guy you looked at once and forgot. Until he sliced open your carotid artery with a straight razor, drove an ice pick into the base of your brain or shredded your heart and lungs with the Colt Python he favored.

Yeah, plenty of dead men made the mistake of looking right past Chuy Reynaldo. Thirty or more, rumor had it. By the hand of a man who looked like his 40-watt burned out at birth. Malo Garza's best killer.

Burch didn't make that mistake when he tumbled to Chuy tailing him in a shiny, deep green Olds Delta 88 the last time he was in West Texas. He dry-gulched Chuy's sorry ass at a roadside tienda *south of Alpine, breaking front teeth by jamming the .45 in his mouth to get his attention for a message to Malo. Tell your boss I ain't gunnin' for him – I got other hombres in my cross hairs.*

Cold-cocked him next, setting Chuy up for the lawdogs to find with joints in the glovebox and ashtray and cheap tequila spilled on his clothes before dropping that dime. Then got his own fat ass faraway gone.

Wasn't the last time he saw Chuy. That frozen moment was burned permanently in Burch's brainpan.

So was the slam-bang squeal of shearing sheet metal and shattered glass. Chuy's Olds t-boning the side of the pickup Burch was in. Chuy's face, plastered with a maniac's smile, behind the yawning barrel of that Python. Burch steeling himself, about to be another dead man who underestimated Chuy's lethal talents and killer drive.

The click of the Python's hammer thumbed to full cock. Eight sharp blasts from above.

No more maniac's smile. No more barrel as big as the mouth of a freight train tunnel. No more Chuy, bleeding out on roadside gravel. Cut down by hollow-points from the .45 of the woman who would give him that bitchin' Cutlass. The one who could still make his heart freeze.

"Don't guess it mattered none to Luis that I wasn't the one who killed his brother."

"Don't reckon it did. Lots of cash in his wallet. About three grand in crispy Grants and Franklins. Like someone whistled him up, fingered you and paid him just before he walked into that store."

"Nothing like long green to juice up a revenge killing for blood kin."

"Made killin' you both business and personal. Besides, you and that crazy blonde were joined at the hip. Didn't matter to him she was the one who pulled the trigger. What the hell ever happened to her?"

"*Desaparecida, hombre. Sin dejar rastro.* Into thin air. A ghost. No forwarding address. A couple of postcards I burned after reading. And that Four-Four-Two I'm driving. Cousin from Tennessee delivered it, title transfer and bill of sale tied up with a neat bow by some lawyer in Atlanta."

"You must have impressed her. Beats hell out of that clapped-out Ford pickup you used to drive. So, lemme ask you this – who knew you were coming out here? Who'd you tell before you hit the road? Landlady? Girlfriend? Buddy? Bartender? Bookie? Get your mail stopped?"

Burch shook loose a Lucky, fired it up and eyed Doggett as he took a deep drag. Doggett fished a pouch of Red Man out of his back pocket and loaded his jaw.

"Meaning you and I both don't believe Luis just happened to see me by some random and miraculous twist of fate and just happened to have a scattergun in his paw."

"Meaning just that. Somebody's up on you. Maybe since Dallas. And that somebody put Luis in play. Far as I know, he was a one-man band. For a while, he was working for the outfit that took Malo's place, but he was a hothead so they cut him loose. Makes him the perfect patsy or cutout."

They fell silent. Burch smoked. Doggett chewed and spat into a rusty Community Coffee can.

"Who'd you blab to?"

"No damn body. Not even you. I decided to wait until I got here to wag chins. I did settle up my bar tab. Which I always do before leaving town just in case I get run over by a semi. You'd have to know me pretty good to know what that means. What I did not do is mention where I was going. I damn sure didn't dance on the bar and yell 'Hey, y'all, I'm headed back to West Texas to get shot at again.'"

"So, who knew?"

"Only the woman who hired me."

"To do what?"

"Find her granddaughter. Last known whereabouts raht c'heer in scenic Cuervo County, Texas, God's own garden spot. Grow a world-class prickly pear in these parts. That's what I'm told."

"Spanish dagger is what we're known for. Prickly pear is for the tourists."

"I'll try to remember that."

"Somebody's been bird-doggin' you so you gotta ask who the old woman talked to."

"I doubt she talked to anybody, but I don't know that for a fact."

"What makes you think the girl's here?"

"Not for certain she still is. Her granny has some letters from her. Several with Faver postmarks. Last one came more than a year ago. Looks like she got herself mixed up with one of those Texas secesh outfits."

"We've got a couple of those."

"A lot of their lingo in her letters but I can't tell if she's a True Believer or a grifter selling the hustle to fleece the suckers. Maybe both. She did mention a lot of tension between factions wherever she was. Had to make a choice or get gone."

"Those folks are crazy as bedbugs. And they fuss and split the blanket quicker than goddam Baptists over the fine points of doctrine only they give two shits about. What else she say?"

"Not a whole helluva lot else. She fell in love with the land out here. The stars and such. She never names the place she was staying. She never names names – just an initial or two. She did say she fell in love with somebody she met wherever the hell she's at. No name. Just initials – T.J."

"Sumbitch. That ain't good."

"Why not?"

"I know a dead man with those initials. Fella chopped up and left in a smoker next county over. Ruined my appetite for days having to smell all that. And the kicker is that I nailed him for gun-running about four years back and he was big into those Texas secede groups."

"So much for a simple missing person case. Got all the makin's of your basic West Texas goat ropin'."

"Never does get dull around here. Not with the bad boys playin' musical chairs across the river. The ones who smoked Malo are getting a run for their money. Rumor has it what's left of Malo's outfit is tryin' to reclaim the throne. Bodies stackin' up like cordwood again."

"Good news. Long as they're killin' each other and not choppin' down decent folks on this side of the river, you can lean back and keep score."

Doggett squirted a stream of brown into the coffee can. Burch expected a smile but got a frown.

"Trouble is, it ain't a game that stays south of the river. You got them letters?"

"Yup. Want to study on them close to see if there's anything else I might find handy."

"Shit. Whoever's on your tail won't know that. Might guess it but will want to narrow it down. You got anybody you trust who can check on the old woman?"

"You bet. I'll dial them up now."

"Make sure they don't go alone. Good chance whoever's on you has visited the old woman and left somebody watching."

"Motherfucker."

Burch made two phone calls. One to Cactus Jack, the other to Johnny Del Rio. He hoped they'd be saviors and call back to say Juanita Mutscher was safe and sound, guarded by their guns.

But he knew better. And blamed himself for bringing death to another's door.

Doggett read the look that crossed Burch's face.

"There's whiskey in that cabinet behind you. Old Crow. Nasty stuff but it gets the job done. Fetch two glasses while we wait for a call back. You can sack out on the couch in here or grab a bunk in a cell – we've got a few open tonight."

"Best make it a cell. That way you can tell folks I'm an asshole you hauled in for blasting one of your citizens. Till we got a better lay of the land, don't want nobody thinkin' we're buddies."

"Is that what we are?"

"We're spilling whiskey together, ain't we?"

"But it's really bad whiskey, so I wouldn't read too much into that if I were you. One other thing – we need to lock up that ride of yours before somebody hotwires it and takes it to a chop shop across the river."

"What'll I do for wheels?"

"You'll enjoy what I have in mind. A visit to the blood kin of another dead man you know."

"Which ghost is that?"

"Dirt Cheap Bustamante."

Doggett eyed Burch, waiting for his reaction. Got rewarded by the look that strolled across Burch's face.

Christ – that fat, motor-mouth popdick. Malo Garza's cousin. Sold clapped out wrecks to wetbacks and dirt farmers. Had a side business of muling some of Malo's brown horse tucked behind the sheet metal of rides he brought across the river.

Danced the hot lead mambo for that pusbag with two sicarios sent to ice Dirt Cheap at his own car lot in the heart of Faver. Chopped them down, saving the auto huckster while earning Willingham's ire. Short salvation. Needle Burnet blasted the sorry bastard two days later with a silenced .45 and tried to hang it on Ma Burch's favorite baby boy.

"Looks like you remember the man. His son took over the car lot. And he's got a Bronco with your name on it."

"How'd you know that?"

"Used to be my rig. He bought it at a county surplus auction last week. County finally got me a new ride."

"Lovely. Still got the sheriff's decal on the doors?"

"Nah, he covered that up with a spray job. Primer gray. You go get that and I'll have your ride locked up in the impound garage. It'll be safe. Got my cousin runnin' it. Don't pay more than $500 for that Bronco. It's a piece of shit."

"Gettin' to be an expensive trip."

"You know, there's still an ol' rich gal 'round here I bet would still love to be your sugar mama."

"Not on your life."

"No? She still speaks fondly of you."

"She speaks fondly of any man she fucks. And there are a bunch of us."

"Haven't had the pleasure. Then again, I hate crowds."

The banter died. They sipped the Old Crow in silence. Doggett was right. It gave rotgut a bad name. Harsh and ill-tempered. Light years away from the Maker's Mark he favored.

And it was whiskey spelled with an 'e'. As in white trash and doublewide dumbasses. Didn't do a damned thing to dent his dread and guilt.

The cast was straight and true, the lure and line looping toward the edge of a half-submerged tangle of deadfall and brush hugging the steep, muddy bank of Lake Texoma.

A soft plunk right where he aimed. A three-Mississippi count then trip the bale on the spinning reel. A slow retrieve, raising the rod tip then lowering to get the lure to rise and fall. Just like Daddy taught him.

He could feel his father's watchful eye and smell the smoke of a straight Camel. He spotted a bulge of water at the edge of the brush.

"Easy, son. Nice and slow. Got something trailin' your bait. Bet it's a hawg."

He took a deep breath and stayed steady with rod tip and reel. He smelled the sweet tang of bourbon vapors from his father's mouth. He felt a dull tug on his line.

"Wait, wait...now hit'im, son. Hit'im hard."

He gave the rod a firm yank. Halfway between their boat and the brush, the water boiled and a big lunker leapt from the water, sun catching the green-black upper body, center line of dark blotches and white belly. The fat lure hung from its jaw, a treble-hook buried deep in the hinge.

"Helluva fish, son. He'll fry up nice for supper."

He felt himself grin. Happy his father was proud of him. Happy he had a hawg on the line. But still locked on the task of reeling this bad boy close and slipping him into the net.

His father had the net in the water. He steered the fish that way. Easy. Just a few more feet. Easy.

Brrrrrrrrrrrraaaapppppp. Brrrrrrrrrrrrraaaaapppppp. Brrrrrrrrrrrraaaaaapppppp.

His eyes popped open. He was sprawled on a jail cell bunk, his windbreaker tucked under his chin like a blanket.

His mouth tasted like mildewed gym socks. His head felt like someone had wrapped an iron hoop around it and hammered it tight. He knew the culprit – that empty bottle of Old Crow up in Doggett's office.

Brrrrrrrrrraaaaapppppp. Brrrrrrrrrraaapppp. Brrrrrrrrrrrrraaaaaaapppppp.

He pushed himself up to a shaky vertical – socks, no boots. He fished out a Lucky and fired it up, then doubled over with a racking cough that forced up a thick, nasty-tasting ball of mucous he spat on the cell's rough concrete floor.

Brrrrrrrrraaaaapppp.

"Hey, asshole – quit fuckin' up my deck."

Burch swiveled his head toward the source of the sound – a short, barrel-chested Mex jailer with a gut the shape of a VW Beetle and a long, thick nightstick in his left hand. The jailer raked the nightstick across the vertical bars of the cell.

Brrrrrrrraaaaapppp.

"You mind knockin' that the fuck off, Deputy? Makes a man want to jam that hunk of hardwood sideways, straight up your ass."

"Sheriff said you weren't housebroke and to make allowances for the hangover you no doubt got. He also wants you cuffed up and in his office right now, so I got no time to dance with you. I'll either club you silly and drag your sorry ass up there or you can go along peaceable."

Burch shrugged, then plopped on the bunk to pull on his boots. He slipped on his windbreaker and held his arms out, wrists touching.

"Peaceable it is, Deputy. Hook me up."

The phone was ringing as the jailer led him into Doggett's office and unlatched the cuffs. Doggett picked up the receiver, listened for a moment then handed it to Burch.

"This is Burch."

His voice sounded like a poor imitation of Foghorn Leghorn.

"Damn, you sound awful."

Cactus Jack. Dread and guilt rapped him right on the iron hoop squeezing his head.

"What'ja find?"

"She's alive, EE. But it's touch and go. Had to get her to the hospital. Found her on the floor. Blood pressure through the roof, the medicos say."

"Which hospital?"

"Parkland."

"What happened?"

"She had visitors. Bad dudes. Four of 'em. Two Mexicans, by their accent, two Anglos who ain't from 'round here."

"She tell you that?"

"She did. Had a few choice words about 'em. Called 'em a bunch of popdick scum suckers. Pissed her off more than anything else. She's a pistol."

"That she is. She tell 'em anything?"

"They asked where the granddaughter is. She couldn't tell 'em because she didn't know, right? They ripped through the house but didn't find anything."

"Say anything about me?"

"Didn't have to. These hombres seemed to know all about you. To tell the truth, this has the earmarks of people just covering all the bases. They didn't lean too hard on her. Didn't kill her. And didn't seem in a hurry to catch up with you."

"Had somebody else on me. Or a couple of somebodies."

"Be my surmise. You best keep your head on a swivel. Holler if you need any more help."

"Thanks, Jack. Will do. Already had a bit of a fracas. Fella tried to turn my head into a canoe with a sawed-off."

"Sounds sporty. Also sounds like you need somebody out there to watch your back."

"You volunteerin'?"

"Shit, no. I'm too old and fat. But Johnny ain't. And I know a few people."

"Lemme check the lay of the land and get back to you on that. Do me one more favor. If she's up to it, ask Juanita if she mentioned hiring me to anybody. It'll flat piss her off, but we need to know."

"Good notion. Keep it low, son, and let me know about sending anybody your way."

Click. Burch looked up. Doggett was standing in the office doorway with two steaming mugs of coffee in his mitts.

"Grab some aspirin outta that bottle in my top drawer. Got your chaser right here."

"You shitbirds woke me up from a damn fine dream. Fishin' with my old man. Had a hawg on the line."

"You don't get many of those, I'd bet."

"You'd win."

Eight

"*W*hat the fuck happened out there?*"

"Motherfucker went cowboy on us. Wanted payback for his dead brother. Got himself dead instead. Old man still has moves."

"You told this dead asshole who you were waiting for. And that ain't a goddam question."

"Not me. One of my crew. The dead motherfucker's cousin."

"Christ-all-mighty on a Schwinn bicycle, why the fuck did you hire the cousins of somebody the mark killed?"

"It was a rush job. Had to grab up who was available. And I only hired the cousin. The one who ran his mouth. Not the shooter. That *pinche cabrón* went off the rails years ago."

"What a clusterfuck. The blabbermouth can tie you to this mess."

"Not anymore. And the others don't give a fuck about him or his *enemistad mortal*."

"By all means, get rid of anybody else honor bound by this blood feud bullshit. Tie it off neat and get this thing back on the simple track it needs to stay on."

"You got it."

"Do I? Not a lot of confidence in you on this end. Client's pissed and wants to send down the Dallas crew. Talked him into letting you clean up your own mess and make it right."

"OK. And thanks."

"You want to thank me, get the fuckin' job done right. You don't want that Dallas crew in your neighborhood. They ain't house-trained. To keep them from pissin' all over you, you shadow Burch,

93

he leads you to the girl. She's got something the client wants. Grab her and bring her here."

"And Burch?"

"Make sure you end all his tomorrows. Client was real specific about that. Put him out of his misery. Might boost your standing with the family of the dead cousins."

"A debt of honor repaid. That always plays well with those who believe in such things."

"And you don't? Thought all you vatos *were bound by the blood oath. Alrighty, think of it as good public relations. But first things first. Shadow Burch. Get the goddam girl. Then ice that old fuck and be a man of honor."*

Click. Dead-line dial tone, scratchy with static.

Alvaro Maldonado, a wiry, sharp-faced man with thinning black hair and acne scars along his long jawline, hung the receiver on the cradle of a pay phone on the backside of a Shamrock gas station, bolted right to the gray concrete blocks next to the solitary restroom door. He tapped out a Camel *filtro* and fired it up, taking a deep drag to chase the stench of piss and shit out of his lungs.

He looked up at the dome of stars overhead and muttered bitterly to himself, quietly flailing away like a Jesuit mortifying his flesh with a birch branch at his own stupidity. And the betrayal of Chuy Reynaldo's cousin.

Pinche Luis. He didn't hire that *chupaverga* because he was one out-of-control dude who never did what he was told. Got booted off the payroll of the Monterrey outfit that blew Malo Garza off his throne. Lucky he didn't get a bullet to the back of the head.

Shouldn't have hired the cousin but needed an extra man. *Pinche Alberto.* Should have known that *bicho malo* would spill to Luis and goad him into killing Burch. Egging him on, but too chickenshit to do the deed himself.

For what? Family honor? The Reynaldos had none. To avenge Chuy? Shit, that murderous sack of shit has been dead for almost a decade. Longer than his master, *El Rey*, the once mighty Malo Garza, blown to bits by a car bomb in Monterrey.

Alvaro used hollow-point insecticide to eradicate the *chincha* Alberto. Two .357 slugs to the back of the head, blowing out meaty chunks of skull, jawbone and brain matter and leaving one big exit crater where the nose and mouth used to be. Body dumped in a deep hole out in the wasted nowhere south of Valentine.

That severed the connection to Alvaro and the rest of his crew but didn't answer a nagging question. How did Luis wind up in that *tienda* the same time as Burch? With a shotgun in his hand, revenge in his heart and bloody payback buzzing in his brain.

Alvaro didn't believe in blind luck or coincidence. And he knew Alberto wasn't part of the two-man team that slipped behind Burch as he left Alpine, aided by a VHF transmitter soldered to the frame of that gaudy muscle car and tapped into the brake light wire for power. With a receiver on the dash, Alvaro's team could run a loose tail on Burch, locked onto the signal from his car. But neither the team nor the tracker could predict Burch's stop at that *tienda* north of town.

By the time they closed the gap and turned into a gravel lot, the sound of gunfire already boomed from the clapboard building with the ristras of dried chili peppers dangling from the porch rafters. Patrons banged through the front screen door, yelling and screaming their way to safety.

One of the team, Beto Quinones, slipped through the back door and saw Luis' body on the floor, the blasted display cases dripping the dregs of shattered jars, bottles and cans across two aisles and the goo and mire of blood and condiments wetly gleaming against the dull linoleum.

Before ducking out the way he came in, Quinones saw Burch, standing at the cashier's counter, smoking a cigarette and looking toward the front door, a .45 in his left hand, hammer back.

Quinones reported to Alvaro from a pay phone closer to town. Alvaro had two slam-bang thoughts:

This fuckup will get me killed.

Find that pinche cabron Alberto, squeeze the truth out of him, make him a ghost.

Earlier in the evening, Alvaro got a call from one of his sheriff's office snitches. A new detail. Luis had five grand in his wallet. Five fuckin' grand. What the fuck? This was a border mutt who had to beg for table scraps, a guy who could barely rub two twenties together. On Christmas Day.

Not a detail he shared with Dallas. Who the fuck would give Luis five large and point the finger at Burch with split-second timing? Told Alvaro there was another player in this game. Make that players. Made him nervous he didn't know who. Needed an answer for that.

But getting back on the target was the top priority. Now. Before the client changed his mind and sent in the Dallas crew. With one eye open for these other players. Had his snitch on the inside. Had another man posted up outside the Cuervo County jail, waiting for the *mayate* sheriff to release Burch.

Burch. That *pinche gabacho* did him a favor by greasing Luis. Saved him the trouble. Saved him two or three hollow-points.

But those slugs wouldn't stay in his pocket very long. He'd use them to put an old man out of his misery. Once Burch found *La Güera*. Once his crew grabbed her up and took her to the client. Dead man walking, waiting for a date with those pocketed slugs.

Only then would Alvaro be free to crow about avenging Chuy and Luis Reynaldo and restoring honor to the family of the fallen. When he got through, they would write *corridos* about the Reynaldos, their killer and himself as the instrument of righteous revenge.

Hypocrisy of the highest order. But like the man on the phone said. Good public relations.

Nine

Rhonda Mae frowned at the image in the mirror, her face twisting into a lemon-rind grimace as she inspected her hair. It was short, Clairol black and looked like somebody used a hacksaw to cut it.

Patches of scalp marked where the blade sliced too close. And stalks of hair flagged where it didn't clip close enough. Made her look like an orphan in one of those Bosnian refugee camps, the ones you saw on late night TV commercials from some bleeding-heart outfit hitting you up for a nickel a day to feed a waif.

Looking like hell wasn't a pleasure to see in the mirror, but it was part of her survival plan. She needed to ditch the long blonde locks and the *La Güera* flash to dodge the *narcos* on her trail and stay alive. Clairol got rid of the bottled blonde until her natural raven grew out.

Stash the tight Guess jeans, plunging tops and needle-nosed red lizard boots that made the customers pant while she jacked up the price. Put them in the same canvas go-bag as the turquoise and silver bracelets and rings. And the case with lipstick, eyeliner and make up. Top it off with a blonde wig well north of a hooker's outfit but far cheaper than anything Dolly Parton would wear.

Baggy men's Wranglers, an oversized cotton sweater, scuffed shit kickers with a wide, mule-shoe toe and an oil-stained Carhartt barn coat were the style now. Maybe an extra-large T-shirt and a denim shirt on warmer days.

Always with a four-inch .357 Colt Trooper stuffed in the belt behind her back. And two speedloaders kept handy in her pocket.

Crazy, dangerous world out there. Full of nigger and spic rapists and murderers, Muslim terrorists, bomb-throwing Commies, wet- backs stealing our jobs, eco-warriors killing cattle and good ol' boy serial killers prowling the highways and streets. A girl needs to know her guns these days. And how to hit what she's aiming at. With the first shot.

That's the rap she spread on thick at the Bar L R, hustling the heifers attending her self-defense and gun safety class while their husbands drank deep from one of Bondurant's secession seminars.

That's why we need to resurrect the Republic of Texas, ladies. To have a place of our own, a land where the Bible is the law and is blessed by God and protected by the gun. Protected by your gun and the gun of your man.

To sell the suckers, she made herself believe every bright and shining word she spoke about the Republic of Texas. She told her- self it was a harmless fantasy that gave hope to desperate people. And she half believed a goodly hunk of her spiel, the part about America being overrun by niggers, wetbacks, Commies and killers.

Down deep, though, she took to heart only one part of her hus- tle. *A girl did need to know her guns.*

Wrap up the fashion check list. Cover up those amber wolf eyes with cheap sunglasses you could buy, lose and replace at any roadside gas n' go. Just like every other Great American on the run – from the law, a jealous husband or a *narco* gun hand.

Top it off with a ratty old ball cap. Hell, they were perfect for bad hair days. And this one was going to last a month. If she lived that long. Cover up the styling disaster and tout your favorite team. Had a ratty burnt orange one that fit the bill even though she didn't give a fuck about the Texas Longhorns.

They were hiding out in a tin-roofed adobe shack on the south end of a hard-scrabble *rancho* in Presidio County owned by the cousin of Armando Ruiz, the man who drove her away from the death screams of Tommy Juan Jaeckel. Armando was once married to one of Tommy Juan's older cousins and the ties of love and loyalty to the younger man survived divorce and death.

One room with a dirt floor and two narrow, iron-framed cots on opposite sides. Two doors. Two windows. One mirror. A wash basin and a pile of MREs scattered on a rickety picnic table, stolen from a roadside rest stop, the initials T H D burned into a wide wooden leg – Texas Highway Department.

Two aluminum folding chairs, the type used to torture the faithful at Wednesday night prayer meetings. A Mossberg 500 pump leaning in a corner near one cot. A full-auto CAR-15 nestling in a corner near the other, occupied by a snoring Armando, sleeping on his back, his right hand on a Beretta 92F tucked near his belt buckle.

Privy out back. Long-handled pump with a stone trough out front. Tarp covered the CJ5 in a mesquite thicket twenty yards away. Outback living at its finest. Rattlers, scorpions and coyotes just part of the shack's dusty, desert charm.

Rhonda Mae grabbed the CAR-15 and slung it across her back. She folded up one of the chairs and tucked it under her right arm, hand gripping the underside lip of the seat. She stepped through the front door and closed it behind her, feeling the hairs on the back of her neck start to crawl.

If somebody's out there, now's the time they'll let it rip. And that'll be the end of me.

Her eyes scanned the thickets and clumps of brushy scrub. Nada. She shook open the chair, plunked it in the sand to the right of the door and placed her pistol on the seat. Leaned the CAR-15 against the adobe wall, butt in the sand.

Stepping over to the trough and pump, she worked the handle to pull up a gush of brown water that slowly became clear. She leaned forward, cupping her hand to get a drink, then ducking her head into the cool, clear flow.

Wet the bandana. Scrub her face and neck. Run it through the neck of the T-shirt to wipe her pits. Wet it again and wring it out. Shuck her jeans below her hips to wipe her pussy and ass. Buckle up then wet the bandana again to drape around the back of her neck.

Damn, but don't that feel good. Park your pistol. Sit yourself down. Take your ease with this bush burp gun across your lap. Let Armando sleep. Got a few more hours. Enjoy the sunset.

Smoke one of his Delicados. *Poached a pack from his jacket pocket, but he won't mind. Fire up an* ovalado, *spit loose tobacco off your tongue, suck down the strong, unfiltered smoke.*

You're crazy for staying here. You should be long gone. But that note from Tommy Juan changed everything. Like a voice from the grave. Gives me an out lined with greenback. One more run.

Also gives me an idea, if I've got the guts to pull it off. And hope. Don't forget hope. Helps tamp down the fear.

The note came to her from Tommy Juan's *abuela*, who lived in Valentine. Traveled down a semi-long line of Tommy Juan's cousins until it crossed over to Armando's kin. Took a few days to get to her. Faster than the Post Office. Slower than the jungle telegraph.

The envelope was still sealed when she got it. Which might not mean a damn thing, since anybody with half a brain could steam one open and re-seal it.

"*If you're reading this*, mi amor, *then I'm a dead man. But I leave you a gift I hope you are able to use, one that will let you get away from this hellhole in some comfort and style.*

"*I felt the walls closing in and the clock running out so I parked a quarter of our stash with a friend. He's a smuggler like us and no friend of the Garzas. His name is Malachi Hulett. He's the son of an old outlaw named Gyp Hulett. Leastwise, that's what it said in Gyp's will that gave Malachi the ranch. Well, Gyp's half. It's in Cuervo County. The Bar Double H.*

"*There's the usual mix of long guns. Ten cases and 5,000 mil surplus rounds. There's also those special bang-bangs that will give the boys a big chubby. You'll know what I'm talking about. Malachi will expect a handling fee – no more than ten percent no matter what that bastard says.*

"As far as selling the hardware, there's an outfit upriver of Ojinaga itching to expand its turf now the big dogs are busy carving each other up. Armando knows them and how to connect. Armando's also the only one who knows where we buried this cache – we gave Malachi a false trail so he only thinks he knows where they are.

"Good luck, mi cariño. *Make the deal, give Armando his cut then be a ghost. I just wish I was by your side. Te amo, mi cielo. Always."*

Back to Cuervo County. Not exactly appealing. Too close to the crew of smugglers Tommy Juan ratted out. His killers, most likely. That's what she believed. She heard some of them turned up at the Bar L R not long after she left.

Reason enough to steer clear of the county named for a crow, the black-feathered symbol of bad luck and death, a carrion-eater happy to feast on roadkill or a corpse hanging from the gallows.

But she couldn't leave Tommy Juan's last gift to her unclaimed. And she couldn't shake the idea blooming in her mind and sinking deep roots in her heart. She couldn't just do what Tommy Juan wanted her to – make one last deal, grab the cash and disappear.

They killed her lover, her best friend, her future. She knew who they were and where they were. What she didn't know, Armando could find out. He had a network of cousins and nephews scattered south of the river that gave him contacts in most of the warring *narco* camps.

Blood kin served them well when she was fronting deals for Tommy Juan as *La Güera,* the sexy, gun-running heartbreaker. They could serve again to turn the flaming red flower in her heart and mind's eye into a fiery reality.

It was blood simple. She wanted payback. Revenge. Served up hot and frothy while the mind and soul stayed ice cold. Something biblical. Straight out of Leviticus, her grandmother's favorite book in the Old Testament.

To preach her sermon of vengeance, Rhonda Mae knew she needed the solid rock of opportunity. Over the river, there were fissures and cracks between the *narcos* warring for dominance along this stretch of the border, gaps a savvy operator could exploit.

Two at the top of the bloody pile were the Monterrey outfit that toppled Malo Garza from his throne and the rejuvenated remnants of his family empire, fulfilling the phoenix myth with a murderous vengeance.

Most of the smaller outfits allied themselves with one of the top dogs. But several, like the crew near Ojinaga that wanted to buy this last cache of weapons, were taking a wait-and-see approach, gathering strength and getting ready to fill the vacuum should the top dogs bleed each other white in stalemate.

This Ojinaga outfit was hungry to expand, willing to pay top dollar for the M16A2s and A3s and AR-15s she had for sale. All of them altered or designed to be full auto. Were they hungry enough to take on the Garzas and their Anglo partners to hijack the cache of weapons trucked from the mesa top the night Tommy Juan was killed?

She was willing to bet a deal sweet'ner they would be – twenty LAWs rockets, three M2 60-millimeter mortars with four cases of high explosive rounds and fifteen M-79 Thumpers with 200 of the 40-millimeter grenade rounds they fired. Thrown in gratis from the cache hidden on Malachi Hulett's ranch if the outfit would go after the cache of hijacked weapons.

Armando's kin told him the Garzas killed Tommy Juan and took the weapons stored on that mesa rancho, but they were still on the north side of the river, hidden after word that a rival's crew got ambushed at a favored crossing. Hidden by who, Armando's cousins didn't know, but Rhonda Mae's money was on the crew Tommy Juan ratted out, the ones operating out of the Bar L R. She also bet they teamed up with the Garzas to kill Tommy Juan.

The mesa cache had been earmarked for the Monterrey boys. Simple enough to get them to do the hijacking if Armando could find out the where and when of the move south. But Rhonda Mae wanted to stay one step removed from the two top dogs. And she wanted payback, not just a jolt of quick cash.

That's why she wanted the Ojinaga crew to do it. Make it primal and brutal. Like smashing a skull with the jawbone of an ass. Clear, true and lethal in her mind's eye.

She needed Armando's help to make it real and would preach her pitch during their backcountry trek to Cuervo County, bouncing in that rusty CJ5 over goat trails and ranch roads. She was banking on blood ties and loyalty. And a taste for revenge straight out of the Good Book.

Vengeance is mine, I will repay, saith the Lord...Whom shall I send? Who will go for us? Here am I, Lord. Send me.

Armando stepped through the door, carrying the other chair and the shotgun. She shook an *ovalado* out of the pack, lit it and handed it over. He nodded, unfolded the chair, parked himself and took a deep drag.

"So, still we go to Cuervo County?"

"*Sí*, Armando, still we go."

She decided not to wait and told him her plan, including the LAWs, stovepipe and Thumper sweet'ner. She told him of the need to find out all they could about the crew hiding out on the Bar L R. They needed to know if these were the motherfuckers that killed Tommy Juan. Armando smoked his *Delicado* to the nub and said nothing until she finished her pitch.

"You don't have to be there. Stay here and let me make the arrangements."

"No, I have to be there. I have to see it through all the way."

"For Tomasito?"

"*Sí*, for Tommy Juan."

Armando looked at her in silence as if gathering the words to convince her to stay. She met his gaze as the seconds ticked by. His head jerked forward in a sharp nod.

"*Bueno,* we go then."

Thwack-crack. Thwack-crack.

Two heavy slugs slammed into the trunk of the cottonwood he was using for cover, missing his head by a couple of inches.

A little chin music. Down the pike. High and inside. One-and-one.

He flattened out and backed away, sliding his body under the thicker cover of creosote and mesquite and a sandy hollow in the ground that gave the illusion of defilade.

Thwack-crack. Thwack-crack.

Two more slugs. One buzzed through the brush just above his head, snapping branches and dropping leaves and sharp thorns on his back. The other smacked the lip of the hollow, geysering sand into his face.

Slider caught the corner. Chaser low, away and in the dirt. Two-and-two. Need better cover.

He spotted a rock to his left and was tempted to bolt that way.

Sucker's bet. He'll nail you before you get halfway. Stay put. Burrow deeper. Stay chilly and enjoy your problem. Keep channeling Loel Passe. Hot ziggity dog and good ol' sassafras tea.

Pure radio cornpone served up every Houston baseball night. Cold comfort from his childhood that gave him a small, bitter chuckle.

He took a deep breath and relaxed. Thought about the tactical trap and finding a way out. The gap between the slug hitting the tree and the sound of the shot told him the shooter wasn't close.

Didn't need to be. Has enough gun to reach out and touch. More gun than the MP-5 he was toting. Also has an elevated perch with a good line of sight over this river crossing. At night. Which meant he had a Starlight scope or better.

Bet on better. Moonless night. Starlight scopes HPD had were Vietnam-era hand-me-downs and weren't worth a shit without moonlight. Buddy of his was HPD SWAT and used to bitch about it all the time.

Thwaaaack-crack. Right down the pike. Now you chuckin' in there, boy.

Hell, this motherfucker probably has a Gen II scope, higher-grade Uncle Sam surplus courtesy of the Mexican army.

Thwaaaack-crack. Thwaaaack-crack.

More sand in his mouth, nose and eyes. More thorns, branches and leaves raining down.

Stay still. Stay chilly. Chilly and still. Gettin' waaaaay too old for this kinda shit.

His rover was off. By choice. Made before he started slithering closer to the river to avoid the crackling electronic giveaway of a rogue transmission. Another buddy of his got shot to shit after forgetting to turn his off before creeping toward a suspect's house. The buddy lived but had to pull the string on a medical because the rounds shattered the bones of both legs.

That fuckin' rover stays the fuck off. My folks know I'm still alive because fuckhead keeps shootin' at me. Sure as hell, there'll be no smugglers crossing this river tonight. No shit, genius.

Those guys backed the hell away as soon as Mister Fuckhead spotted me and took his first shot. Spicer'll be pissed. Fuck him. He's 300 yards away on our side of the river, nice, safe and sitting on his lardass in a command Humvee.

The slow, metallic cough of a Ma Deuce opened up from higher ground to his rear. Tracers lit up the night, drenching Mister Fuckhead's perch. Heavy slugs that could shatter an engine block, churned out by the Deuce ring-mounted on the roof of another Humvee closer to the river. Gulf War surplus handed over to the DEA, a perk of working on a joint task force.

Bet a Gen II scope set up this fire mission. No more thwaaaack-crack. Not from that guy. Not with a lead rain pouring down.

Wake up, shithead. Slither back to safer ground before the cover fire stops. Fuckin' knees are killin' me. Didn't I tell you you're gettin' too old for this shit? Don't believe me, listen to your hunnert-year-old hinges, dumbass.

On the other side of the river, the night sky flared orange and green with tracer and the flash-boom of rifle grenades. He could hear the high-pitched stutter of lighter automatic weapons rising above the slower, deeper chuffing of the Ma Deuce.

Must be those Mexican Marines – El Cuerpo de Infantería de Marina. *Hitting the bad guys before they could get away. Jesus, those hardasses don't fuck around. They kill everybody. At least the blood is on their side of the river.*

With a big rock between him and the river, he turned on his rover.

"Three to Six. Checking in. I say again, Three to Six."

"Where the fuck have you been, Three?"

"Dodging bullets, Six."

"Who the fuck told you to move in so close, Three?"

"Nobody. Did that on my own nickel, Six."

"You blew this op, Three. Get the fuck back here and check in with me, pronto."

"Not a total loss, Six. Mex Marines made hash of the bad guys, sounds like."

"Stay off the 'net and get your ass back here, Three."

"You bet, Six. Looking forward to it."

Willis Quanah "Cider" Jones wasn't in the mood for an ass-chewing. His knees popped, sand stuck to his sweat-soaked clothes, his crotch and every exposed part of his body. He was in dire need of a long drink of water and a short, fat chaw of Red Man.

He didn't need a DEA puke to tell him he fucked up. But he knew Senior Special Agent Donald Spicer, head honcho of this joint task force, couldn't resist the opportunity to smack him in the balls.

Two reasons for that. Jones wasn't a fed; he was seconded to the ATF side of the house from the Texas Attorney General's office, where he worked a paper-shuffling job a buddy got him when the Houston Police Department decided to ease him out to pasture after more than two decades as a homicide detective.

When the ATF said they needed a sho' nuff manhunter for their task force cadre, his buddy floated Cider's name their way. Got him out of the office and back in the harness of the job he loved. Best of all – nobody gave a rat's ass how he got a nickname pinned on him after an unfortunate incident as a rookie cop involving apple cider, Everclear and a spectacular amount of projectile vomiting.

While most of the task force focused on seizing drug shipments, Cider tried to draw a bead on individual gunrunners, their hideouts, their favorite crossings, who they did business with and who they did not.

Not quite a murder cop, but it beat shuffling paper. He missed being a homicide detective, channeling the spirit of his dead grandfather, a Comanche shaman, staring into the eyes of a murder victim.

Waiting for what the victims told him in wide-eyed death. Sifting through what he saw as he squatted on his boot heels and gazed into a set of sightless lenses. Searching for a shard of image, a sense of the horror of this life's last moments or the utter unknowing surprise of having the plug yanked out violently, without warning or time to flinch or record a thought of what was happening.

Sometimes, the eyes told him nothing. At other times, a great deal, silently passing him information that would rise from his innards as he worked a case, causing the tuning fork to vibrate at a faster frequency, clicking confusion into clear focus.

No call for Comanche mysticism on this job. ATF owned his ass, so he made the bang-bang merchants his priority, running snitches on both sides of the river, scraping the rust off his *barrio*

Spanish and drawing up a target list of nine of the top gunrunners working this part of the border.

One top target was already crossed off the list. Tommy Juan Jaeckel, killed by one or more of his competitors, no doubt for ratting them out. Details hardly mattered. Just chalk it up to the lethally high cost of doing business in a very competitive market.

Tommy Juan's killers left the customarily gruesome calling card to mark the demise of a rat. Throat slit, cock and balls sliced off and stuffed in the mouth of a chopped off head. The rest of the body sawed up then everything racked neatly in a giant barbecue cooker and slow smoked to perfection.

That left Tommy Juan's paramour and business partner, a leggy blonde or redhead who called herself a string of fake last names – Adams, Taylor, Martinez, Shaughnessy – all attached to the same fake first name – Rita.

One of his snitches told him she was also known as *La Güera*, a flashy bottled blonde who had the fellas drooling while she fleeced them in gun deals across the river. Fronting for Tommy Juan.

The same snitch told him that Tommy Juan had one last cache of weapons that included some bang-bangs Cider didn't want the bad guys to get hold off. Mortars, LAWs rockets, a bunch of M79 grenade launchers and the 40-millimeter ammo to make them thump.

La Güera. That was his meat. Fuck the DEA – let 'em get their own manhunter. Fuck Spicer.

He knew what Cortez, his last true partner, would say: *Cool your jets, Breed. Take your ass-whuppin' and live to fight another day.*

Fuckin' Cortez, still dogging his ass despite being dead and buried for more than a dozen years, gunned down at the mouth of the world's sixth largest bat cave near Mason, Texas by a muscle-bound black hitman with a squealy voice and a godawful toupee that looked like tar-coated Astro-Turf.

The same burst smashed up Cider's shoulder and killed the ex-wife of the dirtbag they were chasing, a defrocked Dallas homicide cop named Ed Earl Burch. Burch was their top suspect in two drug-related murders in Houston. He and Cortez were sure Burch was a *narco* gun for hire and they'd brought the ex-wife along to talk him into surrendering once he was cornered.

Didn't matter to Cider that the hitman, Willie "Bad Hair" Stonecipher, pulled the trigger that killed Cortez, the ex-wife and three local deputies brought along to help net Burch. Didn't matter that Stonecipher was working for a carrot-topped half-Mex *narco* named T-Roy Bonifacio.

Didn't matter that Burch iced Stonecipher when the hitman went into the cave to chase the ex-Dallas cop and his petite blonde accomplice, Carla Sue Cantrell.

No honor among thieves and killers. No hall pass for Burch.

As far as Cider was concerned, Burch pulled the trigger that killed his partner. Burch set the whole bloody mess in motion. And Burch was a dirty ex-cop. He had no doubt. It chapped him Burch was still breathing the rancid air of whatever hellhole he hung his hat.

He knew what Cortez would say: *You keep blamin' the wrong guy for me gettin' killed. I can't rest until you stop that shit. You can't either.*

The last time he saw Burch face-to-face was in the homicide bullpen of Houston PD. Burch was babysitting the wife of a fugitive financier with mob ties and had gunned down some freelance Mexican muscle who slapped around the wife and tried to give him a buckshot chest tattoo.

The wife still had some of her husband's money – enough to trot out a protege of Racehorse Haynes to get her and Burch off the hook. Burch tracked the husband down in the bowels of the Astrodome, trying to cut a deal with some Vietnamese gangsters in the middle of the Houston Livestock Show and Rodeo. Wound up in a shootout in the middle of the arena, smoking the gang honcho and two others before getting side-swiped by a runaway bull.

Then the wife jumped the tracks, leaving Burch behind along with the bodies of two ex-mercs hired to keep her safe. Wasn't pretty. Shotgun blasts to the chest and face rarely were. Cider worked the scene. Knew the wife was the shooter. Blamed Burch anyway, his hatred again flaring white hot. But he didn't act on it.

He was content to trail Burch as the bent ex-cop chased the wife to a little white chapel just over the river from La Linda for a showdown with her husband. Let the mob or the *narcos* deal with Burch. He'd watch from a safe, comfortable spot and get the body bag sent north.

Didn't happen that way. Burch walked out of that chapel. The wife and husband did not.

The memories and hate were no longer sharp and razor-edged. Harder to dial into clear focus. A sign that time and distance had tempered his bloody obsession. Maybe. Or maybe it was a case of out of sight, out of mind. At least, the conscious part. Maybe that hatred was still buried deep, waiting to rise again, but it was no longer a white-hot burn across the front of his brain.

Cider felt sweat-soaked sand scrape his crotch and shoulders as he walked toward Spicer's command Humvee. He lifted his black ball cap and raked fingers through his wet hair – mostly white now, but still thick – then shifted his MP-5 to keep it from banging his hip. A dark figure stepped out of the Humvee.

Time to face the music. No doubt it would be harsh and tuneless.

"Get your ass over here, Jones."

"Headed right your way as ordered, boss."

"You move slower than my ninety-five-year-old granny."

Cider said nothing and stopped walking only when he was toe-to-toe with Spicer.

"Who told you to move in close?"

"Nobody, but I saw we didn't have anybody posted near the bank on the downriver side of the crossing."

"So, you took it upon yourself to move there without checking with me?"

"Didn't want to risk a radio squawk that might give my position away."

"Sure didn't have to worry about radio silence once that sniper started throwing rounds your way. You know, you blew this op."

"Not with the Mex Marines backing our play. Sounds like they chopped up those *gabachos* pretty damn good. You're just pissed about missing a photo op on this side of the river."

Spicer jutted his face toward Cider. Now they were eyeball to eyeball. The smell of stale coffee and cigarettes flooded his nostrils.

"You can go fuck yourself sideways with that bullshit. You're hangin' by a thread here, Jones. One call from me and you'll be back in Austin, riding that desk with a do-nothin' job."

"That right? You might want to talk to Charlie Boudreaux about that. He's right fond of me picking out targets for his ATF cowboys. Helps keep them on the straight and narrow. You might also give serious thought about pissing off the attorney general of the Great State of Texas while you're at it. Ain't nobody in this state overly fond of you *federales*. Not after Waco. You piss off my boss and things get real frosty right quick for your little joint task force."

"You got a mighty high opinion of yourself for a retread cop."

Cider jabbed a finger in Spicer's face.

"Ain't my sense of self-worth you need to worry about. Best you meditate on what I told you."

Out of the corner of his eye, Cider saw other dark shapes standing and listening. Time to disengage. He turned on his boot heels and walked away, digging a pouch of Red Man from an inside pocket of his tactical vest for the fat chaw he craved.

Spicer kept his mouth shut.

Ten

It didn't take much to give Burch the look of a long-haul trucker – a greasy red Mack gimme cap with a frayed brim, a dark green Hollofil vest with a strip of duct tape patching a tear and jeans worn thin by years of wash and wear.

Throw in a black cowhide biker's wallet with a belt chain and scrape the rust off lingo he learned from riding with his Uncle Lon, a long-haul trucker, and Burch was set to sell himself as a bitter blue-collar chump.

A down-the-drain loser who lost his best ride hauling freight for one of the big national outfits and was scraping by as an indie driver. A man who lost his home and his family because the money he made wasn't enough to keep ground beef in the freezer. Just the kind of guy looking for somebody to blame and something to believe in.

The cap, vest and wallet were loaners from one of Doggett's cousins. Inside the wallet was a fake Texas commercial driver's license good enough to fool a bank teller, well-worn and slightly dog-eared. Edward Earl Slaughter was the name next to his scowling photo, from Fort Stockton, a town he knew because cousins lived there.

The jeans were his. With a little bit of insurance stuffed down the front left pocket – a palm sap, a zippered black leather pouch with a ten-ounce roll of quarters stuffed inside and a web hand strap to give lights-out heft to a hook or haymaker.

Not as nasty as Black Betty, his spring-loaded leather sap, but a small comfort on an undercover run. Call it a sucker punch equalizer. Perfect for the young punk who thought old made a man an easy mark.

He also owned the scuffed up Justins with the worn-down heels and the 1911 tucked in a belt slide holster at the small of his back. Figured a gun-loving secessher crowd wouldn't care about a man packing heat. Might care if he didn't.

But Burch flipped Doggett's script when he ghosted up to Alpine, where he spotted a dented, dark-green 1976 Dodge D100 sitting near the back of a used car lot. A shade more expensive than the primered-over Bronco Doggett wanted him to buy from the son of the late and unlamented Dirt Cheap Bustamante. Right there in the heart of Faver where a lot of eyes were looking for him.

Nope. Not going to happen. Pretty stupid to trust his life to a thin layer of gray covering the Cuervo County Sheriff's Department logo. Not with all those eyes watching. The Dodge was the safer bet – out of town and unknown.

He was a Ford man but felt right at home in this veteran rig. Four speed with a floor shifter and a 318 V-8 that still had a little giddyup. Spare tire riding the driver's side fender of the short stepside box made it look like a rancher's truck. Rust here and there but no cancer. Lots of galvanized steel in the old Dodge.

Brakes were shaky but the tires were fair. Seven Ben Franklins made it Ed Slaughter's, taxes, tag and title thrown in. A single Ben for a brake job down the street at Jackie Montoya's garage, the same guy who gave Ol' Blue, his elderly Ford truck, a top-end overhaul when he blew a head gasket driving to Faver almost a decade ago.

Jackie did good work on Ol' Blue and in the years since moved his shop from Faver to Alpine to tap into a bigger base of customers. Burch missed his old rig with its big straight-six engine and granny creeper first gear. A real stump puller. Sold it to a cousin when Betty Lou rolled up to his door in all her muscular midnight blue splendor.

Burch hated admitting Doggett was right about anything but knew Betty Lou was far too flashy a ride for a private dick trying to run a discreet investigation. Even lust-blinded adulterers would spot him in the big Olds.

The clincher was the sheriff's cousin discovering a tracker soldered to Betty Lou's frame while troubleshooting a battery with barely enough juice to crank the engine. The nasty little transmitter confirmed somebody was on his six, probably before he left Dallas and still out there looking.

Enter that old Dodge. Never seen by nobody with him at the wheel. Never had a sheriff's badge plastered on both doors. And no transmitter to rat him out to the bad guys. That left him a little less beholden to Doggett, which still rankled.

"Just don't fuckin' say 'I told you so.'"

"Don't have to. It's a story that tells itself."

"Whoever it is knows the car's been impounded and probably figures I'm still in your jail."

"That would make them half right."

"Half right is all the edge I need."

They were sitting in the front room of Doggett's stone-walled house, butts in overstuffed leather armchairs, deep whiskies in hand, listening to the pop and crackle of a small piñon blaze in the fireplace. Maker's Mark. His favorite.

Not much bigger than a cabin, the place had a tin roof, a porch that wrapped around three sides, a loft for guests and a back bedroom and bath for the master of the manse, a public man who guarded his privacy by living twenty miles from town, at the far end of a box canyon with only coyotes and rattlesnakes for neighbors.

A barn and paddock out back sheltered three horses, milling around outside, snorting and acting annoyed. The reason? Maybe the Dodge parked inside their crib with the door rolled shut, covered in the chalky dust of the ranch roads Burch took to avoid going through Faver. Inside the house, a white-muzzled blue heeler dozed at Doggett's feet.

Burch lit a Lucky then eyed the room, spotting a Winchester '92 with a long, octagonal barrel leaning against a window frame behind Doggett and a well-worn 12-gauge Winchester Model 12 pump perched on pegs above the front door.

"Expecting company?"

"I'm a cautious man, Burch. Have to be. Besides, if company does show up, I was raised to be a good host and give them a warm welcome."

"Your hardware's a little old-school, ain't it?"

"I thought a man like you would appreciate that – a .45-70 Government to reach out and touch and buckshot if they get too close. Got a 16 in the bedroom with two thirty-round mags for some jungle rock 'n roll. How's that for modern?"

Burch raised his glass toward Doggett. *"Te saludo, jefe."* Doggett smiled his sad-eyed smile and raised his glass in return.

"Got a question for you – where'd you get that Dodge? Cousin Luis says after he slipped you out of jail, you asked him to drop you off at that *tienda* where you had your little fracas."

"Had a friend meet me there. Figured I needed to get out of town a bit, get somewhere people weren't lookin' for me. And I doubted folks who were had the scene of a bloodbath staked out."

"That was damn risky. And you don't got no friends."

Burch smiled. "You'd be surprised. Some folks in these parts are quite fond of me."

"Jesus, don't tell me. I thought you wanted to stay clear of her."

"Sure did. But I needed to slip out of your jail and out of town. Figured getting a ride from somebody the bad guys weren't watching would keep me off their radar screen. And keep me out of sight."

"Hell, you should'a let me in on the play."

"No offense, but your walls have ears and the less you knew the better my chances. I don't know who your boys or your cousin talk to when they're off the clock. Don't know them. Only know you."

Doggett took a long pull from his glass, shook his head and held up his left hand. "Okay. I get it. I'm over being pissed about it. Just got one question – was it worth it?"

Burch grinned and stubbed out his Lucky in a tin ashtray.

"Only cost me a hangover and a sleepless night. And look at that fine Dodge pickup I got for my trouble. A ride that doesn't have a beeper the bad guys can track and doesn't look like the sheriff's old ride."

Salty, sweet and musky. Stronger as his tongue goes deeper, lapping the soft folds of flesh, flicking the button that draws a sharp hiss from above.

Hands and chin wedging the thighs wider. Tongue following the new and inner path. Moans that become a deep howl. Fists beating his shoulders. Sharp nails raking his back, drawing blood.

Thighs clamping his head. A howl that jumps an octave. A high-pitched shriek. Shudders and spasms rocking the bed. Pleas of 'stop, stop.' The tongue stabs and laps, ignoring the pleas, chasing the taste, unhinging the torrent. Then riding the downhill slide.

"Jesus, I forgot about that tongue of yours. Haven't cum that hard in a long, long time."

"Bet you say that to all the boys."

"Only the champion pussy lickers."

"Do I get a belt buckle for that?"

A long, low chuckle. An arching eyebrow. A smile breaking across a broad, fleshy face. High cheekbones and olive skin with a rosy flush. Curly black hair shot with silver and running wild. Heavy unfettered breasts with thick, brown nipples and a silver chain diving down her cleavage.

The earthy allure of a mature Latina. Tall and fully curved. Deeply and frankly carnal. With male and female partners. Sometimes both at once. Nita Rodriguez Wyatt, a rich woman with a string of ex-husbands, most of them monied, including one of Sid Richardson's pups, who left her oil and gas leases that kept her flush.

She was an ex-client. She roped him into coming to Faver almost a decade ago to do the peeper work he loathed – track down a wayward husband, snap a dozen or so steamy photos of no-tell motel mattress frolic, get her off the hook of paying full freight on the pre-nup agreement.

Burch delivered the goods, a done deal that made him want to guzzle a barrel of Maker's Mark to hose down the slime and shame. She paid him his price, picked up the tab for getting Ol' Blue repaired and insisted on a face-to-face meeting to personally deliver a two-part bonus – a hefty check and a night of tequila-laced fucking that left him hungover and frazzled.

Past becomes present. She picks up a ribbed bottle of Dos Reales Tequila Añejo and offers it to him, neck first. Yogi Berra speaks: "It's like déjà vu all over again."

"You look a little thirsty after all that tongue work. Take a drink. Whether I give you a belt buckle depends on how well you do in the saddle, hombre."

"I remember this poison. You gave it to me the last time we met."

"Aw, how sweet. Couldn't have been all that deadly – you're still alive, right?"

"We'll see."

Grab the bottle and bubble it. Save a mouthful to bathe her nipples. Then suck and bite. A hiss then a yelp from above.

"Come up here and fuck me. Let's see how much life you still got."

"You might want to wipe that moony look off your face and pay attention. I got a proposition."

117

"Can't let a man have a moment of carnal reverie in peace, can you? Not my fault you're all alone in your own private Alamo with only a dog and three horses to keep you company."

"You'd be surprised at who shows up at my door. Some want overnight privileges I'm happy to oblige. Some want to fix me breakfast in the morning. It would be rude of me to refuse."

Burch grinned and raised his glass. *"Te saludo, jefe."*

"You still headed out to Bondurant's in the morning?"

"You bet. Trail's ice cold, but it's the only lead I've got so far."

"Check in with me. You know you ain't the only one lookin' for her. The *narcos* want her dead. So does anybody else Tommy Juan crossed. And there's a joint task force workin' this territory. DEA and ATF. Chasin' *narcos* and gun runners."

"Shit."

"Shit is right. Got all kinds of wolves huntin' for her. Stick this somewhere safe."

Doggett scrawled on the sheet of a small, leather-bound notebook, the kind cops carry in their shirt pockets. He ripped out the sheet and slid it across the scarred pine coffee table between them.

"It's my private line. I sweep it myself twice a day along with the rest of my office."

"Ain't you the one with the spy-versus-spy gear."

"Like I said – I'm a cautious man."

"I'll check in when I can. But you don't hear from me in two days, best come runnin'."

Doggett sipped his whiskey, then looked at Burch. He started to say something but hesitated. Burch met his gaze and waited. Silence he had to break.

"Tell me about that proposition."

"Best to show you. Catch."

Doggett tossed a hunk of golden metal that flashed in the glow from the fireplace. Burch managed to catch it with his right hand without spilling ninety-proof from the glass in his left. He opened his hand and saw an oval-shaped badge, broad at the top and narrow at the bottom.

He flipped it over and held it up to the light to read the stamped letters – Cuervo County District Attorney made up two arched lines at the top, Investigator filled a single inverted arch at the bottom.

"What the fuck are you doin' to me here – yankin' my chain to piss me off?"

"Nope. Tryin' to give you something back you lost a long time ago. Tryin' to make you an honest man again. Officially, you'd work for the D.A. 'cause he's got room in his budget for you. In reality, I'd be your boss."

"Well, I'll be a cockbite bastard if this ain't the dumbest idea you've ever had. Jesus Christ, Doggett – ain't nobody going to let me be a lawman again. In Texas or any other damn state. Not with all the shit I stirred up in Dallas and Houston, not to mention here in your own backyard."

"This is West Texas, son. We don't give much of a shit about what went down in Dallas or Houston or listen much to anybody from there or Austin. What counts is what a man does here. And folks that count around here remember you helped take Blue Willingham down and smoked Needle Burnet. I remember you killin' that motherfucker and know you're the reason I'm still standing. You piss me off, but I remember."

A flashing image.

The flame and roar of his 1911. A full mag of fat Flying Ashtrays booming down the narrow hallway of a tin-roofed house an hour's slow crawl south of the Rio Grande.

Blowing Needle Burnet out of his socks before he could put a final bullet in Doggett's brainpan with a .44 Mag. At the ass end of a box canyon at the edge of a piece-of-shit mountain village named Ascensión.

No sign of Christ rising to Heaven in that godforsaken place. Nothing holy about the reason they were there, either. No redemption or resurrection. Just revenge and death.

119

And guilt – they got one of Doggett's cousins killed, a teenager too proud and bound by family honor to go home when told.

"Well, shit. Just two days ago, you were ready to run me out on a rail. Now you want me to come work for you?"

"Ain't life strange?"

Burch felt like his heart was going to explode. And his head. The badge felt like a coal from Ol' Scratch himself, hellish and hot enough to brand his palm. He wanted to throw the damn thing across the room before he sold his sinner's soul to Doggett or any other demon lurking nearby.

But he couldn't. He lost his detective's gold shield nearly twenty years ago, robbing his life of purpose and the sense of higher calling he got from chasing killers to either cuff or smoke – their choice. Always with the dark thrill in the back of his mind that they might just smoke him. Kept him sharp and a second faster.

Never thought he'd ever wear a badge again and spent years helping the scar tissue build with whiskey, pills and women just as rootless, drifting in and out of his bed without a clue or compass. He built a safe, hollow life stripped down to a boot on the bar rail and work with little honor, completed with what was left of his professional pride.

Got damn good at tracking down financial fugitives of Texas' oil and real estate bust of the mid-80s – wayward business partners who skipped town with all the money, bent S&L loan officers who opened the vault to mobsters and con artists, flim-flam masters of the Ponzi scheme. Put some coin in his bank account and let him get shed of Fat Willie, the shyster who once held the note on his business.

When Fat Willie still had him by the short hairs, the asshole would get him to do his dirty work. Usually something quick and slimy. But every now and then, the shyster would throw him into a thicker briar patch. Nasty and violent deals, jackpots with people getting dead as Cain's brother, the law looking the other way and gun hands taking lethal offense to him poking his snout where only the victim's kin thought it belonged.

No badge, but he was a manhunter again, chasing killers, putting his ass on the line, surviving on the savvy instincts of an ex-street cop with a gun and a bad attitude. He was alive again. Until it was over, with the bad guys face down in the dirt and the gunfire a loud but receding echo, leaving him with nothing but an unquenchable longing for what he lost.

Took a cruel, cockbite bastard to offer him that badge. Might as well have slashed his guts open with a rusty bayonet. Cheap and shiny, that metal cut him deep and bloody. And Burch wanted to hold it close to his heart like his life depended on it.

His vision blurred and he felt dizzy. He killed the rest of his whiskey and glared at Doggett.

"You got ten seconds to say what you got to say or I walk."

Doggett topped their glasses with fresh whiskey.

"Here goes. We been talking 'bout the need for an investigator in this county since I took office. Don't need no college boy with a criminal justice degree and a hard-on to be the next DA. Need somebody who walked a beat, knows the streets, knows how to track a killer and don't mind bending the rules and getting his knuckles bloody to get the job done."

"Who's we?"

"Me for starters. And the new DA. Believe you know him. Fella named Sam Boelcke."

As in Santiago Quinones Boelcke, the son of a *Texasdeutsch* daddy and a Mexican mother – the border *menudo* personified.

"You're fuckin' kiddin' me, son. Sam Boelcke is Cuervo County DA? Don't know that he's crooked, but he's compromised, right? Used to date Malo Garza's daughter and do work for Garza's outfit."

"This is the goddam border, Burch. Everybody's got blood ties that run north and south of the river, some good, some bad. They keep you connected unless you cross a line and become compromised."

"You rub up against bad guys and you get tied up whether you want to or not."

"Hear me out. Sam and Valentina haven't been an item in five or six years. And Garza preferred keeping Sam clean, letting him handle his legitimate interests on this side of the river. Sam never was a mouthpiece for Garza or his thugs. And he had other clients. Your girlfriend Nita for one and you for another."

"That's two who think my shit don't stink. Who else?"

"Dub McKee."

"The Ranger?"

"Dub's retired now but he's still got juice around here and up in Austin. Likes to keep his hand in and has become a bit of a power broker. Governor lends him an ear. So does the lieutenant governor, the House Speaker and most of the county judges out this way. He's one of the ones who remembers what you did to help bring Blue Willingham down. He's a tough nut but was sure impressed with you."

"Nice to have friends I didn't know about."

"Fact is, McKee was the one who brought up your name last time we were talkin' about an investigator. Boelcke was keen as soon as he heard your name."

"I'm betting you were the tough sell."

"Yeah, but only because I thought you enjoyed being an outlaw too much to ever want to be tied down by a badge again."

"What changed your mind?"

"The notion that somebody just outlaw enough fits the bill to a T. In other words – you."

"Do I have to wear a stinkin' hat?"

"With that bald noggin of yours, I'd strongly advise it. Sun is fierce out here. You'll peel like a snake without one."

Burch stared at the fire as his brain ticked off the long, slow seconds and measured the angles, odds and lethal permutations of the offer. He tried to breathe deep and steady to rein in his trip-hammer heart. No dice. He looked at Doggett.

"I tell you what let's do. Put this back in a desk drawer and lock it up. For now. Let me get this job done. If I live to see the naked light of day, we'll talk it over again."

"Fair enough. Do the job, don't get killed and we'll talk again."

He tossed the badge back to Doggett when what he really wanted to do was pin it on his chest and dance a buck-and-wing across the cabin floor.

But Burch had that first cousin of a street cop's survival reflexes. Doubt. He was dead certain of that.

Eleven

Burch shambled through the rear entrance of a long conference room with windows on one side and a gray tracked divider on the other that always reminded him of an accordion big enough for Godzilla to play. At the front was a dais with a black steel lectern plumb center with an American flag stage right and a Texas flag stage left.

He spotted a huge coffee urn – aluminum dull, dented and naked. Made a beeline for some caffeine salvation. Filled a big cup. Two sugars. No creamer. Ripped open two waxed paper sleeves of BC Powder and dumped them down his throat.

Hot coffee chaser. A quick, silent prayer to the hangover gods for relief. Maybe one of them would speak to Thor and get him to quit hammering the inside of his brainpan with Mjöllnir.

He lit a Lucky and studied the room, nodding to fellow addicts of the roasted bean and stepping out of their way. Long rows of gray, hard-assed aluminum chairs, the cruel creation of churches and public schools, marched toward the dais, their line broken by a center aisle.

Round-butted Americans already filled half the chairs, the kind you see at any Walmart or Dollar General. A slow-moving line of fellow seekers snaked up the center aisle, peeling off to grab empty seats. Wild-ass guess – about ninety or a hundred in the room. Not a bad haul at $200 a pop.

Burch picked a seat on the last row, just to the left of the center aisle, which would eventually give him a clear line of sight to the lectern that would soon serve as a prop for the star of the show – Thomas "T For Texas" Bondurant, seller of secessionist snake oil and sugar-coated hate to the desperate, the down-and-out and the terminally pissed off.

Plenty of those in the gathering crowd, almost all of them whites of the Bubba and Bubbette type. A few that might have Mexican blood. Maybe. No blacks, Asians or Native Americans. No Jews.

Burch focused on a moon-faced man with a faded green John Deere cap, the brick red complexion of a sure-bet stroke candidate and a belly that could shade a family of six on a picnic. Big Belly had a chunky revolver strapped to his left hip with glossy dark bluing and Pachmayr grips peeking above the holster.

He wasn't the only one packing heat. Burch spotted telltale bulges underneath jackets and shirts of several folks sidling up the center aisle. Male and female. Others were bold as brass, with their iron tucked into a hip holster for all the world to see. Some already seated were fidgeting, squirming to find a way to keep their iron from gouging them in the fat hanging over their belts.

Next to Big Belly, a hatchet-faced woman with unnaturally auburn locks was chopping the air with her hands while braying to someone with blond helmet hair and a Confederate battle banner sewn to the back of a black leather vest.

Male or female, Burch wasn't sure. But he was certain about the grip of a semi-automatic riding the small of the back, jutting above a tooled leather belt. Made him glad of the 1911 snuggling against his own spine. Good move to bring it along. Marked him as a fellow traveler.

I'm a gun-lovin' American – just like you.

Burch sipped his coffee and kept up the scan, looking for someone or something that didn't jibe. Or somebody looking at him while he looked at everybody else.

Relax. Quit thinking about your hangover. Just focus, watch and let it come to you.

To check his six, he stood up for a caffeine refill, shucking his vest and draping it over the chair back to save his seat, letting those who cared to look get a glimpse of his Colt.

This is Texas, by God, and a man's gotta right to protect himself and his own.

He cast a casual glance at the stacked up rear entrance and the lurkers leaning against the back wall. No telltales of a watcher. Nobody snapping their eyes away or suddenly frozen like a statue of studied coolness.

Just the suckers. So far. Keep looking, asshole. Don't get sloppy. Be awake. You'll nap when you're dead.

He filled his cup to the rim and took a long sip, eyes back to the front, watching a tall, stoop shouldered man with a silver-gray ponytail and a ZZ Top beard picking his way through a row of knees, feet and frowning faces to an empty chair at the far end. He had a single-action revolver tucked into a double-loop Mexican holster riding low on his right leg.

Ready for the ghost of John Wesley Hardin or a U.N. black helicopter, right pops? Bet that dude knows every word to "La Grange." Wouldn't mind hearing some of that Lil' Ol' Band From Tejas right now. Might liven up the mood.

Snap out of it, popdick. Pay attention.

At the edge of his vision, he spotted a man standing next to the accordion partition, about a quarter of the way down the far-right aisle, looking his way.

Gotcha, pendejo. Wait, now. Let him think you're fat, dumb and happy to be with all your redneck friends. Wait and let him look… One-Mississippi, Two-Mississippi, Three-Mississippi. Go.

Burch spun to the right, jostling a black-haired woman waiting to get a refill, snapping his eyes toward the watcher and watching the man's panicked move to look at anybody but him.

In a crowd full of the worn-down and pissed-off, the watcher stood out – younger, more muscular and aggressively aloof. Like he couldn't stand the sight or smell of the faithful come to worship Bondurant as he stoked their fears and fantasies.

The bulge of a shoulder rig printed the left side of the man's denim jacket. Burch picked up another detail – the familiar vibe of hired muscle. An ex-con maybe. A thug for sure. Trying to recover his cool by keeping his eyes off Burch.

Okay. Let him off the hook. Let him think you didn't see him. But stay alert. Like rattlers, where there's one there's two. Or more.

Burch shifted gears, looking at the woman while keeping the thug at the edge of his vision. She was tall, with a sturdy, muscular body he bet was honed by ranch work that gave her broad face a ruddy and weathered look framed by dark, thick hair.

Scuffed boots, wash-worn jeans and a faded blue flannel shirt with fake pearl speed snaps encouraged Burch to double down on his guess.

But what caused him to do a double-take that almost took the thug out of focus was a bemused smile, hazel eyes with a bright hint of mischief and deep cleavage revealed by the top two snaps left undone. He also noticed a dark spill on the flannel above her nearest breast.

"Damn, ma'am – I didn't mean to spill hot coffee on you. Bull in a china shop is what I am. Least I can do is make sure you don't have to wear more of that by pouring you a cup."

"Sure you can handle that, Mister Bull?" Her smile widened.

"Might even be able to manage grabbing a napkin or two to help clean up the spill."

She chuckled. "That's the least you can do. And I take it black. Make it the big cup – I need another jolt to sit through these festivities. One just won't cut it."

Burch topped off his cup, filled one for her and grabbed four or five napkins from a stack near the cream, sugar and artificial versions of both. He turned to catch her eye and check on the watcher. Thug long gone but she was waiting for his next move, watching him with a frank, level gaze and her smile dialed down to a hint.

Jesus. All it takes is a set of big tits to take your eyes off the prize. He'll be back. I hope.

He nodded his head toward an empty space along the wall and she followed.

"Gets you out of the line of fire over here. Keeps another big oaf like me from spilling coffee all over your shirt."

She laughed as he handed her a Styrofoam cup – big, black and hot to handle.

"How do you know letting you bump into me wasn't part of my evil plan?"

"I don't. A man can always hope, though."

She took a big gulp of coffee while keeping her eyes on him. Hazel and sizing him up.

"What the doctor ordered. Might help keep me from snoring once the speechifying starts."

She stuck out her hand for a shake. He felt the callouses on her palm.

"Leighanna Burdette. Leigh for short."

"Ed Slaughter. Ed for short."

She laughed again. "I think I can remember that. Now, if I can get you to quit looking at my tits long enough, think you might be able to answer a question?"

Burch felt his face flush and knew his beard didn't hide the rising color.

"Don't get embarrassed, Mister Bull. Old married woman like me likes to know she can still catch a man's eye now and then."

"Well, you caught it, but I do try not to leer or drool. Particularly at a married woman."

"Haven't seen a real reason to slap you yet or tuck a bib under your chin, but it's early."

Her eyes were still on him. Hazel and smiling.

"I'll try to behave."

"Good, because I want to ask if you'd mind me sitting with you to keep the wolves away. My husband and me usually come to these shindigs together. Haul an old Airstream with the dually and save money on the motel. But he got called to work this weekend and our bank account can't afford for him to say no."

"Hauled that Airstream by your lonesome?"

"Mister Bull, I been haulin' horses and cattle all over God's green earth since I was ten. Wasn't about to miss a weekend shooting guns with the ladies. Got a course or two just for us heifers. Full auto, too. Got to put up with another dose of the local gospel, but it's worth it."

"Lady, the answer is not only yes, it's hell, yes. But from the sound of it, I'm the one who needs to ask you to protect me, not the other way around."

She threw her head back and boomed a laugh while slapping his arm. Then met his gaze again. Hazel, smiling and interested.

"Lead on, Mister Bull. I'll try not to snore."

Burch knew he fucked up by letting Leigh sit next to him. He could feel her warmth and felt drawn to those hazel eyes. They did the real talking about mutual attraction and near-future frolic that made casual chit-chat seem like a ping-pong match on a waterbed.

A quick glance showed most of the seats were filled with only a straggler or two slinking down the center aisle. No sign of the muscled-up gun hand.

But it was hard to refocus on scanning the room, looking for bad guys, with this much woman beside him. Harder still when she shifted the chit-chat to more pointed questions, ones that required a ready and believable lie.

"This is your first time here, right? I don't remember seeing you before."

"Right on the first guess. Really don't know what to expect. A buddy told me about this place. Said I might get some answers to the questions I'm asking lately."

"I expect you're asking the same questions most of the folks here are asking."

"Tell me what your crystal ball has to say."

She chuckled.

"Don't take no mystic powers to guess that. You're wondering why your slice of the American Dream now tastes like shit. You want to know who to blame and what to do about it."

"Sumtin' like that. Used to haul loads for the big boys – J.B. Hunt, Werner, Western. On the road all the time, but life was pretty sweet. Had a nice house in Big Spring. A wife and two kids. Time off and a pension. But during that last recession, Western kicked me to the sidelines. Been short-haulin' chickens, cattle and any other load I can get for short pay ever since. Lost the house, the wife and the kids to boot. Got a ratty ol' double-wide in Fort Stockton to sleep in when I ain't on the road."

Leigh was silent, her eyes still on him but her mind someplace else.

"Sorry. Didn't mean to poor-mouth."

"You weren't. Just made me think about what we lost when my husband got the boot from Conoco. Lost that house same as you. Kids are grown and gone. Livin' on my parents' ranch now. Place I grew up. Place I'll probably inherit seeing how my sister and brother live so far away with families of their own."

"I'm guessing it suits you."

"Don't be too sure about that, Mister Bull. Workin' a ranch again ain't what I planned to be doin' at my age but it's familiar. I make a little pin money on the side bookkeeping in town. We get by. But Ben – that's my husband – the shame just eats him up. He comes here lookin' for answers. Something to believe in. Or some-one. And it ain't me."

Anger flashed through the hazel. Then a hint of something else – sorrow or guilt. Maybe both.

"Look who's poor-mouthing now."

"Not hardly. Besides, I started it by whining about my own troubles. A man needs to keep a cork in that shit and keep movin' forward, playin' the hand he's dealt. Deep down, I know there ain't no freebies or pat answers in this life."

"If that's what you believe, why are you here?"

"Curious more than anything else. Like I said, my buddy put a bug in my ear. Plus, I might just be full of shit. Not about the freebies, but the answers to those questions."

Lee took a sip of coffee to fill the silence. Burch broke it.

"Why are you here? Do you buy whatever it is they're sellin' here?"

"Not really, but Ben does. Fills up some holes for him. Gives him some hope. But also feeds his hate. He needs somebody to blame. I don't. Niggers, Jews and wetbacks ain't the cause of our problems. Not that I can see."

"You don't think the white man's getting the shitty end of the stick these days?"

Hazel with a hard glint, searching his face. He grinned to let her know he wasn't serious. She wagged a finger at him.

"Don't you know it ain't smart to poke a stick at a mama bear? Alright, I'll answer your smart-ass question, Mister Bull. Always has been a rich man's world and a poor man's hard dollar. That's the cause of my troubles. Not some other poor folks with a different skin color. And I come here to see the show, shoot those guns and gossip and cut up with some of the other heifers. The ones who ain't as eat up with hate as their husbands are."

"This is Texas. You can shoot any damn place you please. Even that full auto rock n' roll. That's your God-given right as a Texan."

Smiling hazel again.

"True enough. But comin' here gets me out of a rut, with or without Ben. Ain't as much fun as it used to be, though. Had a gal runnin' the gun range for us ladies. Pretty young thing. Tall, blonde and sharp as a whip. Knew her way around every kind of gun and didn't preach at us too much."

"What happened to her?"

"Rita and her boyfriend left a year or so back. Got crosswise with the powers that be or just got tired of the bickering. Kind of like a Baptist church around here, if you know what I mean. Them pulpit politics can get nasty. Heard talk that the boyfriend butted heads with Bondurant. Can't remember his name. Went by initials. T somethin' or other."

Burch felt a chill run up his spine and made his mind go blank to keep a tell from showing on his face. He nodded at Leigh but kept his mouth shut.

A singer with a first name that sounded like hers – Lee Greenwood – took him off the hook, hushing the buzz of conversation as the first few bars of "God Bless the U.S.A." were pumped into the room. Burch hated the song but loved the timing. Quick on the heels of Greenwood's last words came the state anthem, "Texas, Our Texas."

"Guess the show's about to start."

"You're right. Best buckle up, Mister Bull."

Thomas "T For Texas" Bondurant had the strut and timing of a revival tent preacher. He sported slicked-back brown hair in a modified pompadour, an electric blue suit with dark blue piping down the front and a shoulder yoke on the back of the same color. His black boots were pointy-toed and flashed the glossy darkness of fresh-washed coal as he paced back and forth across the stage.

He looked good as he delivered his stem-winder sermon. He sounded good, his lines spilling forth with practiced spontaneity. And he knew it.

"Your great-grandfathers and grandmothers built this land, rooting out and driving off the Comanche and the Kiowa, the red savages who scalped and killed and kidnapped the kin of your ancestors...

"Your grandfathers and grandmothers set the foundation that made Texas prosper, doing the hard, back-breaking work on the ranch, in the cotton field and in the home to make this a civilized country fit for a white man to live free. A Texas where a man could rise as far as his gumption and guts, his vision and sweat, would take him, a place where even the Great Depression couldn't snuff out that promise...

"They passed the torch to your fathers and mothers, who went off to war to whip Hitler and Hirohito's asses, fill the factories that made the planes, bombs and bullets their men needed to win and kept the home fires burning until those men could return home and build the most prosperous nation the world has ever seen, a shining city on the hill where the light of liberty never went dark...

"Texas was the brightest star, the Lone Star beaming on a country where your fathers and mothers could stand tall, walk free and prosper, knowing they were descended from the people who built this land – the white people who made it grow and brought order and peace and wealth. They could be proud of how they picked up the torch and built something even better for their future and that of their children...

"And then came the Great Betrayal that snuffed out that legacy and stole that rightful future away, denying your birthright and claim to the prosperity and freedom vouchsafed by your ancestors and the white man's blood coursing through your veins. I know many of you here today have lost jobs, lost homes, lost families, lost friends and lost your sense of pride and country...

"You've watched helplessly while the Jew, the nigger, the slope and the wetback have taken over this country, claimed the jobs that are rightfully yours or refused to work to suck up the slop of the government welfare trough. Slop that your hard work pays for...

"You've watched as the government of this great land has become a slave of the Anti-Christ and his bloody horns and all-seeing eyes, sending out his jack-booted thugs in black helicopters to crush your freedoms and take away your guns. You've watched as the politicians you elect turn their backs on you and swear fealty to The Beast and the iron-fisted rule of the U.N. and One-World Government...

"You think all is lost. You think you have no future. You're scared and angry about the land you've lost, the country you feel is no longer yours, the flag you want restored to its rightful glory. But I also know this about you – the fact that you are here right now means you're willing to fight and win back the America you've lost...

"That fight starts right now, right in this very state, the Lone Star State, where we will rebuild a Republic that rejects the unjust rule of the taxman and a government that wants to brand you with the mark of The Beast. Yes, my friends, with the Bible and the bullet, we will rebuild the Texas Republic and restore the white man's place as a sovereign citizen and natural ruler over all who live here..."

There was a split second of silence when Bondurant finished his sermon. Then an explosion of applause, wolf whistles, cheers, foot-stomping, amens and Rebel yells as everyone in the room rose as one, making enough noise for a crowd ten-fold as big. Burch and Leigh were also on their feet, making modest contributions to the roar. It was the prudent move given the undercurrent of rage riding just beneath the exaltation.

Bondurant stood at the center of the stage, both arms raised in blessing with palms held high toward the crowd. He was smiling and nodding, his face streaked by rivulets of sweat, his chest heaving to take in fresh gulps of air.

He let the loud praise roll on – two minutes, then five – until it started to wane. He then swept both palms downward, urging the crowd to take their seats. A shuffle, a murmur, some residual amens and wolf whistles. Then silence restored.

Bondurant raised his right hand toward heaven, bowed his head and closed his eyes. The room followed suit.

"Our Father, who art in heaven…"

Voices together as a ragged one. Chanting Christ's prayer, the savior's gift to his disciples.

But the sweet grace of Jesus wasn't in these shared words. No comfort to be found.

Burch conjured a burning cross, a hangman's noose and the smell of sulfur.

"Man likes to preach."

"Hell, yes, he does. Likes the applause, too."

Burch tried to stifle a short snort of laughter but failed. The Lucky he was trying to light took a nose-dive to the floor of the hallway outside the rear exit of the conference room. His lit Zippo singed his moustache.

"You're a mess, Mister Bull. Try not to set yourself on fire. Might have plans for you."

Burch arched his eyebrow as he stuck a fresh Lucky on his lip. He lit the nail then snapped the Zippo closed with a saloon sport's flourish.

"How was that?"

Leigh laughed and slapped him on the arm.

"Oh, so much better. You only burned off a nose hair with that one."

"Saves me from cutting myself with some scissors. I'm going to stretch my legs outside for a bit. Care to join me?"

"Tempting, but I'm going to scare up some of the gun sisters and see when we're going to gather for some hot lead and laughs. Come look me up when you get back. I'm such a delicate flower, I need a strong man to lean on for the rest of the day's festivities."

She fluttered her eyelashes at him. He almost lost another Lucky. Figured he'd better move on before she made him laugh again.

"I'll come find you."

"You better."

He shook his head as he strolled down the hall toward the front door of a vintage ranch house with a miniature conference center tacked on the back. He paused at the edge of the front porch to get his bearings, nodding at people who looked his way.

Big Belly brushed past him, his face sweaty, flushed and split open by an ear-to-ear smile. He looked like a man ready for the rapture. Or the firing line to free Texas from the mongrel horde flying the Commie flag.

"Beg your pardon, mister. So jacked by Brother Bondurant's words I wasn't watchin' where I was going. How 'bout that for a sermon? Damn well about time somebody spoke up for the white man."

"You got that right, friend. Been a long time since I heard anybody talk like that."

Big Belly plowed his way to a line of rocking chair spread along the porch, picking out a silent, wooden victim. Burch headed toward the front steps.

Across a yard of raked sand, ocotillo, soaptree yucca and purple sand verbena, a low-slung barn made of rock and timber stood with its entrance angled away from Burch. The building was topped by a silver tin roof and edged by a hard packed trail that ran past the house, a tractor shed, stone-sided guest cottages, a lot for RVs and trailers and the arid, rocky land beyond.

A rail fence enclosed the side of the barn closest to Burch, its wall marked by the Dutch doors of a dozen stalls, some with the heads of horses poking out of the open tops, watching people flow out of the house.

Near a steel gate fronting the trail, a ranch hand was cinching the saddle of a dun-colored quarter horse, pressing his knee into the gelding's body to get it to exhale so he could take slack out of the latigo. Burch strolled that way, curious whether the place was a working ranch or a dude ranch. Or a little bit of show n' go.

"That's a good-lookin' dun, mister. Like the sandy color and the zebra stripes on the legs."

The man said nothing until he finished tying off the latigo. When done, he looked at Burch with sharp blue eyes that didn't miss a trick. He was short and chesty, sort of like the dun he was saddling, with a neatly trimmed Fu Manchu the color of lead shavings.

"Know horses, do you?"

"No sir. What I know wouldn't fill a thimble. Had an uncle who raised horses. He favored duns and buckskins. That's why yours caught my eye. He'd let me ride the ones too old to buck me off."

The man chuckled. Burch pulled out his Luckies, shook loose a couple of nails and offered them up. The man nodded and picked one, holding it up like he was going to inspect it for flaws and blemishes.

"Obliged. Usually roll my own. Beats hell out of candy-ass store boughts. But this here's kindly a man's cigarette."

Burch lit him up then snapped the Zippo closed. They both draped their arms over the fence rail and enjoyed their smokes.

"What kind of cattle you run on this place?"

"Corrientes, mostly, for stock contractors serving the rodeos. A few Corriente-Black Angus crosses. Them are for beef."

"Heard the Corrientes are tough eatin'."

"They can be if you don't know how to get them ready for the grill. Not a lot of fat on 'em. Kinda like venison that way. Easy to leave it on the grill too long and wind up with a hunk of leather. I like the taste of their meat, but you're right about popping a crown or two if you get a tough cut."

"Think I'll stick to the ribeyes I get in town. As many crowns as I got, sure as hell don't want to pay for them twice because of a steak."

"Smart man."

Burch stuck out his hand.

"Slaughter's my name. Ed Slaughter."

They shook paws.

"Bohannon's mine. Friends call me Wiley."

"Wiley it is, then. Looks like you're headed out so don't let me keep you. Appreciate you letting me remember my uncle. He was a good ol' boy."

Bohannon gathered up the reins looped over a fence rail, then mounted up.

"I'm in no hurry. Them Corriente ain't goin' nowhere. Thanks for the smoke."

The roar of a diesel with a bad muffler snapped their heads toward the front of the barn. Bohannon had to steady the dun, pulling its head to the inside as he used knee and rein for a quick circle to cut off a crow hop.

A Cat D4 rumbled into view, its faded yellow body pocked with surface rust. It stopped near the front of the barn, idling with the occasional pop of backfire. The operator stepped out of the enclosed cab, stepped onto a track then hopped to the ground.

He was tan and lean, with a shock of brown hair and a smooth-shaven, bladed face. He was pulling on a long-sleeved shirt but wasn't quick enough to hide the jailhouse tatts Burch spotted, including a swastika.

"Who the hell is that?"

"One of the guys we got doing construction work around here."

"Looks like he just got out of the joint."

"Mister, you seem like a nice fella so let me give you a piece of advice. Don't let anybody else hear you talk that way around here. And don't ask too many questions. It ain't healthy. Sabe?"

Bohannon sawed the reins into another tight circle and headed the dun up the trail, away from the barn and the idling bulldozer.

Twelve

She glanced back over a naked shoulder and gave Burch his carnal orders.

"You need to fuck me a lot harder to make me cum… And you need to start right now."

Burch grabbed her hips and stepped up the pace. Sweat rolled down his face, his chest, his belly, making a hot, humid junction of grasping pussy and thrusting cock. Salty beads dripped from his bearded chin and left shiny dribbles on the cheeks of her meaty ass.

He leaned forward, pinning her arms flat with his hands, forcing her face into the pillows and sheets, trapping her ass between his slick belly and cock. He hammered away, grunting and gasping for air as the sound of slapping flesh filled his ears. She pushed her ass higher and tighter, taking him deeper.

"Take it…take it deep…take all of that cock…Take it…"

"My pussy's on fire, baby…Deeper…Fuck me harder… UHHHHHHHHAWWWWW…I'm gonna cum… AHHHHHHHHHH…I'm gonna cummmm….Oh, shit…Oh, shit… Here it is…Here it ISSSSSSSS…."

Her pussy gripped his cock as he slammed harder and deeper. He felt her spasms and heard her howls, the sound and sensation sweeping him higher till he felt the cum rise from his balls and jet into her pussy.

He hollered, falling forward, pinning all of her to the mattress, his mouth on her neck as he gasped for air, his eyes blinded by her thick, sweaty hair.

"Sweet Jesus."

They said it together and laughed. They stayed tangled and stunned as their breathing slowed and their bodies cooled. He started to roll away, but she held him in place with one arm.

"Like this, baby…just like this…lay with me for a while."

"No place I'd rather be."

"Jesus…we're a sweaty mess."

"Most of it mine."

"Not all of it. Haven't been fucked like that in a long, long time. Let's do it again real soon."

"Twice back-to-back is about all ol' John Henry can handle these days."

She slithered a hand between them, cupping his balls then stroking his half-hard cock.

"All the more reason to go for three."

The carnal trifecta. With an injury report.

His cock was sore, his knees ached and he felt a lump swelling on his forehead where her knee smacked him during their last, long grind. The rest of his body felt battered and bruised, like he'd just played four quarters instead of three hours of mattress frolic.

Sex as a contact sport. That's what happens when big bodies collide. On an Airstream bed not meant for two XXL humans.

His feet flopped over the edge while his head pressed against the wood veneer of the trailer's back wall. Her curls spilled over his chest, heavy breasts pressed against his ribs, one long leg draped across his thighs.

She snored softly. He wanted to join her in a long nap but craved a Lucky. She stirred and read his mind.

"Can I bum a Lucky off you?"

"You bet, if I can find my shirt."

"Foot of the bed. That's where I popped your pearl speed snaps."

Burch eased out of their tangle and found his shirt in a pile of jeans, panties, boxers, boots and a bra. He dug out a pack and lit two nails, then turned to give her one.

She was resting on her side, looking at him, head propped up by one hand as she reached for the smoke with the other. He let his eyes wander the length of her body – half-dollar nipples that begged for his teeth and tongue, fleshy curves with muscle underneath, wide hips and long, strong legs.

And those eyes. Hazel, sleepy and smiling. Framed by black curls, laugh lines and crows' feet on a broad, weathered face. Striking, mature and carnally candid. No cheap tricks or artifice in this woman. Way past all those little girl games. With a body built to last.

She knew what she wanted and wasn't getting it where she lived. Didn't whine about it. Went and got it where she could and with who she wanted. Then went home to a place she didn't want to be. Even money she'd leave once the familiar soured and she started choking on the bile of contempt for the man too filled with hate to know she was already long gone.

Burch had walked a mile or three in that man's boots. More times than he cared to remember. Wasn't hate that blinded him. Nope. His sins were shame and wounded pride. And a refusal to let any woman who cared about him get too close. A woman like her.

He stretched out on his back and sent smoke toward the trailer roof. She trailed her fingers through his chest hair, pausing to puff, then tracing his chest again.

"Glad you tracked me down. This was a helluva lot more fun than listening to gun gal gossip."

"Almost more fun than a man can handle. You flat wore me out, woman."

"You gave as good as you got, Mister Bull. I'm right fond of that cock of yours. And your tongue."

"Both of them know what they like."

She chuckled, then nibbled on his ear.

"Good. Glad we fucked each other to a frazzle. You look like you need a nap. I sure do."

She took the Lucky off his lip and crushed it out in an ashtray, then turned her own smoldering nail into a dead soldier. Burch was already lights out and snoring.

Whenever you want a solid citizen to spill the beans, never travel in a straight line. And never ask too many questions.

Just enough to get them started. Get them talking. Get them telling you a story. Their story.

Nudge them just enough to steer that tale in the right direction.

Then shut the fuck up and let them take you there, riding along in the passenger seat, looking interested, paying attention. Listening, not talking.

A 'yup' or a 'you bet' will do. Or a one-sentence comment, playing off something the solid citizen just said.

Let them take the long way around the barn. The scenic route.

Don't press. Don't push. You got all the time in the world.

Goes double if they don't know you're a cop or a shamus.

"How were the gun gals?"

"Alright, I guess. Not as many of the ones I like to shoot and cut up with this time."

"'Cause of that young gal who left?"

"Could be. We all kind of took to her – the ones I like, that is. She had the others eatin' out of her hand, too. But we're the ones she favored once the lessons were over."

Her head was cradled in the crook of his right elbow. She started tracing his chest hairs again with her thick fingers.

"Kind of a shame her leavin'. Said she grew up near Dallas but hadn't been home in a long time. Made it sound like she had to leave and didn't think she could go back. Thought she found a home here but was wrong and had to leave here, too."

"Damn shame."

"You bet. She and boyfriend just lit out and got gone. No number or forwarding address. That kind of deal. You ask about her 'round here and get a dead-eyed stare and silence, so I quit askin'. I like to think her and him found a better place, settled down and started makin' babies, but I don't know."

Burch kept his mouth shut and stroked her hair, still tangled from sex and sleep.

"Wish like hell I could find out what happened to her. Only person I can think of who might know is Nancy Jo. Nancy Jo Quartermain. I remember her last name because it's so unusual. She was the cook here. A real grandmotherly type. She and Rita were bosom buddies, but she's gone too."

Burch filed away the name as he caressed her shoulder.

"Can't say I like the silent treatment you got. Not a damn thing either one of us can do, but it does make you wonder."

"Wonder and hope for the best."

He kissed her. She stretched like a big cat then snuggled closer. He let the seconds tick by then lit two Luckies and placed one between her lips. They both took deep drags and jetted smoke toward the ceiling.

"I met a ranch hand while stretchin' my legs. Fella named Bohannon. Seemed like the real deal."

"Wiley? He's a sweetheart. If enough folks want to go on a ride, he's the one that leads it. He knows horses and cattle like a preacher knows his Bible verses."

"Saw something else that was interesting. Guy operatin' a bulldozer rolled up, jumped down and put his shirt on. Sportin' some jailhouse tatts. Had a swastika on his bicep. Asked Wiley about him and got the local version of don't ask, don't tell. More of that silent treatment."

"Sounds like one of Brother Bondurant's reclamation projects. He believes in giving people second chances. Has some ex-cons working here. Construction, mostly. Well diggin'. Heavy work like that."

"Mighty Christian of him to do that but an old prison guard once told me that if you're not real careful, the inmates end up runnin' your asylum."

"I know what you mean. Some of them fellas don't look house-broke but they mostly stay in the background and don't mix with us tourists. Don't seem to mix with the ranch hands, either, come to think on it. They're a little on the scary side so I steer clear of 'em."

"Sounds like another mystery. Also sounds like all may not be as it seems at Brother Bondurant's little *rancho* hideaway."

"Never is, baby. You know that. Still feelin' frisky?"

"Hell, yes – now that you mention it."

There are clicks a man loves to hear – like the ripple of poker chips raked in after slapping a winning hand on the felt.

There are clicks a man hates to hear – like the ratcheting noise of handcuffs as the metal closes and bites each wrist.

And then there's the single, echoing click that causes a man's blood to run cold, his heart to lurch and the seconds to freeze as time slips into a lower gear – like the hammer of a heavy revolver being pulled back to full cock.

Burch stifled a flinch as the big barrel was jammed into his right ear, the front sight gouging a bloody groove through skin-covered cartilage. A hand the size of a first baseman's mitt levered his right arm back and up against his shoulder blade. Breath the smell of an untended outhouse scraped his face and blasted his nostrils.

"Easy, dad, and you won't get hurt. Go hard and you'll get dead."

"Easy it is. You hold all the cards."

"Smart man. Spread 'em."

Burch did as he was told.

The gunman kicked his legs out from under him and shoved him face first into the unforgiving flared side of his own Dodge pickup. Burch managed to break the fall with a left arm looped over the spare tire, but the gunman hammered away that shaky brace with a short chop that felt like getting hit with a concrete block.

Bursts of light flashed across his vision as his head banged into rounded metal of the truck cab then slammed into the dirt. The gravel in his mouth was quickly joined by blood.

Burch let it bleed, steadied his breathing and waited. The gunman flipped up the tail of Burch's jacket and started patting him down.

"Let's see whether you're packin', dad."

"This is Texas, son. Of course, I'm packin'. Thought I was some-place that honored the Second Amendment, not New Jew City."

"New Jew City. I like that, dad. Think I'll steal it."

Burch felt the Colt get yanked from the belt slide holster.

"Lookee here. You ain't woofin'. Got you a very nice Colt .45. Old gun, but an American gun. All metal. No plastic."

"Friends don't let friends shoot plastic guns."

Outhouse breath mixed with a hyena's laugh.

"That's another one I'll have to remember and steal."

"On the house. Now, you mind tellin' me why you dumped me in the dirt like I'm some kinda street thug? Paid hard-earned cash to come down here and listen to God's own truth about why this coun-try's goin' to hell. Gettin' smacked around ain't on the bill of fare."

"Quit whinin', mister, before I give you something to whine about."

The gunman continued his pat down. Down both legs of Burch's jeans, then a squeeze of each boot shaft. Found it – the short black-jack tucked down the inside of the right boot.

"Nasty, nasty, nasty. Bet you'd like to use this to give my skull a workout."

"Never can tell, son."

"Now that I got you defanged, let's stand you up and take a walk. Mister Bondurant wants to have a chat with you. Heard you been a nosy bastard, askin' questions we don't like."

"I asked one question about a guy in jailhouse tatts jumpin' off a bulldozer and got warned off by one of your cowboys. That don't make me nosy."

"We don't like questions even if it's only one. Makes us wonder whether you're one of us or a Z.O.G. agent down here to spy and snitch."

The gunman yanked Burch up to his hands and knees by his right arm then lifted him higher with an easy power that spoke of long hours of prison yard iron and daily spikes of steroids.

Sorry dumbfuck thinks I'm right-handed. He's about to find out how wrong he is.

Burch feigned a stagger, pulling the gunman closer, then stomped a boot down on the man's left foot, drawing a sharp yelp of pain and a sudden loss of balance that made his assailant's head pitch forward.

Tempting target for Burch's left hand, already wrapped around the coin-filled palm sap he pulled from his pocket.

Missed that when you patted me down, fuckhead. Time for a little payback.

Four straight lefts with a loaded fist as he slammed the man into the dirt. A howl and a whoosh of outhouse breath as Burch let both knees smack full force into the man's back while clubbing his head with the coin-ladened left hand.

One last dumb move. The man tried to twist underneath Burch to swing his gun hand around. All that did was present Burch with a face in profile to hammer with his left after pinning down the big revolver with his right. He smiled when he heard the man's jawbone crack.

Fuckin' cockbite bastard. Serves you right for bushwackin' me.

Lights out. Nobody home no more. Burch recognized the gunman as the muscled thug who eyeballed him in the auditorium before Bondurant's sermon. Finger to the man's neck. Still got a pulse.

More than you fuckin' deserve.

Spitting gravel and blood, Burch stood up and lifted the revolver – a blue-black Colt Python .357 with the ribbed, six-inch barrel and Hogue rubber grips. He ran a finger over the front sight and came up with skin and gristle from his right ear.

Memory flash.

Staring down the business end of a Python with the wicked, smiling face of Chuy Reynaldo on the trigger end.

Ready for the Big Adios. Another gringo dumbass who fatally underestimated Malo Garza's moon-faced killer because he looked like a nobody with a ten-watt bulb for a brain.

Chuy laughing at him, savoring the moment. Then Chuy's face disappearing in a bloody mist as .45 hollow-point wiped away that smile. Carla Sue Cantrell, saving his sorry ass one last time.

Burch flipped open the Python's cylinder and eyed the primer end of six .357 Magnum rounds. He pressed the ejector rod and fished out one round – Hornady jacketed hollow-point, 158 grain. Seriously lethal. He snapped the cylinder closed and tucked the pistol under his waistband behind his back.

I earned this goddam gun and I'm gonna keep it. For old time's sake. Gonna put it in a display box. Every time I look at it, I'll think of Chuy Reynaldo and remind myself to never ever underestimate a nobody again.

He fetched his Colt 1911 from the gunman's waistband and slipped it back in the belt slide holster above his left kidney. Then the blackjack he tucked down the inside his right boot. He limped over to the Dodge, opened the driver's side door, then flipped forward the seat back to grab a fistful of zip ties, some bungee cords and an oil-stained tarp.

Grunting and sweating like a pig, he trussed up the gunman with zip ties and bungee cords, then rolled the unconscious body onto the tarp and bound up the package with the cords that remained.

Now came the hard part – muscling this package up on the tailgate and shoving it deep into the short bed box. His battered knees screamed in protest, promising payback that only ice bags, whiskey and Ibuprofen could cure. He made sure the man had room to breathe then eased the tailgate shut and slipped behind the wheel.

Wincing as he fired up the Dodge's big V-8, he kept the headlights dark as he drove away from the gravel lot where Leigh parked her Airstream and rolled to the front gate of the ranch. The cold night air froze his sweat but woke him up as he opened the gate, drove the Dodge through, then closed the gate and wrapped the chain around the post.

Nobody yelled a challenge. Nobody pinned him with blinding light. Nobody shot at him.

He looked up at a full moon in a star-splashed sky and thanked the whiskey gods for getting him through another tight squeeze. His left hand throbbed and was starting to swell. Blood from his right ear matted his side whiskers.

You got damn lucky, Sport Model. That pendejo dry-gulched you and you never saw it coming. Too pussy dazed to stay sharp and on your toes.

Shut up, Wynn. Luck had nothin' to do with it. I had my coin sap ready for trouble just like this.

Coin sap, my ass. You were too fucked out to pay attention. What the hell were you thinkin' beddin' that woman down? Thinkin' with your little head instead of your big head will get you killed.

She was worth the stretch.

Hope so. What now, lover boy? Or should I call you Mister Bull? She sure 'nuff had you pantin' and snortin' like one.

Why don't you do me a favor and go back to dirt nappin' with Elvis?

Elvis ain't dead, Sport Model. You know *that. He's workin' the night shift at a truck stop in Conway, Arkansas. We play pinochle on Wednesdays. I'll repeat the question. What now, lover boy? You can't kill this sumbitch. And sooner or later, he'll be missed and the alarm will sound.*

Yeah, yeah, yeah. Tell it to Elvis while you deal from the bottom of the deck.

Jesus, Sport Model. You know I don't cheat at cards.

Burch dialed up Doggett's private line from a pay phone at roadside *tienda y gasolina* halfway between Marfa and Faver.

Took him more than an hour to get there by back roads from Bondurant's ranch, wrestling the wheel through chuck holes and over rocks while juggling a flashlight to read a topo map Doggett had given him.

Both the Dodge and his trussed-up passenger were somewhat worse for the wear. He had to stuff a rag in the thug's mouth and club him a few times more to quiet him down. Then he had to change the punctured right front tire.

His knees buckled a time or two, his back shot sharp pain into his brainpan and his ear started to bleed again. Glove box. Pint of Cabin Still, the Sportsman's Bourbon. Whiskey splashed on a bandana stung and staunched the ear wound. The rest of the pint dulled the knee and back pain. Also made him long for a Percodan.

"Where the hell you been?"

"Been nosin' around that ranch, rubbing elbows with fellow white trash. Listenin' to a Kluxer preach while picking the pockets of his flock."

"Shouldn't have taken you this long."

"Got waylaid a bit. Had to get untangled."

"Jesus. Can't you put that cock of yours in neutral when you're working a job?"

"Sometimes it's part of the job."

"Gonna get you killed some day. Where you at now?"

"Best you don't know. Got some trash I need you to pick up."

"I ain't runnin' no garbage service for you, Burch."

"This is trash you don't want runnin' loose in your county, Sheriff. One of Bondurant's ex-cons. Nasty piece of work. I imagine you'll find a pile of paper on the boy. Enough to lock him up and throw away the key."

"And if we don't?"

"Hard to fathom you not findin' anything, but if you don't, hold the fucker for a forty-eight or a seventy-two. Need some breathin' room. Jumped me at the ranch and having him disappear is a might bit better than me getting my fingernails pulled until they find out I'm an ex-cop."

"Okay. Where?"

"Remember that adobe shack where I had the gunfight with the barn burner and his keeper?"

"The one you didn't tell us about until way after the fact?"

"That's the one. Ten miles north of town on the west side of the road. Up on a hill."

"We'll find it. You plan on bein' there?"

"Not if I can help it. Need a line on somebody. Woman named Nancy Jo Quartermain."

"Jesus. There's a name I haven't heard since Jimmy Carter was president."

"Used to be the cook at the ranch."

"Used to be a lot of other things, too, bubba. Ran a whorehouse in Alpine. Smuggled weed over the river back in the day when mota and stoned hippies was all we had to worry about."

"Sounds like one of Bondurant's reclamation projects. He likes to brag about giving a second chance to ex-cons. Which is horse-shit, most likely. Word is, she was close to Rhonda Mae and would be someone she'd turn to for help."

"Don't let her last name fool you. Nancy Jo is a Ruiz. And you don't fuck with those folks if you know what's good for you. Full-bore badasses. Mexicans with Apache blood. If your gal turned to her for help, Nancy Jo'd make sure her people gave it. Thing is, she ain't gonna want to talk to no ex-cop."

"Figure it will take some convincin'. That's why I got Juanita's letters to show her. And that note from Juanita her ownsef."

"That'll help, but no guarantee it'll seal the deal."

"True, but it might keep her from fillin' me with buckshot. It's the only edge I've got."

Doggett told Burch how to find Nancy Jo. Burch found her place on the topo map. He hung up and headed the Dodge to that abandoned adobe shack.

Old ghosts waited for him there, ready to serve up memories of buckshot, gunsmoke, hollow-points and a Houston gunsel with a helmet of lacquered blond hair face down in the dirt.

And a back blown open by Flying Ashtrays from the Colt in Burch's left hand.

Burch gunned the Dodge up to highway speed, his mind fully focused on a different mission – dumping the tarp full of trash rid-ing in back for Doggett's deputies to find.

Thirteen

They rolled slow and easy down a narrow and rutted gravel trail centered on the rounded spine of a hogback ridge, occasionally flushing a jack rabbit or javelina out of the thick brush on either shoulder to flash through the Jeep's dim headlamps and dart into the opposite darkness.

For the umpteenth time, Rhonda Mae checked the breech of her .45 to make sure a round was already in the pipe. For the umpteenth time, her index finger felt the first of eight fat boys right where it was supposed to be.

She was wearing the blonde wig, tight jeans and calf-length buckaroo boots with stacked riding heels. A black suede bolero jacket with coin silver conchos completed her outfit.

La Güera. One last time.

She puffed on another one of Armando's *Delicados* as he drove, his eyes straight ahead, ready to twist the wheel right or left to dodge the deepest chuckholes.

They were headed for the house of a dead outlaw, Gyp Hulett, a legendary smuggler of anything that put coin of the realm in his pocket, to meet honchos from the Ojinaga crew and dicker over price and particulars. Hulett's bastard son, Malachi, now owned the house and ranch and agreed to host the sit-down because Tommy Juan had paid him $10,000 for the right to bury guns on his land.

Rhonda Mae and Armando hadn't traded sentences for almost an hour. Didn't need to. They'd already talked over the plan, turning it this way and that, hunting for weak spots they hadn't thought of and giving a short nod to the ones they already knew. Any one of which could get them dead.

While a carpenter might tell you a three-legged stool was more stable than one with four, that measure of steady state didn't apply to a deal with three parties of crooks, liars, killers and thieves. The temptation of the double or triple-cross was always there – two sides ganging up on the third, always revealed at the very last second with a roar of gunfire and the losers face down in the dirt.

The trick was to load the deal up with enough checks and balances to blunt the temptation. That's what created stability. And it could be done with sugar or a stick. Usually both.

There's a bonus waiting for you at the end of this deal. One you want bad. Lots of firepower that will make you the deadliest mother-fucker on the border. But you won't get it until you do all of what you promised – or we get dead. That's the sugar at the end of the rainbow.

The stick sounded like this: If we get dead, Armando's cousins will hunt you down and kill you all. They know who you are. They ain't nice like us. They play for keeps.

That stick wasn't an idle threat. Armando's people had a lethal amount of Lipan Apache blood. Which made them excellent trackers, smugglers and killers for hire. And implacable enemies you didn't want on your trail.

If you iced one of theirs, they didn't give a shit about who you worked for, how many guns you had or the color of your money. They wanted your blood. And wouldn't stop until they hacked it out of you. Even if payback took years to deliver. You prayed they killed you fast and didn't have enough time for the old ways.

In the deal they were driving toward, each side had to be happy with their slice of the pie – guns, money and the promise of more of either. Each side had to respect and believe in the lethal consequences of the double-cross. Sugar and the stick. Greenbacks, guns and Armando's killer cousins.

That meant Malachi Hulett, who loved making illicit money but lacked his father's murderous ferocity, had to be content with the fee paid to let a cache of guns get buried on his land. That money would be doubled by a $10,000 sweetener Rhonda Mae would put in his hand once the meeting was over.

It also meant the Ojinaga crew had to be patient enough to wait for the bonus she was dangling – the rockets, the thumpers and the mortars. And they had to be ambitious enough to whack Tommy Juan's killers – Garza's crew and their Anglo partners – in the middle of a gun-running deal for arms and ammo stolen from a dead man. Rhonda Mae had an ace up her sleeve for *los muchachos de Ojinaga*.

Pulling this off would be doubly sweet for them, tired of sucking hind tit and taking table scraps from the big boys. Killing some of Garza's men and their gun-running partners would send a loud, bloody message that Ojinaga was moving up. Pinching those guns would also be rough justice – Tommy Juan had earmarked the cache for Ojinaga before his killers chopped him up and trucked away the ordnance.

They crept through a series of tight switchback curves to drop off the ridge, rumble over the rocks of a dry creek bed, then started climbing up another set of curves that doubled back on each other to reach the top of a gently rising bench that led to the house Malachi's father built.

Dark and forbidding, it featured the turrets and steeply pitched roofs of a Victorian manse and loomed above the highest point at the rear of the bench, bracketed by higher, saw-toothed crags of bare rock. All that were missing were whirling bats, howling wolves and a sniveling, fly-eating Renfield manning the front door to serve his master.

To their right, they could sense rather than feel the higher, jagged ridgeline known as the Devil's Backbone, the deeper darkness of its looming presence revealed by the utter absence of stars that glittered everywhere else in the frigid night sky.

Rhonda Mae broke the silence. To let loose the what-ifs and angles buzzing through her brain. For the umpteenth time.

"I'm not too worried about the Ojinaga crew. They sure as hell don't want a two-front war – your cousins and the Garzas. And that's what they'd get if they fuck us over."

"*Es verdad.* They know my cousins are *fuerte y duro.* And *despiadado* – how is that *en inglés?*"

"Ruthless. Without mercy or pity. Relentless."

"*Exactamente. Sin compasión.* You harm one of us, you harm us all. And Ojinaga? Their *jefe?* He knows us and how we are. He believes in the old ways – *honor y respeto.*"

"What's his name?"

"Gabriel Morales. They call him *El Duque.*"

"Think he'll show up tonight?"

"It would be good for us if he did. We'd know who is calling the shots. But I doubt it."

"The one who worries me is Malachi. Tommy Juan did business with him but didn't trust him. I sure as hell don't but I'm hoping an extra jolt of cash will keep him sweet."

"The son is not the father. *Es una pena.* The father? *Señor Gyp? Había un hombre.* An outlaw. And a killer. But when he shook hands with you, he kept his word and his end of the bargain."

"Wish we were dealing with him."

"*Claro.* But we can't raise him from the dead. *Por lo tanto,* we deal with the son. Malachi is smart, but he's also weak and lazy. Paying him more money but no more work for him? *Perfecto.* It will encourage him to do what he likes to do – take the easy way. What's the phrase? Path of something."

"Least resistance."

"*Precisamente.* We just pray nobody pays him more than us."

"And we put the fear of God into him. Remind him of your cousins."

"*Bueno.* Give him the cash. Show him the blade."

156

★

"Before we start the business talk, let us share a drink first to the success of this meeting and the friendship it will bring to all at this table. And let me say, *señorita,* the legend of *La Güera* hardly does justice to your beauty."

Rhonda Mae smiled and nodded her head once.

"I'm honored by the flattery of *El Duque,* but even more so by his presence here tonight. That tells me Ojinaga is serious about taking its rightful place and that you, *El Duque,* have your eye on the kingdom and the crown."

It was *El Duque's* turn to smile, nod and salute her with the bottle of Patrón he held in his right hand. He was a tall, angular man with swept back silver hair, a high forehead and an aquiline nose bordered at the bottom by a well-waxed Zapata moustache. Lithe as he moved around the table pouring drinks, he reminded Rhonda Mae of the lethal grace of a jaguar.

He could be forty or he could be sixty. Hard to tell. But a big cat. Still in his prime. A quiet killer. Best to keep that in mind once the drinks were downed and the business began.

They were in the dining room of the house that Gyp Hulett built. The table they sat around was a rectangle of deeply polished pine the color of custard, reflecting the soft, shaded gleam of lights perched on a wrought iron hoop suspended from the ceiling.

Each of the three principals had a *segundo* seated on their flank. Unspoken but assumed: each *segundo* was armed. Armando certainly was with a nine-millimeter Beretta tucked behind his back. She had the Colt tucked behind hers.

Most of the talk flowed between Rhonda Mae and *El Duque.* Malachi was silent, but alert as dickering over price, delivery, timing and method of payment played out. He was content to play the host, refilling their glasses with Patrón as buyer and seller sparred.

"The price you ask – *Dios mío,* these guns must be made of gold, *señorita.* I don't need them to show off for the cameras. I need them to kill."

"Provided your men can shoot straight, these guns will do all the killin' you need. That is, *if* your men can shoot straight."

"My men can kill with any gun you give them, but the price of these guns is higher than Pico de Orizaba. It makes my nose bleed to be in such rarified atmosphere."

"*Por favor, cabellero.* These are brand-new A2s, the latest issue to the U.S. Army and the Marines, not a clapped-out bunch of Mex A1s with rusty barrels and missing parts. Altered to full auto. You're also getting A3s the SEALS use and AR-15s. Also full auto. My goods either come straight from a U.S. military armory or a gunsmith I know and trust. Five cases of them. With 6,000 rounds. And two M-60s with five units of fire each. Not new, but re-barreled, refurbished and tested."

"*Por favor, señorita* – can you not drop the price so I can tell my men I wasn't beguiled by the beauty and wiles of *La Güera?*"

"I'll knock off $3,000 and do you one better – two M-79 Thumpers and 15 rounds each as a sweetener."

"You must really want my men to kill Garza's crew and his *gringo* gunrunners."

"I want my new friend to grow strong and prosper. You take out everybody you see at this deal, time and place provided by us. Finder's keepers on the weapons you find. And those bang-bangs we discussed as the bonus."

She stared into the eyes of the jaguar. El Duque killed off his drink, smiled and slapped his hand on the table.

"*Bueno y sano, La Güera. Bueno y sano.* And now, let us drink to *la vida pura.*"

They walked *El Duque* and his *segundo* to the front door, then stood on the porch as the taillights on his jet-black Tahoe traced the route through switchbacks and hard climbs, disappearing for the dip to the dry creek bed then fading for good as it went over the far side of the hogback ridge.

Rhonda Mae faced Malachi Hulett, handing him a fat manilla envelope she pulled from the inside pocket of her jacket.

"What's this for?"

"Insurance. Doubling down on what Tommy Juan paid you."

"You don't need to do that. Tommy Juan was my friend. You were his woman and I'm happy to help out any way I can."

"That's mighty fine, Malachi. I appreciate your friendship. And your hospitality. But I think there's every reason to do this. Friendship is one thing but cold cash calls the tune. Or maybe it's best to put it this way – we want to remind you of who your friends are."

Armando edged closer to Malachi's side. Malachi took one step back so he could watch them both.

"I told you there was no reason to give me more money."

"It's a gift you can't give back. From your true friends. We want you to have it."

A blur in the darkness. Armando with a knife to Malachi's throat.

"Stay friendly, Malachi. Take the money. But don't get greedy. And don't get stupid. Remember who my people are."

Bang-bang. The sugar and the stick.

★

The hiss and crackle of a radio coming to life.

"See 'em?"

"Not yet."

"Headed your way. Blonde with the guy she came with. In the Jeep."

"Got 'em. What's the call? Stop 'em or tail 'em?"

"Looks like this was just a meet and greet. So, tail 'em. At a distance. Give 'em lots of space till they hit the main road. We gotta find out where they're keeping their guns."

"That's a rog."

Cider Jones smiled as he watched the Jeep swing into view in his night vision goggles. A Gen III. None of that old Vietnam-era shit. Hands free to drive this Blazer four-by. Without headlights. Cortez would be pleased.

He saw the blonde riding in the passenger seat as the Jeep passed and fired up the Blazer.

"Gotcha, *La Güera*. Let's see if we can figure out what you're up to."

Malachi Hulett swung the heavy oak door shut and leaned against it until the latch clicked, then turned the deadbolt knob until the lock clunked in place. Whistling a nameless tune, he wandered into the study and slumped into the burgundy leather swivel chair behind his father's plain, pine desk and pulled a bottle of Knob Creek from the deep bottom drawer.

He uncorked the bourbon bottle and tilted it to his lips, letting the liquor bubble down his throat until he felt the burn in his stomach.

Goddam, how I hate tequila. Gotta torch the taste of that shit with some smooth, hundred-proof corn.

Sipping more, he let time float by, thinking about squeezing more money out of this deal with a deft double-cross. Without breaking a sweat. Or lifting a finger. From the comfort of his father's hilltop fortress, walled in by steep, rocky spires and ridgelines.

Twenty minutes. Thirty. Then sixty.

Think a shit twenty thousand buys me? Wrong. Think a blade to my throat will keep me from making a move? Fuck that. Think I made you a promise? I'm an outlaw and my word means nothing. I'm Gyp Hulett's son. I want more and I'll get more.

The chair swivel squealed like a whorehouse box spring as he spun to face the ironwood credenza behind the desk and pluck a satellite phone off its charger. He flipped out the knobby, black antenna, checked for a link then punched up numbers he knew by heart, cradling the phone to his ear while listening to the beeps, blips and burring of the call bouncing to space and back.

"*Bueno.*"

"They just left."

"*We know. We picked them up turning off that old mining road on the west side of the ranch.*"

"Jesus, they got there fast."

"*They're not alone. Got a rig tailing them.*"

"Who? The law? Or somebody from your side of the river?"

"*We don't know but we'll find out. What do you have to tell us?*"

"They settled on a price. Five cases of A2s, A3s and AR-15s full auto. Two M-60s. Two grenade launchers. Army issue with ammo. Time and place of delivery to be determined."

"*Lotta firepower. We're paying you to find out the where and when. Be nice if you found out where those guns are hidden since it's on your land.*"

"I've got a pretty good idea what part of the ranch Tommy Juan picked to hide his stash. My men have been out there with metal detectors, but we still don't know the exact location. We'll keep looking but if we don't get lucky, we're both going to have to tail them when they make their move."

"*A man makes his own luck, Malachi. The clock is ticking. Don't disappoint us. Your father never did.*"

Click. Malachi silently cussed and reached for the Knob Creek. He bubbled the bottle until the burn filled his brain and washed away the echoing insult.

You're not your father. You never will be. We know it. And you know it.

Fourteen

Ever since his partner got killed, Cider Jones preferred working alone.

His way. His savvy and gut instincts. His moves.

No second guesses. No orders from on high to shut him down. A hunter tracking his prey, locked down and focused on the trail. With nobody to get close to and lose.

That's how he worked his last decade as a Houston murder cop. He had partners but only because the ladder climber in the captain's office made him take one.

To their credit, they let him make the pick. He chose the dead-enders, guys on the way out, treading water, praying to dodge a bullet until they racked up enough points for their pensions.

Partners in name only. None of them were total burnouts or limp dicks. He didn't want to carry dead weight. Some had been top manhunters in their day. But that day was deep in their past.

Somehow, some way, the switch got flipped off on that remorseless drive to run a killer to ground and either slap cuffs on each wrist or give them a hot lead adios. They still knew the moves and still had the smarts. But they no longer had the hunter's heart.

Ray Martinez was the best of this bunch. Four years away from the golden handshake when the captain tapped him on the shoulder. Short, dark and wiry, he favored black suits, tooled leather boots with stacked heels to give him some height and a Browning Hi-Power with most of the bluing worn away. He had a Jorge

162

Negrete moustache and slicked back his hair with jasmine-scented Tres Flores pomade.

In his prime, Martinez had cracked some major cases as a lead detective, taking down a slasher who preyed on prostitutes working the Bissonnet Track and a banker who money-whipped his mistress nurse to slowly kill his invalid wife with arsenic. But he was never the same after a *chulo* gunned down his partner in a Barrio Segundo dive then pumped two slugs into Martinez's gut as the detective blew him down with nine-millimeter hollow points.

"Cards on the table, Cider. You know I've lost my edge. I know you like to work alone. That's why your last four partners have been guys like me. With one foot out the door. But I ain't a total burnout and can still hold up my end as second fiddle."

"What's that look like?"

"Looks like this. We work the initial scene together. We talk every day – maybe go grab a bite to eat or a beer. You tell me everything except what will get my pension pulled. I'll do the paperwork, interview witnesses, pull case files and keep the captain in the loop with a plausible story that will keep him off your back. Never tell the bastard anything we don't agree to tell him."

"That it?"

"No. Never treat me like a shit sandwich and I'll do the same. I'll tell you what I think, with the bark on it. You do the same. We're either partners or we ain't. I've got your back. In the office and out there. I'll go through a door with you if push comes to shove. And I'm still a damn good gun hand if the assholes get frisky."

"Can I give you shit about the smell of that damn pomade?"

"You can try, but the act doesn't change. Neither does the pomade."

"Good thing I like to ride alone. Deal."

Martinez was as good as his word. Didn't take long for Cider to learn his new partner was an ace with a murder book and case files. He also had a long, sharp memory that coughed up details, patterns and a killer's telltales from past cases that fit their murder of the moment.

Smart about office politics, keeping the captain at bay and able to take the long view on a case to prevent Cider from getting so target focused he missed important details lurking outside his vision. Could still tune in to the vibes of a killer and sense what his next move might be.

Good company over lunch or a beer, too. They teased each other about Cider's habit of stuffing napkins in a coffee cup for his post-meal chaw of Red Man and the overpowering, sickly-sweet smell of the pomade in Martinez's hair. It was an echo of the banter with Cortez that Cider came to enjoy, not realizing how much he missed the back-and-forth between two men who like each other.

More and more, Martinez stepped out of the office, riding with Cider to brace a witness, taking the back door if they thought they had a runner. He was a murder cop again, shouldering more than his share, no longer an office-bound second fiddle. When Cider kicked open a door, Martinez followed.

One too many times. A shotgun blast Cider ducked caught Martinez full in the chest. Dead before he hit the floor. Cider emptied .357 hollow points from his Smith & Wesson Model 19 into the scumbag, blowing out the back of the man's skull and shredding his chest cavity.

Too late for Martinez. Cider never picked a true partner again. Just the burnouts. And for the rest of his time at Houston PD, he rode solo.

Fast forward. Cider Jones, older and miles and miles of Texas west of Houston, riding alone again through the ass end of sun-torched country hidden by the star-splashed night. As a retread state investigator loaned out to the ATF instead of a righteous murder cop.

Running lights out. Banking on the night vision goggles to keep him between the ditches and the Jeep in sight.

Humming "Faded Love" and "Waltz Across Texas" to himself and feeding strings of Red Man into his jaw to stay awake. Answering when a squelchy question popped into his Plantronics headset.

He kept his distance, slowing down when he saw their taillights flash but never tapping his brakes, speeding up when they disappeared behind a rise, praying they weren't watching him through a night vision scope of their own, hoping they didn't spot a darker square that briefly blocked the stars when he topped a rise.

Cider knew they were checking their six. He did too because you never knew when the hunter became the hunted. He also knew he was playing a sucker's game. One-man tails always were.

But they needed to keep an eye on that Hulett asshole in case he made a move toward a cache of guns, so Hughes, the ATF agent who watched the mansion meeting in his own Blazer, stayed behind.

And they needed to get up on the other players from that meet and greet. He replayed some back and forth with Hughes.

"Know those other fucks that left in that black Tahoe?"

"Oh, yeah...."

"Care to enlighten me?"

"Some gents from Ojinaga. If they're buying some serious bang-bang, it's about to get real interesting south of the river. Real bloody, too."

"Fuck 'em, long as they're killin' each other."

"You catch on quick."

Cider studied the angles of this intel. The gents from Ojinaga looking to make a move. In a terminal way. More blood. More bodies. More collateral damage. He snapped his attention back to the targets ahead.

So far, so good. They didn't juke or jink. They didn't slow down or speed up. The Jeep kept a steady pace, slowing for curves and the occasional roadkill he also thumped over. He reached for a Dixie cup stuffed with napkins and spat out a mouthful of tobacco juice.

He never saw the dark shape of a one-ton flatbed with a drill pipe bumper hurtling in from his right to T-bone his Blazer. He heard the meaty smack of metal on metal and the sharp crack of shattering glass. Goggles flew from his head, blinding him to the night, ripping away the Plantronics rig.

Cider grabbed the shoulder strap of his seat belt and braced himself. Sparks and shards flew past his face as the view through the starred windshield started spinning. The dark horizon stood vertical before flipping through the compass degrees in a blur, each counterclockwise lurch marked by a hollow boom and the grinding agony of Detroit iron shoved across concrete.

His head smacked against the door frame, then the roof and the rearview mirror as the Blazer cartwheeled toward the ditch to the left of the highway. Cider saw exploding stars and pinwheels with every jolt. Then black.

The driver of the black Suburban tailing Cider topped the rise at highway speed, then slammed on the brakes when he saw a hulking shape in the middle of the road. Skidding to a stop that smoked the tires, he jammed the rig into reverse and tried to spin into a J-turn to escape the kill zone.

Two streaks of flame-lit smoke lanced the Suburban. A yellow-orange ball of flame belched skyward, bursting from the vehicle's innards and lifting it off the road. The stuttering snarl of a dozen guns raked the wreckage from shooters posted behind the hulk in the road and the right-hand ditch nearest the rise.

Three shooters scooted from the hulk to the far side of the Suburban to kill any survivors tumbling out the blind side of the wreck. Two shooters from the ditch did the same. Five or six single pops marked the shooters being thorough, pumping slugs into the heads of seven flame-licked corpses.

From another rise a quarter mile away, Rhonda Mae and Armando watched the action through binoculars.

"Smart to give my cousins a couple of those LAWs. Made it quick and clean."

"Figured they needed the insurance. No skin off our noses. Those rockets were part of Ojinaga's bonus. Thanks, *muchachos*."

Armando chuckled.

"Let's go down there and look it over."

"*Sí*, but this needs to be quick."

"*Claro*."

Seven not-so-pretty corpses all in a roadside row. Pulled from the flames of a Suburban burning bright.

"Most of these *pinche maricónes* are Garza's men. We know them. But two of them are *gringos. Mira esto*."

Ignoring the smell of flash-roasted flesh, Armando and Rhonda leaned over a corpse to look where a Ruiz cousin named Roberto was pointing a flashlight beam – a battling leprechaun flanked by an A and a B.

"Fuck me. That's an Alice Baker tatt."

"*Mierda*. Not so good, *sí*?"

"*Sí*. But at least we know what we're up against. We were guessing before. Now we know. Garza's in bed with The Brand. These are the fucks that killed Tommy Juan."

A cousin standing by the overturned Blazer in the ditch whistled them over.

"What do you want to do with this guy? Shoot him?"

Rhonda Mae knelt and looked at the blood-streaked white hair of the driver. She pressed two fingers against his neck. Strong pulse. Out but not dead.

She flashed a light through the cab of the overturned rig, spotting a dark blue windbreaker crumpled on the headliner holding everything else that tumbled down – loose change, spare mags, speedloaders, a Red Man pouch, maps, binoculars and lots of sand.

The beam picked up two big white letters that reflected the light. An A and a T – and that sure as hell didn't mean the phone company.

"Fuck no, don't shoot him. He's ATF. Cut him the fuck out of there and see what kind of shape he's in. Make him comfortable. Get somewhere safe and call it in. Let this guy and his buddies try to figure out what went down here."

Armando nodded at his cousin. Rhonda Mae winced, realizing she might have stomped on his *macho* by being the bossy bitch in front of his kin. She relaxed when he barked out his own orders. *Macho* restored.

"*Tira a esos dos gringos en un hoyo profundo. Deja los demás ahí mismo.*"

To her: "We make a little mystery for our friends. Bury the gringos. Leave the *federale* and the others. Maybe they had a falling out. Maybe the two *pinche gringos* sold out Garza's men to the ATF. Maybe they just lined them up and shot them but let the *federale* live. Maybe they were smart enough to know killing him would bring too much heat."

"Lots of maybes. You sure the right ears will learn of this great mystery?"

"*Ciertamente. Pinche rinches* will call the Garzas. The Garzas will dial up *el jefe de los gringos.* It won't be a pleasant call. There'll be lots of finger-pointing and suspicion until they get it figured out. Buys us some time."

"Hearing about that ATF agent will twist a knot in their tail."

"*Exactamente.* They won't know what to think about him. And he's out of their reach. Not that he knows what happened. He was out of it when the fireworks started."

Rhonda Mae chuckled: "You got it all figured out, *hombre.* Didn't know you were such a devious fucker."

Armando smiled: "*Yo soy el diablo que usted conoce.* We go now."

"*Sí. Eres el diablo familiar.* And by all means, let's get the fuck out of here, *Señor Diablo*, my friend. Let me have one of those *ovalados*. Need to get the stink out of my lungs. Need to get out of this blonde wig, too. Makes me feel like a Juarez whore."

Fifteen

If you listened to enough speed metal jabber from an Odin-worshipping brother ripped on crystal and pruno, you learned of the potent role the number three plays in Norse mythology.

Odin is one of three brother gods. He suffers three tribulations on the World Tree in his pursuit of the runes of knowledge and power – he hangs upside down for nine days and nine nights, he runs himself through with his spear and he suffers deep hunger and punishing thirst.

Three is also the number of consecutive harsh winters that must pass – with no summer breaks – before Ragnarök, a titanic clash of the gods that marks the end of the world, with the promise of a watery rebirth and renewal.

Cleve Chizik knew all this sacred Norse bullshit because he once shared a cell at Pelican Bay with an A-B brother named Carl Berdahl, a 300-pound man-mountain with a reddish-blond beard that covered his chest and belly and biceps the size of mutant cantaloupes.

Carl demanded everybody call him Beowulf. Nobody argued. Smart silence because when Carl wasn't huffing crystal and guzzling pruno, he was breaking skulls in the yard for The Brand. Or twisting heads until the neck bones snapped. A Viking berserker behind bars.

Nobody wanted to face Carl on a rampage. Just call him Beowulf and watch him nod and smile. Like he was everybody's friend. Everybody wearing The Brand. Beowulf the Benevolent.

Not that Carl ever read the epic Old English poem. He learned about Grendel the Demon, King Hrothgar, Wiglaf, Beowulf, and his wife, Wealhtheow, from a lifer – Quentin Cosby, a professor of ancient literature who chopped up his wife and son with an axe. He was also Carl's punk.

There's another way to look at the power of three – one Chizik's Missouri grandmother taught him during childhood summers he spent on her farm south of Springfield, the only moments of his young life free from violence and abuse.

Bad things come in threes. That's what granny told him. Chizik remembered Carl's Norse jabber. But granny's lesson was more fitting to the shitshow he faced right now.

Three. As in three missing members of his crew. Axel and Dawg – righteous killers called Charles and James on their forged IDs. Riding with a Garza crew chasing a hot tip about *La Güera*. Hadn't heard from them in four days. Supposed to call him every two.

Might mean something. Might not. Chizik's gut told him it did. And he was too savvy a survivor of the yard and the street to ignore his initial instinct. They had a sat phone. And Axel was a precise pro who crossed the T of every order. Dawg would follow his lead if Axel couldn't.

The third missing man was the one who had Chizik grinding his molars and washing down some 'ludes with tequila straight from the bottle to chill his nerves.

Sledge, a newbie and youngest member of the crew. Straight from Huntsville, the toughest prison in Texas after pulling ten of a fifteen-bit for armed robbery. Early release to ease overcrowding. Branded with an ABT tatt that took up most of his muscular back – Aryan Brotherhood of Texas. Blooded with four kills of The Brand's rivals.

Disappeared right from the ranch after spotting somebody who looked like a cop. Heard the guy was nosing around, asking questions about the crew. Sent to go fetch the guy for a hard chat. Gone. Into thin air.

Problem was, he didn't name the guy. Didn't know it. Just described him as a big guy with a beard. That fit half the Texas Secede suckers in the auditorium that day. And it didn't mean much if the guy was a cop – more than a few suckers at each session wore a badge or used to. Lawdogs were common as dirt among Kluxers and white supremacists.

That left Chizik pouring over the registration list, looking for likely targets, starting with the dozen suckers who left the ranch early, before the final banquet. Six of those were couples. One was a solo female. And five lone wolves.

Blowhard Bondurant, the strutting con artist who peddled softcore white supremacy, still had connections from his days as a state senator, including an ex-cop with access to the right databases. Feed the names to that guy and see what comes up. Then play the waiting game.

Fuck that. Only suckers wait. Make a move. Start muscling the sheep about the solo female and the five lone wolves. People gossip. People talk. Find out what they say about these six. See if there's any connection between the six. See if anybody heard or saw something. Run those leads down.

Make another move. Time to get the stash away from this fuckin' place and out of harm's way. Guns and ammo for the Garzas and a load of crank, coke and brown sugar for biker gangs in New Mexico and Oklahoma. Know just the place.

About forty miles northwest of the Bar L R was an abandoned ranch with absentee owners who didn't ask questions when folks wanted to park something on their land. For a hefty fee, of course.

Perfect Plan B hidey hole, too. Rougher country, with deep arroyos, box canyons and steep mesas. Only one way in or out. Unless you were a mountain goat. Or a sidewinder.

Farther from the river and not as handy for a firepower trans-action. But Chizik could run the load up there, leave two men in the old Airstream they kept handy and know the goods would be safe. He pulled out his sat phone and made the call.

The owner's man would meet them at the only gate. Trade the key for ten grand. In cash. Done deal. Chizik took a deep breath and felt the tension loosen its grip. Not for long, though. The sat phone chirped. As soon as he saw the caller's number, the tension clamped down again.

"We got trouble, *hombre. Un gran problema.*"

"We'll deal with it. What've we got?"

"A fuckin' mess is what we got. Five of my men are dead. Their rig got blown up by fuckin' RPGs then they each got a bullet to the brain. The two guys from your crew ridin' with them? Gone. *Desaparecido.* Got an ATF agent who drove his truck into the ditch. Don't know where the fuck he fits in all this."

"What the fuck are you talkin' about, Luis? The crew tracking down the blonde bitch?"

"*Sí. La Güera.* Who the fuck did you think I was talking about? *El Charro Negro?*"

"Who the fuck is telling you this shit?"

"Cops we own. One of them was on the scene. *Aquí está el resul-tado final.* The bottom line, like you *pinche gringos* say, is five of my men are dead. Your two are nowhere to be found. Makes us wonder whether a couple of Judas goats led my men to the slaughter."

"Luis, that doesn't make sense. We both want *La Güera.* And we're about to complete another deal that benefits both of us. Why would I want to fuck that up?"

"We wonder the same thing, *hombre.* Why would you? Perhaps you got a better offer for your goods and services? Perhaps you think you can do better with other partners?"

"To answer your first question, Luis – I fuckin' wouldn't. You know why? Because I'm in this for the long haul, not the quick score. Betraying you is bad for business and bad for my health. It's the quickest way to get me dead. Just ask Tommy Juan."

"Tommy Juan? That *pinche chupavarga* don't hear so good no more."

"Yeah? Well, we both taught him a lesson I heard loud and clear. Don't betray your partners."

"We know you know that. But this matter needs to be settled before we can move forward with this deal. *Mi patróna* wants a meeting. On our side of the river. You can bring a *segundo*, but nobody else."

"Name the time and place. And you can tell Senorita Garza I didn't betray her family and would never do so. Also tell her I have moved her goods to a safer place until we get this figured out."

"*Bueno.* I will call back with the details. And I will tell *La Patróna* what you said. But *hombre*, a word of warning – this meeting is *muy importante* to your dealings with us. And to your health. Speak the truth. She'll know if you lie. Flinch or twitch and you die."

The connection was cut. Chizik stared at the sat phone without seeing it.

That fuckin' blonde bitch. I'll cut her heart out and eat it. After I fuck every hole she's got. After I kill her slow, slow, slow. While she watches. While she screams. While I look her in the eyes.

Up close. So she'll know it's me. The last thing she sees. Slicing her life away. Cut by cut. Strip by strip. Until I slash that throat down to the neckbone. Blood in, blood out.

"Problem solved."

"Nothing a little lead couldn't cure."

"Not much lead can't cure. Gotta say, the bastard didn't flinch, didn't beg for mercy. Just stood there and took it like a man. Didn't even seem surprised."

"No surprise in this. He knew the score. He fucked up once. Got warned and told to get his shit together and the job back on track. Or else. But he fucked up again. The target disappeared and neither the dearly departed nor his crew have clue one where he went. No surprise, this."

"No. Strictly amateur hour. Keystone Kops."

"Gang That Couldn't Shoot Straight, more like. One minute, the target's in jail and they got it staked out. Got a man on the inside, for fuck's sake, lettin' them know what's what. Next minute – poof, the target's gone. No forwarding address."

"We'll find him."

"Fuck yes, we'll find him. What pisses me off is starting from Square One. Could be out there in the desert somewhere. Could be down in Juarez, drinkin' tequila, gettin' sucked and fucked. Could be hiding out on a pig farm in Bumfuck, Iowa, for all we know. Could be back in Dallas, but I fuckin' doubt it."

"Easy, Johnny. We'll get it done."

"Don't call me that. I don't want him to know I'm comin' until it's too late. Last thing I need is him sittin' in some shithole bar hearin' Johnny from Dallas is lookin' for a guy that looks an awful lot like him. That's a whole 'nother heartache we don't need."

"What do I call you, then?"

"I'd tell you to call me Judas, but that's way too biblical for a bunch of sinners like us. Boss will do. Or *Jefe*."

"And where do we go from Square One, *Jefe*?"

"We're gonna two track this one. First, start cutting for sign of blondie. Find out where she's been, who's close to her. Put the arm on them. And we keep the hunt going for the target. He's in the wind but tends to leave a bloody trail. Start lookin' for dead outlaws. Or missing ones – they'll be dead, too, but their bodies might not have turned up yet. Reach out to our friends across the river. Don't mention blondie. Just the target."

"Sounds like you know the target. Friend of yours?"

175

"Yes. From a long time ago."

"What you want done with this guy?"

Silence as both men stared at the corpse of Alvaro Maldonado, face up in the rain-soaked gravel behind an abandoned Shamrock station on the outskirts of Faver, arms outstretched like he was ready to get nailed up on Golgotha.

His eyes were wide open, staring at the Big Nowhere. But his acne-scarred face was relaxed. Free from care or worldly worry. With a faint smile on his lips.

"Leave him. Good message for the other fuckheads."

Sixteen

The rough hemp rope bit deeply into Burch's wrists, tightly binding his arms behind his back, leaving him helpless against the whiplash whims of every twist, turn, bump and axle-snapping hole that cropped up on whatever goat trail they were on.

Didn't help he was also blinded by a thick hood over his head, bound tightly at the neck and scratchy like burlap. Meant he couldn't see what his noggin was about to hit when the rig zigged and zagged. And it was tough to draw air into his lungs.

By Burch's shaky count, they were about an hour off the black-top. North, south, east or west, he couldn't tell, but he bet north. Away from the river.

That was a wild-ass guess, but it made sense if these *hombres* were taking him to Rhonda Mae. She wouldn't last very long hiding out south of the river. Too many eyes, too many ears, too many *ratas* hungry to curry favor with the Garzas and score some *narco* silver.

If they were going to smoke him, they'd have done it by now. And dumped his body. Any hole in this desert wasteland would do.

They bumped and bashed along for another hour. But that was another wild-ass guess. By this time, Burch had banged his head against everything sharp and hard within reach. Not that he could. Every now and then, somebody would slap him on the side of his head. Just because they could.

Whether slapped or whiplashed, he saw exploding stars behind his eyelids. He felt three lumps swelling on his forehead and could tell his nose was bleeding into his moustache. His teeth felt loose. His internal clock was a wreck.

Fuck it. Don't fight it. Enjoy your problem. Embrace the pain. Plot the payback. In spades.

Redneck Zen.

Hours before this joyride, Burch had tracked down the home of Nancy Jo Quartermain, following Doggett's directions and a circle he drew on the topo map.

It was a trim adobe house six miles east of the highway between Faver and Alpine. Topped by a tin roof painted silver to reflect the unforgiving sun. Chickens pecked the sand of a raked front yard.

Burch stopped the Dodge on the ranch road with the engine ticking over at idle, even with Nancy Jo's front door, letting her see him before pulling into the yard. No sudden moves. No presumptions.

He eased out the clutch and rolled slowly up her gravel drive, stopping again with his tailgate just a few yards away from the ranch road. He stepped out of the cab with the file folder that held Rhonda Mae's letters pressed against his chest with his right hand while he raised his left to shoulder height, palm facing the house.

The front door opened, revealing a darkened interior that might as well have been dipped in tar. He kept his hands still and squinted against a sun far stronger than his Ray-Bans.

He heard two quick metallic clicks. First one, then the other. Like the sound of the hammers being cocked on an ancient shotgun. Old gun could still get you dead quick. Burch kept very still.

"Who the hell are you and what the hell are you doin' on my property?"

His answer was slow, but short. Juanita. Knockin' On Heaven's Door. Rhonda Mae. Or Rita. Big Trouble. And the letters between a granddaughter and her grandmother.

"Got them right here, ma'am, if you care to look. They're my bona fides for what I'm about to say. You know her as Rita but I know her as Rhonda Mae. I'm here to help if I can. Take her to her grandma, if she's willin'. At least see her, tell her about her grandma if she ain't."

"I'll give you this, mister. You got sand. Don't know that you can be much help to Rita, but I'll look at those letters and hear you out."

The front door filled with the body of a short, stout woman with thick grey hair, reddish brown skin and fierce black eyes that shot him a look that could cut concrete block. She was cradling an old L.C. Smith double-barreled shotgun that looked longer than she was tall. Also looked like a ten gauge, with muzzles as wide as the Washburn Tunnel.

Both hammers were cocked. Burch hoped the springs were strong.

"How do you want to work this, ma'am? I could hand you this folder and wait till you've…"

"Oh, hell no, mister. I'm not putting this scattergun down until I'm satisfied you ain't a cop or a bounty hunter."

Burch felt his balls try to crawl up into his belly. More than the sun was causing him to sweat like a chain gang pickaxe artist.

"I'm gonna stand right ch'ere and you're gonna read me a letter or two. If I don't like what I hear, I'll blow you right out of those boots you're wearin'."

Burch traded the Ray-Bans for cheap drugstore cheaters, then opened the folder and peered at the sideways stack of letters, each with its envelope clipped to the top of the page. Two of his favorites were near the top.

"…There is something wonderfully raw and beautiful about the land we live on…At night, you can lose yourself in stars that glitter like diamonds and cover all the sky you can see…It's harsh, arid country with its own stark magic. The mountains rise up rocky and sharp, looking like the bones of an ancient and terrible beast ready to tell you the earth's deepest and darkest secrets….I love it and want to stay out here forever…."

Then the second.

"...there are True Believers living here, folks who want to save Texas and keep her separate from a Federal Government that wants to put us under the boot of the U.N. Then there are folks who want to make a quick buck. Lots of quick bucks. I've got a foot in both camps but the tension is thick and I got to make a choice or leave because the middle is no place to be...Everybody has a gun...."

"I loved Rita to death, even though I knew that wasn't her real name. She was always a puzzlement to me, though. One moment, she was a starry-eyed romantic in love with this godforsaken place and swallowing the horseshit Bondurant sells about building a new Texas republic.

"Next minute, she falls for that Tommy Juan, who always was a train wreck waiting to happen, and dives headlong into his foolishness, hustling those guns for him, doing business with the *narcos*. And when Tommy Juan got killed, she had to run for her life."

Nancy Jo sighed then slowly let down the twin hammers on the L.C. Smith and shucked the shells. Old-timey brass cylinders. The kind you'd pack with black powder, buckshot and carpet tacks.

"Come on in, mister. I want to read those letters myself and let you tell me more about this fool's errand you're on."

He burned a Lucky as Nancy Jo read Rhonda Mae's letters, holding them up to a reading lamp beside the moth-eaten easy chair that sagged under her weight.

The shotgun was perched across her lap, its barrels a dull gray that hadn't been blued since Landslide Lyndon cheated Coke Stevenson out of a U.S. Senate seat. Speckled with pitting, the naked steel cylinders were pointed his way, wavering slightly to the rhythm of her breathing.

Every few seconds, he got the full-bore dead man's view of those big black holes that could suck out a man's soul before blasting his body into a bloody pulp. Knowing the shotgun wasn't loaded didn't lessen the pucker factor or dissolve the lead lump forming in the pit of his stomach.

He looked around the room as she kept reading but couldn't see very much in the gloomy light. A few pieces of furniture, well-worn but dusted and squared away. A framed photo he took to be a much younger Nancy Jo, a glamor shot of a dark-haired beauty with flashing eyes, casting a look of carnal challenge over her shoulder. A hint of the whore and brothel madam she used to be.

The air was still, hot and carried the odors of someone who has lived alone for too many years. Bengay, Vicks VapoRub, Lysol, Mister Clean, stale smoke, sour milk, sour sweat and the faint whiff of urine and hopelessness common to old folks playing out the end of their string. He took another drag to chase the smell out of his lungs.

Nancy Jo cleared her throat and slipped the last letter she read back into the folder.

"What's your stake in this? Why the hell should you give a damn about what happens to her? Never met a cop yet who cared about anything other than pinning the blame on the nearest patsy and getting a freebie from one of my girls. And don't you deny being a cop – it's written all over you."

"Ma'am, it's been a long damn time since I've carried a badge. I work private now. Which may make me a lower form of shitbird in your eyes, but there it is. As for why I give a damn about Rhonda Mae, the answer is her grandmother, Juanita. I owe her for turning my back on her and Rhonda Mae and I aim to make amends."

Nancy Jo snorted and shook her head.

"You want me to believe you're a bubba Sir Galahad on a noble quest to save the damsel in distress? You might want to climb down off'a that high horse, mister. I ain't buyin' what you're sellin'."

"This is West Texas, ma'am, not Camelot. Noble has nothin' to do with this deal. I owe an old, dying woman one last look at her granddaughter. Or the news that she's still alive from somebody she trusts who laid eyes on her. That last part is a piss-poor second best, but Juanita Mutscher is tough and takes life as it comes."

"How much is this poor ol' woman payin' you for this wild goose chase?"

"Not nearly enough for getting shot at and clubbed on like I've been if this were just a money deal. But it ain't. It's a debt. More about something you'd find in The Big Book instead of the tales of King Arthur's court."

"You a friend of Bill, mister?"

"No, but quite a few of my friends are so I know a bit about the step where you try to make amends to those you've wronged. And I wronged Juanita and Rhonda Mae by turning my back on them when they needed my help real bad."

"What is it you want from me?"

"I was told you were her friend and might have a way of reaching out to her. I'd like to know if she would see me."

Nancy Jo's eyes narrowed and bored into Burch. He was glad the shotgun wasn't loaded.

"Mister, that's a big damn ask. And if she's in as much trouble as I think she is, she don't have time for no broken-down ex-cop workin' a half-ass twelve-step program."

"No, ma'am, you're right. But she might make time for word about her grandmother. If you're the friend I think you are, you know that's true."

Nancy Jo kept right on staring but said nothing. The seconds stretched out and crawled on by. Burch wanted another Lucky but stayed his hand. She finally broke the silence.

"Mister, I'm gonna roll the dice on you. Even though you stink of cop. You wait right here. I got to run down the road to make a phone call or two. There's beer in the icebox if your throat's dry. I'm takin' the shotgun with me, so don't get no ideas of gettin' cute with that Colt behind your back."

"Wouldn't dream of it, ma'am."

Seventeen

By the time they reached their deep outback destination, the sun was low and about to duck below the mountain peaks. The breeze he felt through his sweat-stained shirt was cool with the promise of colder still.

After the hours he spent with a burlap sack over his head, the light was still strong enough to make Burch blink. He wanted his Ray-Bans. He craved a Lucky. But his hands were still bound at the wrists behind his back.

He felt cold steel brush against his wrists before a quick slice freed him from the hemp. He rolled his shoulders and shook his arms to loosen them up.

Shades. A smoke. Then a looksee. On his flanks were five men, four lean and one chunky, all wearing pearl speed-snap shirts with fancy stitching across the chest and shoulders. The chunky one had a Zapata moustache and was giving him the Evil Eye.

"You the one that kept slappin' me?"

"*Sí, cabrón. Me dio un gran placer.*"

"Slappin' my head gave you pleasure, huh?"

He took a sidestep toward the Chunky One then pivoted, putting all his fat and muscle behind a left hook that caught the man squarely on the jaw, distorting his face and sending slobber and blood flying from his mouth.

The man staggered. Burch cupped his palms together, passing a leather pouch to his right hand, then shifting his weight and launching an overhand punch that flattened the man's nose, crunching cartilage with hard knuckles loaded with a little something extra.

The man dropped with a beefy thud that sounded like raw meat slapped down on a butcher's block. Down and out. Burch slipped the coin sap back into his pocket.

"Pleasure has its price, *pendejo*."

That drew a laugh from a few of the Chunky One's *compadres*. Didn't stop them from pulling their pistols and pointing them at Burch, fully cocked.

"*¡Guarda esas armas! La Güera lo quiere vivo.*"

The command came from a man striding toward them from the craggy shadows, his features caught by the dying light as he drew closer.

Swept back black hair, frosted with gray. A broad face with a high forehead, sharp cheekbones and stubble the color of coal and lead, an ugly mix that begged for either a razor or a chance to sprout into a full beard. A hawk nose that was a few inches left of plumb. Reddish brown skin. Lots of *Indio* blood.

"You better come with me before Carlos wakes up. *La Güera* wants you upright and still breathing."

A gravelly voice in a low register. Like his vocal cords were damaged.

"You mean Rita?"

"*Sí, hombre.* Or Rhonda Mae, if you prefer. I know that is the name of her birth, but it's been a long time since anybody called her that. *Muchachos* here still call her *La Güera*, but it's not a name she'll use much longer."

"Why not?"

"I let her tell you that."

"They call Rhonda Mae *La Güera*. What do they call you? *¿Cuál es tu nombre?*"

"Armando. Armando Jesus Ruiz."

One of the Chunky One's *compadres* hustled up and handed Burch the folder with Rhonda Mae's letters to Juanita.

"*Dale su arma también. Podría necesitarlo para dispararle a Carlos.*"

The man laughed and pulled the Colt from his belt and handed it to Burch. Burch popped out the mag then checked the breech. He popped the mag back in, nodded a thanks to the man and slipped Ol' Slabsides into the belt slide holster behind his back.

"Think I'll really need to shoot Carlos?"

"*Probablemente.* And I don't really give a shit because he's not one of my cousins. You might also need that gun for company we've got coming. They're supposed to be friendly, but you never know. *¿Quién puede decir?*"

"And my blackjack?"

Armando nodded to the stocky young man waiting for orders. The youngster slipped the braided leather blackjack to Burch, shaking his head and a finger at him while making the universal *tisk-tisk-tisk* sound with his tongue. *Naughty, naughty gringo.* Burch tucked the short black weapon down the inside of his right boot then smoothed the leg of his jeans over the leather top.

"*Pinche pendejos* missed that cute little coin purse in your pocket. Where we're going, you'll need more than a roll of quarters in your fist."

"Much obliged. Felt naked without them."

"*Yo lo creo.*"

"You could leave here right now. With me. I'll take you to see your grandmother."

"Can't do that. Not right now. There's something I've got to do."

"Getting dead ain't a got-to."

They were sitting in canvas camp chairs parked in front of a weathered wall tent with rolled up flaps that looked like a prop from

She Wore A Yellow Ribbon. With fabric checkered by patches, it was a poor and distant cousin of the cavalry canvas that served as a stage for John Wayne and Maureen O'Hara during their charged scenes of love shot through with loss and bitter anger.

Burch could see Rhonda Mae's hair was chopped short and dyed black beneath a faded Longhorns' ballcap with a frayed brim. She had just finished cleaning a CAR-15 when he first walked up and gave him a stern, defiant look with a jut to her jaw.

Reminded him of her mother, the stripper and part-time hooker.

Naked in the rain with a fresh-killed boyfriend at her feet.

Flashing him that same look.

Just before she jammed a .357 Colt Trooper under her jaw and blew off the top of her skull.

Grisly memory.

He shook it off to focus on Theda Bayer's daughter. Rhonda Mae. Locking in on who she is right now. Not the whacked out and reckless teenager he bailed out of drug busts and a gangbang at a biker bar all those years ago.

That girl was long gone. The woman he was sitting next to now had steel in her spine and anger in her heart. He could see it in those amber wolf-eyes she got from her mother and the air of stubborn grit gifted by her grandmother. Still reckless, maybe, but with purpose.

Faded Levis, scuffed ropers and a dark gray T-shirt hid her curves with a baggy look that was the sartorial opposite of Armando's crew and their needle-nosed boots and fancy-stitched *ranchero* shirts.

Not the *La Güera* look he expected. For now, the glitzy trappings of that persona were strewn across a cot inside her tent – blonde wig, designer jeans, tooled boots with stacked rider heels, tight bolero jacket.

Burch thought her down at the heels look better suited this hideout camp of gunrunners and wished the crew would follow

186

her lead. Most were blood kin to Armando Ruiz, which also made them distant cousins and nephews of Nancy Jo, a Ruiz despite the Quartermain surname she got from a husband enjoying the eternal quiet of a granite tombstone for the past thirty years.

Don't need no needle-nose boots or fancy stitches, *pendejos*. No gloss of Hollywood glamour necessary. Not even the hint of Villa and his Immortals. *La Revolución* is a distant myth and memory, and its ghosts aren't welcome here. This is a dust-choked and dirt-cheap haven for everyday outlaws hiding from rivals and lawdogs.

Tents and lean-tos were hidden by thickets of mesquite trees, creosote brush, ocotillo and yellow paloverde scattered along the floor of a small box canyon with a hidden exit through the boulders.

Camouflage netting was strung through the stubby branches of trees and brush, shading the tents and covering the spots where trucks and Jeeps were parked, including three canvas-topped, 6 x 6 military rigs with Mexican Army markings. Inside the back of each were high stacks of wooden cases painted olive green with black stenciled letters.

Burch lit two Luckies and handed her one, snapping the Zippo shut with his left. He watched her slip a bone-handled knife into her boot.

"Nice blade. Always good to have an ace in the hole. Never know when you'll need to get up close and personal."

She ignored him. He tried again.

"Nice hidey hole you got here. All the comforts of home."

"It'll do until we get done with some business."

"Guns or drugs? Or a little of both?"

"What do you care? You quit being a cop a long time ago."

"Never did quit, hon. They took my badge. And you never can quit being a cop, even when you ain't no more. Not really."

"Question still stands – why do you care what I do?"

"Your grandmother, Juanita. She wants to see you before she dies. And she don't got long. She sent me and I owe her."

"I remember you bein' around back then. Married a local gal but it didn't stick. Don't remember you ever bailin' me out of jail. Granny was always the one pickin' me up."

"I was the guy who pulled the string that sprung you. Until I didn't."

"She cussed your name a time or two when you stopped lending a hand. I remember that. I remember J.D. trying to defend you and her not buying it. But by that time, I was living with Danny Ray, who wasn't worth a shit as a father. He flat let me run wild."

"Never did understand how a scumbag like him got custody of you."

She chuckled, low and mirthless.

"You're smarter than that. He bribed the judge hearing the case and the chief judge of the family court. Fix was in, mister."

"How'd you get shed of him?"

"Kicked him in the balls then stuck the barrel of a Smith & Wesson 686 in his mouth the first time he tried to fuck me. Walked out the door and never looked back. Had to hit the road. Couldn't go home to Juanita."

"Yeah, not with that custody order still in play."

"There you go."

"Takes me longer than most, but I manage to figure it out."

She chuckled again. No bitterness this time.

"I remember you being a funny guy, quick with a joke."

"The jokes buy me time to get my brain in gear."

She finished her smoke and snuffed it in the sand with a boot heel. Then she field-stripped the butt, sticking the paper in a pocket and letting the tobacco scatter to the wind. He handed her the folder with those letters to Juanita and the grandmother's scrawled plea to come see her.

"I brought you these to remind you of what Juanita means to you. Or meant. Sheet at the top is her note to you."

188

Her head jerked up at the barb, her wolf-eyes flashing in anger. Burch was glad she was no longer cradling the CAR-15.

"Where the fuck do you get off trying to tell me how I feel about my granny? Worse than a Baptist preacher piling on the guilt. You helped us once but that was a long fuckin' time ago. Too long to count now."

Burch said nothing and let her blast wash over him, meeting her glare with the empty gaze of card sharp. He wasn't surprised to hear the voice of his dead partner giving advice he didn't need.

Bad move, Sport Model. You really put both boots in the horse-shit there. You got one choice – just plow ahead. You apologize and she really might just shoot you for being both a dumbass and a limp dick.

Shut up, Wynn. Go back to your dirt nap with Will Rogers. I'm busy trying not to get shot here.

Another blast.

"You say you're here because you owe her – well, your debt don't mean a damn thing to me. And I ain't in the absolution business. Go see a goddam priest if your guilty conscience is getting too heavy to carry. Plenty of them around."

Enough of this shit. Either shoot me or shut up. But you're gonna hear what I have to say.

"Here's the deal – I've read those letters. I know the woman who wrote them loves Juanita. And when I let myself study on it, I realize I love her too. She wants to see you one last time and I'm here to take you to her when you're ready to go. In the meantime, I'm here to keep you from getting killed in the middle of whatever jackpot you've gotten yourself into."

"Look around here, mister. Does it look like I need another gun hand to keep me safe? More to the point – does it look like I really need to be a babysitter to an old fart like you?"

"Don't let the grey beard fool you. I still manage to hold my own."

"You want to take care of me again after all these years? Want to be my bodyguard? Fine by me. It's your funeral."

"More likely, it'll be somebody else's funeral. Folks cross me and tend to get dead. Tell Armando to ask around about me. He'll find out I still don't need no rockin' chair. Not yet."

The anger in her eyes flamed out like a sputtering gas grill sucking on an empty tank. Fatigue caused her face to sag. She didn't break her stare at him, but her mother's defiant glare was gone.

In its place was a look of both curiosity and calculation. *Who is this grizzled wreck? Can I trust what he says? Can I trust him? Did Juanita really send him?* That last question was easy to answer with a phone call or two. The rest was something only gut instinct and a survivor's guile could cure.

"You got any whiskey here? I could use a drink while you tell me what we're up to and who we're up against."

"Thought you said you never quit being a cop even when they take your badge away."

"That's on the inside of me, deep in my heart. On the outside, I find I occasionally like the outlaw life."

"What does your heart say about that?"

"Not a damn thing. I tell it to shut up and enjoy the ride."

She grinned, then ducked into her tent and popped back out waving a fifth of Old Grandad. Nasty stuff. But it would have to do in this hideout for everyday outlaws with no real need for glitz or glamour.

Eighteen

Doggett grimaced as he stepped inside the Airstream and started clocking the murder scene. His nostrils registered the coppery scent of blood riding above the common stench of any outhouse or toilet.

His eyes recorded the overturned chairs, the arterial spray that climbed the back wall, clothes scattered on the floor and the naked body of the big woman on the bed.

Her eyes – glassy, wide open and sightless. Her mouth – gaping in a frozen, silent scream. Her breasts – bloody from sliced off nipples. Her torso – pocked with cigarette burns. Her legs – splayed wide with blood pooled between. Her throat – sliced deep from ear to ear.

"Jesus Christ, she died damn hard."

"You bet she did. Need to catch the cockbites who did this. Pronto."

"Must be some low sumbitches. Goddam animals."

Stan Walton, his chief deputy, stating the obvious to blow off steam, like the safety valve popping on a pressure cooker. Walton was ex-Fort Worth P.D., steady and smooth, kept the paperwork flowing and had just the right touch with the dozen deputies and five civilians in his office to keep everybody in line without being an asshole about it.

Like Doggett, he did a tour as an M.P. but never served in C.I.D. and didn't have a murder cop's instincts or savvy. Knew how to rope off a crime scene and take notice of the basics. Gutsy enough to kick down a door. But the train stopped there. Truth was, he was glad to see Doggett walk through the trailer door and take charge.

"We got an ID?"

"Texas DL on her. Leighanna Burdette. Rural route address near San Angelo looks like. Ran the plates. Rig is registered to a Benjamin Burdette but with an Odessa address."

"Which one expires first?"

"The plates."

"Go with the DL, then. Folks who move will update that before they do the plates so they can go to the bank and do business in town. Unless some asshole with a badge pulls them over and writes them up."

Walton gave him a quick briefing. An elderly rancher named J.L. Nelson found the parked Ford dually and Airstream tandem while taking a backroad shortcut to his house after a Sunday night service at the First Baptist Church in Faver.

The rig looked abandoned. Nelson stopped, checked out the truck's crew cab with his flashlight and knocked on the trailer door.

No answer.

The door was unlocked. He turned the handle as he called out a greeting. He ducked his head inside, played his flashlight across the innards then screamed. He also slammed the door shut and vomited his sanctified casserole supper all over his Sunday best Larry Mahans.

Shaking and stinking, he drove his '68 Ford pickup home and told his wife what happened. She called it in to the sheriff's office then fetched a bottle of Old Hickory for her shell-shocked husband, who sat on the steps of their back porch muttering to himself and trying to wipe the vomit off his boots with a bandana.

J.L. Nelson needed him some Jesus to get over this spiritual trauma. He also needed a snort of 86 proof to prepare himself for the Lord's healing grace.

Doggett doubted the murder took place on the shoulder of this gravel road. Seldom used, but not quite deserted enough for a torture session and a killing. No clue about the kill scene. Not yet. No clue where the woman had been and how she wound up here. Not yet. All he could rule out was teleportation by aliens, but even that wasn't a certainty.

Quit worrying about all those 'not yets.' Work what you got in front of you.

He eased closer to the bed, squatting on his heels to scan the body, the bloody wall spray, the night table and the floor. Ashtray with butts on the night table. A crumpled white pack with a red bull's eye, discarded after the last cigarette was lit. He felt a tingle of recognition but relaxed so he wouldn't spook what his subconscious was trying to tell him.

Easy. Don't scare a colt already headed into the paddock. Let him come to you.

Near the foot of the bed, scattered around the corner nearest him, a short trail of clothes. He could trace a broken line – jeans, shirt, boots, bra and panties. Didn't look like they were torn from her body by the killers. Did look like they were peeled off in a hurry.

He studied a break in the line, a void big enough for something that pulled the jeans and shirt away from the bed when it was moved. Another nuzzle at the back of his mind.

I know you're there. Take your time. I'll wait.

A short, square-mouthed wicker waste basket with a honey oak stain played peek-a-boo from under the night table. Couldn't see it when standing. Could while squatting. Doggett rose from his crouch just enough to flash a penlight around the innards. Wadded up tissues and what looked like three grayish white sausage casings. Sharp poke in the forebrain.

There you are. Knew you'd show up when you were ready. Got somethin' for you. A juicy ol' apple. Looks like the lady had a gentleman caller before she got killed, didn't she? Did he let in the killers or was he gone before they got there?

"Coroner on his way?"

"After he guzzles some more Dutch courage so no tellin' when or what kind of shape he'll be in."

Doc Battles. Been Cuervo County Coroner since the late 60s. Threw a damn good barbecue and was likeable enough to keep getting elected every four years. A large animal vet by trade. Knew his cows and horses.

Learned just enough human anatomy in three decades to get you a time of death and a preliminary cause if the latter was bloody and obvious. And this one was.

"Crime scene? Get hold of Katie?"

"On the way."

Good news. Katie Navarro had the chops Battles never would. She would spot details that would help him get a bead on that gentleman caller and the killer. Or killers. This didn't look like a one-man job.

And he had a hunch about the victim's last welcome guest. Hoped he was wrong. Doubted he was. But he'd cool his mental jets and wait for Katie.

Doggett felt a nip of pain in his bad leg as he stood straight. He fished a pouch of Red Man from his jacket pocket and loaded up a chaw. He felt Walton's eyes on him, waiting, not wanting to break his train of thought.

"Yeah, Stan."

"Found these. Pamphlets from that ranch run by Bondurant, the ex-state senator."

"You mean the home for wayward Kluxers and pissed off folks who want Texas to leave the Union?"

"That's the one."

"Good find. Gives us a reason to go roust that blowhard asshole and take a good look at what he's got goin' on out there. No tellin' what kind of cockroaches we might find."

"You don't want to tell Settles about this. He's kindly tight with Bondurant. Or used to be."

Deputy Brad Settles.

A holdover from the Blue Willingham days. A Kluxer with a badge. A pipeline to the Willingham loyalists, the *gringos* who used to run the county and anybody else who would slip him some cash.

A shithead Doggett dearly wanted to get shed of but too clever to give him a reason.

"I believe it's Deputy Settles' turn to pull the midnight trick at the jail, ain't it, Stan?"

"Now that you mention it, I believe you're right."

"Remind him when we get back to the office."

"He won't like it a damn bit, but I'll enjoy his discomfort."

"A man's got to take pleasure in his work. Enough about our favorite deputy. Let's back off and wait for Katie. And Stan – when we go out to that ranch, it'll be me, you and Bobby Quintero."

Quintero was his best gun hand – an ex-Army Ranger and sniper he met through one of his cousins. The cousin and Quintero had served together during the ragged final days of Vietnam. Bobby also pulled some nasty duty in Nicaragua, El Salvador and the Middle East. Black ops shit in places where nobody was a good guy and everybody could get dead.

When Doggett brought Bobby along, he expected trouble to get lethal. Real quick.

Stan let out a long, low whistle. Doggett looked at him and smiled.

"You'll come heavy, too. That Model 12 you like. Bobby'll bring whatever he favors. We're not there to play checkers with that asshole."

Doggett knew what Walton was thinking. Bondurant contributed to his campaigns. Not a huge amount but enough to get a phone call returned. Then again, Bondurant money was in the campaign coffers of most of the incumbents in Cuervo County.

Doesn't buy you shit, pendejo. Not when it's murder.

★

"What's your read?"

"Think you're dealin' with two events here, Sheriff. One right after the other. The vic had a roll in the hay with somebody. Then she got tortured and killed. Cutting her throat caused her to spray the walls and bleed out, but it looks like they tore her up inside. I don't know what they jammed up there, but it ripped her up. I'll make sure to point that out to Battles and whoever handles the autopsy."

Doggett kept his hunches to himself and let Katie Navarro tell the story. He'd ask a question or two but that would be it. *Let the evidence speak. Don't jam it into your working theory to make it fit.*

Navarro was short, wiry and intense, with big, dark eyes that gave off enough energy to crank up a semi. Her straight, black hair was pulled back in a ponytail and tucked under a dark blue ballcap with CCSO embroidered above the brim – Cuervo County Sheriff's Office. Those same white letters were stenciled on the back of the windbreaker she wore, which hung off her thin frame like a tent.

She spoke with her hands, chopping the air and pointing to objects in the room as she made each point. She jabbed the index finger of her right hand toward the ashtray then raised it toward the ceiling.

"Boyfriend was a smoker. They both were. Or both enjoyed a smoke after fucking. Butts in the ashtray are the same brand. Lucky Strikes. Just like the pack says. Three of the butts have lipstick on them. The others don't."

"Lucky Strikes. No filters. Old school. Think it was an older guy?"

"Not sure about that, Sheriff. Got a lot of the younger *machos* pickin' up the *Delicados* their *abuelos* used to smoke. Old school is making a comeback. Besides, the boyfriend had enough lead in his pencil to go three rounds. Wish my boyfriend could do that."

Doggett coughed. Navarro grinned. She liked needling him and making him feel uncomfortable. He envied her boyfriend but knew his age placed him firmly in the carnally irrelevant camp of the *abuelos*. In her eyes. And the eyes of just about every woman he met these days. With a few notable exceptions.

Navarro continued ticking through her checklist, marking each point with a raised digit. Middle finger came next, raised in the air to form a V with her index finger.

"Hard to say but I'd guess that we're not talking a lot of time between rolling in the hay, getting killed and getting found. The lip ends of the cigarette butts are still damp. You can feel that the semen in the condoms isn't cold. The blood is still pretty fresh and hasn't coagulated that much."

Ring finger up next. Bad news comes in threes.

"I can tell you there are rope burns on her wrists that show she was bound. There's also some bruising at the corners of her mouth that look like she was gagged. No sign of gag or rope though."

Pinky made it four.

"The cuts were deep and almost surgical. With a scalpel or a straight razor. No hesitation. The cutter knows how to use a blade. He got bloody, though. I expect we'll find drip stains on this dark carpet between the bed and the door."

Five with the thumb.

"My guess is there were two killers but once they got her bound up and gagged, the rest of the ride could have been solo. Feels like a double-team though. One working her down low, the other cutting and burning her with cigs. Can't tell you if lover boy was one of the two."

"I kindly doubt he was. Got a pretty good idea who he is. You'll find his prints scattered around this trailer but he ain't our killer. Just a guy who draws trouble like shit draws flies. Ol' Mister Death follows him around like a black cloud. Leaves bodies behind like folks used to leave calling cards."

"Sounds like a guy who needs a whole lot of leavin' alone."

"Wish I could."

They fell silent and waited for Doc Battles to show up so Katie could tell him what he'd never figure out on his own.

Nineteen

Valentina Garza wanted them to hear her coming. *Let the sound fill them with dread.*

She smiled at the thought as the taps on her riding boots made a raspy ring along the slate floor, echoing down the long, cool hallway that ran between her father's study and the large dining room where four men waited for her arrival, lit only by wall sconces that cast a muted yellow light.

They had been waiting for exactly twenty-nine minutes by the twenty-four-karat gold Cartier Tank Francaise on her left wrist. It would be thirty by the time she entered the room.

Two of the men worked for her – Gustavo "El Tiburón" Portales, the head of the Garza family's drug smuggling and gun-running operation and his second-in-command, Francisco "Azul" Sanchez.

Tibby and Azul. Both were the main *machos* in the family's *narcotraficante* resurrection, raising it from the ruins of her father's empire, wrecked by his rivals after he was killed by a car bomb in Monterrey.

It took a lot of sweat, money and blood to rebuild but she felt her father's guiding hand and heard his voice in the small hours past midnight, giving her strength, guile and ruthlessness that were gifts to his only daughter.

She had to kill four of his trusted lieutenants who thought they should wear his crown, snuffing them out with the nine-millimeter Browning Hi-Power her father always favored, the pistol with the golden G inlay on each rosewood grip, her eyes glittering as their boots rattled on the ground in a death they didn't expect.

The gun was tucked to the small of her back. Her people knew it wasn't there for show.

Valentina entered the room, her curls, long and black, flowing over her shoulders, her face a stone mask, her dark eyes cold as she looked at each man as he stood to greet her. She had her father's height. They either had to look up to meet her gaze or level their eyes straight ahead.

Dead level.

"Thank you for waiting, *señores*. We have much to discuss and only a little time to do so."

Chizik nodded his head and spoke.

"It's an honor to meet you in person, *madrina*. I hope we can settle this matter and continue the relationship that benefits us both."

She ignored the compliment and the pitch.

"Be seated, *señores*. I trust you have a drink if you're thirsty. If not, you need only ask."

A linen napkin, folded into a triangle and tented, was in front of every chair, guarded by a glass tumbler. A clear glass pitcher, sweating condensation, was centered at arm's length for easy refills.

She stepped to the head of the table. Tibby pulled out her chair and tucked it behind her as she pulled the pistol out, placed it on the table and perched like a lithe cat ready to pounce.

She looked at Tibby and nodded, then locked her eyes on Chizik, who remained standing.

"*Señor* Chizik, I can understand your wanting a swift conclusion to this meeting so you can continue sucking the golden teat of the Garza family, but I demand a satisfactory answer to the question at hand."

Chizik took his seat. She could tell he was angry and didn't like answering a woman's questions. Too bad. She could also see him rein in his anger and resume the look and tone of subservient respect he was smart enough to know was his only chance of success. That and telling the truth. Or as much of the truth as needed to salvage the deal.

"I can tell you that I don't know what happened to the men from my crew who were with the men you lost. Did they go rogue and sell out your men? I doubt that but don't know for sure. Are they buried in the desert somewhere to create distrust between us? Did a rival do this? That would be my bet, but I don't know for certain."

"What do you know, *señor*? We can't continue on doubts and bets."

"I know that I'm not trying to crawdad out of this deal and take my goods to somebody offering me a higher price. I know I gave you my word when we struck this deal and give it again now. I know I'm in it for the long haul."

"You want me to believe your word is your bond so we can continue to do business. In the present circumstances, that's the only answer you can give if you want to leave this room standing up. Even if I choose to accept this answer and not feed you a bullet, it's clear that you've been compromised and may have a traitor in your midst."

"I agree and have taken the precaution of moving your goods to a safe location. It's a place known only to myself and my trusted *segundo,* Jack Reese, who is with me today."

Chizik turned his head away and made an open-handed gesture toward Reese, a burly man with bushy red hair and beard and a lurid scar that sliced diagonally from the middle of his forehead, across the ridge of his eyebrows and down the right side of his face. Reese gave a short nod of respect then looked her in the eye.

With one fluid motion, Valentina swept her father's gun off the table, cocked the hammer and sent four hollow-point slugs slamming into Reese's face and chest. Blood splattered the table and

Chizik's face. He looked startled and angry, but didn't break eye contact with her, letting his man's blood drip off his chin and stain his off-white shirt.

"That's one less person who knows."

"He was my friend and brother."

"You can buy another. What you can't buy is our renewed trust in you. Fortunately, there's a way you can earn that back."

"Who do I have to kill?"

"Somebody you already want dead. Someone you'll enjoy killing. As slow and as painfully as you like."

"Who would that be?"

"You call her *La Güera*. We know where she'll be. And when."

Chizik stared at Valentina, his eyes stony and cold, then snapped open a linen napkin and wiped the blood from his face. Azul handed him a folded piece of paper. Chizik nodded once then stalked out of the room, his boots sounding like a sledgehammer striking the stone floor.

Bobby Quintero craved a gallon of black coffee strong enough to float a railroad spike and a steaming plate of *migas* with deadly pieces of *chile pequeña* lurking under the eggs. For dessert? Fire up a 64-ring maduro cigar.

He settled for a strip of venison jerky, a couple of coffee beans to crunch between his molars and a sip of warm, gypy water. Dessert was a fresh chaw of Red Man. As he stuffed stringy tobacco into his mouth, a thin line of light ribboned the crags and folds due east of the brushy rise of rocks and boulders he picked for a one-man observation post.

Dawn coming. With big heat to follow.

He fussed and tugged at the camouflage netting hanging from the creosote branches, closing the gap above his head, then scooted deeper into his hidey hole, digging out the odd stone or three that dug into his belly and thighs.

He ditched his Starlight scope, a heavy, Vietnam-era bastard, and picked up his binoculars. Resuming his scan of the backside of the ranch below, he was careful to cup his hands around the front lenses of his binoculars to cut the risk of a giveaway flash in the rising light.

This was the second dawn of Bobby's recce of the ranch. The Bar L R. Thomas "T For Texas" Bondurant's place. *T, my pimply brown ass. Try B for Blowhard. Maybe S for Shitheel. Or P for Pendejo.*

The night before the first dawn had been long stretches of dull tempered by a silence that strangled the clock. Bobby started his vigil just after sunset, dropped off by Doggett then slipping into the creosote, mesquite and Spanish dagger about a mile from the ranch and working his way to a pile of rocks across the road from the pipe gate entrance.

Wait and watch. Rinse and repeat. Time was frozen but Bobby didn't mind. The stillness of this scrubby outback calmed him. His breathing and heartbeat slowed, but his mind and senses were sharp and clear.

Brought back memories of long-range ghosting after *Sandinistas* in The Nick. Back in his Ranger days. Scouting for the *Contras*. Bunch of coke-addled and corrupt scumbags who loved to shoot up women, children and oldsters in any jungle village they visited. Pigs and cows, too.

Backcountry free-fire zone. Sickened a man's soul. Left him tainted and dishonored no matter how much distance he and his Ranger buddies kept from the *Contras*. Took Bobby a long time to get over that.

Putting his recce skills to work for Sudden Doggett was a redemption of sorts. So were the other duties of being a deputy. He liked the life. The lines were clean and clear. Protect Joe and Janey Citizen. Put the bad guys away. Or put 'em down. He spilled only bad blood these days. So far.

He chewed his coffee beans to say awake. He crossed his legs and leaned back against a rock still warm from the sun, a .308 FN FAL with a folding stock resting on his lap, his face wrapped in thin muslin mottled in tan, ochre and burnt umber. More reach-out-and-touch with the FN than the CAR-15 he carried in the jungle, better for the desert flatland.

Watch and wait. No action at the gate. In or out. Rinse and repeat. A low rumble to his right. A mile or two up the dirt and gravel road. The noise got louder and closer. A dark, low-slung shape rolling his way.

Closer still.

A low rider with dual exhausts and a chopped roof. Chevy Impala. '63 or '64. *Ranchera* music riding above the rumble, trumpets rapping notes into the night air. Bobby counted five men in the car. They swung into the entrance and a man stepped out of deep shadows to open the gate.

Damn. Didn't see that fucker. How long have you been there, cabrón! Hombre's got skills. So do I, buddy. So do I.

Bobby trained his Starlight scope on the driver leaning out of the window to talk to the man who opened the gate. *Well, hello Santiago Cruz. Been a while. How was your graybar vacation, homey?*

Cruz did a nickel for possession of stolen goods and car theft – a lightweight beef for a guy with his nasty reputation. Used to do wet work on this side of the river for Malo Garza. Got lots of people dead. That was the talk. Second in body count only to Chuy Reynaldo, Malo's favorite hitter, now taking the same dirt nap as his dead master. And Elvis.

When Malo got blown away by that car bomb in Monterrey, Cruz disappeared from Cuervo County, a gun hand without a master. Lot of those around with the frequent turf wars of the cartels. The Mexican version of *Ronin*. There were rumors of Cruz sightings. On both side of the river. Usually tied to a particularly grisly killing.

But details were sketchy and unsubstantiated by hard proof. Kind of like a sighting of Sasquatch or, more apt, a *Chupacabra*, that hairless, grotesque animal of myth and legend said to suck dry the blood of livestock. And children.

But nobody really knew where Cruz was until he got pinched in El Paso while sitting on hot jewelry, electronics and a cherry Porsche 911 and equally fine '67 Mustang fastback with the 428 cubic-inch Cobra Jet engine stuffed up front.

Musta just got kicked loose, mi carnal. Didn't see no paper letting us know of your new status. No courtesy call from the TDOC. Not that they gave a fuck about opening the gates on another killer, setting him free to resume jacking up his body count in some shithole border county.

Now you show up at a ranch full of visiting bubbas and bubbettes who hate blacks, browns, slopes and kikes, blaming them for the fallen fortunes of the white man who they think built this country. Stoked up on Bondurant's sermons of resentment, hate, victimhood and scapegoating. Packin' heat and lookin' to use it.

What the fuck, homey? Why are you rollin' into this den of heavily armed rednecks? At midnight, sure. So the guests can't see your brown ass. But why at all? Workin' for the Garzas again now that Valentina is resurrecting her father's old outfit? Now, THAT would raise some interesting possibilities for this midnight call.

Maybe Bondurant and the Garzas are between the sheets, with cover from the hate sermons, the redneck sheep, 'Texas Secede' and that scraggly herd of thin, spooky cattle. Not that high a step between fleecing the loser lambs with hate they want to hear and running drugs and guns across that river.

Not for a high stepper with the morals of a hyena.

Bobby reported this to Doggett when the sheriff picked him up in a battered CJ-5 shortly after dusk about a mile up the rutted *caliche* road to an abandoned ranch. Three miles east of his first drop-off point. A longer hike, but a safer play. Safer play with the Jeep instead of the sheriff's Bronco, too.

"Santiago Cruz. Man was off the radar screen so long I thought he was dead. No – I was sure he was dead. People who blasted Malo sure didn't want to leave one of his primary hitters alive."

"Then he gets picked up for those Mickey Moust charges. Shit, with the number of bodies he's dropped, the fuckin' *pendejo* gets pinched for that?"

"Never did take that bounce at face value, Bobby. Didn't make sense to me. Cruz had a big target on his back. Maybe he thought being in prison was safer than out on the streets. Lame, I know, but I never thought that much more about it. Until now."

"We're gettin' some critical mass here. First we got that 'roid-head Brotherhood fucker your buddy plucked from the ranch and dropped on us. Now Cruz."

"Cruz showin' up tells us Valentina Garza is rebuilding her father's organization. We sort of knew that in bits and pieces. This is another piece. A big fuckin' piece. Second thing we know is, Bondurant is more than a blowhard hatemonger. He's partnered up with the Garzas and the Brotherhood to run drugs and guns."

"Good place for it. I need to get in there tonight and find out who else is on that ranch besides the sad-sack losers Bondurant takes to the cleaners. Find out how many hard pipe Brotherhood fuckers are holed up in there."

"A look-see only, Bobby. Don't slit no throats. Not yet."

"You take all the joy out of a man's work."

Doggett jammed the CJ-5 into gear, drawing a grinding metal protest, then headed further east before cutting north, tracing a long, wide loop toward the backside of the Bar L R. He was headed for a drop point not far from the pile of rocks Bobby was perched on now.

Ten hours had passed since Bobby watched Doggett's Jeep slowly fade into the darkness. Plenty of chores to while away those hours. Like finding a gate along the rear fence line and studying the deep tracks of heavily laden trucks in the dust of the rutted track leading into the ranch.

Like waiting forty-five minutes to see if anybody showed up before hopping the gate and staying off that track to ghost-walk deeper inside the ranch. With only his Starlight scope, a penlight and the FN for company. Four extra mags, too.

Like sticking to the brush and pausing every ten yards or so to scan ahead with the scope. And study his backtrail. Squatting in the rocks, thorns and dust with camouflage netting wrapped around his shoulders and mottled muslin masking his face.

Always the smart move. Every time. Even when nobody was there.

He spotted a lone figure moving toward the back fence, shoulder-ing a rifle of some sort. Couldn't tell what. Face uncovered, showing up through the scope like a big, green marshmallow. He watched as the man turned to parallel the fence, walking away from him.

In his Ranger days, he might have left a calling card. Body bled out in the dirt. No ace of spades. Not his war.

After an hour, Bobby found a sidetrack. Heavily used. By ATVs, maybe. Not big trucks. Lots of foot traffic. No sign of horse or cattle. He crept down this new path, keeping to the brush and his stop-and-scan routine, enjoying the familiar discipline of moving at night through Indian country.

During one stop, he heard scrabbling to his left. Bring the scope around. Javelinas. Five of them. Startled and scrambling. Wait until they disappear into the brush. Move forward. About ten feet. The angry, dry buzz of a rattlesnake. Freeze. Buzzing rattles to his right. Cut a wide loop to the left. Might be a mate nearby.

He slipped toward a bowl-shaped depression, rimmed with boulders and tough to see until you were right up on it. Maybe fifty yards wide and a hundred yards deep. Bobby sidled to the edge, checked for rattlers then lowered himself between two of the bigger rocks to watch and wait.

With the night scope trained on the opposite side of the bowl, Bobby could see the outlines of a rectangular metal building with a flat roof. Bigger than a double-wide, looking like temporary barracks thrown up near an oil rig or remote construction project. A job in the outback, which is what West Texas is all about.

No lights. Need to find out if anybody's home. But not right now. Be patient. Watch and wait. Seek and ye shall find. Ask and it shall be delivered unto you. In the form of a man opening the door, slinging a rifle on his shoulder and lighting a cigarette that flared like an acetylene torch in the scope.

Piss-poor light discipline. None, really. Dumbass also let himself get silhouetted in the door frame by the faint glow from inside. He watched the man walk south on a trail toward the front side of the ranch, sweeping a flashlight beam back and forth in front of him.

Strictly amateur hour. And more than a little strange. They seem just as worried about keeping an eye on Bondurant and his sheep as making sure the back door stays locked on a guy like him. On the slow creep from the back gate, he had expected to slip up on a sentry or two and give them a wide berth. Not just one guy walking the back fence.

Slack, shoddy and half-ass. Whoever these dudes were, they weren't military. Which was fine by Bobby. Made it easier.

Stay chilly, hombre. Don't get fat, dumb and happy because these guys are. Slack and shoddy are contagious. Worse than the dengue or blackwater fever. You don't want to catch either all by your lonesome out here.

Might ruin your day. For good.

Next to the building, he spotted a light pole with a motion sensor. *Coño!* Meant he had to slip along the near rim, deeper into the bowl, before crossing, staying well behind the invisible beam of the sensor. He waited another thirty minutes before making his move.

As he edged toward the deeper end, he sensed rather than saw the outlines of something man-made, taller and wider than the glorified double-wide serving as a barracks. Scope didn't tell him much. Not enough ambient light.

He took a detour. Sense became shape. A big shed of some kind. Not much more than six stout poles and the rafter frame for a metal roof. No walls.

Tall and deep enough for a couple of tractor-trailer rigs. But that was just a guess since the space was empty. Wide enough to also house what looked like a bulldozer as he walked even closer to the only mechanical beast taking shelter in the dark.

Next to the dozer was a waist-high stack of something covered by a dark tarp big enough to cover five times more of the mystery cargo's cousins.

Bobby moved to the far end, ducked under the tarp and kneeled, pulling out his penlight. Wooden crates, two wide and four tall, minus a couple missing from the rear corner where he stood.

Gave him sheltered space to pan the small beam of light across the top and sides of two crates painted a dull green. Very military. Very familiar. Then he read the stenciled, yellow lines. Rifle, Caliber 5.56 mm, M16A3. Quantity: 8.

Well, fuck me runnin'. Rare bird 16s. Full auto instead of the three-round burst. Made for SEALs and Seebees. Got to be 50 tucked away in these crates.

Old guns. Armory rebuilds, most likely. But still able to light up anyone on the wrong side of the muzzle. Odds favor more of the same wherever those absent rigs are parked. And the ammo to feed them.

Bobby snapped off the pen light and slid from under the tarp, standing straight and still, letting his eyes readjust to the dark. He put the scope to his eye and swept his back trail. For another ten minutes.

He smiled as the dumbass with the swinging flashlight bloomed into the scope.

Lord helps them what help themselves.

Dumbass didn't head for the barracks. He kept walking toward the back fence line, swinging that light like a dirtbag Diogenes.

Meets the other nighthawk before doubling back. Probably. Gives me fifteen minutes for one more chore. Good deal.

Bobby slinked between the boulders along the barracks side of the bowl lip, then crept along the back wall of the building and listened.

Sounded like a handyman's orchestra of dueling power tools in there – buzzsaws, chainsaws, drills and grinders. He separated the sounds and did a rough tally – seven distinct melodies of snoring loud enough to wake Elvis and Patsy Cline.

Wait a second. Make it eight. Bump the manpower tally to nine, adding one for that rarest of birds, an *hombre* who didn't snore. Throw in the two nighthawks and make it eleven.

Time to vámonos and đi đi mau. That last part was a favorite phrase of his old platoon sergeant, a 'Nam vet who survived some hairy shit during his three tours. It meant slip back out the way he came in, *muy pronto,* and hit the hidey hole before dawn.

Watch the back gate in the cool morning air. Snooze during the heat of day. Wait for Doggett to pick him up after sunset. Serve up his latest recce jewel.

Dead easy.

Not so fast, hombre. Don't get slack like these jokers. Stay sharp and frosty. Like a blade of ice. Slicing through the cool desert night.

Wait for the dumbass to make his return trip. Slip across his back-trail and head for the exit. Watch for the guy with the marshmallow face to show up then reverse course.

Slow and sure. Because sure is certain and certain is fast. Anything else is a dead man's move.

"How the fuck do you know where they'll meet?"

"My cousin. He's with *El Duque.*"

"And how do you know *La Güera* will be there?"

"Because she was there when they *cerrar un trato* – how to say *en inglés*? Strike the deal?"

"Close enough. But just because she was there to make the deal doesn't mean she'll be there to deliver the goods."

"My cousin says *El Duque* is convinced she will be to make sure nothing goes wrong."

"What are you trying to sell me, here? She'll be there to personally guarantee customer satisfaction? To *El Duque*? Like he's buying a refrigerator from her? Or a car?"

"*Sí*. But don't make light of this. My cousin says she wants *El Duque* to go to war with the Garzas to avenge the death of her lover. *El Duque* wants to do this anyway, but he's very taken by her *amor immortal* and desire for *vengaza*."

"That and she's almost giving the guns and other goodies away. And *El Duque* is gonna need that firepower if he's taking on the Garzas and knows a good deal when he sees one."

"*Sí*. As you say."

"Do you know where she is right now? Does your cousin?"

"No. She is with Armando Ruiz, who often worked with her dead lover and is very loyal to *La Güera*. No one wants to fuck with Armando and his family. They are *indio,* Apache some say. Comanche say others. Not pure of blood, but the *indio* is *muy fuerte* in their veins."

"So, they've got Apache or Comanche blood. What's that supposed to mean? Are they shapeshifters?"

"Ain't talkin' no spook story. Not these guys. They flesh-and-blood scary motherfuckers. A force unto themselves. They do wet work for the cartels, special jobs. Local and on the road. But strictly *independiente*."

"Free agents?"

"*Exactamente*. They also know the land and how to live off it, silent and unseen. If they don't want you to find them, you won't."

"Okay, let's go with what you do know. When?"

"Three nights from now."

"Where?"

"I will show you on a map. This side of the river."

Cider Jones grunted, partly from the pain shooting from his cracked ribs and bruised shoulder – lovely parting gifts from the one-ton flatbed that T-boned his rig. But mostly, he was venting contempt for the romantic notion of eternal love between drug dealers and gunrunners.

Revenge was another matter. That he understood. He also knew the power of having tribal blood in your veins. His was Comanche, from his mother's side of the family, Quanah Parker's descendants.

During his days as a murder cop, he'd stare into the unseeing eyes of victims. Sometimes, he'd see the horror of their last moments. Other times, nothing. Then came the rare moments when a tunnel would open in his brain and he'd gain an unspoken knowledge of the killer, shapeless but growing stronger as he worked the case and caught the scent of his prey.

But that was a long time ago. He'd lost that gift. Gone for good. Just like his gold shield.

Cider spread a topo map showing both sides of the river on the table between he and his informant, a weasel-faced Mexican named Enrique López, a small-time dealer who liked to shoot up and snort his own product and needed that extra snitch money to make ends meet.

López didn't look like much. Rail thin with a scraggly moustache and lank black hair. Most wouldn't give him a second glance. But that was his gift. He could fade into the background of a *cantina*, unnoticed by hard-drinking *hombres* talking trash, bragging about deeds they didn't do and, every now and then, spilling a dirty little cartel secret.

And he had cousins on both sides of the river who traded what they knew for a twist of coke or horse. Information from López led the task force to two righteous takedowns of gunrunners and a tidy little haul of northbound Garza product. Also led to that bloodbath that could have been Cider's last roundup, but that wasn't López's fault.

Cider already had three hundred dollars in his pocket, ready to fork it over to his solid-gold snitch. But first things first.

"Show me on this map where *El Duque* and *La Güera* will consummate this celebration of eternal love, vengeance and firepower, Enrique."

Lopez smiled, then stabbed the map with a dirty index finger, marking a backcountry crossroads.

"Aquí."

Cider snorted a disgusted chuckle.

Well, shit. Right in Malachi Hulett's backyard. Might as well be right in our laps. Either dumb as a dried-out cow patty or smart as a coyote trickster.

Hard to tell.

Twenty

*C*hizik *dives in the dirt, right eye blind from blood jetting from a brother's carotid artery, brain registering the shotgun boom and smack of a cop's slug tearing through the dead man's neck.*

Rolls left twice. Back-to-back booms with the telltale chinnnnng-chinnnnng in between. Slugs buzz the empty air where he was standing a split second ago. Sees the second muzzle flash with his left eye. Fires twice that way. Two fireballs shatter the dark again. Hears a heavy grunt and a thump to the ground.

Rolls left again. Scrambles behind a rock, staying low. Drags a shirt sleeve across his right eye. Clears some of the blood. Vision still blurry. Blinks hard, three or four times.

Vision clears. Blood gone. Eveready's blood. The brother who never said no when one of the crew wanted a blowjob or a backdoor ride. Wizard mechanic who kept every motor on the ranch ticking true.

The man craved dick. Who gives a fuck? He was a brother. Blood in. Blood out. The Alice Baker way. A rough benediction.

Listen and wait: Chizik still, with a .44 Magnum in his right hand. Dirty Harry's favorite, a Smith & Wesson Model 29. Four shots left. Go ahead, make my day, motherfuckers.

Gunfire echoes, front and rear. From the ranch and the crew shack. Nothing nearby. No fresh incoming. No rounds trying to write his name. No sounds from the cop he shot. No moans. No motion.

Time to reload. Flip open the revolver's cylinder, shuck the two empty shells, slip in two fresh rounds. Hand howitzer ready for more action.

He could see Eveready's corpse, a blacker lump on the dark, desert ground.

You got something I need, brother. Two somethings. I'll take that full-auto '16 with the two thirty-round mags taped side-by-side. And the new burner in your shirt pocket, fresh from the stack you brought to the crew yesterday to swap out.

Listen and wait: then crouch low and duck walk to the corpse. Eveready on his back, dead eyes wide and surprised, a gaping neck wound already drawing flies. Fish out the burner. Slide the '16 from under the body. Check the mag, the breech and the safety. By feel not sight. Risk the sound. Then get gone.

Jaw muscles tight. Molars grinding. His sweet set up in ruins. No turning back now.

Walk away. Now. Keep walking. Head on a swivel. Dodge the lawdogs. Disappear.

Those stupid motherfuckers. Lazy cocksuckers. He and Jack moved most of the guns and ammo to the new hide, using muscle and forklifts from the well-paid owner to off-load and tie down tarps to cover the stash. Did all this before crossing the river to choke down Valentina Garza's shit. And wipe Jack's blood off his face with a linen napkin.

Jack was dead. Sledge, Axel and Dawg were missing, location unknown. No forwarding address. Might be a hole in the desert. Might be a hellhole Mex jail.

Had a clue on Sledge. Disappeared after being sent to fetch one of Bondurant's sheep for being way too nosy for his health. Big dude with a salt-and-pepper beard and biker's limp. Smelled like a cop.

Maybe. Told Bondurant's gatekeepers he was a truck driver out of Fort Stockton. Slaughter. Ed Slaughter. Checked with one of his coke-whore snitches in DPS. Slaughter had a current commercial driver's license with a Fort Stockton address.

That didn't mean shit, though. Dead easy for the law to gin up a fake ID for one of their own and slip it into the DPS database. Sent a biker associate to the Fort Stockton address. Nobody home when the biker kicked down the door of the deserted doublewide. Dead end.

Next step. The woman Slaughter was boning. Leighanna Burdette. A ranch regular who liked to get frisky when her husband wasn't with her. Sledge had his eye on her before he vanished. Even crept her trailer for a lacy but soiled souvenir before making a pass. She turned him down. Flat. Too bad. She needed a friend with an Alice Baker mark.

Chizik handled this one personally, dragging Eveready along to help bind and gag the big cow and hook up her trailer. They drove out to a dark, deep stretch of the Big Empty and started their special Q&A session.

She didn't know much more than they did. And they had to hurt her bad to get that. Chizik took a moment to admire her big, meaty tits before slicing off the nipples with a straight edge. Eveready rammed a Mag-Lite in and out of her cunt, then started burning her body with a cigarette.

Chizik ended the fun by slitting her throat. Blood gushed and sprayed everywhere. He watched the light go out of her hazel eyes. He was hard as kiln-dried hickory, his cock bulging his jeans.

Eveready sucked him off. Chizik returned the favor. For the last time, turns out. Can't make a dead man cum, no matter what Mick Jagger sings.

Chizik felt his cock twitch at the memory. Down boy. No time for that. Mind back on business and those four missing men. One thing was certain – they kept the others in line. Put some iron in their spines with a boot or two up the ass. Without them, the rest were lame and suspect if he wasn't around, Alice Baker brothers or not.

All these fucks had to do in his absence was cart a few cases of bush bang-bangs and ammo to some small-time buyers. Could have done that with a pickup or panel truck.

Told them to also move about ten keys of coke and a dozen bricks of Mexican brown. Stash it anywhere but the ranch. Ditch the crank, too.

Get it done and the place would be wiped clean. They'd be home free and ready to pose as innocent construction laborers on hand to help Bondurant turn the ranch into a Mecca for disgruntled and hate-fueled Bubbas and Bubbettes.

Dead easy. Too easy for his remaining crew of fuckups. They got the job half done then decided to call it beer-and-bong thirty before loading up the last five or six cases. Almost shit a brick when he saw the tarp and crates and started cussing Dog and Dirty Charlie.

About an hour later, the lawdogs hit the front and back gates, busting through in Humvees and Broncos. Locals and feds.

The guns and drugs his crew didn't move meant maximum federal time for anybody stupid enough to get caught. Disengage and disappear was the smart play. Gunfire told him stupid and dead was the hand being played. By his crew and Bondurant's people.

Kiss these shitheads bye-bye. Brand or no brand, let 'em eat lead. Chizik knew he could still salvage his deal with the Garzas. Knew it in his bones. All he had to do was slip out a back exit only he and Jack knew about.

Duck and dodge. Find that tarp-covered Jeep about a mile inside the brush. Dial up some new A-B foot soldiers. He knew just who to call.

Then find that bitch and snatch the life out of her. *La Güera.* Track her down. Kill her slow. Savor it. Chop off her head and serve it up to Valentina Garza. A dead bitch for a bitch he knew he'd kill. Once he had that Garza money in his hand.

★

Sudden Doggett almost shot the man who saved his life. His sights were centered on the man's chest, his finger ready to squeeze that trigger like a long-lost lover, when his brain registered that his target's arms were raised, one hand holding a lever-action rifle with its barrel pointed toward the sky.

"Put that goddam rifle on the ground! Now! Don't think – do it!"

The man crouched down on one knee, careful to keep the barrel pointed away from Doggett as he gently placed the rifle on the ground, then staggered slightly as he rose, holding both hands high.

Doggett recognized him but couldn't remember his name. Ex-con. Rustled cattle and farm equipment. Did his time then rattled around town making a poor man's dollar doing day work for any ranch that would have him. Pretty fair hand. But strictly a saddle for hire when times were busy. Not to trust and sign on for the long haul.

Hadn't seen him in a while. Wasn't all that surprised to find him at a fucked-up place like this, a sham outfit serving as a front for gunrunners and drug smugglers. Mighty glad he was here considering the old hand just jacked the lever four times to blow a big-bellied redneck out of his socks as he was leveling a shotgun at Doggett's back. Buckshot would have ruined his day and got him dead.

Doggett kept his head on a swivel, his gun hand steady, as he walked up to the old cowboy. Gunfire still popped here and there. But it was mainly mop-up time now that the big firefights had cooled down and the bodies could be counted.

"I know you, but I can't put a name to your face."

"Bohannon, Sheriff. Wiley Bohannon."

"That's right. Mind like a sieve. Getting so I have a hard time rememberin' my own name."

"Wait till you get my age, Sheriff."

"Many thanks for knocking that bandit off my tail, but I'm still gonna have to cuff you and pat you down till we get everything sorted out here."

"It's a tangled damn mess for certain, but I'm in no hurry. Got a Ruger thumb-buster tucked behind my back you'll want to pull. And a folding knife in my right front pocket."

Doggett spotted one of his deputies, Zell Benteen, walking past with a shotgun at the ready. He whistled him over while freeing Bohannon of his Ruger and knife.

"Cuff Mister Bohannon here and take him wherever we're gathering up folks. But hear this clear, Benteen – the man just saved my life so I want him treated proper, not like a scumbag. *Sabe?*"

"Sheriff, you mind if I rolled a smoke? I'm a little jittery and it might calm my nerves. My fixin's are in my right jacket pocket."

"Don't mind at all, Wiley. Deputy, pat the man down and pull out his fixin's before you cuff him."

"You bet, Sheriff."

"Wiley, how'd the hell you wind up here?"

"You mean how come an ex-con like me who should know better ends up in a den of thieves? Simple, Sheriff. Nobody else would sign me on full time. These folks would and all we had to do was put on a show and make it look like this was a workin' ranch. Chuck was good and the bunkhouse was dry. And they pretty much left us alone to cowboy these damn Corrientes long as we minded our own business."

"Didn't you know what was going on here?"

"Hard not to guess, Sheriff. Bondurant kept company with some pretty scary characters. But if you wanted to live and keep cowboyin', you learned to not ask too many questions and look the other way if you saw somethin' you shouldn't."

"Well, I hope it was worth it, Wiley. I truly do 'cause I can't guarantee you won't get the hammer dropped on you by the damn feds. I'll put in a word or two with these folks, though. I owe you that."

"Glad to do it, Sheriff. They hired me and my saddle. Not my guns. I took their money, though, so my hands ain't clean. Deal with the Devil and there's always hell to pay. Got to cowboy the right way for two years, though, so I can't complain. I know how to do time."

"Hope it don't come to that."

Cider Jones winced at the *thunk-thunk-thunk-thunk* of rounds smacking his Humvee as it skidded to a stop just short of a bowl-shaped depression lined with boulders and lesser rocks.

He heard the M-60 hatch gun open up, throwing rounds at muzzle flashes on the other side of the bowl and what looked like two doublewides spliced together end-to-end. The harsh glare of a powerful pole lamp stabbed out the dark, lighting the rim and dirt below, marking a killing ground nobody could cross.

Cider rolled out the passenger side door and hit the ground as more rounds slapped the thin sheet metal of the Humvee, an unarmored Army cast-off. Full-auto incoming. A loud and rapid tattoo.

A scream from the driver's side startled him. He shook it off and scrambled forward on all fours, hugging rock at the rim and keeping his head down as he shrugged an M-14 off his shoulder.

He knew and trusted this rifle. Fired it to qualify as a marksman in the Army reserves years ago, toting its heavy weight on many a weekend warrior march in the Texas heat and cold.

Asked the ATF boys to get him one before this mission. And five extra 20-round mags, each nestled in the foam-lined segment of a pouch riding his left hip. Lesson learned the hard way from that river crossing clusterfuck a few weeks back when a cartel sniper had him in his crosshairs and he didn't have enough gun to shoot his way out of trouble.

Fuck that MP-5. I can reach out and touch these bastards with this. Never catch me bringin' a popgun to a big-bore fight again.

Cider looked along his side of the rim and spotted two more Humvees about 50 yards to his right. Neither had hatch guns. Doors on both were wide open. Dark forms were scattered behind the rocks, hiding from the glare, returning fire from the other side.

He also saw a body sprawled beside the nearest vehicle. One of the good guys down. Not good. Not enough firepower to suppress the bad guys.

Gotta flank these bastards. Gotta kill that goddam light.

From his brainpan to the hatch gunner's reality. Cider watched tracers from the 60 walk up the pole then engulf the lamp, triggering an exploding cascade of sparks right out of a Hollywood classic.

Roy Hobbs swings…Way back…Way back…It's goodbye, Mister Spaulding…

Darkness. A sudden return. Snap the night vision goggles into place. AN/PVS-5s. Old but decent hardware. Battle tested and still used.

Good enough for a grunt in the Persian Gulf, good enough for me.

Rounds splattered against his rocky shield, dust and stony chips the only damage.

To his left, a thud and the rippling sound of fabric sliding across dirt and stones shot his heart into his throat and sent his pulse into the staccato stratosphere of a jack rabbit zanged on Black Beauties. Cider rolled right and swung his rifle toward the threat.

"Easy, brother. Friendly here. Damn, you're jumpy."

All said in a low gravel-growl laced with a slight Mexican sing-song. One of Doggett's deputies. The ex-Ranger who creeped this ranch without a warrant and found the stash of full-auto 16s and ammo that whistled up this raid. This time, with a warrant.

"Scared the shit out of me. Lucky I didn't blow out your candle."

"Yeah, that would've ruined my night. Hey, flip up those goggles and let your eyes get used to the dark again."

"Why would I do that?"

"Because they slow you down unless you train with them a lot and the other side don't got 'em."

"Based on your off-the-books visit nobody's supposed to know about but everybody does."

"Yeah, but the scumbags don't know that. Neither does the judge who gave the warrant for this raid. Not that he'd give a shit if he did. These are bad *hombres* and they need to be taken off the board."

"Where we goin' in such a hurry?"

"Got a little trick I want to pull and need your help. You're the only other guy on our side carrying a .308 besides me. Got a way to slip 'round behind these assholes and hammer 'em. But we both need something with a little more punch and range."

"We flyin' the black flag on this?"

"You bet. They smoked one of ours. ATF guy, I think."

"You picked the right partner, then. That's who I'm workin' for."

The deputy grunted.

"C'mon then."

They were perched behind the rocks above and behind the right end of the barracks, marking positions of the gunrunners by their outbound muzzle flashes, careful to keep their heads low so they didn't get clipped by friendly incoming rounds.

Took them thirty minutes of duck walking and quick dashes to get where they were. Along the way, they passed to the rear of the storage shed with the bulldozer looming in mechanized slumber. The deputy pointed out a tarp-covered rectangular lump and shook his rifle. The full-auto 16s they came to snatch.

While waiting to make their next sprint across open ground, the deputy leaned in and spoke.

"I'm Quintero. Call me Bobby."

"Jones. Call me Cider."

"Story behind that, I bet."

"Tell you when we get back."

"*Un optimista.* I like it."

Cider counted five shooters below them. They were now playing the long game, conserving their ammo with single shots or three-round bursts. No more Mad Minutes of emptying thirty-round mags full auto. They moved between shots, but not far.

Tracers from the other side struck rock, bounced skyward. Or punched through the thin aluminum of the barracks walls.

Bobby leaned in again.

"Let's whack a couple and see what happens."

"Tough to see where to aim."

"They're between you and their gun. When you see a flash, aim a click behind and a click lower. Freehand. Don't dial it in. You don't got time."

"OK."

Bobby disappeared to his left. Cider settled in behind his M-14 and waited. The moon was bright enough to give him a sight picture with the iron peep and front blade. He saw an outbound muzzle flash, front and far right.

Breathe. Exhale. Pause. Blade a click behind. A click lower. Squeeze.

Boom. Grunt. Thud. Clatter against the rocks below.

Duck. Hug the rock.

Slugs spatter against rock. His rock. Sweet rock. Friend forever rock. If-you-could-cook-I'd-marry-you rock. Blink away the muzzle flash blindness.

Two shots. Near left. Bobby. Another grunt. A scream. Two thuds. Three down. Two to go.

More of that deadly snap and buzz. Overhead. Not close. Scattered.

They know we're back here but don't know where. Guessing game. Hide-and-seek. Time to scoot and grab fresh rock.

Sorry, ex-rock-of-mine. Love in a firefight is fickle.

Mop-up and body count. Doggett, sitting in a rocker on Bondurant's porch, doing a mental tally.

Three from Bondurant's flock of sheep, including the one Wiley Bohannon smoked. Four wounded. One circling the drain.

Five bad guys, all sporting Aryan Brotherhood tatts. One wounded. Two banged up but smart enough to surrender. Fingerprints taken from the living and the dead to see if they matched any from that murder trailer. Already found a match to that A-B asshole sitting in his jail, the one Burch buffaloed. And one of the survivors. Needle City for those fucks.

Two lawdogs – an ATF agent named Pierce and one of Doggett's own, Stan Walton, his chief deputy. They found Stan face down in the brush to the side of the trail running toward the back of the ranch with the back of his skull blown out by a hollow point. Found one of the dead bad guys, too.

What the hell, Stan? Why were you way out there?

Doggett felt a sharp twang of guilt. Back at that murder trailer, he had pushed Stan to prove his mettle. Not hard. But enough. In front of two deputies he outranked.

Did it for the worst of reasons. Mad about the woman found tortured and murdered. Mad about Bondurant. Mad at himself for ignoring T for Texas and his Kluxer shitheads for far too long.

Took it out on Stan, an easy target, a brave enough lawman, but not a gunfighter. Put him on the spot. Told him he was coming along to brace Bondurant.

Action: Bring your shotgun. Come heavy and ready to shoot.

Reaction: Stan played the hero, chasing two bad guys all by his lonesome, nailing one, getting killed by the other.

Doggett didn't spare the spiritual lash. He wasn't much of a Catholic, but knew his soul deserved it.

You're a heartless bastard. Got a good man killed by questioning his manhood. Killed trying to prove up to a shitheel like you. His blood's on your hands, asshole. And his death will stalk your dreams.

Doggett dreaded those future night visits. Knew they'd start the moment his head hit the pillow. He also knew he'd feel the full force of that guilt in the daylight hours when he delivered the sorrowful news to Stan's widow and kids.

Just desserts, pendejo. Suck it up. Need to pick up one of those rope whips the Jesuits use. The one with the seven cords bound together with the three knots the end – one for each day the crucified Christ was in the tomb.

A voice broke through his mental mortification. Bobby Quintero. Told him he and some geezer ex-Houston homicide cop seconded to ATF waxed four A-B guys doing an Alamo at their barracks. Wounded a fifth.

"We packed up those 16s and the ammo. Forty-eight full autos. Ready to hand over to ATF."

"No, they go to our crib first. Press conference will be at our place with the guns on display, not some fed hangout. You found those guns, even though we can't say so. This is our case and it ties directly to a murder in our county."

"Got it."

"And Bobby? Nice work out there. Took some real bad people off the board and got these guns out of circulation."

"*Gracias,* Sheriff, but I had help. He got two and I got two. We'll split the guy we just winged."

"Like to meet this ancient warrior who had your back."

"You might like him. He's old school. Carries an M-14. Limps like you but still gets the job done."

"A gamer. An *hombre* with some grit."

"You bet."

Bobby lingered. Doggett knew he was about to drop the second shoe.

"Sheriff, I don't think we got all the guns they had out here. Plenty of space to store a lot more. And I think one or two of these guys got away. They might have another stash somewhere."

"One day at a time, Bobby. Chalk up today's haul as a win. Tomorrow, we start chasing anybody who got away and hunting for that other stash."

Another deputy, Dick Belsky, stepped on the porch and whispered in Doggett's ear. Doggett nodded and pointed to the porch floor.

"Bring some of it right here."

Belsky nodded and left.

Shouting from inside the house. More like a bull's bellow. Righteous anger at full boil. Bondurant. Doggett eased out of the rocker, shook Quintero's hand and stepped through the front door. The volume of the bellowing doubled. Dogget knew a headache was about to drop the hammer.

The sheriff stepped into a large front room Bondurant used as his office. Bondurant was handcuffed to a chair in the center of the room, yelling at Sam Boelcke, the Cuervo County district attorney, DEA Senior Special Agent Donald Spicer, head of the joint task force, and the ATF's task force honcho, Charlie Boudreaux.

A florid-faced man with a bad blond combover, a big belly and a suit that fit him like a teepee sat on a leather couch on the sidelines, a battered briefcase at his feet. Bondurant's lawyer, probably. One of Doggett's deputies, Sheila Quick, stood watch over the room with her butt perched on edge of Bondurant's desk.

T for Texas was in full pulpit roar, preaching that Z.O.G gospel.

"You and your federal friends here have staged another jack-booted raid on law-abiding American citizens with absolutely no cause, violating their rights of peaceful assembly, free speech and bearing arms to protect themselves from an assault on their freedom like this. You have blood on your hands, killing members of my organization who were acting out of fear for their lives from the vicious Gestapo tactics of your thugs…"

"That include the fat bastard in bib overalls who tried to saw me in half with a shotgun, Mister Bondurant? Fella tried to shoot me in the back before one of your cowboys shot him."

"We only have your word on that, Sheriff. And I don't think that counts for much now that you're in league with the oppressors of the Zionist Occupational Government. All of you have the blood of patriots on your hands."

"If there's blood on anybody's hands, it's yours, you pusbag piece of shit. Luring folks here to take their money and fill them up with hatred and the fantasy of a new Texas republic. You wound them up with your preachin' and seven of 'em were dumb enough to grab a gun and throw down on officers of the law. Three of 'em are dead and another soon will be. That's on you."

"If I were you, Sheriff, I'd disassociate myself from these federal henchmen as quickly as possible. You, too, Mister District Attorney. Get ready to lie like hell and call yourself a dumbass dupe of their evil ways. Neither one of you will want to be pilloried for allowing another Waco or Ruby Ridge to happen here in Cuervo County."

"Looking forward to being in the national spotlight, Bondurant? Sure you can stand the heat?"

"I am indeed looking forward to telling the truth about this assault on American freedoms and the blood of patriots you spilled here today. I look forward to standing in the docket with Gerry Spence as my attorney. I look forward to being on *Nightline* with him, getting interviewed by Ted Koppel. With Gerry Spence by my side, I can stand any heat you want to throw my way."

Doggett started to respond. Boelcke held up his hand to check him.

"I'm touched by your concern about my future and that of Sheriff Doggett, Mister Bondurant. And I'm pleased to see you're already preparing for your day in court by thinking about hiring Gerry Spence. He's a legend and I'll really have to step up my game to battle with him."

"Gerry Spence will fillet you like a channel cat and deep fry you right in the middle of the courtroom. You'll wonder why you ever thought you could be a lawyer after he gets through with you."

"Maybe so. He's mighty stout. But I'm wondering whether Mister Spence will want to sully himself with your case once he learns you're charged with having nearly 50 fully automatic weapons on your ranch without the proper permits. And I wonder what he'll say about you harboring fugitives and violent criminals here?"

"We don't harbor fugitives and criminals here. We give a second chance to people who have already paid their debt to society. We give them the opportunity to change their lives and learn an honest trade like carpentry or operating heavy construction equipment."

"What about those automatic weapons?"

"I don't know anything about that. If I had, I would have reported it to the proper authorities and turned the weapons in."

"I don't think your partners would have liked that."

"What partners? I have employees and contractors I've hired. That's it. What do you mean by partners?"

"Those gun thugs who were so anxious about keeping us from seizing those weapons. The ones who killed an ATF agent and one of Sheriff Doggett's deputies."

"That's regrettable, but you can't blame me for their deaths. You're the ones who stormed in here like the U.N. Gestapo. And I know nothing about those weapons you mention. It sounds to me like men I gave a second chance succumbed to the temptation of easy money to run guns behind my back."

Doggett heard the heavy thunk of boots on the porch. He leaned his head into the hallway and whistled.

"Bring it in here, boys."

Belsky entered the office, shouldering a heavy bag that might have been feed or maybe cement. He was followed by a DEA agent carrying two double-wrapped bricks with more readily identifiable contents. The bricks had a black scorpion stamped on top of the brown paper of the inner wrapper, visible through the clear outer layer of Saran wrap.

"Take a load off, Dick, and drop that bag to the floor. Looks to be a heavy sumbitch. Mister DEA man – kindly place those bricks on the desk."

"What's the meaning of this dog-and-pony show?"

"It's not just guns we're talking about. A little birdie told us about a hidey hole you got underneath your barn where there might be some contraband. Gave us a reason to expand the warrant a bit. Took us a while to find our way in but man, was it worth it. Got a bunch of ammonium nitrate and diesel fuel down there."

Doggett kicked the heavy load Belsky had carried and dumped.

"In bags just like this. Enough to blow up the county court-house two or three times over. Or another federal building like Oklahoma City."

"This is a ranch, Sheriff. We use fertilizer in our pastures and diesel fuel in our tractors and construction equipment."

"Must be gold-plated stuff to keep it hidden away like that. And I ain't quite finished. We also found about a hundred kilos of cocaine. That's major felony weight – way above the threshold for trafficking. What's that mean, Mister District Attorney?"

"It means Mister Bondurant is looking at serious prison time for trafficking in guns that are no doubt stolen from a federal arse-nal and for trafficking in cocaine. We also found crystal meth and heroin. As for the fertilizer and diesel fuel – while they're not illegal in and of themselves, the amount you have on hand is well above the needs of a ranch of this size. And we've found timers, wiring and other material that can be used to trigger an explosive device."

Doggett stepped up and stared into Bondurant's eyes. "You're fucked, *pendejo.*"

The after-action briefing was anything but formal – just a group of lawdogs standing in the barnyard, drinking cowboy coffee brewed up on a Coleman camp stove set up on the tailgate of Doggett's Bronco. A bottle of Old Crow made the rounds as a sweetener. The federal boys waved it off. Still haunted by the ghosts of Prohibition.

Dub McKee, the retired Ranger and emissary from the governor's office, kicked it off after taking a pull of bad bourbon directly from the bottle. Doggett called him to Cuervo County while they were waiting on the warrants for the raid, looking for some Texas political muscle to keep those federal teetotalers in check.

McKee was a tall, beefy man with a long, florid face, hazel eyes that could pierce a killer's heart and a gravelly, parade-ground voice that never needed a bullhorn. Wearing a dark gray Stetson with a come-and-go dip to the gently curled brim, a midnight blue windbreaker and a pearl-handled 1911 on his right hip, he still had the commanding presence of the Ranger he was for more than thirty-five years.

"Sorry about your man, Sheriff. Yours too, Charlie. When a peace officer gets killed, we all feel the loss, no matter what our badges say. State, federal or local don't matter worth a shit when one of us bites the dirt."

Nods, hard stares and bowed heads all around. No matter how big an asshole you were, turf didn't count at a time like this. That and the finger-pointing would raise their ugly heads again soon enough. In about five minutes, more than likely.

"Okay, now. We know Bondurant is gonna start baying about Ruby Ridge and Waco as soon as he makes bail, ranting about jack-booted thugs and black U.N. helicopters. The governor needs every one of you sumbitches to go over the evidence and your actions to make sure we met every letter of that goddam warrant. Work with Mister Boelcke and a guy from the state A.G.'s office named Augie Bryant, who should be here soon. I'm assuming you federal boys already have somebody on the way."

Nods from DEA Senior Special Agent Donald Spicer, the head honcho of the joint task force, and the ATF lead, Charlie Boudreaux.

"Next item. When the shitstorm breaks, the governor wants Sheriff Doggett out front. He's already called Lloyd Bentsen and John Tower to wire it up with the president and Attorney General Reno."

Spicer glared at McKee.

"The joint task force I run was specifically formed to stamp out gun-running and drug smuggling along this stretch of the border. We've done exactly that by raiding this ranch. Asking us to take a back seat to the sheriff here is a bit much to swallow."

"I don't want to hear it, Donnie. You'll chew and choke on it. And you'll damn well like it. You *federales* still got the skunk smell on you from Waco and Ruby Ridge. Guilt by association with the Fibbies. Believe y'all could stand a spell of being out of the spotlight."

Spicer's face turned deep red.

"Besides, your boys didn't come up with the intel on this little jackpot. Sheriff Doggett's man did. We've got his little extracurricular reconnaissance properly papered over to make it all right, tight and legal, don't we Sheriff?"

Doggett nodded and pointed at Boelcke, who patted his briefcase.

"Good. Another thing, Donnie Boy. The tip on the fertilizer and blow came from that old cowhand who kept our good sheriff here from getting blown away today, not from any of your or Charlie's snitches, right?"

Doggett nodded, then ducked his head to smile at the way McKee kept sticking it up Spicer's ass. Spicer kept glaring at the old

Ranger. McKee returned the stare, smiled and made a point of peeling back his windbreaker to let Spicer see the Ranger badge pinned to his snap-buttoned white shirt.

"That's right, Don. This badge being back on my chest tells you I ain't some retired civilian you can jack around and ignore. And Reno's office is sending down some legal mumbo-jumbo to put me in charge of making sure this shitshow gets cleaned up nice and tidy. Already got the governor's blessing. In writing."

Spicer's face turned scarlet and his eyes bulged out. Doggett half expected the man's head to take an Exorcist spin while he started growling or speaking in tongues. Didn't happen. Spicer turned on his heel and stomped away, raising small clouds of dust that trailed his exit.

McKee gave the knife one more twist.

"Don't worry about your task force getting credit, Don. You'll be right there at the press conference when Sheriff Doggett gives you and Charlie lavish praise for providing much-needed support to take down this snake den of gunrunners and drug traffickers hiding behind the American flag and all this Christian patriot and Z.O.G. shit."

McKee smiled at the men still in the barnyard circle. Quintero and Jones walked up, their long guns shouldered, standing a few paces behind the others. Their desert BDUs were filthy and torn. Sweat-stained dust streaked the black face paint they sported for night work, making them look like Cheyenne Dog Soldiers.

"Well, boys, lancing a boil like that is always painful and unpleasant. Always necessary, too. Charlie, you got any problem with what I've said?"

"You know I don't, Dub."

"Well, that's because you've got sense, Charlie. Always have been one of us more than one of them."

"Afraid you might not have drained all the pus out of that boil, Dub. Spicer ain't through, yet. He's going back to work the phones to get your head stuck up on a pike."

231

"That's what he *thinks* he's gonna do, Charlie. He'll pick up that phone alright. But he's about to find out he no longer runs this task force and is getting called back to the home office to explain why some sheriff out here in the mesquite thickets of West Texas found a stash of cocaine, meth and heroin he didn't. He'll get to study on that question for a spell while wondering whether it would be better for him to go ahead and retire."

"Damn, Dub. You play for keeps."

"You know me, Charlie. Best study on what's about to happen to Senior Special Agent Spicer of the DEA as a cautionary tale. This is your task force now. Unless I say it ain't. And I suggest you make Special Agent Jones, who's been kind enough to join us, as your deputy and liaison to me. That work for the both of you?"

Jones was glad his face was masked and hid his surprise. Battlefield promotion he didn't expect. Charlie Boudreaux shot him a look and a smirk.

"I'd be dee-lighted to make Cider Jones my deputy, Dub. He's the only one of my crew who's done any sho'nuff lawman work. The rest are just trigger pullers and dumbass muscle."

The circle was smaller an hour later. Just McKee, Doggett, Boudreaux and Jones. A fresh pot was brewing but the Old Crow was long gone. Chaws and coffin nails for dessert. No glazed donuts.

"What's next?"

"The man who murdered my chief deputy, Dub. Goes by the name Delbert Lucius McCoy from Lubbock. That's the name on Bondurant's employee roster. Phony as a three-dollar bill. We beat his real name out of one of those A-B boys who didn't get dead. Says we're looking for an ex-con named Cleve Chizik. Headed up the gun-running and drug smuggling going in and out of this ranch. Already wanted for a similar operation run from a ranch about forty miles from here."

"Mighty bold move to set up shop again in the same county, Sheriff."

"Bondurant gave him top cover, Dub. We think he might have had some other help. Somebody inside my office. One of Blue Willingham's holdovers. We're running that down now that we have our hands on Bondurant's files."

Charlie Boudreaux shook his head.

"Surprised that Alice Baker fuck talked no matter how bad you beat on him. Thought the Brotherhood believed in the skinhead version of *omertà*."

"Hell, Charlie – not even the wops believe in that shit anymore. Dagos rat each other out in a heartbeat if they get in a tight."

The circle got quiet. Averted eyes. Sudden interest in a boot toe stirring dust.

"What? You fellas look like church ladies after somebody farted during prayer meeting."

A nervous chuckle from Charlie.

"Since when did you get so sensitive, Charlie? Can't let you boys have all the fun with the Kluxer talk. Hate me some greaseball wiseguys and like to call a spade a spade. Unless he's a wetback."

Guffaws all around. McKee started laughing so hard his face turned beet red. Then he started coughing like a man who had swallowed his chaw. Boudreaux pounded the Ranger's back. Sure enough, he hacked up a stringy wet ball of yarn the size of a tangerine.

"Dammit to hell, Sheriff – you done got me with that."

Doggett grinned and formed a pistol with the fingers of his right hand. Dropped his thumb like a hammer while sighting down the fingers at McKee.

"Bang. Bang."

Raised his fingers to his lips and blew away the imaginary gun smoke.

"I'm done pulling y'all's leg. One more thing about that blabbermouth A-B fucker. We found this little piggy's prints in a trailer where a woman got cut up, sodomized and murdered. Facing a Big Needle bounce clarifies a man's mind. Even a mind rattled by a leather sap."

Charlie laughed then strolled over to check on the coffee pot. Wrapped a bandana around the pot handle to pour for the others before filling his own cup.

"Careful, boys. This coffee's damn hot. And strong enough to outkick a mule."

"Only way we like it, Charlie."

"Back to Chizik, Sheriff. What are we doing about him?"

"Bobby Quintero thinks he knows the path Chizik took to get away, Dub. He's found a side trail and is cutting for sign right now. Back side of the ranch. He thinks the trail will lead him about a mile west of the back gate."

"Damn fine. We need to get on the tail of that sumbitch right quick because we figure he's got another big load of guns hidden somewhere that he needs to sell for getaway cash, right?"

Nods all around.

"What's next on our honey-do list?"

Cider Jones spoke for the first time.

"We know we got another outfit getting ready to sell weapons to some Ojinaga *narcos* looking to start a war with the Garza gang just over the river from here. The Garzas are rebuilding their organization and reclaiming turf lost after Malo Garza got blown up by a car bomb in Monterrey a few years back. The Ojinaga crew wants to knock 'em out before they get much stronger."

"What do we know about these gunrunners, Agent Jones?"

"My snitch tells me they got a mixed bag of weapons to sell, Ranger McKee. Full-auto M-16s, bloopers, mortars and LAWs rockets. And all the ammo needed to keep those bang-bangs well fed. The outfit is led by a flashy blonde known as *La Güera*, who's hooked up with the Ruiz family, a bunch of badass freelancers with *indio* blood who do wet work for cartels up and down the border. "

"You're kindly obsessed with this *La Güera* gal, Agent Jones."

"Not only yes, but hell, yes. Ever since she and her crew almost killed me by T-boning a flatbed into my rig a few weeks back. I'd surely like to nail her hide to the wall in my office."

"He's not the only one, Dub. *La Güera* was the girlfriend of a murdered gunrunner named Tommy Juan Jaeckel. I popped him for selling stolen guns and he drew a six-year sentence. Got out way early by ratting Chizik to Charley's folks, which wrecked the sweet set up the A-B had at that other ranch. Then Tommy Juan started selling guns to Chizik's customers, with *La Güera* as the front who turned their heads and got them to cough up the cash."

"Jesus, that was bold and stupid at the same time, Sheriff."

"Not a move you'd make if you wanted to live long. Tommy Juan's body was found out in the boonies one county over, stuffed in a big barbecue smoker with his head, arms and legs chopped off and his cock stuffed in his mouth. We figure Chizik and his crew caught up with him and did the cutting and chopping before firing up that smoker. Might have had help from folks said to be his biggest customer, the Garzas."

"Damn. We got a line on this *La Güera*?"

Cider jumped in.

"We do. My snitch gave me the time and place. Three nights from now. West side of the Hulett ranch."

"Sweet Jesus, Jones – when were you gonna tell us this?"

"I'm telling you now, Sheriff. Been a little busy with this goat ropin', though."

"Easy, fellas. Plenty of time to regroup and do what we need to do. The way I see it, we're runnin' down two forks of the same trail. One for *La Güera*. The other for Chizik. Charlie, we need more manpower. See how much you can rustle up. I'll do the same. We better get crackin'."

235

Sudden Doggett held up his hand.

"One more thing. I've got an undercover man with *La Güera's* crew. Can't reach him so I don't know whether he's alive or dead. But if he's still kickin', he'll be next to *La Güera*. Promised the girl's grandmother he'd bring her home to see her one last time."

"Who is this *hombre*, Sheriff?"

"You know him well, Dub. Ed Earl Burch, that ex-homicide cop out of Dallas."

"You finally hired that sumbitch like I told you to?"

"Yeah, but you know I was reluctant. Man has his particular charms and skills, though. Thought it best to bring him back into the law enforcement tent rather than having him out there rambling around like a wrecking ball."

Cider was stunned, unsure whether he heard the name of a man he loathed. It took him a minute to play back the tape in his brainpan and a minute more to speak up.

"I got a big problem with havin' Ed Earl Burch on this case. He was a bent cop in Dallas and got my partner killed in the Hill Country. Everywhere he goes, people get dead. More often than not, smoked by bullets from that 1911 he carries. He's crooked as they come and a loose cannon to boot."

"The way I hear tell, he saved your shot to shit ass during that same fracas. And it was some crazy spade hit man who did the shooting, not Burch."

"May not have had his finger on the trigger, Ranger McKee, but he was the one who put everything in play that got my partner killed and left me with a shoulder that's able to forecast the weather."

McKee frowned then locked his eyes on Cider.

"I'm going to tell you this once, Agent Jones. The man's done the Lord's work in this county. Help us get rid of a real snake-in-the-grass crook and traitor to the badge. That would be Sheriff Doggett's predecessor, Blue Willingham.

"Burch don't care much for the rule book, but he damn sure gets things done. And his heart's always been in the right place. You best get used to him being a part of this deal and a man who'll be wearing a badge again, workin' for Sheriff Doggett. If he don't get killed first."

Doggett delivered the benediction.

"I hired the man, Cider. And I have a very high regard for the guts and savvy he brings to my table. Swallow your pride and hate or go home."

Twenty-One

One of the skills stolen by old age and battered knees was a street cop's staple – the ability to stand in one place for hours on a stakeout, in the heat or the cold, dark thirty or high noon.

Could be just inside the recessed doorway of a darkened store-front, with the backsplash of icy rain soaking your boots and jeans. Or swallowed by the breathless heat under the only hunk of shade in the withered West Texas outback.

Didn't matter. Had to stand still, rock solid, keeping your eye-balls on a place or a target. Taking it all in, brain automatically recording the comings and goings. You might shift your feet or weight to stave off the stiffness and fatigue.

But that was it. No stomping your feet to restore circulation. No rocking backwards and forwards. No overt motion that might give you away. Stand still and take it. Hit the record button on your brain. Watch and wait. Eat the pain.

Back when he wore a badge, Burch could do this for hours – behind a camera mounted on a tripod in some fetid apartment, in a doorway in the dark just down the street from a suspect's house, peering around the shadowy corner of an office building with the parking lot asphalt still blasting the day's heat into his face and lungs.

In his thirties, he could tough it out even though both his knees sported zipper scars from the surgeon's knife, jagged and ugly part-ing gifts from the gridiron. *Bring it on. I'm a young man still in my prime. I'm one of Dallas' finest, strong and tough. Leave me out here forever. I don't give a shit. I can hack it.*

In his fifties, the closest he got to prime was the dark blue ink of a USDA inspection stamp on a thick ribeye just before it hit the flame at the Hoffbrau. Six arthroscopic surgeries on top of the old tendon and ligament repairs sucked up torn cartilage and shaved bone spurs, leaving his knees with no natural cushion.

Bone on bone. No more standing stakeouts for hours on end. He carried a fold-up canvas camp stool on any outing that might force him to post up outside his car, its metal legs wrapped in tape to muffle any metallic giveaways.

No more jogging, either, which used to be his favorite way to shed the pounds and offset the bourbon and Luckies. No fuss. Just throw on some shorts, a raggedy-ass T-shirt and jogging shoes and hit the street. For five miles. Maybe more. Usually less. Turn off the brain and move.

Now he had to haul his ass down to the Y on Akard to pedal a stationary cycle to nowhere, climb imaginary steps on the Stairmaster, glide the rivers of his memory on the rowing machine and bang through leg curls, leg extensions and leg presses on the torture machines that promised to strengthen the muscles around his knees so he could walk without a cane. Just a slight limp a physical therapist told him he hid very well.

He also hit the heavy bag, slipping on the gloves and bashing through five rounds of combos – crosses, jabs, uppercuts, hooks, straight punches. Three minutes a round. Ignored the rope. Did the crunches and pushups. Boxed a bit in the Army. Wasn't worth a shit, but he liked the discipline. Kept him sharp.

The bag led him to Rocky Alvarado, a retired Marine gunnery sergeant who taught Y youngsters the basics of boxing and tutored oldsters on the street skills of close combat. Trained a few cops, too, but Burch shied away from those classes and stuck with the oldsters. After a month of getting knocked around by the gunny and geezers ten or fifteen years older, Alvarado took him aside for some one-on-one coaching.

"You're a big guy with two lights-out punches – a left hook and a straight right. You're light on your feet, but that ain't sayin' much 'cause you only got a quick first step. That's why you get clobbered when you get aggressive – you ain't got the legs to dance out of harm's way.

You CAN take a punch, which is a good thing because you're gonna get tagged. So best bet is to either come out of nowhere and put 'em down or let them come to you, take a punch or three, let them get overconfident and nail 'em."

"I need an edge."

"Other than a gun or knife?"

"Right."

"Ever use a sap or blackjack?"

"A time or three. Used to carry one when I rolled in a squad car. Still got it."

"I'm not talking about one of those big, spring-loaded jobs that stick out of your back pocket like a baseball bat. Talkin' about something smaller, easier to conceal. I know a guy up in Denton. Fix you right up."

The gunny's buddy was a 300-pound bruiser named Maxwell – no first name or initials – with shoulder-length white hair, a dandy walrus moustache and a blurry USMC tatt on top of his right forearm. He made the six-inch blackjack Burch carried in his boot and the coin sap that carried about five dollars in quarters.

Alvarado taught him some new tricks to use with both, including the sleight of hand with the coin sap he used on Carlos. Added a little extra to his money shots – left hook, straight right. Worked out righteous on a cocky *tejano* who mistook him for a washed-up rent-a-cop. Which was only a few towns over from the truth.

But Burch knew he couldn't count on everybody underestimating him. He knew he needed something to make up for the merciless erosion of strength and skill driven by the clock that never stopped. Until it did.

Cheat, Sport Model. Cheat, cheat, cheat then cheat some more.

Don't listen to that jarhead about takin' a few shots then knockin' 'em down. That's way too much of a fair fight for an ol' dude like you.

If you can't just shoot 'em right away, sap their brains into next Friday. Don't go toe to toe. Sneak up on their blindside and coldcock the sumbitches.

His dead partner was right. Cheat. With whatever was handy. A lead pipe. A sap. A gun. A baseball bat. Brass knuckles. A rock. He didn't wear a badge and was no longer bound by the law. Do them before they did you. Or just as soon as you could.

After all, Wynn. I'm a wily, crafty veteran.

Now you're talkin', Sport Model. Old age and treachery beats youth and talent seven times out of ten.

What happens the other three times?

You get dead.

Marvelous the thoughts that rumbled through your brain when you were headed to a jackpot where all your chips might get cashed. You couldn't just pass off the buzzing and snarling in your skull as pre-game jitters. You could get your game face on to deal with that.

This here was a whole other level of bad juju. Driving toward men who were armed to the teeth and would just as soon shoot you dead if they didn't like your looks. And give it no mind. Like taking a piss or lighting a cigarette. Boom. You're dead. Fellas, let's go get a cup of coffee.

Either you could screw the lid down tight on your fear and sack up to stay frosty or you couldn't. Behind Door Number Two, fear blew out your circuits like grabbing a 220-volt live line. You ran. If you could. Dead meat if you couldn't.

For all those years as a beat cop and a homicide detective, frosty was Burch's middle name. He could hold his mud, as his old football coach, Branson T. "Buzz" Lyle, loved to say. Tighten up, sack up, gear up and meet the bad guys. Make their livers quiver. Burch, tough, bold and relentless, always answered the bell.

But in those wilderness years after he lost his gold shield, Burch felt hollowed out and aimless. No core. No center. No soul. A man without purpose.

When he first hung out his shamus shingle, he stuck to easy work. Running down deadbeats who owed money to his lawyer, Fat Willie Nofzinger. Chasing runaway wives and teenagers. Bail skips. Occasionally stooping to do divorce work, which made him feel as slimy and battered as a ten-dollar whore after pulling the train for a biker gang.

He found a safe and lucrative niche – chasing financial fugitives from the oil and savings and loan busts that flattened Texas in the mid-1980s.

There was no ringing bell to answer. And Burch wanted to keep it that way. His Justins wore a rut between his brownstone apartment on Marquita Street, a converted barber shop off Mockingbird that served as his office and Louie's, where most nights he hung a boot heel on the footrail and knocked back Maker's Mark with ice-water backs.

Then he met Carla Sue Cantrell, a petite blonde who double-crossed gangsters and *narcos* for a living. She introduced herself by firing a single fat round from a Colt 1911 that barely missed the top of his bald head before smacking into the wall behind him, showering sheetrock on his *huevos rancheros con salsa verde* and refried beans.

Pissed his pants in reply. Stuffed a bandana down his Wranglers to soak up the wet.

Dragged him across Texas and into Mexico on a run where they were both hunters and the hunted. Gunning for a crazy *narco* named Teddy Roy Bonafacio, a wiry killer who was half-Mexican and half oil field white trash and thought he was an Aztec Jaguar Knight. Believed in heart sacrifice.

T-Roy killed his partner and order up a hit on Carla Sue's uncle. Code of the Thin Blue Line and Code of the Hills called for them to get T-Roy dead by any means necessary. Burch and Carla Sue were also fugitives, pursued by a Houston homicide cop named Cider Jones who still blamed him for the death of his partner.

Didn't matter that they saved his sorry ass from bleeding out in front of the world's sixth largest bat cave near Mason, Texas. Jones still wanted Burch dead. Or buried under the nearest prison.

Their relentless pursuit felt like something straight from the brainpan of Herman Melville. Except the object of their murderous obsession wasn't a white whale – it was a raving psychopath with bushy, flame-red hair who trafficked in the hellish rituals of an ancient *bruja* who blended the beliefs and blood sacrifice of both voodoo and the Aztecs.

Madness followed the moment Carla Sue smoked T-Roy with .45 ACP hollow-points, coring out one eye, leaving the other to stare with the unblinking remorselessness of a shark after his head *thunked* on altar stone inches from Burch's face. Even dead, that eye still wanted to kill.

Nightmares of being trussed naked to that altar, eyes bulging in terror as a giant winged serpent descended from the overhead gloom, tongue flicking to taste Burch's fear. Visions of T-Roy, rising above him like a zombie, holding a bone-handled knife high above his head.

Brains and gore dripping on Burch from a blasted eye socket while that single shark eye stared. No rescue from Carla Sue. A cruel laugh and a kiss-off instead. T-Roy plunging a glistening blade in his chest again and again to carve out his heart.

His own screams ripping him from the horror, fumbling for bourbon and Percodan to throttle back his hammering heart and slam those demons into their holes. Gobble those pills and bubble that bottle until his stomach burned.

The terror could smack him at any time, day or night, favoring the small, quiet hours after midnight or before the sun was fully above the horizon. Night sweats, dawn shakes and vertigo. White knuckles gripping the armrest of an easy chair.

Whiskey and pills were his salvation, a pharmaceutical sacrament chased with ninety proof that granted him a numb and chilly grace to get through the working hours.

And with that grace emerged a strange and shaky dichotomy. When he was focused on a case, all his skills and savvy as a cop were right there, at his fingertips. And the demons stayed in their holes. For hours at a time. Until the work was done. And it got real quiet.

He learned self-medication in moderation. Half a Percodan. Four fingers of Maker's. Repeat as necessary. That staved off the dawn torment and stretched the hours when he could be a walking, talking and semi-righteous shamus.

Carnal healing helped. Of all the woman still interested in sharing his bed, only one had that kind of touch – Carol Ann Gunther, a county clerk administrator and fellow Louie's regular. She'd drop by and help him fuck those demons into oblivion. On those nights, they left him alone. And he slept like a dead man.

His comeback was slow but steady, paced by the drink and the dose. Hours turned into days and days turned into weeks. He picked up more cases and started raking in the dough, chasing those financial fugitives he knew how to hunt so well.

He started living again, feeling like a shamus. Far short of being a murder cop, but still useful. Until Fat Willie roped him into a Cuervo County divorce case by promising to forgive the note on his business.

Finding dirt on a rich bitch's wayward husband dropped him into a murder case Doggett's predecessor, the utterly bent Blue Willingham, didn't want to touch – the killing of rancher and community pillar Bart Hulett.

Hired by Hulett's outlaw cousin, Gyp, Burch was a manhunter again. And it almost got him killed. In West Texas. Again. But he cracked the case, blew away some bad guys that needed to get dead, hammered a nail or three in Willingham's coffin and savored the satisfaction he thought he'd never feel again.

It gave him back his sense of honor and the pride of serving something bigger than himself. Only an asshole would call it justice.

Weaned himself from the pills but kept the Maker's. Started dating Carol Ann like a proper main squeeze. Until he fucked that up when a much younger Louie's waitress sideswiped him around closing time for naked sport.

Still felt like a cop again. With Doggett dangling a gold shield in front of him. But this was the first time he was going up against the baddest of the bad while clean and somewhat sober.

With a clear head and too much time to think. Too many minutes to wonder whether this would be that time he'd reach for that cold, inner killer and come up empty handed.

"This is where doubt stops being your friend and starts being an enemy, Sport Model."

"Now you tell me."

"Two sides to every coin. You're lookin' at the flip side right now and doubting your ownsef. That's fatal."

"Had too much time to think."

"Don't think, Sport Model. It hurts the ballclub. Which is only you. Just be."

"Now you're going all Caddyshack on me, Wynn. You tellin' me to be the ball? That all you got for wisdom?"

"If you study on something other than doubt, you'll see you still got it. You blew away that asshole who tried to turn your head into a canoe. You coldcocked the prick who bushwhacked you at that ranch."

"Didn't have time to think about that. Just reacted."

"Tells you what you need to know. And all you need to know. You still got it."

"And if I don't?"

"You get dead. But you won't give a shit. Dead people never do. I didn't."

"You in heaven or you in hell, Wynn?"

"*Kindly hard to tell, Sport Model. Place I'm at is cool, semi-dark and indoors. Like a regulars' bar that ain't too crowded. Bartender looks like Joe Frazier. Doesn't talk much and pours heavy. Got a pool table in back.*"

"*Sounds damn near idyllic.*"

"*It's not half bad. Suck it up, Sport Model. Stay frosty.*"

Armando Ruiz strolled up as he was tucking the blackjack into his boot.

"*¿Listo para ir, hombre?*"

"You bet I'm ready. Let's go."

Cold and steady. Like he needed to be. Right now.

Twenty-Two

Chizik crouched in the jagged rocks near the bottom of a saw-toothed ridge as six dark shapes lumbered into the darkness below. He was flanked by nine Garza *sicarios* and the only other member of his crew who slipped out of Bondurant's ranch – a short, swarthy A-B lifer named Quint.

He watched the trucks through a borrowed night scope and smiled as they neared a semi-circle of night-black Tahoes and tricked-out pickups with fat, off-road tires and jacked up chassis – the Ojinaga crew, hungry to pay up and grab the weapons in those trucks.

Too hungry. And that made them sloppy. No security thrown out to guard their flanks. Stupid, too. Light bars from a few pickups were switched on, casting a glare toward the approaching trucks.

The newcomers were *La Güera's* crew. Not quite as sloppy. They stopped well short of the light. Kept their headlamps dark. Also posted two shooters on each side of their trucks. But those men stayed close and were easy to see. More worried about the Ojinaga boys than any unseen danger lurking in the dark.

Chizik flashed a hand signal to the Garza *jefe*. The *sicarios*, clad in black and wearing face masks, crept down from the rocky perch to get kill-zone close. He knew ten other Garza trigger-pullers were creeping in from the opposite side of the trail that ran through flat, rocky ground between his vantage point and another ridge to the west.

He swept the night scope across the line of trucks and picked up two Jeeps in back. His lips curled into a mirthless grin as he spotted a flash of white climbing out of the first Jeep. *La Güera.* She was flanked by two big men, then joined by four others from the second Jeep before moving toward the front of the trucks.

He tapped Quint on the shoulder and they slipped through the rocks and crept toward the trail. Chizik's eyes stayed on *La Güera,* whose blonde locks marked her in the darkness.

Fuckin' bitch. Gonna take my time and carve you up.

Burch kept his head on a swivel as he slowly walked along the edge of the trail toward the lit no-man's-land, his body between the bobbing blonde wig in his peripheral vision and the darkness to his left. This forced him to carry the Winchester Model 12 pump like a right-handed shooter. Tricky for a natural lefty, but a skill he still had.

He swept the rifled barrel of the twelve-gauge in sync with his head and eyes, a deer slug in the chamber, safety off, index finger just above the trigger guard, ready to throw the gun up to his right shoulder and blast the first muzzle flash from the darkness. He was sweating like a pig under a Kevlar vest.

Armando was walking point ten yards ahead, carrying a CAR-15, the short barrel dividing the invisible angle between the Ojinaga crew just ahead and the deep black on his left. His cousins manned the trucks to their right, standing on running boards or leaning out of cabs, armed with M-4s, M-16s and the occasional FN FAL with the collapsible stock.

The four who climbed out of the last Jeep walked together another ten yards behind Burch, loosely grouped around their shortest member, who wore a ratty Texas Longhorns baseball cap with a chewed up bill.

Burch passed one of Armando's men standing guard a few yards to the left of the trail. The sentry faced the darkness, but Burch could tell the man was keeping one eye on the Ojinaga crew.

Not ideal. Wished they had sent a few more men deeper into the dark. Too late now. Play the cards dealt.

A young man's voice from under the false blonde locks.

"*Esta maldita peluca es como papel de lija. Es rascarme el infierno del cuero cabelludo.*"

"Shut the fuck up, *pendejo*. And keep looking pretty."

"*Coño!* You got me dressed up like *un manfloro.*"

"More like a *travesaño*. We gave you falsies. Big deal. You still got your dick. You're also wearing body armor. Not too many trannies wandering around with a bulletproof vest. Now, shut the fuck up and twitch that ass. Work it like *La Güera.*"

Next up – a string of Spanish profanity, muffled by the blonde wig. Bartolo Contreras, a thin, light-skinned Ruiz cousin barely out of his teens. They outfitted him as a *La Güera* decoy but he sounded like he was starting to lose it.

Then Burch noticed him straighten up and start swinging his hips again. Natural, not exaggerated. The boy loved *La Güera* and would do anything for her. Even take a bullet. *Hang tough for fifteen more minutes, kid. Hope you don't get dead.*

Straight ahead, *El Duque* stood at the center of six of his men fanned out in a gentle curve a few yards inside the edge of the light. Gentle, but deadly. Only *El Duque* was empty handed, clenching a long, thin cigar between his teeth. But even he had a matte chrome semi-automatic stuffed down the front of his pants. His honor guard held full-auto hands, a hodge-podge of MP5s and AKs, even an ancient M3 grease gun, with the barrels pointed down.

A showy courtesy. *El Duque* was nothing if not polite and a believer in the niceties of Mexican business rituals. Behind their *patrón* and his honor guard, though, the rest of El Duque's men kept their guns pointed at Armando, Burch and the cousins in the trucks. The cousins mirrored this deadly pose.

Armando stopped about twenty feet in front of El Duque. Burch kept himself and Blondie about five yards further back. The others fanned out in front of the first truck. *El Duque* spread his arms wide in greeting.

"*Buenas noches,* my friends. I'm so pleased to see you again and honored that the lovely *La Güera* is here to ensure everything is done to our mutual satisfaction. We've waited a long time for this night. Now that it's finally arrived, let us do our duty diligently but with some degree of urgency so we can all travel swiftly to places of safety and comfort."

Armando managed a short bow and sweep of his left arm. The pistol grip of the CAR-15 was in his right hand, its barrel pressed against his leg like an officer's sword. His words had a gravelly flourish that surprised Burch.

"*Es realmente un honor hacer negocios con un hombre íntegro, un hombre de palabra. Esperamos que el negocio que hacemos aquí esta noche sea el primero de una asociación larga y rentable.*"

El Duque stared at Armando, puffed on his cigar then threw his head back and laughed toward the stars.

"*Qué maravilloso. Hablado como un verdadero caballero.* We've long known Armando Ruiz for his fierce courage and his formidable fighting skills. Who knew he could be so eloquent?"

"My words are those of a beggar compared to *El Duque* or *La Güera,* but she's asked me to speak because an illness has left her throat raw and painful. She can only whisper but wanted to be present for this important moment."

"It pains me to hear this. She is a brave woman, *La Güera,* truly living up to her famous name as well as the love she has for her Tommy Juan and her desire to see his death avenged."

El Duque bowed deeply toward the *La Güera* decoy. Burch growled at Contreras.

"Smile at that bastard, put your hand over your heart and bow your head."

"He's not my type."

★

"*Bravo One to Six...Deal is going down. Got Blondie looking at money. Got buyers moving to the trucks to check out the goods...*"

"Six to One...Roger that. Everybody hold. We wait until Bravo One tells us the buyers are done with their looksee and take over the trucks. We move on my command. I say again: on my command."

Charlie Boudreaux flexed his shoulders and rocked his head from side to side to work out the kinks of too much time sitting still in a Humvee, then resumed sweeping the darkness with night vision binoculars. Waiting. Watching.

From his vantage point, he could see the line of trucks. They looked like Matchbox miniatures. In monochrome green. The people looked like ants, upright on their hind legs. Some carried twigs that could light up the night. Others didn't.

Boudreaux watched a group split from the buyer colony to clamber into the back of the trucks. He couldn't tell which ant from the seller colony was *La Güera*. Had to rely on Bravo One, who was much closer to the action, for that level of detail.

Bravo One was Cider Jones, leading from the front, running the risk, toting that borrowed M-14 the ATF would never pry out of his hands. Unless he was dead.

"*Bravo Four to Six...Got beaucoup movement on my flank. Moving toward target area.*"

Boudreaux tossed the binoculars onto the dashboard and swept up his hand mic.

"Bravo Six to Four. Say again last."

"*Bravo Four to Six...Lots of movement. Headed toward target area. Any good guys late for the party?*"

"Negative, Four. Our folks all accounted for and holding position."

"*Bravo Two to Six... Got movement here. Headed toward target area. Haven't spotted us.*"

"Bravo Six to Two and Four… How many unknowns your position?"

"Two to Six… Hard to say. Estimate a dozen."

"Four to Six…Same-same. Make it a dozen."

Shit. Unknowns moving on the northern and southern flanks of the target area. Brushing past two of his six four-man outposts. Safe bet these newcomers weren't friendly. To anybody.

"Bravo Six to Bravo One, Three and Five…Any unknown movement?"

"Bravo Three to Six…Negative movement."

"Bravo Five to Six…Negative movement our area but we can see the movement near Bravo Four."

"Bravo One to Six…Same-same. Negative movement. Got two guys watching our back door. Me and Torres are eyes on the main players."

"Bravo Six to all Bravos…Do not engage unless fired up. I say again: do not engage unless fired upon. Let them pass. Repeat. Let them pass."

Need more bodies. Need more firepower. Pronto. Time to dial up McKee, the old Ranger, holding the reserves about four miles back.

"Bravo Six to Alpha Six…You copy my traffic? Any movement in your area?"

"Alpha Six to Bravo Six…Copy yours. Unknowns to the north and south. Negative to east and west. Negative movement in our area."

"Bravo Six to Alpha Six…Request moving up firepower and manpower but no engagement new threat. I say again: no engagement."

"Copy and concur, Bravo Six. Let the scumbags chop each other up. We'll move up but wait till the smoke clears then grab the weapons and any survivors."

"Bravo Six to all Bravos…Grab some rock, hunker down and watch the fireworks. We'll move in when the shooting stops."

Cider Jones was closer to the action than need be. Should have been uphill a few football fields away with the other raid commanders. Should have left the scout duties to the younger dudes who learned the art of the sneak and peek in the military.

Couldn't help himself. Had to get close. Had to crawl through the rocks and sand. Had to see for himself. Had to sift through the green images of scumbags selling the goods, hoping to get lucky, hoping to spot the sorry bastard he blamed for his partner's killing.

What he did then was between him, his Comanche ancestors and the ghost of his dead partner, Cortez. Depending on that spiritual coin flip, the 'how' was easy – the borrowed M-14 at his side.

He was comfortable with this old gun. He knew from the fracas at Bondurant's ranch that he could reach out and touch somebody with this iron. Even in the dark. He also knew that in the firefight that was about to light up the night, nobody would notice him shooting a sorry bastard named Ed Earl Burch.

Two figures stepped into the harsh headlamp light. A man, bearish and limping, and a thin blonde with tall cowboy boots.

There's the sorry bastard. And that La Güera bitch.

Jones brought the M-14 front and center, gluing his right cheek to the stock and lining up the sights. First on the man. Then on the woman. Good sight picture. Good deal.

A hiss in his ear from Torres.

"What the fuck are you doin', man? They said no engagement."

"Boy Scout rules – always be prepared. The show's about to start. And those two ain't gettin' away."

Two Dallas thugs tracking Burch and Rhonda Mae sheltered behind rocks perched high enough to monitor all the action playing out below.

One a boss, tall and wiry. The other hired muscle, short and steroid thick. Both watching through binoculars.

"Awful lot of people down there. Awful lot of guns."

"*Sí, jefe*. Shaping up to be a real train wreck."

"You bet. Got the buyers and sellers. Got the law ready to pounce. Now we got these other *hombres* creeping in. Doubt they'll be friendly to buyer or seller, but I could be wrong. Could be a double-cross."

"What's our play?"

"We sure as shit don't want to go down there. A man could get dead real quick doin' that. I think our best bet is to set up at that Y with the main trail, post another man where the main trail hits the highway and have one more watchin' the jail. See if we get lucky and spot our man and our girl handcuffed in the back of a cruiser. Or a getaway rig."

"Sending them now."

A low voice giving instructions. A mic keyed twice in reply.

"And if this don't work?"

"Well, goddam Juan, don't you know the Good Lord hates a pessimist? Have faith, brother. Ask and it shall be given unto you. Seek and ye shall find. Weren't you payin' attention in Catechism Class?"

"Nope. Too busying tryin' to get my hand up Juanita Diaz's dress."

"I remember her. Girl could suck the chrome off a Cadillac bumper. What's she up to now, I wonder."

"Whore in Fort Worth, last I heard. If she ain't OD'd."

"There you go with that pessimism again, Juan. Let's raise up the hope she's alive and well, still putting her considerable oral talents to good use in Cowtown."

The kid making a show of checking the money bag. Teeth clamping a penlight. Fingers riffling the bill bundles. Pausing to brush blonde wig strands from his sweaty face.

ZIZZZZZZZZZZZ. CRAAAACK! An angry lead hornet and the Devil's handclap. Incoming round buzzing the right ear. Burch pivots left, shotgun to shoulder. Pumps four slugs at the nearest muzzle flashes. Close and rushing closer.

More jacketed hornets. More handclaps from Ol' Scratch.

Burch turns toward the kid, crouching as low as his knees allow. Sees El Duque's head explode into a red mist. Hears slugs smacking into Armando's back, knocking him face first into the dirt.

Grabs the kid by the back of the collar with his left hand, hauling him toward the truck at the front of the line. Blonde wig drops to the dirt.

Get out of the light. Get to the dark. Grunting, sweating, vision juddering with effort. Pushing the kid, forcing him to move, stumbling, catching the fall. Knees screaming.

More bodies dropping, toppling from the truck cabs. More Ruiz blood in the dirt. More muzzle flashes from the opposite side of the trail. Hornets and handclaps from both flanks.

Crossfire trap. Craziness and confusion. El Duque's men slow to realize the real threat. Lighting up the targets already in their sights – Armando's cousins. Whacking the wrong guys. Getting whacked before wising up.

The cousins not as confused. Turning their guns to light up the darkness on the flanks. Didn't matter how smart they fought. Didn't matter where the bullets came from. They still got dead.

Lead slapping flesh. Screaming from the kid. Dead weight that almost takes Burch down. Ditch the shotgun. Grab the kid with both arms. Dive to the dirt and wrestle him under the bumper of that first truck. Wince at the whack and ping of rounds smacking sheet metal.

Gurgle and rattle from the kid. Two fingers pressed to his neck. Shit. Gone. Adios, muchacho. Time to make sure he didn't make the same final exit.

Crawl to the back of the truck. Dust clogs the nostrils. Breathe through the mouth. Suck down more dust. Gag and cough. Squeeze past the transfer case.

Slither across the gap fronting the next truck. Glimpse shooters crouched by bumpers, firing toward both flanks. Squeeze past a dead man with half his face blown away. Grab his blood-spattered gun and a couple of mags. Keep crawlin', old man.

Gotta get to Rhonda Mae. She was three trucks from the front rig when the shitshow touched off. Wearin' that fuckin' flea-bit Longhorn cap. Too fuckin' stubborn to sit this one out. Not happy about the decoy wearing her wig.

One truck after this one. Keep crawlin', you fat bastard. Nothing but ringing in his ears now. Gunfire deaf.

Dirt and sweat stinging his eyes. Deaf and semi-blind. Helluva bodyguard. But not dead. Yet.

Get to Rhonda Mae, you cockbite motherfucker. Keep crawlin'. Keep your promise to an old woman at death's door. Least you owe her, pendejo.

Third truck. Bodies piled at both ends of the front bumper. Scramble like a three-legged sloth across the gap, pistol grip of the dead man's gun in the left hand. A '16. Looked old enough to be full auto. Hope so.

Bodies under the chassis. Half of them dead. The other half still pumping rounds at muzzle flashes on both flanks. Wet smack and a final grunt. One more muchacho tagged for the permanent dirt nap.

Crawfish to the nearest man still firing. Tap his shoulder and croak into his left ear.

"¿La Güera?"

"¿Que?"

A bellow this time.

"La Güera. ¿Dónde está?"

"Allá atrás, pinche gringo. Detrás de las ruedas."

Eyes to the rear. Rhonda Mae prone behind the rear pair of wheels on the left side of the six-by, her face and Longhorn ballcap lit up by the muzzle flash of her CAR-15.

A short crawl across dead bodies to her side, wincing at the thud and reverb of slugs tearing up corpses. She was slapping in a fresh mag, her body fully behind the wheels. A glance his way, eyes flashing in the darkness.

"Thought you were dead."

"Hard to kill."

"Hah. Still the joker. Armando?"

"Saw him get hit and go down. Don't know he's dead. El Duque got his head blown off."

"I liked that old man. Didn't trust him. But I liked him."

"The ol' boy had style."

"Bartolo?"

"Gone."

A sharp cry from her lips. A quick roll to the front edge of the first wheel. A long burst from the CAR-15. Reverse roll to swap mags.

"Nailed two."

"How can you tell?"

"They're close enough to see now."

"All the more reason to get gone. Now."

"I want to stay and fight."

"Why? So you can be a beautiful martyr to the memory of Tommy Juan?"

"Fuck you, old man. I ought to shoot you dead right now."

"You're too young to be the star of a corrido that turns getting dead into a beautiful lie."

No answer. Another quick roll to the front edge of the wheel. Four short bursts. A fifth long burst to empty the mag.

"Two more. Now get the fuck out of here and leave me alone."

"No can do. I made a promise to your grandmother."

Summer storm lightning from her eyes. A quick, short punch with the coin sap in his right hand. One bounce of her head against tire rubber. A teetering pause on his shoulder. A slide down his chest to rest in his lap.

A yell to one of the few still living.

"La señorita está herida. Tenemos que sacarla de aquí."

"Vamos a llevarla al Jeep."

Thirty yards to the two Jeeps. Need a shitload more firepower to make it that far. A fuckin' shitload. Now.

Profane prayer draws a heavenly answer. The thumps of an M-79 sending blooper rounds into the darkness, a sound from his Army days. The flash and crump of those rounds tearing into those murderous assholes trying to kill them all.

"C'mon, darlin'. Let's get you the hell outta Dodge."

Blonde wig in the dirt. Skinny puke with falsies, a flashy vest and buckaroo boots just a few yards away, lifeless eyes locked on the stars, neck ripped open by a high-powered round.

A decoy. A La Güera lookalike.

Chizik screamed. Frustration. Rage. Fury that fueled his zig-zag sprint down the left side of the lined-up trucks. Juking. Ripping a burst from his AK. Chopping down a shooter taking aim his way.

Where is she? Where did that bitch go? Want to rip her head off. Empty a full mag up her cunt.

He grinned, ducking as rounds ripped overhead. Diving away from dust blossoms stitching a deadly dirt line straight toward his body. Rolling and popping up in full stride. Cutting left. Then right. Slapping home a fresh mag. Knocking down two more mooks.

Find that bitch. Find her now. Nothing else matters.

Reaching the last truck. Skidding along the rear bumper. Stomping on bodies. Nailing a mook firing blooper rounds at his guys.

Chizik froze. Shadow of a big man shouldering a load. Heading to a Jeep. Almost there.

It's HER! I know it's HER!

Legs dangling down from the big man's right shoulder. Shooters guarding the flanks of the big man and his cargo. Big man limping badly, pushing to cover ground, carrying her like a side of beef.

That bitch! That fuckin' bitch! Need you dead. Right here. Right now.

Straight line sprint. Chopping down the shooters. Screaming "La Güeraaaaaaa! I got you, bitch! Got you now! Gonna slice you wide open and watch you bleeeeeeed!"

Skidding to a stop as the big man spun around. A frozen flash of recognition – THAT guy, that fuckin' guy nosing around the ranch like a cop. Thought you was a ghost, motherfucker. Fuckin' make him one now. Shouldering his AK.

The big man, dumping his load, raising his left arm and emptying a mag of Flying Ashtrays into Chizik's chest and face.

Eight bucket-mouthed Fat Boys. Punching holes. Gouging huge exits from the Chizik's back. Blowing out skull fragments and brain tissue.

"Not today, you cockbite motherfucker. Not in this lifetime or the next."

Sending Chizik straight to Hell. The 1911 Express. No transfers. No stops.

Twenty-Three

The ranch road was rough as a cob, all rocks and potholes and washouts. More of a goat trail, a path for javelina, mule deer, pronghorn, horse and rider. Or the occasional jaguar. Not the first choice for four-wheeled travel. Not even in a Jeep.

It sure wasn't the route Rhonda Mae and Armando chose to lead their trucks to the killing ground Burch was inching away from. That was an interstate compared to this, a real backcountry boulevard – bumpy, rutted and rocky but fairly well-traveled. No dice for a getaway, though. It would be chicken-hawked by lawdogs and bad hombres of every kind.

Not a smart way to truly get gone and get safe. A good way to get dead, though. Not what Burch had in mind as he muscled the old CJ5 over rocks and through potholes with the headlamps dark. Wincing as it bottomed out with a bang to the oil pan or transfer case.

Keep your foot off the brake pedal, dumbass. Don't cause those taillights to fire their bright red flares. Let the gearbox govern the speed. Low-low and slow. The only way to go.

Rhonda Mae was still lights out in the seat beside him, head lolling, body trussed by a seat belt tightened down to the max, ratty Longhorn cap missing in action. She stirred now and then, groaning when the bumps were particularly bad, but clinging to unconsciousness like a fifth grader who didn't want to wake up and go to school.

Burch had no clue exactly where they were headed. Roughly the opposite direction as the way they came in, he figured. He didn't much care, long as he put some crawling distance between them and the badge boys and what remained of those rival cartel gunsels.

Keep choppin' each other up, boys, while me and the little lady slowly slip away. Shit. Little lady my ass. The girl's a hardcore outlaw. A hustler. A killer. And an old woman's granddaughter. Don't forget Juanita and her one true last wish.

Bang! A jolt that rattled Burch's teeth as the Jeep caromed off a big rock to the sound of shearing sheet metal. Dead stop with a dead engine.

"Who the fuck ever said you knew how to drive?"

"Your granny, for one."

"Fuck you, Gramps. You should have left me back there to die with Armando. Who gave you the right to butt in and decide my fate?"

"Same answer, Slick. Your granny. I'm workin' for her, not you. And she made that decision a couple of weeks ago. Put me in charge of making it happen."

"Paid you, too. Wouldn't be here if she hadn't crossed your palms with a bunch of Benjamins."

"Thas' raht, sugar. I'm a mercenary fuck. Just like you."

Burch unbuckled the seat harness and swung his legs out of the Jeep with a loud grunt. He stood up slowly, listening to the bone-on-bone grind from both knees. He felt his way toward the front of the Jeep until he found where the rock had ripped away the left front fender and bent the bumper up and back like a bull sporting a single horn.

He hunkered down, facing the left front tire, running his hands over the treads, checking the sidewalls for gashes and puncture wounds. He reached behind the wheel, first for the shock, then for the strut. Both were still there.

He grabbed the tire with both hands, rocking it back and forth, putting his weight behind it. Felt tight. No wobble. Felt full not flat. Lucky break.

Now for the engine. He popped the hood latches, lifted the hood and propped it up. He grabbed the flashlight out of his pocket, ducked under the hood and lit up the engine. He checked the four-banger's plug wires and carb hoses. He smelled warm oil and the faint scent of gas but not the heady stench of a flooded carb.

He eased the hood back down and snapped the latches closed. He climbed behind the wheel, pumped the accelerator twice then reached for the keys and breathed a silent prayer as he turned the ignition. The starter ground through a cycle or two but failed to wake up the engine. He fed the carb more gas.

"C'mon you motherfucker."

The four-banger wheezed back to life. So much for prayer. Better off throwing F-bombs.

"Think you can get us out of here without turning this rust bucket into a total wreck, Gramps?"

"Still got three fenders and an engine that runs, don't it?"

"That don't give me comfort."

"You never have been a child of faith, have you, Slick?"

"God ain't ever done me no favors. The Holy Peckerhead's fucked me over a time or two. But favors? None from that sorry bastard."

Before they could think about being stupid and dead, they rolled up on the T where the side trail hit a wider ranch road. Looked like it ran north-south. Looked like the run south might take you to the blacktop between Faver and Valentine.

Burch shifted out of low-low, gunned the engine and turned left.

Brrrrrrrrrrrr-rap. The long, metallic rip of an automatic weapon. Sounded like an AK. Sparks flew from the Jeep's hood and along its right flank. *Brrrrrrrrr-rap.* Burch and Rhonda Mae ducked their heads and slouched their shoulders as if vinyl seatbacks could stop high-velocity lead.

As they barreled out of the kill zone, Burch could hear the growl of a big engine firing up behind them. He spied the ghostly track of another side trail ahead and to the right. He turned sharply, flirting with a rollover as the tires on his side left the road and the body rose before banging down sharply as he straightened the wheel.

Thick brush crowded both sides of the trail. Nowhere to run but straight ahead. Then two sharp curves – left, right – and a steep drop toward a dry creek bed.

Nowhere to hide. Until there was.

"Pull over there, Gramps! There! Right there! Fuck, you passed it."

Burch slammed on the brakes, jammed it into reverse and juddered the Jeep to a narrow opening in the brush. He swung the ass end through and backed up until he ran out of room.

Comfy little alcove. Long as you ignored the thorny branches reaching out to claw your face open and the rough brush swallowing the rear of the Jeep clean up to the roll bar. Damn near idyllically claustrophobic.

Rhonda Mae unbuckled and squeezed out of the Jeep, grabbing her CAR-15 and stuffing some fresh mags into the pockets of her baggy pants. Burch did the same with the blood spattered M-16 he took off the body of one of Armando's dead cousins. He had a mag in the well topped with 20 5.56 green tips, a steel-cored penetrator round, and one more mag to stuff in the back pocket of his jeans.

"We got one chance to hose these guys down as they pass, Gramps. We're dead meat otherwise."

"I'll get over to the other side of the trail."

"No time for that. I'll pick a spot nearest them and stay low. You post up on the other side of the opening. Hammer the cab. I'll hammer whoever's in back. And try not to hit me, motherfucker."

"Yes'm."

They hustled to the mouth of their brushy little alcove. Rhonda Mae ducked under a creosote bush and crawled to the side of the trail. Burch mirrored her, slipping into the brush on his side of the opening and picking a standing spot behind a mesquite tree that gave him a clear line of fire.

Faint light only from the stars and a rising quarter moon. The trail a ragged, ghost-gray ribbon flanked by jet-black brush. Engine roar grew louder. Dark hulk of a short bed pickup looming large, rolling closer. Bad hombres trying to run them down and snuff them out.

Fuck that.

Burch centered his sights on the windshield, his mind registering the outline of three targets – driver, passenger and the poor bastard riding bitch. He let his breath out slow until it bottomed out, then held it and squeezed the trigger.

Muzzle flash lit up the night. He shifted the barrel in short arcs, firing quick bursts of green points that shattered glass, sliced through metal and punched through the flesh of his targets.

First, the bitch in the middle, then the driver. He could see them twitch and jerk as the rounds struck home. Bloody ragdolls, dead the first few seconds he cut loose.

Rhonda Mae opened up, chopping down two guys standing in the back who were using the truck's light bar to hold on and stay upright. Until she blew them down.

The truck swerved left, nosing into the brush, swinging the passenger into Burch's sights as the scumbag leaned out of the door window, firing a MAC-10 his way until the green points blew open his chest and skull. The shooter spasmed and twisted like a man with the St. Vitus dance, his gun hand flying up and back, sending a spray of lead toward the stars.

Burch held down the trigger until the mag was empty and the bolt catch locked. Dropped the empty, slapped home his only spare then pulled back the charging handle to fill the chamber with a fresh round.

Spent brass piled around his feet glittered in the starlight. Burch was deaf as a brick from the gunfire. He opened his mouth and flexed his jaws, bleeding off the muffled pressure from his eardrums.

Pop. Burch could hear again. Just in time to be scared shitless by loud, short bursts from Rhonda Mae's CAR-15, delivering *coups de grâce* to five dead fuckheads who deserved neither grace nor mercy.

"Might want to save that ammo, hon. Pretty sure them fellers are deader than Elvis."

"Elvis ain't dead, Gramps. Just makin' sure these cocksuckers are."

Rhonda Mae pressed the muzzle of the CAR-15 to the head of the dead driver and fired a single round.

"Quit, now. Choppin' these boys into dog meat won't bring back Tommy Juan."

She spun to face him, leveling the gun muzzle to point at his chest. She jerked her head toward the bullet-streaked truck and its bloody cargo. Her voice was brittle. Her words were angry and bitter.

"Don't put your mouth on him, old man. Not 'less you want to end up like them."

Burch stood still, his eyes holding hers. He said nothing, letting time thaw out to start the seconds ticking again. Her anger passed like squall line scudding over a dry and thirsty land. She smiled and shook her head.

"You know, for a badass who wants to be my bodyguard, you're pretty squeamish about blood and guts, Gramps. Besides, I thought you liked a little walk on the outlaw side of life."

Burch snorted a laugh and dug through his pockets for a crumpled pack of Luckies and his Zippo. He lit a crooked nail and took a deep drag.

"Jesus wept. Helluva pair of outlaws we are, Slick. A regular Bonnie and Clyde. And you know what happened to them."

They were home free, rolling on blacktop, the Jeep in high gear with its four-banger thinking it could bust the double nickel but barely cracking fifty. Nobody chasing them. Nothing but stars and dark wasteland in their eyes.

The ride was a little cockeyed, with a hard front-end pull to the left, forcing Burch to hold the steering wheel a few ticks to the right to track a straight line. Straight toward Valentine and a left turn just a few miles east of town down an old smuggler's trail that would disappear them deep into the outback.

Truly home free if they made it that far. Truly fucked if they didn't.

Burch felt the pressure ratchet of the past forty-eight hours ease up a notch. He wasn't relaxed. He was alert and knew they couldn't afford to be fat, dumb and stupid. But that grinding, high-tensile band of tension around his head wasn't as fierce. It was still there, but he had room to breathe and shift his brain out of squirrel-on-meth overdrive.

He found and lit another Lucky with his left hand and enjoyed that first deep and sweet drag. Eyes dead ahead on the dark black-top ribbon.

"Lemme have one of those, Gramps."

"Bad for your health, Slick. But your call."

He glanced her way as she snaked a hand into his shirt pocket. Just in time to get blinded by the sudden glare of high-beam head-lamps that lit up a spike chain that snaked across the crack-laced blacktop.

Too late to avoid. Too late to slam on the brakes. Fatal to do either. Just keep the wheel straight and pray as the spikes punctured the tires and turned the Jeep into a cartwheel of torn metal, shattered glass and broken bodies.

Truly fucked instead of home free.

Burch rose from the blessed blackout of the nearly dead to a resurrection of searing pain.

He was deep in the gravel of a roadside ditch, coughing up blood, struggling to breathe, mindful that any movement was rewarded with a quick spike of agony.

Jagged white bone poked through the bloody skin of his right forearm. Blood flooded his mouth and blinded his left eye. His left foot was unnaturally cranked at an angle that gave him a good chance of kicking his own ass.

The Justin for that foot was gone. So was the sock.

Rhonda Mae. She alive or dead? He raised himself up with his left forearm to find her. Got a gopher's glimpse of the blacktop crown and the crumpled metal tangle of the Jeep.

The pain slammed him back to the gravel. A familiar face slid into view, way too close for the stench of too many cigarettes, coffees and onion-laced burritos blown into his face from a mouth framed by the silky flow of an expansive Zapata moustache.

"That's the ticket, *mi amigo*. Rest easy. You gave it a good run but now it's over. You tried to save her, but you didn't. We have her now. And soon that won't matter to you."

His addled brain tried to find a name for the voice and the face.

"Who the fuck are you?"

His voice sounded like he was gargling gravel. He spat out a glob of blood and tried again.

"Who the fuck are you?"

"I heard you the first time, *mi carnal*. You know who I am. You've probably got another concussion. Not your first, right? Not to worry. It will come to you in a second. And in *another*, that won't matter either."

"I know who you are, you cockbite motherfucker. Del Rio. Johnny Del Rio. We used to be partners. Now you're just another shitbird scumbag."

Del Rio chuckled, but his dark eyes were cold like frozen coal.

"Clearly, we scrambled your eggs a little bit but didn't make a dent in that nasty temper of yours. Or that nasty tongue. We could still cut that out for you, my friend. As a last rite. So, try to be nice."

"Kiss my ass, Johnny. Who you workin' for these days, partner? The cartels? We did what we had to do to survive way back when, but we never sank that low."

"Stick that hypocritical shit up your *culo, pendejo.* You sound like a Baptist preacher who rants about sin and damnation on Sundays but fucks the church secretary every Saturday night. And tells himself that isn't so bad because she is a godly woman.

Johnny looked up, shouted something in Spanish too fast for Burch to catch to someone he couldn't see. Then he looked down again at Burch. There was a sadness in his eyes. For both of them. For the stand-up cops they both used to be. But no salvation.

"Such horseshit you talk, *amigo.* Once you cross that line, sin is sin no matter how much you lie to yourself. Black is black, no matter how much you try to make it grey. You can tell yourself one sin is worse than the other and one sinner isn't as bad as the next, but that's a lie."

"We used to have a code. And a line we wouldn't cross."

"And I'm telling you that was a lie we told ourselves to feel better about the bad shit we did. Planting evidence. Shooting scumbags in the back. Rat-fucking a bad cop or crooked D.A. Taking money from one scumbag to fuck over another. Yeah, we got some folks off the hook who were getting railroaded. But who paid us to do that? People who were even worse than the cops and prosecutors doing the railroading. We told ourselves we were righteous and sold ourselves that line of crap with all that talk about living a code and having a line we wouldn't cross."

"Fuckin' too bad for you, Johnny. I still live that code and won't cross that line."

"You're still feeding yourself that steady diet of holier-than-thou horseshit, Burch. You're pathetic. I watched you torture yourself over losing that gold shield and having to do all those shitty things we both had to do to keep our heads above water. Watched you drink yourself toward an early grave night after night at Louie's. And take all those jobs from Fat Willie that made you puke. Never did understand why you didn't just ice that bastard. Some guys would'a paid you good money to do them *that* fuckin' favor."

"Never was a killer for hire. And didn't know you really cared."

"I did back then. I don't now. Let me bring up some more fond memories of you. I watched you try to redeem yourself by taking on cases that nobody with half a lick of sense would touch because it made you feel like you still had that gold shield. Instead of walking away and taking the smart money for an easier job, you'd make these suicide runs that nearly got you killed. And for what? Redemption? A chance to reclaim your soul and a piece of that badge you lost?"

"Keep talking, Johnny. I never knew I was such a sucker in your eyes. But who gives a shit about how they look to a scumbag like you?"

"Not just my eyes. Everybody's eyes. Everybody who counts."

"That everybody include Jack?"

"Who do you think had your back all these years? Guys like me and Jack. We gave a shit about you. Guys who wanted to clip you got cold feet. Didn't want guys like me and Jack gunnin' for them. When you finally got rid of Fat Willie and started making some big bucks, we all thought you'd finally smartened up. About damn time, we said. Better late than never."

"Now that you've told me what a dumbass I've always been and what a smart guy you always were, why don't you tell me who's paying you. Who wants Rhonda Mae more than her grandmother?"

"Don't kid a kidder, my friend. Your brains aren't scrambled that much. Who has always wanted Rhonda Mae more than that old lady?"

"Fuckin' Danny Ray Mutscher. The daddy who got her hooked on smack. The daddy who wanted to fuck her. She almost blew his balls off with a .357 for that."

"See? I knew you could put the pieces together. He wants her. He pays enough money, he gets her. All we had to do was keep a tail on you. Lost us a time or two because you still got moves but we caught up."

"How'd you get on me in the first place?"

"Hell, *amigo* – we've been on you since before you left Dallas. That Lucy gal who runs errands for the old woman and sometimes sleeps on the couch? She works for us. Dialed us up as soon as the old woman blabbed about hirin' you."

"Figured it was something like that. Why does daddy still want her so bad?"

"I don't know. And I don't really care. What I do know is Danny Ray's a big wheel with lots of serious friends on both sides of the border. Dixie Mafia and cartel types. And what I care about is he pays me lots of cold cash to do his bidding. That means we pack the daughter up, deliver her to daddy all wrapped up with ribbons and bows. What he does with her after that is none of my fuckin' business."

"Nobody's a ghost. Anybody can be found. And if you find them, you can reach out and touch them. Permanently."

"Is that what you're telling me you're gonna do? Chase Danny Ray down and save his little girl? I always said you were a funny guy, but this is really rich. Busted up in a ditch in West Texas and making threats you'll never live to carry out. Like I said. Pathetic."

"You know better, Johnny. I don't make threats. I make promises I always keep."

"I remember. That's why it's time to end this lovely chat and show you some mercy."

Johnny stood up and pulled out a nickel-plated Browning Hi-Power, racking the slide to put a round in the pipe. He pointed the pistol at Burch's head, taking aim with eyes that were now cold and flat.

"Goodbye, my friend. I hate to do this, but you've needed killin' for a very long time. Hate that it's me having to pull the trigger."

"Go fuck yourself, Johnny. I'll see you in hell."

"No doubt about that, my friend. Be joining you some day. But not today."

Burch braced himself for a blinding flash that would send him to the Big Nowhere, locking his eyes on a man he once called his friend, ignoring the yawning mouth of the barrel that would spit out the bullet to end his life.

Stay frosty, Sport Model. Buy you a whiskey when you get here.

Be along shortly, Wynn.

Four quick, loud metallic barks caused Johnny's face to freeze in final surprise, a hole in his forehead and three more in his chest. His dead hand spasmed and jerked the Hi-Power's trigger, blasting the bullet meant for Burch into the gravel an inch from his head and scorching his face with powder burns.

Johnny's body folded like a tattered Gulf Oil road map and slammed down on Burch. Burch screamed, the pain blowing out the nerve circuits of his brain and body.

"Sweet Jesus, that hurts."

At least you ain't dead, Sport Model.

Not hardly. Not yet. But it might be an improvement.

Last words, spoken and imagined, before the long, black fadeout.

Twenty-Four

Burch was buzzing along in a haze of high-grade hospital pharmaceuticals, his mind's eye focused on a woman he used to fuck a long time ago.

A long-legged and rangy strawberry blonde with a terminally bad attitude. Built like a power forward with big tits. Sex with her was a contact sport and always left him battered and bruised. And always ready to come back for more.

Savannah Crowe, feckless, lethally carnal and dead a long time. He missed her.

"Nice to see an old man with a busted head, a broken arm and a shattered leg can still get a hard-on, Gramps."

"Bad habits take a long time to die, Slick."

"Bet they're gonna have to chain that thing down when they bury you."

"Best use plenty of pole barn nails and some concrete blocks to keep that coffin lid shut. Ol' John Henry has been known to wander."

"Jesus, Gramps."

"Keep him the hell out of it."

Rhonda Mae laughed. Burch tried to join in, but sharp pain from his busted ribs stopped him cold. Only so much those high-grade drugs could do.

"What are you doin' here? Thought you went to see Juanita."

"Just got back. Been gone a week. Spent every waking hour with her with an ankle monitor strapped on and this Ranger here chained to my wrist. Another one sat outside her room with a shotgun in his lap."

"Hospital?"

"No. At the house in her own room. Hospice care. She said to hug your neck and give you this."

Rhonda Mae handed him a long, fat manilla envelope battened down with red string looped in a figure eight between two stout circles of equally red oaktag. His zoned-out brain had trouble unwinding the figure eights. She had to un-dally them for him.

Inside was a thick stack of $500 bills and a folded sheet of plain white tablet paper. Nothing fancy. The kind you used to find at any corner drug store or five-and-dime.

He nodded toward a bedside table that held a capped plastic cup with a straw and a worn, hard-cover copy of *Islands in The Stream*, a Hemingway novel he was reading for the umpteenth time, published years after the author blew his head off just like his daddy did.

"Hand me my specs, Slick."

He slipped on the cheaters with his only free hand, then smoothed out the paper on his lap to read. It was a letter from Juanita, written in a spidery hand that wandered about in crooked, black-ink lines.

My Prodigal Friend,

I can never repay the debt I owe you for finding Rhonda Mae and sending her to me. Before you set out on this journey, you said you wanted to make things right between us.

You did more than square the deal and she tells me you almost got killed in the bargain. If that's not above and beyond true friendship, I don't know what is.

I call it something else – love. The kind you're supposed to find in a family but often don't. If you're lucky, you find that love with a rare friend you value more than your own kin.

It's a special bond and I count myself double lucky that you returned to my life and restored that connection. Yes, I cussed your name more times than I can count but that doesn't matter now.

I don't know how much longer I have to live in this nasty old world. Not very much, I'll wager. But I feel such peace and calm knowing you are a part of my family again and have given me a priceless gift in my final hours.

When we saw each other last, you talked about redemption. You meant for yourself and your past sins against me. But I think redemption is a two-way street and a shared state of grace.

Rhonda Mae tells me you're too busted up to travel. Call when you can so we can say good-bye. And don't even think of raising Cain about the money. I'll get Rhonda Mae to whack you with my cane.

With much love, I am your friend and your kin,

Juanita Mutscher

Tears flooded his eyes, rolled down his cheeks and into his beard. He choked back a sob, then parked his useless macho and bellowed out his first long, hard cry in a very long time. Over anything.

His face felt flush and swollen. Clear mucous ran from his nose and clotted his moustache. His vision was as blurry as a car windshield caught in the middle of a frog-strangling deluge. He did not give a solitary fuck about how he looked or who saw him let the floodgates loose.

Rhonda Mae handed him a Kelly-green bandana. He honked his nose until both nostrils were clear, then wiped the tears and mucous from his beard and moustache.

"She loved you too, Ed Earl. She died last night."

"I know."

She hugged his neck and gave him a peck on the cheek.

"This is for me and her. A double good-bye."

"Figured as much. WITSEC, right?"

"Right. I'll spill what few beans I've got to the feds and the Rangers, then disappear down a rabbit hole."

"I owe you one for snuffing out Johnny's candle before he could do the same to me."

"We're even."

"What about daddy?"

"That worthless cocksucker? In the wind. Dodging attempted kidnapping and murder charges for our little shindig and a couple of murder beefs."

"That's a problem. Danny Ray's a man what needs killin'."

"Agreed. And I'd be glad to do it on sight. Word is, though, the greaseballs want him whacked for some shit he pulled in New Orleans and he's pissed off the Sinaloas. Don't believe we'll have to worry about him anymore."

"You can't afford to think that way and you know it. Eyes in the back of your head. And get a cold piece. I don't give a shit what the feds say. Stay safe. Stay out of trouble."

"I'd give you the same advice, Gramps, but I know you're a hard case and a hopeless cause."

"Smart girl."

When Dub McKee came calling, Burch had his pharmaceutical buzz on medium low. Carnal visions of lethal ex-lovers weren't rolling through his brain like a porn video and he didn't have a hard-on.

McKee rapped his knuckles on the safety rail of Burch's hospital bed, pulled a chair up close and plopped down with his left leg crossed and his Stetson smoothly dismounted and perched on the tip of his boot. Smooth trick only a Texas lawman could pull.

"You with us today, hoss? Last time I dropped by you were raving like a drunk wetback on a ten-day bender."

"Thing I like most about this hospital, Dub. The food sucks but the drugs are high grade."

"Doc says you're healin' up fine. You'll never be able to walk through a metal detector without setting it off, but he thinks you'll be able to walk again without a cane and with no worse a limp than you've already got."

"You're leavin' something out, Dub. That exquisite torture they call physical therapy."

"Ain't no hill for a climber like you, son. You're double tough and will chew up everything they throw at you and spit it back at 'em. I know. I got faith in you."

"But you ain't gonna be the one doin' all that chewin', Dub."

"True. But I got the power of prayer and I'll be sending some on your behalf as you eat up all that pain."

"Enough preachin', Dub. Why don't you tell me why you're really here."

"Don't rush me, son. I'm a half-ass politician these days and have to practice my witty and charming. Business can wait. I brought a little present for you."

The old Ranger reached in the pocket of his steel gray, double-yoked Western blazer and pulled out a pint bottle of Maker's Mark. A pretty little bottle of ninety proof bourbon whisky without the 'e' but with the dipped red wax over the top. Just like a grown-up fifth.

McKee fetched two plastic cups, pulled the string that unraveled the wax then poured until they both had four fingers of liquor to sip.

"Mighty fine. Knew it was the brand you favored. Now that I've had some, I know why."

"You did your homework. They'll make a politician out of you yet, Dub."

"They call it constituent service. Question is – is you is or is you ain't my constituent?"

"You've got my vote, Dub. Now tell me what it's going to cost me."

"Got a little proposition for you, son. One I think you'll like."

Burch did. What McKee had up his sleeve was simple and marvelously devious. And like most brilliant ideas, it ignored the rules and jurisdictional lines and bureaucratic red tape that kept a lawman from doing his job.

Burch was pretty sure it was illegal and knew it violated a slew of regulations, but McKee's proposition went something like this:

Burch would take the gold shield Doggett was offering and officially be an investigator for the Cuervo County D.A. – Sam Boelcke. That was one piece of fiction because his boss would really be Doggett. Made sense since Boelcke was a fine contract law attorney but didn't know shit about tracking down bad guys and building a case.

That would be the everyday set-up. McKee added another twist. Burch would also be seconded as a special investigator to the state attorney general's office, answering to McKee. Sort of an on-call gig where he knew he'd get dialed up early and often.

"I see a need for a man with your particular talent for slinging shit all over the walls and bustin' up the good china. So does Doggett. Need you to help clean up the Bondurant mess and that cartel clusterfuck. Doggett doesn't mind sharing you and appreciates the extra money we'll put in your pocket because Cuervo County can't afford to pay you what you're really worth."

Burch took a sip of Maker's. He pined for a Lucky the nurses wouldn't let him have.

"I got one question – do I ever have to work with that cockbite motherfucker Cider Jones?"

"You don't have to worry about Mister Jones. Notice I say 'mister' because the man's been cashiered and is no longer in the state's employ. No longer has a badge. He's a civilian and he don't count."

"How'd that happen?"

"We know he took a shot or two at you and that boy posing as your girlfriend during that goat ropin' where all them cartel boys got dead. Dug a .308 slug out of the boy's body."

"Bartolo Contreras? How'd you find out Jones was the shooter?"

"Not too many guns of that caliber were present – leastwise, we didn't find any .308 brass scattered around. Jones was carrying an M-14 and proved he was pretty good with it out at Bondurant's ranch. Dropped more than his share of baddies. Dug some .308s out of those boys that matched the one from the youngster."

"Doesn't absolutely prove he pulled the trigger that killed Bartolo."

"No, but we also got a sworn statement from an ATF agent who was right next to Jones when he fired those shots. Said Jones was aimin' for you and who he thought was *La Güera*. We could've rolled the dice and tried to nail him. But a murder cop doesn't last too long in prison. Better to use the goods we had on him to convince the man to turn in his badge and keep his pension."

"Damn. I knew the man hated me bad and wouldn't mind seeing me get dead. Hell, he trailed me all the way to Mexico one time just to see if I *would* get killed. But I never thought he'd pull the trigger himself."

"He did, son. Now, do we got a deal?"

"We got a deal, Dub."

"Good. Now let's enjoy the rest of this bourbon. Believe I've got another pint in my pocket."

"That'll work."

Better wake up, Sport Model. Your phone's about to ring.

Shut up, Wynn. Need my sleep.

You'll sleep when you're dead. Wake your ass up and take this call. You ain't gonna like it but you got to take it.

It's Jack, ain't it?

Yup. Cactus Jack, his ownsef. You know he's the one who set you up and sic'd Johnny on you. You know he's the one who's been callin' the plays for Danny Ray Mutscher.

I know.

Then you know you got to get Jack from the vertical to the horizontal. Real permanent like. Otherwise, he's gonna find another Johnny to send your way. And Rhonda Mae's.

278

Burch popped his eyes wide open. The phone next to his hospital bed rang. He picked up the handset on the third ring.

"Jack."

"How'd you know it was me, ol' hoss?"

"Been thinkin' about you. Quite a bit lately."

"Thought they had you too zapped on painkillers to do much thinkin'."

"That they do, Jack. But hate's a powerful antidote to even the best drugs a hospital can serve up."

"What the hell are you talkin' about, boy? Them drugs have fried your brain."

"Cut the shit, Jack. I know. I know you set me up and sent Johnny to grab Rhonda Mae and ice me. I know you're working for that fuckwad Danny Ray."

"Bullshit, boy. You don't know a goddam thing."

"I know, Jack. Look for me real soon."

Burch hung up the phone. He was wide awake. His heart was pounding and he wished he was in the same room as Jack with the Colt in his hand. His mind was clear and cold. No haze, no buzz.

Pharmaceuticals didn't stand a chance against a truly murderous hate. Burch savored the feeling. Meant he was starting to be his old self again.

Twenty-Five

As soon as a hint of dawn outlined the jagged rocks of the box canyon that surrounded the three sides of Doggett's cabin, Burch grabbed his cane, shouldered a borrowed M-1 Garand he had a growing fondness for and thumped down the front porch stairs to start his daily six-mile walk.

Three miles up the canyon and three miles back. With a break in between for water and a couple of granola bars. Get it done before the merciless West Texas sun dropped the hammer faster than Judge Parker gaveling a horse thief into a hangman's noose.

Truth be told, Burch didn't really need the cane. Not after four months of torturous physical therapy to break up the scar tissue and restore flexibility and movement, weightlifting to strengthen the muscles that supported shattered bones held together by titanium surgical plates and these long, morning walks along the scrubby Jeep trail that ribboned the middle of the canyon.

But he liked the smooth, jaunty style of this hand-made gift from Hanque Curtis, a retired Florida murder cop he met in the late 70s while tracking down a small-time Dallas hood who murdered his girlfriend, running him to ground in Tampa. Hanque handled the arrest and wrote up the extradition request to the judge who ordered the hood shipped to Texas and a date with the Big Needle.

His Sunshine State buddy crafted the cane shaft from Cuban mahogany – only fitting since Hanque was married to a far younger Cubana who gave the nickname for Henry a Havana spin. The wood maestro joined the mahogany to an end piece of some mysterious

South American hardwood with a hexagonal brass tip and topped the creation with a curved handle made of spalted hardwood marled by iron filing swirls.

Held lightly in his right hand, the cane helped him keep time on his walks and balanced the Garand slung butt-side-up over his left shoulder, a habit he picked up from the old vets of World War II and Korea still serving in his armored unit when it was stationed in Germany in '67. When pulling guard duty in the rain, they said, keep the muzzle pointed down to help keep the inside of the barrel dry and rust-free.

Also gives your silhouette a lower profile on the march, they said. Makes it harder for a sniper to dial you in. Good to know any time you were slinging and schlepping an M-14, the Garand's younger, full-auto brother with the 20-round box magazine, even if you weren't worried about getting whacked by a Waffen-SS sniper.

Burch hated the M-14, which he considered an unwieldy and hard-to-handle weapon, wild as a buck on full-auto. He preferred the Garand, the rifle he qualified with in basic. He liked its heft and balance and the hard kick of the .30-06 that punished a trooper who didn't get a firm cheek weld and a solid shoulder pocket for the metal butt. It was the only long gun he could truly reach out and touch somebody with using just the iron sights.

He particularly liked the Garand slung over his shoulder, an armory mutt with a Harrington & Richardson barrel and receiver of Korean War vintage, a smooth Winchester trigger group and a well-worn stock darkened by years of rubbing with linseed oil, the wood showing dings, dents and the faint outlines of inspection and proof stamps but no serious cracks.

During some of his walks, Burch unlimbered the Garand and nailed bottles and cans at 100 yards on a half-assed range Doggett had marked off near a canyon wall. Kept it in the black on a standard paper target at 200.

Burch loved this rifle. He planned to offer the deputy who owned it two grand to keep it. He also dusted off his 1911, punching paper, knocking down cans and blasting bottles at fifteen yards or less.

An old-school metal Army canteen and cover was clipped to his belt. Around his neck, he wore World War II surplus M3 6x30 binoculars given to him by his uncle, a vet. Carried these as a cop and a shamus. And used them to scan the walls of the box canyon every time he took a walk. Going out and coming back in.

Both accessories amped up the Garand's G.I. chic. So did four eight-round en bloc clips of .30-06 jingling softly in the pockets of his jeans – two on the left, two on the right. Spares for the rounds already loaded. Made from stamped metal, they gave off the famous Garand *PING!!!* when the last round was fired and the clip was ejected.

Burch knew he looked slightly ridiculous carrying all this surplus hardware to the occasional coyote or javelina that crossed his path, but they didn't seem to mind and he didn't give a shit what they thought. He was a walking reclamation project, pushing himself to get his body in shape and his mind and reflexes sharp enough for the street, where the cardinal rule was this: *Be quick or get dead.*

These long walks also helped him sweat through a bad case of terminal piss-off. One too many motherfuckers tried to kill him and he wanted payback. When he woke up in the morning, his jaw ached from grinding his molars. When he scanned the rimrock, he hoped to see somebody pointing a gun at him. He was angry and spoiling for a fight.

When he got tired and sore and needed a jolt of motivation, all he had to do was run a playback reel of this latest West Texas sojourn and all the shitbirds who tried to blow out his candle. From Luis Reynaldo, who tried to turn his head into a canoe with a shotgun when he first rolled into Faver for killing his older brother almost a decade earlier, to Johnny Del Rio, his old partner who was ready to give him a nine-millimeter *coup de grace* until Rhonda Mae put a bullet in his brainpan.

Playback punching through the hospital drugs. Rhonda Mae telling him how she saved his sorry ass:

"There were four of them, Gramps, and they were careless. They grabbed me up but didn't pat me down. Didn't find the knife in my boot."

"Big mistake a pro doesn't make."

"Stupid gets you dead. Stabbed two of them in the heart, grabbed a Beretta from one. Got the drop on the third. He ran. Smoked your buddy before he could do the same to you. Nailed the runner when he came creeping back."

"Killer moves, Slick. Smooth and fast. Sure saved my sorry ass."

"You're welcome. That old Ranger says he'll take me to see Juanita before they throw me in jail. You have something to do with that, Gramps?"

"Never can tell."

Then there was Jack, his wily old mentor and friend, the man who helped him get sober and back on his feet when he lost his gold shield.

Cactus Jack, the original string puller who played all the angles with a master's touch. Throwing sand in his eyes by checking on Juanita while sending an old partner after him with a killer's gleam in his eye and a bullet with Burch's name on it. Ol' Jack, calling the shots and taking Danny Ray Mutscher's money.

Payback was mandatory. But he couldn't breeze into Dallas and fill Jack up with Flying Ashtrays. Not if he was going to take that badge. He'd have to borrow a page from the Cactus Jack String-Puller's Playbook and set things in lethal motion from a distance. He already knew who to call but hated the idea of remote revenge.

Getting even with Danny Ray Mutscher would be a steeper climb. The man had money, power and nasty friends. He was on the dodge and wouldn't be easy to find.

Burch would have to pray on this a bit, have a little talk with Jesus to make it right, then get the Devil to help him take Danny Ray from the vertical to the terminally horizontal.

If all that don't get you off your ass and steppin' lively, I don't know what will, Sport Model.

Got to get back to fightin' trim, Wynn. Always gets a little sporty out here in West Texas.

They do play for keeps out there. Good to see you gettin' back in the groove.

Got no choice. Got people to see and scores to settle.

That you do, Sport Model. Stay frosty.

You bet.

Burch had the sheriff's cabin to himself. Preferred the solitude it offered. Doggett was shacked up with his main squeeze of the moment, a waitress named Juanita. But he knew his time was just about up.

He also knew he was close to ready. Once the sawbones cleared him for street duty, he'd have about two weeks to fish or cut bait on Doggett's gold badge offer. Maybe three. Stay or go. Wear it and own it for good or get gone.

McKee's proposition made it mighty tempting to stay. But he had his doubts about getting tied down by the rules no matter how much freedom Doggett and the old Ranger dangled in front of his snout.

For now, he was giving it a trial run, clipping it to the left side his bullhide gun belt for short runs into town, just in front of the leather holder for two spare mags of Flying Ashtrays. His Colt 1911 nestled in a cross-draw holster on his right hip, an El Paso Saddlery 1920 model with basket stamping and a russet stain. A gift he gave himself for avoiding a dirt nap with Elvis.

Less conspicuous than the shoulder rig he favored. Handier for the ride into town in his old Dodge pickup. Made him look like one of the boys instead of a pimp. He still didn't own a hat, though. Wouldn't get one until he made up his mind.

He did wear his gun metal gray Ray-Bans with the smoked green lenses, just like every other swingin' West Texas dick with a badge. Got his beard trimmed boxer close, too, but kept the moustache full enough to comb and wax.

He pretended he had all the time in the world to decide, content to go visit Doggett or Boelcke two or three days a week, talking about cold cases and hotter numbers they wanted him to handle.

Mop-up on Bondurant, the Alice Baker shits and a joker named Santiago Cruz, a resurrected *segundo* from Malo Garza's crew that Bobby Quintero spotted slipping into the ranch, presumed to be working for the dead drug lord's daughter. Cruz had a woman in Valentine. Might be worth bracing him there to rattle his cage and see what fell through the bars.

Same-same trolling on that cartel clusterfuck – sifting through the files of twenty dead gunrunners, drug smugglers, scumbags and trigger-pullers that nobody gave a fuck about except their kin. And you couldn't always count on kin.

Burch wasn't kin but gave a fuck about two of the dead – Armando, a loyal, stand-up guy he liked a lot for a stone-cold killer, and the kid who posed as *La Güera*, Bartolo Contreras, who had a crush on Rhonda Mae and would do anything to prove his love. Getting dead was proof enough.

Doggett also mentioned one case that made Burch wince – the murder of Leighanna Burdette, the woman he was halfway to falling in love with even though she didn't know his real name. She called him Mister Bull. And she died a horrible death because of him.

"You were bangin' her and your prints are all over her trailer. It's our bet it's your DNA on Lucky Strike butts found in her ashtray and the semen in three condoms chucked in a waste basket by the bed."

"So what? You know I didn't kill her. I want in."

"We're not letting you within a hunnert miles of this case. We think we've got one of the shitbirds who tortured and murdered her – the A-B goon you wrapped up and gave us for an early Christmas present.

Lifted his prints from the trailer. You smoked the other one – Chizik. We think there's a third guy, an Alice Baker boy called Road Dog. Found his prints, too. Texas boy named Lonnie Jim Barker. He's Dub's meat. You stay out of it. A defense attorney would have a field day with you on the stand. You're toxic."

Not a chance that would happen. McKee had him wired up.

Burch pulled case files and brought them back to the sheriff's box canyon hideaway to study, a cup of coffee or glass of whiskey by his side. Flanked by a pack of Luckies and the Colt. He ignored the bottle of Percocet on the kitchen table.

The files called his name. He took a sip and read. He took a drag and grabbed the next file. Manna for a murder cop. One grabbed his interest. Alvaro Maldonado. Hispanic male, dead from gunshot wounds, two to the chest, one in the head. Body found behind the shitter of an abandoned Shamrock gas station north of town.

Alvaro was a local boy, born and raised in the Faver *barrio*. But years back, he'd been busted a time or two in Dallas. For pimping. And possession. The vice perfecto. A couple of phone calls to an old buddy who wasn't a friend of Cactus Jack gave Burch the arresting officer's name – Johnny Del Rio.

A thread or a dead end, Burch didn't know. But a name always led you to another name. And another. Maybe all the way to Danny Ray Mutscher, the cockbite who hired Johnny to kidnap Rhonda Mae and kill him.

A big maybe. Work what you got if you want more. And keep walking those long walks. With a Garand looped over your shoulder. Because the gunfight you're itching to have might just come calling.

Home stretch. Sweating like a mule. Rounding the last bend of the trail back to Doggett's cabin, he heard the throaty roar of V-8 muscle headed his way on the road from town, trailing a plume of dust.

He raised the binoculars to get a better view. A resale red Cutlass ragtop that looked a little too familiar. A '72 with the white top raised. A younger cousin of the midnight blue '68 hardtop sitting safe under a tarp in the county impound lot run by Doggett's cousin.

He let the binoculars dangle and unslung the Garand, clicking the safety off, but keeping the muzzle angled toward the ground.

The Cutlass barely slowed as it turned into Doggett's dirt drive, slipping sideways and slinging gravel and dirt. He raised the Garand as the driver slammed on the brakes and the Cutlass slid to a stop about a yard short of where he stood.

A petite blonde with blue eyes that looked permanently startled climbed out of the car. His heart froze. It was her. Carla Sue Cantrell. Her ownsef. Hurtling back into his life again.

"Is that a rifle in your hand or are you just glad to see me, Big 'Un?"

"Depends on whether you're here to pick up where we left off last we saw each other or working for somebody who wants me dead."

"I could never kill you, Big 'Un. Not when we could be doing things that would be a lot more fun for both of us."

"Step inside the house, then."

"Not before we've said a proper hello."

Carla Sue closed the gap, pushed aside the Garand and pressed her taut body against his girth. Her hair smelled like sandalwood, spearmint and sweat.

She reached up to pull his head down to her level for a kiss that was all mouth, tongue and teeth, with the promise of more carnal frolic than a man could handle.

"Damn, you ride a girl hard. Had me screamin' so loud I was speakin' in tongues."

"Did I make you see Jesus?"

"No, I was too busy fuckin' the Devil's younger brother."

"I'll tell Brother Lucifer you said hello."

"Family will have to wait. I'm not done with you yet."

Burch was on his back, his head and shoulders propped up on pillows. Carla Sue stretched across his body like a cat, rubbing the nipples of her bell-shaped breasts against his chest. While reaching down to stroke his balls and rising cock, she flashed him a lust-laced grin, framed by deep laugh lines that weren't there a decade ago.

Her eyes flared a brighter blue, her thick hair tangled, her face flushed, turning the crescent-shaped scar on her chin crimson. She leaned in to stab his mouth with her tongue. He pressed his fingers into her pussy. She moaned through a kiss she didn't break.

Burch grabbed her hips and pulled her body toward the headboard as he ended the kiss and slipped underneath her. She knew what he wanted and straddled his face. He put his tongue back to work, lapping the sweet saltiness between her legs, flicking her joy button. Her thighs pressed against his ears, muffling the sound of her moans, gasps and cries.

"Right there. Riiiiight fuckin' therrrrrrrrre. Damnit, gimme that tongue. Work that clit. Unnnhuh, unnnhuh, unnnhuh.... Work it..."

Lifting one leg and then the other, she slid down his body, pausing to let him tongue and suck each breast before pressing her face close to his and kissing him fiercely. She grabbed his hardened cock and tucked it inside her pussy then placed both palms on his chest to raise herself above him while rocking her ass up and down.

A hard ride that started slow then picked up speed, her breasts bouncing and glistening with sweat, her startled blue eyes locked on his, her mouth a wide O sucking in each ragged breath. He grabbed her hips and matched her pace with upward thrusts of his cock. They both smiled.

The sounds of wet, slapping flesh got louder. So did her cries and pleas to fuck her harder. His grunts and growls added the right carnal bass notes. They were in that rare groove of two people who were flat natural partners in bed and didn't need much coaxing or coaching on the moves each other craved. On the other hand, they both enjoyed profane encouragement.

"Slam that pussy, Big 'Un. Slam it harder, harder, haaaaarddder... Thas' it, thas' it... Oh, fuuuuuuck, fuuuuuuck, I'm cuuuuuuming...."

Burch bellowed as he came deep inside her. She collapsed on top of him, her face next to his, her lips nibbling his neck and ear, her tongue seeking his mouth.

"So fuckin' good. So, so, sooooo fuckin' good. You really got me that time, Big 'Un. I missed getting got that good by you."

"Phone lines have always been open, Slick. And you know where I live."

He reached over her to swipe his Luckies and Zippo from the bedside table. He lit nails for both of them.

"You know why I had to stay away."

"I do. You double-crossed two Mexican *jefes de narcotraficantes*, ripped them off for a buttload of cash and product and had to get yourself gone for good to live long enough to enjoy that loot. I get needing to do all that. What I don't get is you showing up right now, right here."

"A little bird told me you were stupid enough to come back to West Texas. Knew you'd step in the shit again with people who wanted to get you dead. Figured you might could need me to save your sorry ass again."

"Not good enough, Slick. The people who want to kill me are small timers compared to the big mules wanting to see you dead. The people gunnin' for you are a whole 'nother, other serious kind of trouble. With lots of long green motivation."

"What if I told you all of those big mules have bought the Big Adios? Malo Garza you know about – got blowed up in Monterrey. Same with Flores, the other *narco* I double-crossed."

"Heard about his demise. Shotgun blew his head off while he was playin' cards at a *cantina* in Piedras Negras. Up close and personal. Shooter got away and ol' Emeliano's bodyguards all disappeared."

"Grisly and very public. Something gentlemen of the Sicilian persuasion might do to somebody who crossed them. Sicilians out of New Orleans, perhaps. So, that's two of the big mules off the board. The third was a politician in Mexico City, very high up, with fingers in all the cartel pies. He died in his sleep two months ago. Natural causes, they say, although we both know a man who can make a murder look natural with just the prick of a needle."

"So that's why you're free to show your smiling face around this desert paradise again? And free to offer your services to the highest bidder once more."

"Always said you were one smart *hombre*, Big 'Un. For an ex-cop."

"Thing about those services, Slick, is they tend to draw another bunch of big mules who want you dead and have the money and long reach to make that happen. My enemies are just people I've pissed off with my natural good looks and charm."

"You piss people off walkin' into a room. That's why you always need to have somebody watching your back."

"I ain't no toddler, Slick. While I'm grateful to anybody who has saved my ass, especially you, most of the time I've had to fend for myself. Backup is rare for guys like me and I've gotten used to working without a net or a partner."

"What if you didn't have to do that no more, Big 'Un? Go it all by your lonesome, I mean."

He took a drag off his Lucky and looked her in the eye.

"You offerin' to be my partner, Slick? Already got an offer on the table that gives me back a gold shield and all the partners and back-up a man like me can stand. What are you willin' to put up?"

She cupped his balls then squeezed his cock.

"This, for one. Lots and lots of this. Non-stop and no long goodbyes in between."

"Temptin', I'll admit. You still got some moves that make a man beg for more. Not bad for an up holler white girl from Tennessee with some North Dallas gloss. What else you puttin' on the table? Don't wanna play 'less you're all in."

She laughed and slapped him on the chest.

"It ain't just bed partners I'm talkin' about, Big 'Un. Or goin' to Reno to get hitched and start playin' house, no matter how much that might appeal to the both of us. I'm talkin' business partners, working together on a score that'll make us both rich and take some scumbags off the board to boot. How's that for all in?"

"Temptation just got a whole lot sweeter."

"Beats the hell out of a pot metal badge coated in gold leaf. Don't know why you'd want to go back to that. Not after the way you got run out on a rail for smacking a pimp. What is it? Redemption? Guilt? Go see a preacher. You been walkin' the wild side for way too long to be a cop again. And I think you like being an outlaw but won't admit it. It's who you are now. Not that piece of pot metal."

She was the third person to preach this hard gospel to him in the past six months – Rhonda Mae, Johnny, now her. There was a truth there he didn't want to see, blinded for so long by his stubborn belief in the golden badge and its promise of salvation and redemption. It was the final lie he kept telling himself and the main reason he leapt at the offer by Doggett and Dub without thinking it through.

Even when he had a badge, he was never one for the rule book or the letter of the law. It was that higher calling that kept him hooked, that sense of duty and belonging he lost when they stripped away his shield and tossed him out on his ear.

The truth Carla Sue was trying to get him to see was this – he'd been out in no-man's-land for so long, telling himself he still stayed true to the lawman's code while making moves that bent and broke that code more often than not, that he could never go back.

Truth be told, he liked being the outlaw he said he wasn't. Maybe it was high time to admit it, ditch the gold shield fantasy and move on. Couldn't live in the twilight forever.

"I got some scores to settle."

"No shit. I can help with that."

"Those scumbags you're talkin' about – anybody I know?"

"Valentina Garza for one. She's tryin' to rebuild her daddy's empire and some folks I know don't want that to happen. They were banking on those Ojinaga boys putting a stop to her but those fellas got blown to shit in that goat ropin' you got yourself in the middle of."

"Who else?"

"This one might really interest you – the fella who bankrolled those Aryan Brotherhood mutts runnin' guns from that ranch full of Kluxers that got busted up. He's already set up another crew at a ranch down by Presidio to feed the Garzas all the weapons they need. My folks want him stopped."

"This fella got a name?"

"Sure does. Danny Ray Mutscher. Yeah, THAT guy. Guy who sent your ex-partner down here to pop you. My people say he was real specific about wanting you dead."

Bingo.

Maybe the gold shield could wait. Maybe it couldn't. Maybe he didn't need it anymore. Behind every maybe was a doubt. Burch was dead certain of that.

About the Author

J im Nesbitt is a lapsed horseman, pilot, hunter and saloon sport with a keen appreciation for old guns, vintage cars and trucks, good cigars, aged whisky without an 'e' and a well-told story. He is the author of four award-winning, hard-boiled Texas crime thrillers that feature battered but relentless Dallas PI Ed Earl Burch – *The Last Second Chance; The Right Wrong Number; The Best Lousy Choice*; and his latest, *The Dead Certain Doubt*. For more than 30 years, Nesbitt was a reporter, editor and roving national correspondent for newspapers and wire services in Alabama, Florida, Texas, Georgia, North Carolina, South Carolina and Washington, D.C. He chased hurricanes, earthquakes, plane wrecks, presidential candidates, wildfires, rodeo cowboys, migrant field hands, neo-Nazis and nuns with an eye for the telling detail and an ear for the voice of the people who give life to a story. A diehard Tennessee Vols fan, he now lives in enemy territory – Athens, Alabama – and is working on his fifth Ed Earl Burch novel, *The Fatal Saving Grace*. To learn more, go to his web site at: https://jimnesbittbooks.com